SONNETS OF SUMMER SORROW

[A NOVEL]

ALASKA TUKEN TEGI

Sonnets Of Summer Sorrow

Print edition ISBN: 9798864431658

E-book edition ISBN: 9798864431658

Published by Kindle Direct Publishing

First Edition: December 2023 8

Printed and bound in Great Britain by Kindle Direct Publishing.

❧ Created with Vellum

Mea columba, Em
Amor omnia vincit.

ALASKA TUKEN TEGI

SONNETS OF SUMMER SORROW

This novel is fiction, except for the parts that aren't.

SONNETS OF SUMMER SORROW

PROLOGUE

Dear Theodore,

From the moment I was born, I was shattered. My delicate pieces were swallowed by the sea; shattered by expectations out of my grasp, by empty seats at dinner tables and closing doors. The turbulent waters washed away what was left of my shattered being along the beach for all to admire and cherish.

And they would indeed, admire. They would indeed, cherish.

But then, they'd walk away.

From the moment I was born, I had a knife in one hand and a wound in the other: my past beats inside me like a second heart. I fear if ripped open I will be found unsightly; recollections and dreams knotted up in a reasonably attractive bundle of flesh.

I remember what this flesh has gone through.

I dream of what it may go through.

From the moment I was born, I was an angel; golden light shrouded a body breached with little red numbers. Nothing but sweet confessions danced around my empty head. But now, there's something peaceful in the massacre of my senses; only viewing the earth merge with the sky.

And when the clouds collapse, you'll find me caving in on myself, melting into the concrete.

After I was born, I cradled death in my arms and asked for it not to consume me; not to weigh me down into the ground; to pursue me strongly. My legs ached to run at the promise of a thousand tomorrows, and yet, the earth was still so unknown; I am only familiar with one coast, when I know there are lands I am meant to meet. I know there are mountain tops I am meant to greet, and oceans where I am to sink and swim deep. I know that there are woods calling for my footsteps; for my exploration into the earth's lungs.

I want to see it all, and I want to breathe.

I want to remember that I am just as alive as everything around me.

After I was born, the stars were still there to be observed; the gale still rushed to be heard. We may not be moving together anymore, but isn't it beautiful how the world keeps spinning anyway? How in the sunshine the ground is warm and the grass pales.

How my heart thumps and never rests.

After I was born, we met in the summer I turned seventeen; when the sun bellowed and currents spilt softly in the distance. I found words for everything, in melodies, in the rise and break of summer sunsets. How I found words for what you said and the words you did not.

I still remember that. Do you?

When we met, I was born again. My delicate pieces were held in your gentle hands, my love beat inside me like a second heart, the stars were still there to be observed. We awakened every morning, we chased existence relentlessly; how fortunate we were to be in such an ephemeral life.

For all that, this ground has changed and all the earth has been recreated, we were there in the Oxford sun.

When we met, my life started to seem alright, nice even, less shattered, less wounded. Because when I told you things, they seemed to rest more lightly on my shoulders because you held them on yours too.

In a solitary life, there are rare moments when another soul dips near yours, as stars once a year brush the earth.

Such a constellation you were to me.

When you had left, the world was too quiet without you nearby. I walked around all day knowing that I was going to die in the same universe you loved me in. I was homesick for a place I was not sure even existed anymore;

one where my heart was full, my body loved, and my soul understood.

Grief is all I have left of you, so yes, I do hold onto it.

After you had left, I didn't want to know another person so deeply they felt intertwined with my own self. I did not want to feel like they made a home in the cavity of my chest. I did not want to give another person my everything again.

I cupped my relationships in my hands like sand, and all the same, watched them slip away from me.

They say as time goes on you forget, but as time goes on I remember.

After you left, I concluded with an aching finality that all the could-happen possibilities were gone, that doing whatever you wanted, whenever you wanted was over.

Our future doesn't exist anymore.

Everything is in the past and will stay there.

After you left, I realised we were the perfect match and not the perfect love.

Wind folded around my body, silent and soothing as it embalmed me. It reminded me that I was not done searching, and though I do not know what I am looking for,

I know it resides on the horizon,
in letting my eyes devour all I can see.

From the moment I was born, I was always the lover, never the loved. But I came to realise that one day, the right person will know how to hold my love. The right person will choose me just as deeply as I chose you. I will not have to quiet the way I care; I will never feel like I am too much. I will not have to beg for the love I deserve — I will not have to fight for someone who isn't fighting for me.

One day, I will understand that it never mattered how tightly I held onto our love, how intensely I tried, because one day, the right person will find me.

And the right person will finally stay.

I am choosing to let go now. I will not lose myself for the possibility of us any longer.

Alaska

not out of fear, but excitement, for something wonderful happened. Everything I needed was revealed to me in a split second, like suddenly knowing all the answers to a difficult test or the exact route to an impossible destination. I saw it all before me, in an instant that instantly disappeared yet made its mark. I intuited that when I was ready, I held the key. Skating was a language without words where the mind must bow to instinct. I excelled in school yet nothing before skating gave me the tools to express the inexpressible.

I honestly can't remember much else about those years except a certain mood that permeated most of them, a melancholy feeling that I associate with reading chapters from Yanigahara's *A Little Life* on Sunday nights. Sunday was a sad day — early to bed, school the next morning. I was constantly worried my manuscripts were disfigured — but as I watched the fireworks go off in the night sky, over the floodlit cityscape of London, I was consumed by a more general sense of dread, of imprisonment within the dreary round of school and home: circumstances which, to me at least presented a sound empirical argument for gloom. And since all this had been true for as long as I could remember, I felt things would doubtlessly continue in this depressing vein as far as I could foresee.

From as far back as I can remember, my first feeling was one of loneliness; the warmth of a hand evaporating from my shoulder. I felt as though my existence was tainted, in some subtle but essential way.

Those feelings had seemingly exemplified after the assault.

I suppose it's not odd, then, that I have trouble reconciling my life to those of my friends, or at least to the lives as I perceive them to be. Adeline was brought up in such a magnanimous style that even the gossips were impressed — private schools, summers in Oxford, winters in France. And Asli; a Turkish upbringing vitally present in her in every respect, from the way she shook your hand to the way she told a joke. Consider even sweet, dulcet Serena, if you would; an American childhood, a big house in the suburbs, with sailboats and tennis rackets and golden retrievers; summers on Cape God and tailgate picnic during football season.

And then there was you, *Theodore*. We do and did have everything in common with each other, a knowledge of philosophy and the weeks spent together in each other's company. And if love is a thing held in common, I suppose we had that in common, too, though I realise that might sound odd in light of the story I am about to tell.

How to begin.

During high school I went to a private school in New York City, Brooklyn, after moving away from London at eleven (I was opposed, as it had been very plain that I was expected to uphold our generational titles, one of the many reasons I was in such agony to leave) and, during my six years there I studied Classical Literature as a fulfilment of my love for language.

I did well in Literature, excelled in it even, and I won many awards in the Classics department my junior year. It was my favourite class because it was the only one held in the campus library — no smell of formaldehyde, chalkboards or teenage deodorants, and instead, I found myself surrounded by endless shelves of novel collections and academia-bound pillars. Initially, I had thought with hard work I could overcome my fundamental distaste for STEM subjects, that perhaps with even harder work I could stimulate something like a love for them. But this was not the case. As months went by I remained uninterested, if not downright sickened; by my study of biology; which came so naturally to my sister who studied veterinary nursing; I was held in contempt by teacher and classmate alike in what seemed to me a doomed and Pyrrhic gesture.

Eventually, I switched my focus to English Literature and let my days be consumed by writing and prose. I drew comfort from books and writing letters.

Littera scripta manet.

Oddly enough, it was Louisa May Alcott who provided me with a positive view of my female destiny in her novel, *Little Women*. She gave me the courage of a new goal, and soon I was crafting short stories and spinning long yarns for the memories of past and imaginary loves. From that time on, I cherished the idea that one day I would write a book full of letters; the only issue was that after the assault, I stopped writing for I feared that the words which had once given me sustenance were in danger of spiritual starvation. I feared them losing their sense of purpose, falling into fattened heads, floundering in a mire of spectacle. Finance and vapid complexity. The words that spilt from the memories, black memories, they couldn't stop. Their stories were wearing me alive, turning me inside out.

And so, I cut all my words out.

My heart was too full of them.

Like a baby harp seal, I was all white, thickly bandaged, heavy as clubs. I carried with me a tender kit — as I used to call it — almost everywhere I went. When I look back on those years, all I can remember is how sad and tired, and unloved and unpretty I was. I had to cut it all out, getting smaller and smaller until I was nothing. I became bitter and untouchable. I craved affection but the mere thought of someone caring for me made my stomach turn.

For a while, I lived only for skating and told myself there was no room for anything else; not love, not school, nor scraping the walls of memory; I devoted myself completely and only to those sacred hours of the day which I spent on the ice. Skating provided the warmth of a miracle. My mind became a muscle of discontent, my sole desire was to astonish. When stepping onto the ice, all else faded.

I still have a hard time talking about what had happened, nevertheless writing about it; because even if I sometimes use the word abuse to describe certain things that were done to me, in someone else's mouth the word turns ugly and absolute. It swallows up everything that happened: everything that I pretended that the assault was when it really wasn't. I had myself convinced those months were a love story. I needed them to be. Otherwise what were they?

Why suffer for something ordinary? And from what I knew, I knew from books, and books lied, they made things prettier.

I thought less and less frequently of this, it was true, but my days outside the rink smeared into one; most of the time I felt I was floating, trying to pretend that I didn't occupy my own life, wishing I was invisible, wanting only to go unnoticed. Things happened to me and I didn't fight back the way I once would have; sometimes when I was feeling hurt I was still conscious of those years that were gone: my rages, my cries, my struggling. Now I was the girl I wished myself to be. Now I hoped to be someone adrift, a presence so thin and light and insubstantial that I seemed to displace no air at all.

This is the poem scratched onto the walls of my throat.

No one had heard it, but it was there.

But, in the nature of humans, against all odds, against all logic, we *hope*. I slowly started to come to terms with what transpired all those years ago; after having lived in a state of victimhood for all those years, I realised how much I had sacrificed and relinquished for my formative despair. Of course, I was a victim. But I refused to live like one anymore. And so, I stayed soft; I could not let the things that had hurt me turn me into a person I was not.

Sometimes I forget how I got there.

Sometimes I forget how much I didn't want to survive.

I was motivated more by a fear that if I didn't move forward, I would somehow slip back into my past, the life I had left and about which I would tell none of them except for you. And it wasn't only me who possessed this quality: Oxford was populated by the ambitious. It was often the only thing that everyone there had in common. So I studied Literature and liked it better. But I didn't like New York any better. I don't think I can explain the despair my surroundings inspired in me. Though I now suspect, given the circumstances and my disposition after the assault, I would've been unhappy anywhere, in Biarritz or Caracas or the Isle of Capri, I was then convinced that my unhappiness was indigenous to place. Perhaps it was. While to a certain extent, Milton is right — the mind is its own place and in itself can make a Heaven of Hell and so forth — it is nonetheless clear that New York was modelled less on Paradise than other, more dolorous cities.

Though I had a confused idea that my dissatisfaction was bohemian, vaguely Marxist in origin (when we had just moved abroad I made a fabulous show of socialism, mainly to irritate my parents), I couldn't begin to understand it; and would have been angry if someone had suggested that it was due to a strong Puritan streak in my nature, which was in fact, not the case. I knew that after the assault I needed something to change; a sign, a blue star promising the grace of a new tomorrow. *Kharisma.*

Not long ago I found this passage in an old notebook, written when I was fifteen or so: 'There is to me about this place a smell of rot, the smell of rot that ripe fruit makes. Nowhere, ever, has the hideous mechanic or birth and copulation and death — those upheavals of like that the Greeks call *miasma*, defilement — have been so brutal or been painted up to look so pretty; have so many people put so much faith in lies and mutability and death. The reputed last words

7

of French writer, Francois Rabelais: *Je m'en vais chercher un grand peut-être; tirez le rideau, la farce est jouée.* I go to seek a great perhaps.'

And so, I wound up in St. Catherine the summer I turned seventeen.

I lit on St. Catherine by a trick of fate. My sister had attended their summer course several years ago, and with my parents weighing expectations of me to live a prospective life, I too signed up for a promising summer at Oxford University.

Junior year, I had spent dozens of hours studying photographs from the college campus as though if I stared at them long enough and longingly enough I would, by some sort of osmosis, be transported into their clear, pure tranquillity. Even now I remember those pictures, like pictures in the storybooks I loved as a child. Radiant meadows, fields vaporous in the trembling distance; leaves ankle-deep on gusty autumn roads; bonfires and fog in the valleys; cellos, dark window panes, rain.

St. Catherine's College, south-east England. Established in 1981. Student body, 800. Non-collegiate. Progressive. Specialising in the liberal arts. Highly selective. *Nova Et Vetera.* New and old.

St. Catherine's College, south-east England. Even the name had an austere. An Anglican cadence, to my ear at least, which yearned hopelessly for England again and was dead to the sweet dark rhythms of little mission towns. For a long time, I looked at a picture of the dormitories resident students nicknamed 'staircases'. St. Catherine was suffused with a weak, academic light — different from Brooklyn, different from anything I had ever known — a light that made me think of long hours in dusty libraries, old books, and silence.

The months subsequent were an endless dreary battle of

paperwork, full of stalemates, fought in the trenches. Even today I do not fully understand the chain of events that brought me to Oxford, and yet, less than a year after I'd sat down on the gold-shag carpet of my room in Brooklyn and impulsively filled out the questionnaire, I was getting off the bus in Oxford with two suitcases and foreign currency in my pockets.

When I stepped off the bus after a long anxious night that had begun somewhere in the States, it was six o'clock in the morning. The sun was rising over the fields, birches, and impossibly green meadows; and to me, dazed by the night and no sleep, Oxford was like a city from a dream. And it was from that moment, whether I realised it or not, that I was given the opportunity to change my life, and was ready to do whatever it took to make it happen.

The world doesn't give you things, you *take them*.

CHAPTER TWO
NOVA ET VETERA

ON MY FIRST DAY AT ST. CATHERINE'S COLLEGE, THE STORM was a glazier. The wind spun glass from a stained glass depiction of a saint no one knew. It was a cathedral for cold morning July, a place for the grey, bitter month that everyone hated, to come and hide and pray for mercy, to pray to stay, when everyone wanted it to leave.

I trailed my luggage into staircase sixteen and made my way to the twenty-fourth dorm room. My bleak room contained a meagre bed, neatly made, two straight-backed chairs, a sage washstand and a bureau — without any mirror — and a small table. There were no drapery curtains at the dormer windows, no pictures. All morning, rain had been pouring down upon the roof and the little room was like a refrigerator for cold. It seemed to me that the dormitories weren't even dorms — or at any rate, not like the dorms I knew, with cinderblock walls and depressing, yellow lights — but white clapboard houses with green shutters set back from the commons in groves of maple and ash. All the same, it never occurred to me that my particular room, wherever it might be, would be anything but ugly and disappointing. I took a few books and piled them against the wall, reading some, browsing others. I enjoyed the silence, the singular moment to breathe.

When the first ray of sunlight hit my window, a knock flurried through the other side of the wooden door. "Come in," I yelled, and immediately was greeted by my new neighbour, the occupant of room twenty-three. With heavy dark-blonde hair and an epicene face as clear, as cheerful as grace, she introduced herself to me.

"Hey!" she exclaimed, leaning with elation against the doorframe. "My name is Adeline, I'm your new neighbour." Perhaps most unusual in the context of Oxford — where pseudo-intellects and teenage decadents abounded, and where black clothing was *de rigueur* — she wore pale clothes, particularly white.

"Hey, it's nice to meet you," I said, reaching out my hand. Her expression brightened as she leaned over and shook it vigorously. "I'm Alaska."

She chuckled softly. "Alaska?" she asked. "Like the country?"

"I suppose so," I said warmly. "Are you in room–"

"Twenty-three," she smiled. "Last year's dorms were so much nicer."

I raised my eyebrows curiously. "You've been here before?" I asked.

"Absolutely," she said proudly. By now, she had entered my room and was sitting on the white cotton covers. "This is my third summer at St. Catherine's College, and when this block is over, I'll be doing another two weeks at Balliol."

"Balliol?" I asked, confused.

"You know, the other university branches?"

I was unsure of what she meant but nodded cordially. I looked around my single room again, the wallpaper chipped on the ends. "I'm guessing we're sharing a bathroom."

"What?" she asked, peering into the darkly lit room beside me. Two bureaus stood below a rectangular mirror; one toilet; two showers. Our reflections looked ghostly and disfigured in the poorly-lit room. The freckles scattered across her olive cheeks appeared as little angel kisses crowning around a pair of radiant brown eyes.

"I suppose we're getting the full college experience," I chuckled.

"Okay," Adeline said, eyes bursting with optimism again. "This is going to be so much fun. Picture this: mornings together, evenings together..."

"I love the sound of that," I smiled. "We're going to be like a domestic couple on their honeymoon."

"That depends," she said. "Whether you're already coupled or not."

Once again, I was unsure of what she meant. "What do you mean?"

She laughed softly. "I'm asking whether you're in a relationship or not."

"Oh," I chuckled, looking down at the linoleum floors. "Devastatingly single."

"That'll change very soon," Adeline said, her smile more callous and almost bent like a warning sign. This time, I did not ask her what she meant and instead smiled back. What I would never admit to anyone who'd met me was how desperately I wanted to be loved, I didn't think I could say it. How I wanted someone to hold my wrists and kiss my palms and smile at me, and want me, I wanted to be wanted and I didn't know how long poetry or songs would substitute for that longing. Nevertheless, I was deeply grateful to have found someone like Adeline, to have found a type of person that made the entire lonely plain of Oxford seem somehow less lonely.

We walked down to the convocation together; passing the

great elm, passing flurries of students, billowing clouds in the sky. In the hall, the Oxford crest hung on a banner behind the podium — a white saltire on a blue field, a long gold key and sharp black quill crossed like swords in the foreground. Below was the motto: *Nova Et Vetera.* I'd heard a variety of translations, but the one I liked best was: *Things Both New and Old.*

It was one of the first things Ian, the head director, said at the convocation. "Good evening, everyone. *Nova Et Vetera.*" He had appeared onstage from the shadows of the wings, a spotlight on his face striking the rest of us into silence. Ian was a strange man — tall, quiet but forceful. Most notably, he was bald. He had a large hooked nose and little square glasses so thick that they magnified his eyes to three times their natural size. "If you are sitting in this room tonight," he said, "it means that you have been accepted into the esteemed Oxford family. Here you will make many friends, and perhaps a few enemies. Do not let the latter prospect frighten you — if you haven't made any enemies in life, you've been living too safely. And that is what I wish to discourage." He paused, chewing on his words for a moment.

"He's gone a bit off the wall," Adeline muttered.

"I encourage you to live boldly," Ian said. "Make art, make mistakes and have no regrets. You have come to Oxford because you prized something above money, above convention, above the kind of education that can be evaluated on a numeric scale. I do not hesitate to tell you that you are remarkable. However–" his expression darkened. "Our expectations are adjusted to match your enormous potential. We expect you to be dedicated. We expect you to be determined. We expect you to dazzle us. And we do not like to be disappointed." His words boomed through the hall and hung in the air like an odorous vapour, invisible but impossible to ignore. He let the unnatural quiet linger far too long, then abruptly leaned back from the podium and said, "We plan to prepare you for it as best we can. The future is wide and wild and full of promise, but it is precarious, too. Seize on every opportunity that comes your way and cling to it, lest it be washed back out to sea." Ian smiled dreamily, then checked his watch. "Goodnight."

And he was gone from the stage before the audience could even begin to clap.

———

After the convocation, I wandered St. Catherine's in a dream, my head spun but I was acutely, achingly conscious that I was alive and young on a beautiful day; the sky was a deep painful blue, wind scattered the red and yellow leaves in a whirlwind around me. I hoped the weather would be cool for my lunch with Adeline, but outside the sun started to blister and was only getting hotter.

I entered Franco Manca; a tiny, beautiful restaurant with white tablecloths and bay windows opening onto the streets of Oxford. The customers were mostly middle-aged and prosperous ladies with frosted lipstick, challis skirts, mixed with country lawyers in Vermont fashion. When Adeline walked through the parquet doors she brushed beside a tall, tanned figure that appeared incredibly feminine, well-dressed and soft. She took a seat next to Adeline in front of me. "Alaska," Adeline said, gesturing towards the ornate figure beside her. "This is Asli. She's our other neighbour in room–"

"Room twenty-two," she said. Her voice echoed softly through the walls of Franco Manca. I smiled at her, apprising her complimentary brown eyes and hair, she was absolutely breathtaking. Her clothes were neat and matched well together, and her dark curls brushed over her shoulders.

"It's lovely to meet you," I said.

"Me too. I was worried about making friends until Adeline knocked on my door this morning," she said.

"Funnily enough, Adeline also knocked on my door this morning," I chuckled. "That's how we met."

Adeline's expression flickered from us to the door; we heard the hinges open and close; until a slip of cooling breeze curled around us. "I also knocked on Serena's door," Adeline confessed.

"Serena?" Asli asked.

Gesturing towards a blonde light that inched towards us, "This is Serena," Adeline clarified.

"Hi," she said, with a faint American accent. Her voice was terribly sweet and soft, almost breathless. We ordered pizzas and spent the afternoon getting to know each other. Adeline was French, Asli was Turkish and Serena was, in fact, American. All three of them were grouped in Psychology classes by a trick of fate; I, on the other hand, had elected to study Philosophy, Literature and Modern History in an effort to rekindle what had been lost so dearly to me after the assault.

In spite of this, after a single and albeit bleak afternoon in Franco Manca, I strangely felt at home in their company; as if I had already known and loved them for years. I felt an inexplicable kinship with these people, though I had no way to interpret my feeling of prescience.

In the evening, when the group of us lay splayed in someone's room (a candle burning, a joint burning as well), the conversation turned to my friends' childhoods, which they had barely left but about which they were curiously nostalgic and certainly obsessed. They recounted what seemed like every detail of them, though I was never sure if the goal was to compare with one another the similarities or to boast of their differences, because they seemed to take equal pleasure in both. They spoke of curfews, and rebellions, and punishments, and pets and siblings, and what they had worn that had driven their parents crazy, and what groups they had hung out with in high school and to whom they had lost their virginity, and where, and how, and cars they had crashed and bones they had broken, and sports they had played and bands they had started. They spoke of disastrous family vacations and strange, colourful relatives and odd next-door neighbour experiences and teachers, both beloved and loathed. I enjoyed these divulgences more than I expected — these were real teenagers who'd had the sorts of real, plain lives I had always wondered about — and I found it relaxing and educational to sit there late at night and listen to them. My silence was both a necessity and a protection, and had the added benefit of making me appear more mysterious and more interesting than I knew I was. "What about you, Alaska?" a few of them had asked me, and I would simply shrug and say, with a smile, "It's too boring to get into." I was astonished but relieved how easily they accepted that, and grateful too for their self-absorption. None of them really wanted to listen to someone else's story anyway, they only wanted to tell their own.

And yet my silence was not unnoticed by everyone. Sometimes during these sessions (I had begun to think of them this way, as intensive tutorials in which I could correct my own cultural paucities) I would catch Adeline watching me with an indecipherable expression on her face, and would wonder how much Adeline might have guessed about me. Sometimes I had to stop myself from saying something to her. Maybe I was wrong, I sometimes thought. Maybe it would be nice to confess to someone that most of the time I could barely relate to what was being discussed, that I couldn't participate in everyone else's shared language of childhood pratfalls and frustrations. But then I would stop myself, for admitting ignorance of a language would mean having to explain the one I did speak.

Although if I were to tell anyone, I knew it would be you. And increasingly was I certain that you knew something. (Knows what? I'd argue with myself, in saner moments. You're just looking for a reason to tell him, and then what will he think of you? Be smart. Say nothing. Have some self-control.) But this was of course illogical. My past's very strangeness both insulated and isolated me: it was near inconceivable that anyone would guess at its shape and specificities which meant that if they did, it was because I had dropped clues like a great ugly unmissable plea for attention.

Still. The suspicion persisted, sometimes with an uncomfortable intensity, as if it was inevitable that I should say something and was being sent messages that took more energy to ignore than they would to obey. They couldn't see that I had a secret as big as me. A secret that replaced me.

Returning to my room, I couldn't help but feel a sense of familiar solitude and surrealness. By then, it was evening and the prismatic air pressed on everything that needed it there on the earth; the moon fired itself on the steam and spread light through the underbrush of carpet. Infinite possibilities seemed to swirl above me as I stared at the plaster ceiling. It seemed to me that the vibrating patterns overhead were sliding into place as the mandala of my life. I sat on the bed during twilight while the walls went slowly from grey to gold to black, listening to a soprano's voice climb dizzily up and down somewhere at the other end of the hall until the last light was completely gone. The faraway soprano spiralled on and on in the darkness like some angel of death, and I couldn't remember the air ever seeming as high and cold and rarefied as it was that night, or ever feeling farther away from the low-sun lines of dusty Brooklyn. I closed my eyes and clasped my hands tightly on either shoulder trying to imagine if that was what it would have felt like to have a person hold me again. I hoped it was warmer than I remembered.

My life, I thought. But I wasn't able to think beyond this, and would keep repeating the words to myself — part chant, part curse, part reassurance — as I slipped into that other world that I visited when I was in such pain, that I knew was never far from my own but that I could never remember after: *my life*.

Eventually, something passed through me and I fell into a deep sleep.

In the morning, the sky lit an hour before the sun showed, and the scent of evergreens was the suggestion of the day's falling rain; a wet, green shadow helmed in white. I looked out to the bare trees, arterial, observing how they reached out to the earth and sky above. The cold had already crept against my window panes and into the air of the room. Frost quickly trailed through the thin fabric of my bed covers and raised the hairs against my legs. As I grabbed my laptop and threw it into a bag, I met Adeline in the bathroom before heading down to breakfast together.

I roamed campus like a sleepwalker, stunned and drunk with beauty. In the dining hall, the overhead lights towered across each table, basking them in a soft, flame-like glow. Me, Adeline and Asli settled for a cold breakfast since the line for anything hot was just too long. Nevertheless, we were scheduled to arrive at the marquee in approximately ten minutes.

We placed our trays down next to Serena and looked around at the blur of other students; a group of red-cheeked girl's laughs carried faintly over the velvety, twilit room and fused into white noise around me. I looked down at my sad frozen breakfast, it grimaced back at me. "Are you all excited to start our courses today?" Adeline asked joyously.

"I'm nervous," said Asli. "I've never taken Psychology before."

Serena took a sip of her latte. "I'm excited, I can't wait to meet everyone."

"Me too," I said. "This is my first summer course."

Asli and Serena agreed alongside me as Adeline continued to speak with her usual cadence. "You know, the counsellors are planning to be much more puritanical this year."

"How come?" I asked.

"They were less strict last year," she shrugged. "And so, it was pretty much chaos; people sneaking out, people sneaking in, anything you can think of really."

"I'm guessing that's what the evening shout-out is for," sighed Serena.

The marquee acted as the college's sanctuary, the ever-present home amid such change. It had a sweet, musty smell and was so dim it seemed almost gaslit; the walls were pale with the light of potted palms and the ceilings were so high they made my head reel. Each night we were called to the marquee's dreary, plastic walls for what was called the evening shout-out. This nightly routine was scheduled sharply for ten o'clock and any signs of lateness would result in probing glares from each councillor, and occasionally a firm word or two from Ian. The shout-out was supposedly implemented to inform students on course updates or scheduled activities by the college; when in reality, we quickly learned why it was called the shout-out.

All that ever happened was that we were shouted at for breaching the rules.

Unlike the other colleges (like Balliol or Huges) St. Catherine's held up their trinity of three directives like a standing patron: no alcohol, no smoking, and most importantly, no mix of genders in the staircases. Any violation resulted in immediate suspension.

We still broke these rules anyway.

On our way to the marquee, trees creaked with apples on the red ground beneath, the heavy sweet smell of them rotting drifted among the steady thrumming of wasps around them. The shock of first seeing St. Catherine's elm tree in the morning, rising up in the light as cool and slim as a ghost, the leaves wild and disordered against the skyline.

Upon entering, a breeze stirred the heavy, moth-eaten velvet curtains, ruffling against a line up of fold-up chairs. The wooden planks were bounded by cracks where saplings had pushed through. I left my friends in Psychology and retreated to a cylindrical table bound by a milky scrap of paper labelled: *Philosophy, Literature and Modern History*. I placed down my belongings and looked across the table, the faces of my classmates shone dramatically in the morning sun and endless chatter blurred into a fused bellow in my ears. For a while, I sat malleable, made of clay; clouds careened through the marquee and the summer sun bleached the long marsh grass.

Suddenly, in a swarm of cigarette smoke and dark sophistication, you appeared like a figure from an allegory. You were angular and elegant, precariously thin, with nervous hands and a shrewd of dark brown hair. I thought (erroneously) that you dressed like Alfred Douglas, or the Comte de Montesquieu: beautiful starchy shirts with Italian cuffs and a great black-coat that billowed behind you as you walked.

For a long time, I would return to this moment, a moment in which a young man approached me with a confident stride, as the perfect little crack in an extraordinarily brief window of opportunity. It could have almost never happened. I try to figure out the part that chance played, to assess the nature of risk that led to our encounter, but I never succeeded. We were in the land of the unthinkable.

"Hey," you said, leaning against the round table. Your voice was thick in some unidentifiable European accent. "My name is Theodore. Are you also in group one?"

I was taken aback by your nonchalant nature, and for a moment, struggled to speak. "Yes, I am," I said finally. "My name's Alaska. It's nice to meet you."

You furrowed your brows and there was a deftly silence to which I believed I had said something that had somehow upset you. Then you tilted your head with a playful smile. *"That which the sea breaks against."*

"What?" I said, erroneously confused. "How did you–"

"Derived from the Aleut word, *Alyeska,* right? Or were you perhaps named after the country?" you said, mockingly. Side by side, we were very much alike, in a similarity less of lineament than of manner and bearing, a correspondence of gesture which bounded and echoed between us.

I paused for a moment, unsure of how to respond again. You rolled your eyes and started to turn around. "And your name is Theodore?"

"Correct," you scoffed, looking back at me uninterested.

"*Kharisma.* The divine gift of the gods," I said. "Derived from the Greek, *theos* meaning god and *doron,* gift."

You smiled at me.

"Correct again," you said, more warmly than before; at the edges, your lips curled like a purring cat in the sun. That first time we spoke, I felt it, an ache. Like a little electric burn before my life changed.

"How did you know that?" you asked curiously. "Most people don't."

"I love to read," I shrugged. "I suppose I could ask you the same thing. Most people think my name is derived from the country or the state. I don't know which one is worse."

You laughed softly. "I read a lot as well," you smiled again. "I also write a lot."

"I write too," I said, taken aback. I was charmed by this

conversation, and despite its illusion of being rather modern and digressive (to me, the hallmark of the modern mind is that it loves to wander from its subject) I can see that you were leading me by circulation to the same points that were also adorned by yourself.

"And what does a person with such a romantic temperament seek in the study of Philosophy?" you asked this as if, having the good fortune to meet someone so similar to you, was anxious to extract my opinion while I was still captive in conversation.

"If by romantic you mean solitary and introspective," I argued. "I think romantics are frequently the best philosophers."

You listened to me talk, eyes fixed on mine, apparently entranced by my answers. Never had my efforts been met with such attentiveness, such keen solicitude. You seemed utterly enthralled that I was tempted to embroider a little more than perhaps was prudent. "The best romantics are often the best philosophers?" you challenged. "You mean to say you stick with the ideals of Burke or Carlyle."

"Not necessarily. I'm more of an Absurdist," I said. "I love Camus."

You seemed to contemplate this for a moment. "Have you read *The Myth Of Sisyphus*?"

"Of course, it's one of my favourites."

You grinned at me and for a moment I saw a faint glimmer spread through your eyes. *"This very heart which is mine will forever remain indefinable to me. Between the certainty I have of my existence and the content I try to give to that assurance, the gap will never be filled—"*

"Forever I shall be a stranger to myself."

We both smiled at each other.

"It's one of my favourites too," you said.

So skilfully and engagingly, that I was quite disarmed, you

led us deftly from topic to topic for the rest of that morning. And I am sure that in this talk, which seemed only a few minutes but was really much longer, you managed to extract everything about me that you needed to know. I did not suspect that your rapt interest might spring from anything less than the richest enjoyment of my own company, and though I found myself talking with relish on a bewildering variety of topics — some of them quite personal, and with more frankness than was customary — I was convinced that I was acting of my own volition.

I wish I could remember more of what was said that morning, only that meeting you was like walking into the sun after a terribly long winter.

After the induction, we walked to our lecture hall in Pitt Rivers Museum; famous for displaying the archaeological and anthropological collections of the University of Oxford in England. It was a small building on the edge of campus, old and covered with ivy in such a manner as to be almost indistinguishable from the landscape. On our walk, flowers filled the streets, climbing several stories high, foxglove and like missiles while roasting in the early July sun. I can feel them still, the sap pulsing in their veins, pushing their way to the sky. These streets were a poem waiting to be hatched.

I look back and remember how it was all so close then, the rays of the sun, the sweetness, a sense of time lost forever. After all, you knew nothing of me and I knew less of you then. But it's like that sometimes, you can know an imperfect stranger like no one else.

Downstairs were the lecture halls and classrooms, all of them empty, with clean blackboards and freshly waxed floors. Once at the entrance of Pitt Rivers, we found ourselves in a long, deserted hallway. Enjoying the noise of my shoes on the linoleum, I walked along briskly, looking at the closed doors for numbers or names until I came to one that had a brass card holder and, within it, an engraved card that read *Oxford University*. We stood there for a moment and then passed through the doors.

The lecture hall was a beautiful room, not an office at all, and much bigger than it looked from the outside — airy and white, with a high ceiling and a breeze fluttering in the starched curtains. In the corner, near a low bookshelf, was a big round table littered with teapots and Classic books, and there were flowers everywhere, roses and carnations and anemones, on the desk, on the table, on the window sills. The roses were especially fragrant; their smell hung rich and heavy in the air, mingled with the smell of bergamot, and a faint inky scent of camphor. Breathing deep, I felt intoxicated.

I took the second row of seats, not too close to the front desk. I emptied my bag and took my seat, feeling the ruffles of your trench coat brush against my shoulders. "I'm definitely sitting here," you said, placing your belongings next to mine. "We still have so much to talk about." I looked up and into the darkness of your eyes; they looked like real gold, glinting in the drowsy summer sun which poured through the window and soaked in yellow pools on the oak floor — voluptuous, rich, intoxicating. Sitting next to you, I felt a weight pressing me out. I felt covered; something dark in me retreated for what felt like the first time. I felt pathetic admitting it to myself, but having you there — not just in my life, but sitting next to me — helped. For the first few hours, we didn't speak much, but your presence steadied and refocused me. I thought less of everything. It was as if the necessity of proving myself normal to you really did make me more normal. Just being around someone that knew nothing of me was soothing, and you were able to quiet my mind. As grateful as I was, though, I was also disgusted at myself, by how dependent I was, how weak. Was there no end to my needs?

I felt sometimes like a camera, shocked when people noticed me. I was a little infatuated with you. I wanted to know everything I could, as if, per the *Dune* novels, all of those details might have conferred some greater mastery over the objects of my desire. There was a code to it all, it seemed, something underneath the smooth rhythm of day and night, and that was what I wanted to crack.

Our first professor was a man in his late thirties and sat in an armchair by the window. His face looked out at me. It was a small, wise face as alert and poised as a question; and though certain features of it were suggestive of youth — the elfin upsweep of the eyebrows, the deft lines of nose and jaw — it was by no means a young face, and his hair was snow white. He wore optical glasses and dressed somewhat similar to a stay-at-home father. "I suppose you're all here for Philosophy, Literature, and Modern History," he said with a dreary Scouse accent. "Let's begin, shall we?"

In my clearest memory of him, each class started almost drowsily but soon went at a pell-mell pace. Not frantic, but operatic. Occasionally he'd pause, check his notes in a brief silence, and launch in another direction as we finished making our notes and the sound of our writing died down. Every now and then, we'd exchange glances or an accidental touch and continue writing. Our professor would allow us five-minute breaks periodically, every thirty minutes of our two-hour class; he had a theory that pupils learned better in a pleasant, non-scholastic atmosphere, so I'd take each break to smoke a cigarette outside, feeling more virtuous each time I kicked a filler into the trash. Sometimes, you would join me on my excursions absorbing the heat of each other's company in contentment. "I hate our professor," you sighed on the second morning.

"He's nice—"

"I can tell he doesn't give a shit about philosophy," you said. "All we ever talk about is literature."

I thought of him kindly, but I did agree with what you said. "It has only been two days," I offered.

You took a long drag of your cigarette. "I suppose so," you said and then chuckled. "I hope he gets fired."

I laughed at this, but in retrospect, you might have jinxed it as that very morning, on the second day of classes, our professor had curiously disappeared. He was replaced by substitutes for the entire day; although the idea was rather pleasant, they droned on for hours about history and writing techniques, not particularly applicable to our syllabus but just to use the time I suppose. The whole class couldn't wait to make it to our early morning break. We walked far, all the way to Oxford University Park — soon to become a daily routine of ours; every morning, at ten thirty to eleven we'd walk all the way over to the park, order lattes and smoke a cigarette or two — on that specific morning though, the light from the sun was streaming directly into your face; in such a strong light that most people would look somewhat washed out, but your clear, fine features were only illuminated until it was a shock to look at you, at your dark and radiant eyes, glowing warm as honey. I thought of that line from *The Iliad* I loved so much, about Pallas Athene and the terrible eyes shining. Leaning back, you took a sip of your coffee before opening your eyes. "What?" you asked, smiling.

"Nothing," I said.

"You know, it's weird."

"What is?" I asked.

"It feels like I've known you my whole life," you said, lighting a cigarette. You were a little shy, and when you smiled it was as if we were in a movie and the soundtrack changed. You were deeply tanned from staying in the Italian sun all day. I knew your name was an angel's name — an archangel, really. Which only made you glow more in my eyes.

I was young enough, naive enough, to imagine we could be friends. It was fantasy. I was learning there was a gulf between us that could not be carelessly crossed by my longing. I reached for the pack and lit one of my own. "You know what else is strange?"

"What is?" you asked.

"I feel exactly the same way," I said, placing the cigarette in between my lips and inhaling deep.

"Imagine if we were close in a past life or something?" you joked.

I chuckled and reached for my coffee. "I bet we were best friends. Or maybe married for fifteen years."

You laughed at the latter. "Maybe you were my arch nemesis."

"That literature trope where you don't know whether you feel love or hatred for me?"

"Imagine that," you said. "But I'd prefer that honestly."

"How come?"

"That would imply you want to be my lover." You grinned widely, the ends of your lips curled playfully again. I laughed rather loudly, placing my coffee back onto the table in front of us. You tilted your head with a cocky smile. "What's so funny?"

"Nothing," I mumbled through my laughter. The generosity of your affection unsettled me. First, there was the matter of the attention itself: I had never, never received anything so grand. Second, there was the impossibility of ever adequately repaying you. And third, there was the meaning behind the gesture: I had known for some time that you respected me, and even enjoyed my company. But was it possible that I was someone potentially important to you, that you liked me more than just a classmate, but as something else? And if that was the case, why should it make me feel so self-conscious?

I was frightened of everything, it sometimes seemed, and I hated that about myself. Fear and hatred, *fear and hatred*: often, it seemed that those were the only two qualities I possessed. Fear of everyone else; hatred of myself.

"You need to stop saying 'nothing' to everything I'm asking," you smiled.

"I'm being ambiguous, is it not working?"

"Absolutely not," you laughed.

"For some reason it's not as successful of a seduction method as I'd hoped," I said, and smiled at you, a little, and you smiled back. "But, if you're proposing it as an offer," I trailed on. "I wouldn't mind it."

"What as an offer?" you asked again.

"Nothing."

We both smiled at each other and headed back into class. I wanted to know you better, but during those early days, I had been reminded that the process — getting to know someone — was always so much more challenging than I remembered. I always forgot; I was always made to remember. I wished, as I often did, that the entire sequence — the divulging of intimacies, the exploring of pasts — could be sped past, and that I could simply teleport to the next stage, where the relationship was something soft and pliable and comfortable, where both parties' limits were understood and respected.

During my lunch break, I met with Adeline, Serena and Asli again. The air of the coffee shop was imbued with the rich aroma of freshly brewed espresso and the gentle hum of lively conversations. Sunlight streamed through the large windows, casting a warm glow on the vintage-inspired wooden tables and leather chairs. We bought a sandwich and pastry each, all presented with an artistic touch; powdered sugar between the cracks, warm jam, or sprinkled almonds. "These look amazing," said Serena and we all agreed. The gentle clinking of cups and the faint murmur of music in the background made the hour pass by in a haze.

When I returned to Pitt Rivers, the familiar outline of a broad and academic man sat tensely at the front desk. I glanced around at the other students, their expressions were similarly clouded as to why Ian was sitting in our professor's chair. Suddenly, the doors cracked open and it was, in fact, our professor who wordlessly walked down the aisle. Like a branded maiden he picked up a few books that were scattered across the desk and left the room. We watched from the windows as he disappeared into the rain, never to be seen again. We looked back at Ian as he fidgeted with his round spectacles before releasing a heavy sigh. "As you know, the past day has been nothing up to Oxford standards. Because of this, we have decided *mutually* to merge both Philosophy groups with one another." The air stung with permanence. "Starting tomorrow, group one and group two will be mixed together. It will stay this way until the end of the course. I understand that this has been a very inconvenient situation for everyone involved, but the lecturer of the other group is a very respectable woman."

"Meaning she isn't," you whispered to me with a coy smile. We packed our things and left the room.

Upon returning to the dormitories, I suppose I was only a little depressed, now the novelty of the unknown had worn off. Nothing was more disorientating than insomnia. I spent the night reading Freud until four in the morning, until my eyes burned and my head swan, until the only light burning in St. Catherine was my own. When I could no longer concentrate on Freud, and psychoanalysis began to transmute itself into incoherent triangles and words, I finally went to sleep, only to wake up again a few hours later.

I walked to Pitt Rivers, the outside air was cool and still, the sky a hazy shade of white peculiar to summer mornings, and the flowers lining the sidewalk were now drenched in dew. The hedges and acres and acres of lawn surrounding the Museum were covered in a network of webs that caught the dew in beads so that it glistened white as frost. Behind me, a cool voice whispered in my ears. "Good morning." Startled, I turned to see you lowering into the seat next to me again. "Are you always up this early?" you asked.

"Almost always,' I said, looking through the hazy windows. "It's beautiful here, but morning light can make the most vulgar things tolerable."

"I know what you mean," you said, and I figured you did. We'd often see each other in the very early mornings, almost dawn, when the streets were empty and the light was golden and kind on the grass, the chain-link fences and the solitary scrub oaks. Other students began to trail into the room.

"How are you feeling about our new professor?" I asked.

Your brows furrowed. "If she's anything like the substitutes, I think I'll shoot myself."

I laughed tiredly. "Nothing could be worse than the substitutes."

"Right again, Alaska," you smiled.

Suddenly, the doors burst open carrying a strong breeze behind the stark outline of a petite and peculiarly dressed woman. "Alright," she said, looking around the classroom with a steady gaze. "I hope we're all ready to leave the phenomenal world and enter into the sublime."

Our new professor was a woman named Louise Vincent and at the beginning of class, she would unpack her long, thin thermos of coffee and a bag of Brach's singly wrapped camels — the ones with the white centres. Prior to her studies at Oxford, Louise was awarded a first-class honours BA in Human, Social, and Political Sciences and an MPhil in Political

Thought and Intellectual History. She was unarguably smart, a true academic, but she really rounded the class with her integration of humour and striking charisma. She wore optical glasses, curiously enough the same kind as Ian's: old-fashioned, with round steel rims. She might have been beautiful had her features been less set, or her eyes behind the glasses, less frayed and bespectacled. Louise had an eccentric crux about her, that's why she was so easy to learn from and listen to, even to want to be like.

"We don't like to admit it," said Louise, pacing around the room. "But the idea of losing control is one that fascinates controlled people such as ourselves more than almost anything. All truly civilised people — the ancients no less than us — have civilised themselves through the wilful repression of the old, animal self. Are we, in this room, really very different from the Greeks or the Romans? Obsessed with duty, piety, loyalty, sacrifice? All those things which are to modern tastes so chilling?" I looked around the classroom and then to you. "And it's a temptation for any intelligent person, and especially for perfectionists such as the ancients and ourselves, to try to murder the primitive, emotive, appetite self. But that is a mistake."

"Why?" said Mellisa, a brown-haired girl sitting across the room, leaning slightly forward.

Louise arched an eyebrow, her long, wise nose gave her profile a forward tilt, like an Etruscan in a bas-relief. "Because it is more dangerous to ignore the existence of the irrational. For example of what happens in the absence of such, think of the Romans, their emperors. Think, for example, of Tiberius trying to live up to the command of his stepfather Augustus. Think, of the tremendous, impossible strain he must have undergone. The people hated him. No matter how hard he tried he was never good enough. Before he died, old and mad, he wrote a letter home to the Senate: *May all the Gods and*

Goddesses visit me with more utter destruction than I feel I am daily suffering." She paused. "The Roman genius, and perhaps the Roman flaw," she said, "was an obsession with order."

We moved on to Socrates and spent the hours discussing his theories, his principles and his calculations. But nothing seemed to interest me greater than his death. When faced between exile and death, Socrates came forward and chose death:

> *The difficulty, my friends, is not to avoid death, but to avoid unrighteousness; for that runs faster than death.*

Much of what I loved about literature was also what I loved about Socrates — archetypes at play, hidden forces, secrets brought to light, buffered by cruel turns of fate. I wanted to feel powerful in the face of my fate. I wanted to look over the top of my life and see what was coming. I wanted to be the main character of a story and its author. And if I were writing a novel about someone like me, that would be exactly what would lead her astray.

See, there are two kinds of people, I think: those who want to know the future and those who do not. I've never met anyone ambivalent about this. I have been both kinds. For now, I think I know which one is better, but I'm prepared to change my mind again. But if I told you I could tell the future, you would laugh at me.

And I would laugh at myself too.

CHAPTER THREE

SOME THINGS COSMIC

The chronological sorting of memories is an interesting business. Prior to my first days in Oxford, my recollections of that time are distant and blurry: from here on out, they come into a sharp, delightful focus. It is here, that the stilted mannequins of initial acquaintances begin to yawn and stretch and come to life. It was days before the gloss and mystery of newness, which kept me from seeing anything with much objectivity, would wear off — though reality was far more interesting than any idealised version could possibly be — but it is here, in my memory, that they cease from being totally foreign and begin to appear, for the first time, in shapes very like their bright old selves.

I too appear as something of a stranger in these early memories: watchful and grudging, oddly silent. All my life, people have taken my shyness for soulfulness, a bad temper of one sort or another.

At any rate, this was the week that things started to change, that the dark gaps between the street lights began to grow smaller and smaller, and farther apart. It's easy to see things in retrospect. But I was ignorant then of everything but my own happiness, and I don't know what to say except that life itself seemed very magical in those days. Everything somehow fit together, some sly and benevolent providence was revealing itself by degrees and I felt myself trembling on the brink of a fabulous discovery — my future, my past, the whole of my life.

I had so many happy days with my friends that when they fall from this vantage they merge into a sweet and indistinct blur. On Wednesday morning, the last, stubborn wildflowers finally sprouted and the wind became dull and died away. And on that warm afternoon, when the sky was like lead and the clouds were racing, I spent the day outside with Adeline, Asli and Serena, walking around town altogether. They treated me in a happy, offhand manner which implied I had known them much longer than I had. Adeline I was fondest of and spent the most time with — we were neighbours, of course. I enjoyed her company and always got along with her. Though I often looked forward to seeing her and thought of her tenderly and often, I was more comfortable around Asli. She was a lot like my other friends back home, impulsive and generous. She was always relaxed and never seemed to carry any boat of judgement alongside her.

But I digress.

I awaited Philosophy class with acute curiosity that morning. The dining hall was open at six, though at that hour of the morning, there were no students. I went upstairs and got myself a cup of coffee and sat around my room fully dressed for quite some time. And it was with something of a thrill that I looked at my watch and realised that if I didn't hurry, I'd be late. I grabbed my bags and rushed out; halfway to Pitt Rivers, I realised I was running and forced myself to slow to a walk.

I had caught my breath by the time I opened the back door. The odour of disinfectant and chalkboard cleaner, combined with the monotonous chant of conditional verbs, put me into a kind of trance, and I sat at my desk swaying slightly with boredom and fatigue, hardly aware of the passage of time. "Are you feeling okay?" you asked. "You seem tired."

"I am," I sighed. "I think I woke up too early again."

You raised a curious eyebrow. "Early?" you asked. "Weren't you almost late—"

"Almost,' I said. "*Almost* late."

You chuckled softly. "How about another morning coffee then?"

I smiled. "You read my mind."

On the walk to the University Park, you were gluey with sleep, your head tipped over, lips apart. I walked next to you, awake with the thrill of being close to you, and the knowledge I had of your mind from all of those hours of lectures. I wanted nothing more than to slip a kiss on your mouth right then, but it was only pure lust, not affection, and the imagined scene of it turned in my mind like a worry stone as we passed again along to road's dangerous curves.

It was a summer of wanting impossible things.

In the park, the chill sky, misty with fine rain near the treetops, made even the familiar landscape around Oxford seem indifferent and remote. The fields were white with fog, and the top of the coffee shop was entirely obscured, invisible in the cold haze. We lit a cigarette, drank our coffees, and continued routine conversation about whatever was on our minds; we didn't necessarily have to have a topic to discuss, or a new theory of some kind, conversation even flowed when our lips had stopped moving. When you leaned back in your chair, in that same indifferent and detached manner, I found myself unintentionally mimicking the gesture. "You know," you said with a mischievous glint in your eyes. "Socrates would be envious of our philosophical coffee dates."

The corner of my mouth raised playfully. "Is this a date now, officially?"

You chuckled, taking a sip of your warm latte. "Well, not a formal one, but it certainly feels like a promising start."

I felt a faint blush tint my cheeks. "Don't count your luck."

"That's all I ever do," you smiled, eyes glistening in the waning sun. "Anyway, I'm enjoying Louise. She's smart, she's funny..."

I rolled my eyes playfully. "Would you rather be dating Louise or me?"

"Is that an offer?"

"In what mad world is that an offer, Theo?" I laughed.

"In a philosophical one: *there is always some madness in love—*"

"*But there is also always some reason in madness.*"

"Nietzsche!" We laughed together.

You leaned forward and rested your hands against the table. "What do you want, Alaska?"

I tilted my head and paused for a second. "What do you mean?" I asked nervously.

"What do you want?" you repeated. "Out of your life?"

The sun billowed in the high sky making it hard for me to see. I looked down into my lap and fiddled with the hems of my jacket. "Well, for my friends to be—"

"No," you chuckled. "What do you want *for you?*"

I thought to myself solemnly and reached for my coffee cup. I was afraid that if I opened myself I would not stop pouring. "I want to feel secure enough to be truly free. I have always been...fighting for what's mine, running from things, just surviving. I want to feel safe enough that I can just be free," I sighed. "Now you, what do you want?"

"A philosophically mad offer," you smiled and then suddenly your expression dropped.

I frowned. "What is it?" I asked.

"Shit," you said. "Time."

"What?" I asked again.

"It's time. We are actually late now."

"Oh shit," I laughed as we grabbed our belongings hysterically, spilling pools of coffee against the sandy pathway. The door opened and a hush fell as Louise slipped in and closed the door quietly behind her. A sudden wind rustled through the birches and the smell of wood smoke in the air had a quality of memory; there it was, before my eyes, and yet too beautiful to believe. "Aristotle says in *The Poetics*," said Louise, "that objects such as corpses, painful to view in themselves, can become delightful to contemplate in a work of art."

Rain suddenly began to drum on the high windows, and the floodlights, shining through the glass, cast a pattern on the walls as if dark rivulets of water were streaming down them from ceiling to floor. "Aristotle also says that time crumbles things. And so, Alaska, Theodore, on time tomorrow please." We smiled sheepishly at each other as I opened my notebook and began to write down every word that came from Louise's mouth. Suddenly you whispered to me, "How come I've never seen you use your laptop in class? You bring it out every day, but I've never seen you actually use it."

I sighed. "I don't have an English adapter. I don't have the time to buy one either."

You seemed to contemplate this for a moment. "Why don't we leave it to charge in my room after class? I have an adapter in the bathroom."

I took a moment to think; I was slightly wary of the force of your personality but the extremism of your offer was appealing as well. With each day I trusted you a little more, and at times I wondered if I was making the same mistake again. Was it better to trust or better to be wary? Could you have a real relationship if some part of you was always expecting betrayal? I felt sometimes as if I was taking advantage of your generosity, your jolly faith in me, and sometimes as if my life circumspection was the wise choice after all, for if it should end badly, I'd have only myself to blame. But it was difficult not to trust you: you made it difficult, and, just as important, I was making it difficult for myself — I wanted to trust you, I wanted to give in, I wanted the creature inside me to tuck itself into a sleep from which it would never wake.

But what was I willing to do to feel less alone? Could I destroy everything I'd built and protected so diligently for intimacy? How much humiliation was I ready to endure? I didn't know; I was afraid of discovering the answer.

But increasingly, I was even more afraid that I would never have the opportunity to discover it at all. What does it mean to be a human, if I could never have this? And yet, I reminded myself, loneliness was not hunger, or deprivation, or illness: it was not fatal. Its eradication was not owed to me. I had a better life than so many people, a better life than I have ever thought I would have. To wish for companionship along with everything else I had seemed like a kind of greed, a gross entitlement. But I was, after all, a teenager. And like many teenagers, I wanted to be more powerful than the world around me. "If it's not too much trouble..."

"Never," you said and we turned our attention back to Louise.

"After all, what are the scenes in poetry graven on our memories, the ones that we love the most? Precisely these. The murder of Agamemnon and the wrath of Achilles. Dido on the funeral pyre. The daggers of the traitors and Caesar's blood — remember how Suetonius describes his body being borne away on the litter, with one arm hanging down?"

I raised my hand to speak and Louise offered me a gentle nod. "Death is the mother of beauty. Beauty is rarely soft or consolatory. Quite the contrary. Genuine beauty is always quite alarming."

Louise smiled back at me. "Well said, Alaska."

All afternoon it fell, warm rain, dripping from the eaves and pattering on the pavement. The buildings that lowered at the horizon were swallowed up in the fog and the world seemed light and empty, dangerous somehow. Walking back to campus, the wet grass flattened beneath our feet while threads of smoke floated up from our filterless cigarettes, burning dangerously at our fingertips. The rain pricked at us like wood sparks off a fire, a tea-stained white stretching endlessly across the sky. Each droplet looked stained, ripping everything off the ground, your dark hair now soaked, curled like a branch against your forehead. I could feel a vibration in the air, a sense of hastening...

Sometimes, when there's been some sort of situation and reality is too sudden and strange to comprehend, the surreal will take over. Action slows to a dreamlike glide, frame by frame; the motion of a hand, a sentence spoken, fills an eternity. Little things — a cricket on a stem, the veined branches on a leaf — are magnified, brought from the background in achingly clear focus. And that's what happened then, walking over the meadow to your room. It was like a painting too vivid to be real — every pebble, every blade of grass sharply defined, the sky so blue it hurt me to look at it.

You invited me into your room and in the overwhelming stillness, between our echoless footsteps, my pulse sang thin and fast in my ears. I sat very still, trying not to think. It seemed as if I was waiting for something, I wasn't sure what, something to lift the tension and make me feel better, though I could imagine no possible event, in past, present, or future that would have either effect. It seemed as if an eternity had passed. I looked up at the clock. Scarcely a minute had gone by.

Your room was more private than the old oak-floored dorms that I lived in on campus. You had a wide range of furniture, upholstery, light and dark woods. Everything was too quiet. I traced a finger along the walls. I reminded myself, *you need to be awake and aware.*

I don't know. I suppose I should have had a better idea of what I was letting myself in for. Still, our connection seemed to be so simple, like a dropped stone falling to the lakebed with scarcely a ripple. We took our friendship as something docile, an ordinary weight (gentle plunk, swift rush to the bottom, dark waters closing over it without a trace) when in fact, it was a depth charge, one that exploded quite without warning beneath the glassy surface, and the repercussions of which may not be entirely over, even now.

I suppose, in those days of getting to know each other, we'd simply thought about this too much, talked of it too often until the scheme ceased to be a thing of the imagination and took on a life of its own. I see, now, how quick it was. And it is impossible to slow down this scene, to examine individual frames. I see now what I saw then, flashing by with the swift, deceptive ease of a first love. There you were, like a miracle: sunlight streaming behind you into the room.

I looked into the deepness of your eyes and began to feel it then, the pull, a chill coming from an opening inside of me. It echoed across your carpet floors and back into my chest. You took a seat beside me and slowly, we inched closer to one another, until the tips of our noses touched. Then, you drew my lips in for a kiss. At that moment, I went blank, my very self, erasing myself. It had been a long, long time since anyone had kissed me and I remembered the sense of helplessness I felt whenever it happened, and how I was told to just open my mouth and relax and do nothing, and now — out of habit and memory, and the inability to do anything else — that was what I did, and waited for it to be over, counting the seconds and trying to breathe through my nose.

Finally, you stepped back and looked at me, and after a while, I looked back. When you kissed me again, I had that sensation I always had when I was a child and being kissed, that my body was not my own, that every gesture I made was predetermined, reflex after reflex and reflex, and that I could do nothing but succumb to whatever might have happened to me next.

Maybe enough time had passed so it would be different. Maybe I was wrong, maybe you were right: that this wasn't an experience forbidden to me forever. Maybe I was really capable of this. Maybe I wouldn't be hurt after all. You seemed, at that moment, to have been conjured, like the offspring of my worst fears and greatest hopes and dropped into my life as a test: one side was everything I knew, the patterns of my existence as regular and banal as the steady plink of a dripping faucet, where I was alone but safe, and shielded from everything that could hurt me. On the other side were waves, tumult, rainstorms, excitement: everything I could not control, everything potentially awful and ecstatic, everything I had lived my life trying to avoid, everything whose absence bled my life of colour. Inside me, the creature hesitated, perching on its hind legs, pawing the air as if feeling for answers.

Don't do it, don't fool yourself, no matter what you tell yourself, you know what you are, said one voice.

Take a chance, said the other voice. *You're lovely. You have to try.*

This was the voice I always ignored.

This may never happen again, the voice added, and this stopped me.

This will end badly, said the first voice, and then both voices fell silent, waiting to see what I would do.

I didn't know what to do; I didn't know what would happen. I had to find out. Everything I had learned told me to leave; everything I had wished for told me to stay. *Be brave,* I told myself. *Be brave for once.* And so, I bit against your lower lip and brimmed the edge of my teeth against it. I felt the warmth spread across our bodies. I began to squeeze the memory of you above me out, not so much even the sight of you as the feeling I had, of an aurora of heat and skin above me. I knew there was no way for me to feel the heat of you through the memory of chill water rain. Yet I did.

My hand reached to caress your face, drawing slowly over your cheekbones. For a fraction of a moment, you were not yourself again. I felt the skin of deep memory, the touch of someone long gone. I brushed the thought away as your head lay lowly against my chest and the birch trees were a pale fire running slowly across the cracks of your blinds. My arm cast a glow through the moonlight dawning in and it was in that first moment, resting beside you, that I realised I was on the other side of something and I didn't know what it was.

I waited to find out.

Back in the sixteenth staircase, the wood-plank floors were dark like molasses. Cool to the touch like a lake rock passed to me by someone who held it briefly. Screened windows ran the length of the dormitory. Despite the stretch of endless summer, heavy rains had caused the skylight to leak and my bed sheets were stained with rug-coloured streaks that seemed to contain a language of their own that drifted in and out of my sporadic thoughts. I changed my clothes, couldn't decide what to do with the ones I'd taken off, thought of washing them, wondered if it might look suspicious and finally stuffed them at the very bottom of my open wardrobe. Then I sat down on my bed and looked at the clock.

I sat in my room in silence for a long time, thinking. After New York, I had sworn I would never again do this to myself. I knew you would never do anything bad to me, and yet my imagination was limited: I was incapable of conceiving a relationship that wouldn't end with me being hit, or being screamed at, with me being made to do things I had told myself I would never have to do again. Wasn't it possible, I asked myself, that I could push even someone as good as you to that inevitability? Wasn't it foregone that I would inspire a kind of hatred from even you? Was I so greedy for companionship I would ignore the lessons that history — my own history — had taught me?

But then there was another voice inside me, arguing back. *This is the one person you feel like you can trust,* said the voice. *Theo is not him, he would never do that, not ever.*

It was time for dinner and I hadn't eaten all day but I wasn't hungry. I went up to the window and watched the rain droplets whirl in the high arcs of light above the dormitories, then crossed over and sat upon my bed again. I ran my fingers over the areas of skin that now resembled plucked leather; the scars had always been a constant reminder that the assault was real and not just some terrible nightmare I could force myself awake from with a pinch on the arm. They felt like stretched velvet, the brail of my skin. I shouldn't have liked any aspect of the one thing that ripped my life out from under me, even if it was simply the way it felt beneath my fingertips. But those flaws of mine were blanketed in pink highlights, put on display for the entire world to see; a permanent reminder of the months that destroyed all the best parts of me.

I suppose I loved my scars because they had stayed with me longer than most people had.

Minutes ticked by. Whatever anaesthesia had carried me through the day was starting to wear off and with each passing second the thought of sitting all night, alone, was seeming more and more unbearable. I turned on a playlist, switched it off, tried to read. When I couldn't hold my attention on one book I tried another. Scarcely ten minutes had passed. I picked up the first book and put it down again. Then, against my better judgement, went downstairs and dialled your number.

You answered on the first ring.

We walked through the rain until we approached Magdalen Boat House; the land took a downward slope. A thick fog lay in the crevice below, and by degrees, we descended, and the world sank from view. I have vague memories, like impressions on glass plates, of the old boathouse, a circular band shell, an arched stone bridge. You, beside me, stood out sharp and almost hyperrealistic, a wrath form far from light and strangely substantial in the mist. The undergrowth of the bridge was peaceful and desolate; the dock trackless and undisturbed beneath the falling rain, but also closed off by a large, iron fence. We tried pulling the gate open, but it had been locked twice, one padlock at the top and another at the bottom. I thought hastily to myself, *we could climb over.* "I think we should climb over," you said, emptying your pockets and handing over the contents.

Stepping on the metal bars, I almost slipped on an icy step and pitched, face forward into one of the large spikes in front of me. A few raindrops were one thing, but I had not thought it to be possible for the weather to change as suddenly and violently as this. Almost everything was buried in rain, an expanse of clean, unbroken water droplets stretched blue and twinkling as far as I could see. My hands were raw and my elbow felt bruised. With some effort, I made it over the fence.

We sat together under the bridge, sheltered from the

endless rain, and lit a cigarette each. The flame from your lighter was the only visible light source in miles. We watched the lake heave in the dark, the currents spilt softly around us against the lake. I drew my knees to my chest: nothing. Nothing hurt, nothing even threatened to hurt: my body was mine again, without complaint or sabotage. I closed my eyes, not because I was tired but because it was a perfect moment and I knew how to enjoy them. "This is beautiful," you sighed. "Have you ever been here before?"

"No. Never," I said. "Climbing over fences isn't usually a part of my daily routine."

You rolled your eyes sarcastically. "I feel so..."

"*Eirene.*"

"Exactly," you agreed. "*Nothing matters and few things matter at all.*"

"Nothing ever matters," I chuckled. "*If we believe in nothing then everything is possible.*"

"Ms Absurdist," you smiled.

'Mr Existentialist,' I smiled back, resting my head against your shoulder. The narrows of river emptied into a wide lagoon and I saw upon its surface a singular miracle. A long curving neck rose from a dress of white plumage.

"Swan," you said, sensing my excitement. It pattered the bright water, flapping its great wings, and lifted into the dark sky. The word alone hardly attested to its magnificence nor conveyed the emotion it produced. The sight of it generated an urge I had no words for, a desire to speak of the swan, to say something of its whiteness, its virtuosity and pureness, the explosive nature of its movement, and the slow beating of its wings. I struggled to find words to describe my own sense of it. I felt a twinge, a curious yearning, imperceptible to passersby, to you, the trees, or the clouds. You looked at me and ran a delicate finger over my arms. "You mentioned you like to write," you said, softly.

"All the time," I said.

"What about?" you asked and I paused, slightly embarrassed. "You can tell me," you laughed, nudging me slightly.

"I write prose, but mostly letters," I said. "Letters to people who have ever impacted my life in some way."

"What's the typical response?" you asked, and I must've made some estranged face for you laughed momentarily. "That bad?"

"I've never sent a letter," I said. "They're too honest, but they're good for me to have...to remember."

You inched closer. "Remember what?" you asked. Whenever you asked me questions about myself, I always felt something cold move across me, as if I were being iced from the inside, my organs and nerves protected by a sheath of frost. At that moment, I thought I might break, that if I said anything the ice would shatter and I would splinter and crack.

So I waited until I knew I would sound normal before answering. "Remember the things that have made me the person I am right now," I said. "Some letters are good, others are bad. It all depends on the memories."

You seemed to like this answer and smiled. "Would you ever write me a letter?"

I scoffed. "If you get too close, I'll turn you into poetry."

At the low edge of the sky, a bright smear suddenly appeared. The slow-burning, light peeled like struck bells at the speed of its passing. A bright tear in the night's dark belly. "I write letters too," you said, looking out at the rippling currents. "But not to people, to myself. I have some of the excerpts—"

"Yes," I said immediately as a slight embarrassment tinted my cheeks.

"Yes, what?" you laughed.

"Yes, I would love to hear them," I said, feeling the warmth of your body through the water rain.

"They're in Italian, so bear with me as I translate them," you said, reaching for your phone. The white ultra-violence shone across your face in soft flashes. "*Angeli custodi, protettori dell'amore.* The mockingbirds." The sound of your voice dissolved in my ears; think of a dream with the outer surface of a storm, and the insides like the surface of days as you have sometimes found them. I closed my eyes and listened. Everything was suddenly, irrevocably calm and quiet:

>*"Da diversi anni quando vedo un uccello immagino che esso sia una reincarnazione di mio padre (for several years now when I see a bird I imagine it being a reincarnation of my father), o almeno uno dei tanti occhi attraverso cui lui mi guarda (or at least one of the many eyes through which he watches me)...*
>
>*Sarà per l'aria disinvolta e pensierosa che mi trasmettono, sarà per il loro spirito di osservazione (may it be for the nonchalant mood that they transmit me, may it be for their perceptiveness), sarà per la loro camminata che mi ricorda il suo passeggiare con le mani incrociate dietro la schiena (may it be for their walking that reminds me of him wandering with his hands crossed behind the back)...*
>
>*Ah, se solo credessi in queste cose! (Ah, if only I believed in these things!) Se credessi nei defunti che ci guardano queste sensazioni diventerebbero per me verità, ma ahimè sono costrette a rimanere soltanto un piacevole sogno (If I believed in the dead, watching these sensations would become for me truth, but sadly they are forced to remain just a pleasant dream)..."*

You finished and suddenly it was dark. The blue expanse of July's night wrapped us in as part of its blue, cold snapped at our noses, and the water freezing inside of the dock tore apart the fibres of wood with the wind. For a moment, a bitter sadness seemed to permeate the air, rising like a suffocating gas. You rest your head in my arms. I held it gently in my hands, helplessly at peace. "You should let people hear you," I finally said.

"You're hearing me," you said. "That's enough for me."

"I want the world to hear you."

When the rain dissipated, our shoes were muddied, our clothes were drenched and smelt strongly of tobacco. I made out the trace of your eyes in the dark, then leaned forward to kiss you — long, slow and deliberate. Softly, you drew in your breath and your hands went down to my waist and before I knew it, more from a reflex than anything, you pulled me in even closer. Your mouth was soft and had a mannish taste, like tea and cigarettes. You pulled away, breathing hard, and leaned to kiss my throat. My vision swam. I closed my eyes.

It was a relief to have you there and simply be in your arms. Something felt different. We sat there for a long time, intimately, listening to the rainfall. As rainwater swept in a stream down to the lake, it was a bit windy and the sounds of currents seemed to amplify the call of somewhere else, more surreal than real. It was then that the sky blurred into the horizon, and amidst the quiet, you looked at me and said, "Alaska. *Nobody sees as we do.*"

And in that space of time, it was as if we were the only two people in the world.

When I got back to my room, I fell on my bed without taking off my coat or shoes. The lights were still on, and I felt weirdly exposed and vulnerable but I didn't want to turn them off. The bed was rocking a little, like a raft, and I kept a foot on the floor to steady it.

There was no hope of falling asleep this early and I wished

I had a glass of water. The room was hot and my throat was dry from smoking, leaving a bitter taste around my tongue.

I envisioned a glacier sliding into an intimate hot spring, surrounded by walls of impenetrable ice.

It was then that a familiar intensification overcame me. I was at once liberated and trapped: I wasn't abandoned; I was chosen, I was given a chance at loving again. There were too many sentiments I couldn't express in those days because frankly, it wasn't in my scope to expect, hope or ask. But now, I was given the chance to do so and was selfishly, callously taking the chance; but the misgivings of my past always lingered at the back of my mind.

I always had two longings and one was fighting the other; I wanted to be loved and I wanted to be alone, always. I suppose, I wanted to be loved only to prove it possible: to tell the world that someone saw me as a conquest, that above all else, I was worthy of the risk, the effort. I wanted you to serve as the evidence that I was not as damned as I thought I was, otherwise everything that seemed to touch me left me indifferent. But the night was all so beautiful, it signalled the ushering of endless days of unknowing to come. When morning light finally steamed across the thin coverlet, it was as if I had been enveloped into a strange, chemical calm.

Things were changing at a speed I never dreamt of.

I woke up at five-thirty on Thursday morning — by courtesy of the piercing, demonic shrill of the fire alarm — in absolute agony.

It was like waking from a nightmare to a worse nightmare. I sat up, heart pounding, slapping at the blank wall for the digital clock face until the terrible realisation dawned on me that it was not, in fact, my own alarm going off. Strange shapes and unfamiliar shadows crowded horribly around me; nothing offered any clue as to what was happening, and for a few delirious moments I wondered if I had set the alarm off myself in my sleep. There were shouts far away, somewhere downstairs in the dormitory; doors slammed, confusion grew, voices shouted down voices and then one hoarse voice rose above the others. I took a deep breath, then closed my eyes, exhaling sharply, annoyingly, then fell back in my bed as if I'd been shot.

I fell asleep and slept very soundly for a couple of minutes until I was awakened by a knock at the door. Seized by fresh panic, I fought to sit up in the tangle of my sheets, which had somehow got twisted around my knees as the door creaked open. Adeline was in the doorway. She stood with one hand on the knob, looking at me like I was a lunatic. "Alaska, the fire alarm has gone off," she said, sharply.

"I'll be right out," I murmured sleepily, and lay in bed for another minute or two, trying to collect my thoughts among the noise, then stood up, found my clothes, dressed as best as I could in the dark, and left by the time the drill was already over.

It was one of those mysterious, oppressive days in Oxford. Walking around campus felt like I was in Olympus, Valhalla, some old abandoned land above the clouds, like memories from a former life, isolated and disconnected in the mist. The neighbourhood felt like an overgrown village where time passed a little more slowly.

Drizzle and damp. I still smelled like wet clothes after yesterday, everything was dark and subdued. Huge, rain-splashed pains of glass — tinted grey so they made the day seem drearier than it was — walled us in on three sides of the cafeteria. I found Adeline and Serena talking over another cold portion of an English breakfast and took a seat right next to them. A misshapen old janitor trudged in with mop and pail and began, with weary grunting noises, to slop water on the floor by the beverage centre. What a morning.

I sighed into my cup of coffee. "I can barely open my eyes. I'm so tired."

"Apparently, people didn't come out of the dorms fast enough. I heard a counsellor say they might redo the alarm again tomorrow," Adeline said.

"They must be out of their minds," said Serena. I nodded silently and took a long swing of coffee.

"Where were you last night, Alaska?" Adeline asked. "We couldn't find you anywhere."

Last night?...My eyes widened as the night's events came back to me in some sort of Technicolor. "Oh," I sighed. "I was in town with Theo."

All three of them exchanged perplexed glances. "And who's Theo?" Asli asked excitedly.

"He's this Italian guy from my Philosophy class," I said, unwilling to present any further information.

"So..." Adeline asked. "Were you guys in town last night, *together*?"

I took a sip of my coffee. The grainy expresso burned down my throat. "Yeah, but it was raining so we sat under a bridge and–" I caught myself smiling and forced myself to stop. "We talked, it was nice."

"Nice?" Asli asked. "That sounds really sweet."

I nodded and played around with my cold breakfast. "It really was," I said, slightly uncomfortable by the attention. I differed to change topics. "Anyways, how was Psychology?"

"Plato's four divine madnesses, and what are they?"

Louise called out to the classroom of half-eager and half-tired faces. "Why does that obstinate voice in our heads torment us so? Could it be because it reminds us that we are alive, of our mortality, of our individual souls — which, after all, we are too afraid to surrender but yet makes us feel more miserable than any other thing? But isn't it the pain that often makes us most aware of self?" I looked over and you seemed conflicted. I could feel something brewing, something unnervingly quiet in the air. I kept my suspicions to myself; enduring things is what I did best, gritting my teeth and bearing them. But after our coffee-run, where you had seemingly alternated between affection and moodiness, there was a quiet between us for most of the day, a silence. I pretended not to know what it all meant. I still felt a cold ache climbing over.

"It is a terrible thing to learn that one's aches and pains are all one's own. Even more terrible, as we grow older, to learn that no person, no matter how beloved, can truly understand us. Our own selves make us most unhappy, and that's why we're so anxious to lose them." As Louise continued talking, I couldn't hear anything but a voice inside me, a voice, reading to me from the handbook, lower than my own. The voice hinted at directions, possibilities, even as it pressed forward, inexorable, to the next word in line. *Defect, defection, defective, definition, definitive.*

On the next page, I peeked. *Demon.*

When class was over, the room was all motion. Sounds of zippers and textbooks flipped over one another around me as other students passed in winking colours and pillowed sounds. As I was packing my things, I looked at you again but your eyes seemed hazy, disfigured, almost glassy. Outside, the sun was low, burning gold through the trees, casting our shadows before us on the ground, long and distorted. We walked for a long time without saying anything. The air was musty with far-off bonfires, sharp with the edge of twilight chill. There was no noise but the crunch of our shoes on the gravel path, the whistle of wind in the pines; I was sleepy and my head hurt and there was something not quite real about any of it, something like a dream.

Suddenly, you stopped and put a finger to your lips. In a dead tree, split in two were perched two huge blackbirds, too big for crows, too big for mockingbirds. You had never seen anything like them before.

"Ravens," I said. We stood stock-still, watching them. One of them hopped clumsily to the end of a branch, which squeaked and bobbed under its weight, the other one followed with a battery of flaps.

They sailed over the meadow, two dark shadows on the grass mimicking our own. You laughed for the first time that day. "Two of them for the two of us. That's an augury, I bet."

"Or an omen."

We continued walking back to St. Catherine, and the sky was cold and empty. The sliver of moon, like the white crescents of summer twilight, floated in the dim. I was unused to those dreary summer twilights, to chill and early dark; the nights fell too quickly and the hush that settled on the meadow in the evening filled me with a strange, tremulous sadness. I heard you sigh as you directed your gaze directly into my eyes. "I need to talk to you about something," you said. As soon as you had begun, I experienced a familiar dizziness, stomach-lifting nausea, and I looked down and waited until the cement became cement again and I would be able to walk.

"What is it?" I asked, faintly, warningly.

"I don't want to upset you," you said.

"I can't think of a single reason to be upset with you," I said.

You deeply exhaled. "Look. I love talking to you but I don't know how to feel about...*this*." I had a familiar feeling hinting at the direction of our conversation but vowed to stay silent. I felt in those minutes my body's treason, how sometimes the central, tedious struggle in my life was my unwillingness to accept that I would be betrayed by it again and again, that I could expect nothing from it and yet had to keep maintaining it. "Things are happening too quickly, maybe even too easily."

My science classes in Brooklyn had taught me that breathing turned the air inside us to a carbon, a little different from smoke, but a little like it. We had this in common with flames. We were just slower.

I took a breath, waiting. Impatient.

"I'm not saying that I don't want this," you rambled. "I mean, I'm not sure if I do. I need to think about it"

I sighed quietly. "That's okay. Maybe take some time to think about it and we can talk about it later?" I watched the buds sprouting, the sun lifting, my heart stunned and my voice caught in a stillness. "Thank you for telling me how you feel," I said. "Always be honest with me and I'll never get upset."

I was nothing because that is what nothing says. When we pulled closer to campus, I suddenly stopped. I couldn't bear to look at you or hear your voice and kept my gaze pointed at the ground instead. "When you have some idea of how you're feeling, we can talk about it," I finally said, but my voice was more assertive and protective than I had meant for it to sound.

"Alaska," you whispered. "I'm...I'm sorry."

I sighed. "Never be sorry for me, *please*."

When you didn't say anything, I turned around and walked back into the cityscape. This moment, I thought of as a slight parting of worlds, in which my memories washed up from the loamy, turned earth and hovered before me again, waiting for me to recognise it and claim it as my sentence.

Its reappearance was defiant: here it was again, an unsettling voice seemed to say to me. Did you really think he wouldn't abandon you? Did you really think things could be different? Eventually, I was also made to question how much of the prior days I had edited — edited and reconfigured, refashioned into something easier to accept — from even the past few years since.

What I was looking for was what seemed to vanish then. I learned from you, that often contradiction is the clearest way to truth.

CHAPTER FOUR
NUOVI INIZI

THERE WERE TWO WAYS OF FORGETTING. FOR MANY YEARS, I had envisioned (unimaginatively) a vault, and at the end of the day, I would gather the images and sequences and words I didn't want to think about again and open the heavy steel door only enough to hurry them inside, closing it quickly and tightly. But this method wasn't effective: the memories seeped out anyway. The important thing, I came to realise, was to eliminate them, not just to store them.

So I had invented some solutions. For small memories — little slights, insults — I relived them again and again and again until they were neutralised, until they became near meaningless with repetition, or until I could believe that they were something that had happened to someone else and I had just heard about it. For larger memories, I held the scene in my head like a film strip, and then I began to erase it, frame by frame. Neither method was easy: I couldn't stop in the middle of my erasing and examine what I was looking at, for example; I couldn't start scrolling through parts of it and hoped I wouldn't get ensnared in the details of what had happened, because I, of course, would. I had to work at it every night, until it was completely gone.

Though they never disappeared completely, of course. But they were at least more distant — they weren't things that followed me wraithlike, tugging at me for attention, jumping in front of me when I ignored them, demanding so much of my time and effort that it became impossible to think of anything else. In fallow periods — the moments before I fell asleep — they would reassert themselves, and so it was best to imagine, then, a screen of white, huge and light — light and still, and hold it in my mind like a shield.

After we had talked, I dreaded the thought of the day ahead. What I did experience when alone was a sort of general neurotic horror, a common attack of nerves and self-loathing; every cruel and fatuous thing I had ever said or done came back to me with an amplified clarity, no matter how I talked to myself or smoked to shake the thoughts away, each one paraded before me, one by one, in vivid and mordant splendour. In those days, I would let the thoughts interrupt me, and there would be times in which I would come out of that spell and find my hands still wrapped around the plastic covering of a pen poised over a piece of paper sitting before me, or still holding a book half on, half off the shelf. It was then that I began comprehending how much of my life I had learned to simply erase, even days after the assault had happened; and also that somehow, somewhere, I had lost that ability. I knew it was the price of enjoying my life now, that if I was able to be alert to the things I now found pleasure in, I would have to accept the costs as well. Because as elusive as my memories were, my life still came back to me in pieces. I knew I would endure them if it meant I could also have friends and a newer, brighter future; if I kept being granted the ability to take comfort in others.

And so, around four-thirty, I went to meet with Adeline in Westgate.

Westgate shopping centre was the central hub for teenage proclivities; cafes and commercial outlets lined each wall, bustling crowds could be seen entering in and out from the streets. Whenever we had nothing to do, Westgate was always our best bet for an enjoyable afternoon.

Walking through Radcliffe Square, I was impatient, even desperate. I began to notice how much summer stretched over the city, fragile, like remembering fragments of an old dream. I knew that eventually, you would have decided what this was if it was anything at all, but I couldn't seem to stand the waiting; it crawled through me because of my refusal to admit defeat. For the rest of the afternoon, I hung onto the possibility of redemption. I asked myself: did he regret it? Was it only a stroke of singular madness? A tragic, wrongheaded, even grotesque error? And then suddenly, I couldn't see anything past your rejection; negating everything that transpired between us, one body against the other, the image completely erased.

Adeline and I sat at a third-rate cafe bar called Maya's. In the centre of my own disorder, my mind was going in circles. When repeating the exactness of how you phrased things to myself, I could no longer identify any of them, like the small evidence of a crime gone cold. I tried speeding up the story, then slowing down, figuring I'd collide with myself and break the loop, but to no such luck. So instead, against my better judgement and most rather peculiarly, I asked Adeline for advice. "I think he's an asshole," she said.

I shrugged. "I kind of like him."

She parted her hair in the centre, using the curved talon of her forefinger as a comb. "I don't. He's just making things more complicated than they need to be."

I reached over and cradled my cup of coffee in my hands. "It's only two weeks anyway."

Adeline pinched a piece of the rich, auburn croissant on the table, holding it up to the skyline. "Lovely piece," she said profoundly. "Not quite the way it's made in France, though.'"

I looked at the defenceless pastry as she took a bite. "'No?"

"It has no character, not enough flakes," she said. "It's insulting to the French."

I laughed and then it went silent.

"I think he was quite rude," she said. "He pretty much called you easy."

I sighed. My coffee sat staring back at me with discernment. "That's his way, I guess. See, his mind is always up in the clouds with Plato or something."

"Seems like a bit of an excuse," Adeline said, lips wide and thin. "As long as you're happy."

I smiled ingenuously back at her. "I'm always happy, as long as I'm with you..." I looked back at the pastry again. "And this very mediocre, not very French croissant."

Serena joined us. She looked particularly angelic, her blonde hair windblown, in a white tennis sweater and tennis shoes. I sat staring out at Westgate in a sort of trance. To say that dinner went badly would be an exaggeration, but it didn't go all that well, either. Though I didn't do anything stupid, exactly, or say anything that I shouldn't, I felt dejected and bilious, and I talked little and ate even less. Much of the talk centred around their Psychology class to which I was not privy, and even Adeline's kind parenthetical remarks of explanation did not help to clarify. I left early, told them I'd catch up on work, and backed out of the cafeteria, my face burning under the collective gaze of cool, curious solicitude. It was getting cold and my head hurt and the whole day had left me with a keen sense of inadequacy and failure which grew keener with every step. I moved relentlessly over the evening, back and forth, straining to remember exact words, telling inflexions, any subtle insults or kindness I might have missed from our conversation, and my mind — quite willingly — supplied various distortions.

Just as I turned the corner, I saw you standing by the dormitories; brows arched and looking very sombre, as if what you were thinking was of the gravest importance. I took a step closer and peered as far as I could risk behind the corner. We locked eyes, and there was a terrible loneliness and sadness in your expression, and then it was gone, and you seemed to come back to yourself. You motioned for me to come over and I did, hesitantly. I took a seat on the stone ledge beside you and we both didn't say anything for a while. "I've been thinking," you said as the sky darkened in the distance. I nodded silently. "I'm still not sure."

I exhaled slowly, unjustly annoyed. "I'm not sure I quite understand," I said.

"I'm not making much sense, am I?" you asked, looking into the horizon. "I wanted to clarify things with you, but I'm just as confused as I was this afternoon."

"It's okay," I said gently. "If this isn't what you want, I won't be upset–"

"That doesn't feel right either," you sighed.

"We only have ten days," I said. "There isn't any kind of pressure or expectation. I would hate for you to feel that way."

You seemed to contemplate this for a moment; eyes stuck on the horizon, picking at the cylindrical bend of your cuticles. The ghost of my own distorted reflection receded in the curve of night bending until you looked back at me and smiled. "I like what's happening now," you finally said. "I'd like to continue with *now* if that's the case, if there are no obligations between us."

My thoughts collided into each other; *you need to take your chance, you are not damned.* I inhaled sharply and forced a smile. "Sure, no obligations," I said solemnly.

You stuck out your arm with a reticent smile. *"Nuovi inizi?"*

I shook it cautiously. *"Nuovi inizi."*

White sky. Trees faded at the skyline, the fields gone. We walked through campus, hands deep in our pockets and the crunch of feet was unbearably loud. The dormitories were black and silent, and the big parking lot behind your staircase was empty except for a few faculty cars and a lone green truck from maintenance. Inside, the hallways were littered with shoe boxes and coat hangers, doors ajar, everything dark and quiet as the grave.

My hands dangled from the cuffs of your jacket as if they weren't my own. I never got used to the way the horizon could just erase itself and leave me marooned, adrift in an incomplete dreamscape that was like a sketch of the world I knew — the outline of a single tree stood in the grove, lamp-posts and chimneys floated up out of context before the surrounding canvas was filled in — an amnesia land. I don't know why I remember that now, or why it made such an impression on me, but I felt watched, distracted. "I think we should turn down the blinds," I said.

"Anything for my darling," you derided.

I rolled my eyes as you made your way to the windows. "Why, thank you," I chuckled softly.

As you pulled down the blinds, I wrapped my hands around your waist and planted a few soft kisses on the back of your neck. You snickered before turning around and pulling me in for a deep, but gentle kiss. We lay on your duvet for a while, exchanging breathless kisses into sleep, pressed up against each other. I felt the heat of your skin pass right through me like I was made of glass. I was just about to close my eyes as you sat up, smiling at me with a gaze of strong epiphany. "I think I figured it out," you said suddenly. "What if I only saw you when I wanted to? And then when I didn't...you could just *fuck off.*"

I went silent and sat upright against the headboard. I could instantly feel something inside myself become alert. *What did you just say?* I glared into your eyes, they were malicious and unrelenting. We were both quiet for a long time.

"That only works for one of us," I said eventually.

You didn't say anything and instead pulled me into another kiss, but this time it felt untethered and strange. Those words were kinetically trailing me but in a certain way, not that everything 'went black', nothing of the sort; only that time was cloudy because of some primitive, numbing effect that obscured each and every one of our more intimate moments. I felt somewhat inebriated and caught up, and it was only later, in solitude, in memory, that the realisation dawned: when the air was cold; when I had left your room; when I looked around and found myself — quiet — I found myself in an entirely different world than when with you. And so, I let your words run over me and turn transparent.

I didn't have the courage to let them ruin you.

Months later I would come to regard this as one of those moments where you learn to trust your first instinct. For instance, I always told myself something wasn't what I thought it was because I was trying to scare myself off what I knew was true.

For now, though, the dim room was whirling at what was now an incredible speed, with every moment I took to breathe a series of luminous spots were dark around the edges and clung to your ceiling. And as you kissed me, I tried to decide, if you liked secrets better than kisses. Then, quite unexpectedly, like some godly saviour, there was a knock at the door and then a flurry of knocks. Without a word, we lay very still until it went quiet.

There was another knock at the door. We sprang apart.

Your eyes were wide. We stared at each other, and then the knock came again. You swore under your breath, bit your lip. I, panic-stricken, started to say something but you made a quick, shushing gesture at me with your hand. "Fuck," you whispered. "I thought that nobody saw us come in here."

"I suppose that's what we thought—"

More knocking, more insistent this time.

"Who is it?" I asked.

"We know who," you said. "This can't be good."

"What are we supposed to do?" I asked.

Glancing desperately around the room, your eyes fixated on the wardrobe beside us. "Get inside," you said.

I raised an eyebrow. "You want me to get inside of your closet? This isn't a movie—"

"Any better ideas?" you asked. I bit my tongue. You rolled your eyes and smiled. "That's what I thought. Now get inside, *quick*."

I closed the door behind me, but a slight crack left open made me feel somewhat exposed. My heart pounded, bewildered with fear. I watched as you ran a hand through your hair, unlocking the door. That's when I saw the flash of red, the glow of crimson shooting through the room. "Hey, is everything all right?" you asked. The two counsellors looked at you dubiously. You jostled around your cardigan and turned to the counsellors with a watery, intense gaze. "I was asleep. I'm sorry it took me so long to open up," you said. The counsellors were leaning with one elbow against the door frame, their red lanyards slung into careless loops around their necks, almost like a noose.

When they took a step into your room, their eyes intensely peered around, like they were searching for something unknown. "We heard that a female was in your staircase," I heard a male voice say. "Could we look around your room?"

You ran another hand through your messed-up hair. "Of course," you said. "Come in."

Something that I can only describe as an icy blast swept over me. Before they had entered all the way, I could see the glint of their red lanyards through the crack. I tried to clear my mind but my breath was held tight. I'm sure yours was too. We made brief eye contact and you smiled; I felt, all at once, very nauseous. For a moment, my mind was numb, too, agreeably registering any of the events unfolding in front of us. *Keep still, keep silent,* I repeated to myself, more of a comfort than anything else. "It looks clear," they said finally. I listened to the hinges of your door close and slowly took a step outside the closet. We remained silent for another minute, waiting for the sounds of their footsteps to fade into white noise. We held up our hands next to each other. They were both shaking. "What the fuck just happened?" you whispered, slightly breathless. We laughed softly and leaned in for an embrace.

When we pulled apart, I shook my head. "Next time, we need to be more careful," I said. "I didn't think anyone saw us outside."

"Me neither," you said. "I do like the idea of a *next time* though."

I scoffed, nudging you gently from the side. "Luck, Theo," I said. "Don't push it."

You smiled, cupping my face in your hands and leaned for a kiss. "Okay," you said. "More careful, we can do that."

"Maybe if you weren't so noisy," I joked.

You pulled back, with a playful expression across your face. "Noisy? Look who's talking–"

"*I was asleep, so sorry,*" I mocked and then mimicked a yawn.

"You know, Alaska," you said. "When people are asleep, they usually don't make any noise."

"Not you," I scoffed. "You're definitely a loud sleeper. I can tell."

"Enlighten me with your evidence," you smiled.

I felt my cheeks flush. "I don't have any yet," I said, "but I'm working on it. Anyways, I think I should go. I'm not looking to get kicked out on the first week."

"They wouldn't kick us out," you chuckled. "Maybe trouble, but not expelled."

"I'm not willing to risk it...time for me to *fuck off*, I guess," I said half-jokingly, but your expression immediately darkened in the moonlight. You didn't say anything for a while.

I opened the door and you led me to the back exit. As I entered back into the night; the air felt strangely cold again, almost painfully so. I turned around and when we looked at each other again, it felt like we were lost in a state of two-way desire.

For the rest of the day, I struggled to pick myself back up without you. The feeling of love transported me, it made me happy, but at the same, it consumed me and made me miserable. The way all impossible loves are miserable; I am acutely aware of the impossibility. Difficulty, I could cope with; there is beauty in the hope of conquest. But impossibility, by nature, carries with it a sense of defeat, a limit of time.

A terrible storm came around me, bringing down with it the night; stars beamed reaching out across the dark horizon and, for me, a bout of hallucination. Voices spoke to me in the roar of the night, in the hissing wind: *You need to hide,* they whispered, *you need to protect yourself.* From what, I was unsure of, but the prospect of ignoring these warnings was such that death, to me, seemed preferable. I looked down into the empty courtyard and was startled to see that a dark, motionless figure had materialised under the lamp, populating and growing with intensity. I squeezed my eyes shut. When I opened them again, I saw nothing but grass blades whirling in the bright cone of emptiness beneath the light. I turned to see Asli standing in the doorway. "Hey, it's almost ten," she said. "Let's go to shout-out."

I don't know why the campus insisted on making such a production of these shout-outs because, by the time all students arrived, we were invariably nervous and exhausted. They were a dreadful strain for everyone, councillors included, and this particular evening I found myself less able to conceal the evidence of stress, in my uncomfortable outerwear clothes, and with my less-than-extensive knowledge of campus regulations. The others were more practised at this particular dissimulation. Though at the time, I found those evening shout-outs wearing and troublesome, I now find something very wonderful in the memory of them: the dark cavern of a room, with vaulted ceilings and overhead lights crackling above, our faces luminous somehow, and ghostly pale. All students joined together, the mix of laughter and shouts as the councillors tried hush over us in desperation. I liked too the specific and unexpected companionability of the place. There were times during the day when everyone was there at the same time, and at moments, I would emerge from the fog of my writing and sense that all of them were breathing in rhythm, panting almost, from the effort of concentrating. I could feel, then, the collective energy they were expending filled the air like gas, flammable and sweet, and would wish I could bottle it so that I might be able to write from it when I was feeling uninspired, for the days in which I would sit in front of my notebook for hours, as though if I stared long enough, it might explode into something brilliant and charged.

When we arrived, the lights were beating in a whirlwind near the ceiling. And I wouldn't have been at all surprised if the long mahogany drapes had simply vanished into thin air, a magic casket of some sort. As the shout-out progressed, I was relatively at ease, in the clear, any feelings of anxiety subsidised as the minutes passed on. This was until I stood up to leave and heard my name being called from the front. "Alaska Greenwood...could all students whose names were called, please stay behind before dismissal." I felt the old cold twist through my bones again and then it was all forgotten, the warmth, the lights; like I had never been warm in my life, ever. And just like that, my mind had spiralled once again. Things got white around the edges and it seemed I had no past, no memories, that in reality, I had been on this exact stretch of luminous, hissing road forever.

You checked me sideways. "Did they just call your name?" you mouthed across the marquee. I silently nodded, receding into myself.

I don't know what exactly was writhing with me, for I was in a bad fix. I grew irritated the longer dismissal took, and decided to walk through the crowd to the councillors myself. I wandered from light to light, stepping from the world of warmth and people and conversation overheard until I was stood facing one of the counsellors. "Hi, I'm Alaska," I said. "My name was called out...I was wondering if everything was alright?"

"Surname?" he asked, his expression dismantled and pressed.

"Greenwood."

"Let me check the list," he said, scrolling down on his tablet. My superstitions began to transform themselves into something like mania. I became convinced, in those short and very fragmented seconds, that it was only a matter of time before I had fallen into what I had feared so much and spent so much time avoiding, *disappointment*. "I see," he said, chewing on each word slowly. "You were late to class today, feeling sick apparently. We wanted to check in and ask if you needed medication."

Silence abounded me, mixed frantically with confusion. I felt irritated and slightly aggravated. "Everything's fine," I said. "I wasn't feeling well earlier, but I'm fine now."

"That's good to hear," he said, still staring down at the tablet. "Let us know if there's anything we can help with." I nodded and turned back to my seat. *All of that for nothing,* I thought to myself. I felt nauseous.

You were waiting, reading something on your phone. I tapped your shoulders lightly and you looked up, estranged. "Is everything alright?" you asked. "Was it about this evening?"

I shook my head. "No, but I thought it was too," I said tiredly. "They just asked me if I was feeling well." I looked outside the curtain drapes and the figure had suddenly reappeared amidst the darkness. As it moved closer towards the marquee, I squeezed my eyes shut again.

"You seem stressed," you said, noticing my sudden change in demeanour.

I sighed and looked outside again. The figure had disappeared. "It's fine," I said. "Nothing you need to worry about."

You stood up from your seat and we were now facing each other. "Well, you worry too much, Alaska," you said lightly. "Trust me, relax a bit."

I raised my eyebrow. "How have you come to that conclusion?" I asked, unnerved.

"Let's just say, I think I know you pretty well already," you smiled. "You need to calm down."

I exhaled slowly. "Truthfully, I mostly feel calm around you."

You brushed your arms against mine as we made our way outside of the marquee. "Then I'll make sure to be around you all of the time," you said. "If that's what you want, of course."

If that's what you want, I thought to myself sombrely, but instead, smiled back at you. "Actually, I really hate you," I joked. "I never want to be around you ever again."

You seemed to pick up on this and laughed casually. "Wow, really?" you asked. "Because I was actually feeling the same way. You distract me all of the time in class, it's very aggravating."

"So I'm distracting and aggravating?" I teased. "What a compliment, Theo."

The cold air cloaked in and around us. "That's my forte," you said, planting a soft kiss on the centre of my forehead. "But really, I mean it, Alaska," you said. "Calm down a little."

"Really, Theo, I mean it," I sighed. "Mostly with you."

Walking back to the dormitories, the cold was deep, and before long my legs to knees were prickling and numb. When I finally made it inside, light seemed to thin and vanish into a distant haze; the moon ran down the sky and spilt against the grass, wild lupines raised in the cones of blue in midnight air and I began to bring myself back together, piece by piece.

Looking over the evening's events, there is a part of me, I see now as reckless. People would risk anything for a little bit of something beautiful. Still, the small rule-hating self within me did not die. Reading the story of *Zelda Fitzgerald* by Nancy Milford, I identified with her mutinous spirit. I felt instantly confined by the notion that we were born into a world where everything was mapped out by those before us.

L'appel du vide.

I struggled to suppress my destructive impulses and worked instead on creative ones, like my final essay. The assignment was a two-paged paper on either philosophy, literature or modern history — awfully surprising, I'm sure.

I'd only written a page and I started to hurry through the rest in an impatient and slightly dishonest fashion. The value of the composition, Louise said, was not that it gave one any particular faculty in the subjects that could not be gained easily by other methods but that if done properly, off the top of one's head, it taught one to think more analytically. One's thought patterns become different, she said, when forced into the confines of a rigid and unfamiliar philosophical tongue. Certain common ideas become inexpressible; other, previously undreamt-of ones spring to life, finding miraculous new articulation.

By eleven, the air was clear and very still. Then, suddenly, I heard footsteps approaching, and low hums of voices from across the door. Thinking it was Adeline, I rushed to the door with excitement and swung it wide open, but only a flash of red gleamed back at me, taunting. "Oh," I said, facing the group of counsellors huddled between the stairwell. "Is everything all right?"

"You're Alaska, right?" one of them asked, almost bitchily. She glared at me with big, blue orbital eyes. For a second I didn't know what she meant.

"What? I mean, yes, that's me," I managed out, unconvincingly weak, and chuckled. I felt slightly embarrassed. "Is there something I can help with?" I asked.

The same woman gave me a catty, sideways look. "Can we have a look in your room?" she asked. "And if there's *someone* inside." To my annoyance, the evening's episode followed and caught me by the arm still.

No end, barely no solace.

I don't know what I expected, but the counsellors obviously had been kicked out of orbit by the possibility of something rebellious happening; to have the villainous suspects caught in hopes for a pay rise. There was nothing I could do but let them in, and soon enough, the group of four counsellors had shuffled awkwardly into my room, looking around with small, weak orange flashlights that were almost comical.

Though not untidy, exactly, my room verged on being so. I

was slightly embarrassed. Books were stacked on every available surface; the table was cluttered with papers, empty coffee cans, boxes of chocolates and galoshes that made passage difficult for the counsellors in the small room. Clothes were scattered on the floor and a rich confession of posters were hung from the door; not to mention, my nightstand was littered with more empty coffee canisters, leaky pens, and on the foot of my bed laid my skates with their guards and soakers on the carpet beside them. It was painfully obvious that I would not have invited anyone in here. "Have a good night," the same, snide woman said eventually, closing the door behind them.

Alone again, I locked the door, barely feeling the earth and ground. I sat on the unkempt carpet, waiting for time to pass through me, but my body was unhinged, disturbed again. I was too tired to care though; even as I looked through the window, the columns of grass fields standing tall in dark corners would appear to me in its true whispering, smiling menace, an airy angel of death. My irritation and perplexity were growing stronger, kept in motion by a ridiculous sense of unease. I turned on the lights and looked through my books until I found a Benedict Wells novel I had brought from home. I had read it before and thought that a page or two would put me to sleep, but I had forgotten most of the plot and before I knew it I'd read fifty pages, then a hundred.

Several hours passed and I was wide awake. The radiators were on full blast and the air in my room was hot and dry. I stood to turn it off and heard the knuckles of my bones cracking, disjointing with each step. I began to feel thirsty. I read until the end of a chapter, and then I got up and went to get a glass of water.

The staircase was spotless and deserted now. Everything smelled like fresh paint. I walked through the kitchen — pristine, brightly lit, its creamy walls were eye sore that late in the night. Walking back to my room, I was startled to hear a hollow, tiny tune from the twenty-third room. *Adeline's room*. I knocked on the door and allowed myself in, sitting at the edge of her bed. "Hey, how are you?" I asked, watching as she rearranged a box of jewellery on the floor.

"Crazy," she said. "Today has been such a crazy day. Psychology is boring but I did meet this guy from Honduras."

"What's his name?" I asked, shuffling around among the bedsheets.

"Vasil—something," she shrugged.

I raised a sceptical eyebrow and laughed. "Sounds riveting," I said sarcastically.

Adeline laughed and fiddled with her jewellery. "How about you?" she asked.

I sighed. "I wanted to ask you something again" I said, looking at the lamplight and then back to Adeline. "I'm really sorry if it's a burden to you I—"

"Alaska," she smiled softly. "Don't apologise. What is it?"

I felt ashamed bringing our world out into the open to be judged, but something about Adeline's character was ridiculously receptive that I felt as though, her and I, had built a sanctuary where we could say anything to each other and it would never leave. "I was with Theo earlier, and he said this... strange thing to me."

"Well," she said, picking at her jewellery box. "What did he say?"

I threw my hands in the air in exasperation and sighed. "He said: what if I only saw you when I wanted to. And then, when I didn't, you could just fuck off."

Adeline's face dropped. She placed another piece of jewellery down and looked me directly in the eyes. "He said that?" she asked.

"Yeah, I didn't know what to say," I said, looking at the

carpet. "I just told him that it would only work for him, then we moved on."

We were both silent for a moment. "Alaska," Adeline said, her tone suddenly serious. "That's messed up."

The air felt slightly heavier. "It's okay. I'll talk to him about it tomorrow," I said, knowing I wouldn't, not knowing you would.

That night, I had a dream: At Greene Street I parked in the garage and rode the elevator up past the silent floors, clinging to the cage-door mesh; I was so tired that I would slump onto the ground if I didn't. The building was a sepulchral around me. I stepped into my darkened apartment and was feeling for the light switch when something clotted me, hard, on the side of my face and even in the dark I could see my tooth project itself into the air.

It was you; I could hear your breathing and smelt your scent, even before you flicked the master switch and the apartment became illuminated, dazzlingly, into something brighter than day, and I looked up and saw you above me, peering down at me. Even drunk you were composed, and now some of your drunkenness had been clarified by your face, and your gaze was steady and focused. I felt you grab me by my hair, felt you hit me on the right side of my face.

You still hadn't said anything, and then you dragged me to the beige sofa, the only sounds were your steady breaths and frantic gulps. You pushed my face into the cushions and held my head down with one hand, while with the other, you began pulling off my clothes. I began to panic, then, and struggle, but you pressed one arm against the back of my neck, which paralysed me and I was unable to move; I could feel myself become exposed to the air piece by piece — my back, my arms, my thighs — and when everything had been removed, you yanked me to my feet again and pushed me away, but I fell, and landed on my back.

"Get up," you said...

I woke fairly early again but slept terribly, which wasn't a new sensation for me. Early morning came like an open grave, a dark cold slot in a haze of summer, the cold was permeating and almost numbing against my skin. I opened my door to use the bathroom and saw Adeline wrapped in a towel, standing outside of the shower. Streams of condensation beaded against the mirrors. No one said anything for a moment, the morning cold was too intense for us to even try.

There was a great deal to do in class that day, especially for Philosophy group one. Since we had missed three lectures (on account of our first professor disappearing), we were a great deal behind. On Tuesdays and Thursdays it might be pleasant to sit around and talk about Literature, or Philosophy, but the rest of the week was taken up in Modern History and prose composition and that, for the most part, was brutal, bludgeoning labour, labour that I — being older now, and a little less hardy — would scarcely be able to force myself to do today. I had certainly plenty more to think about besides the coldness which apparently had infected my classmates, once again, the crisp air of solidarity, the cool way their eyes seemed to look right through me.

The hall rose in acres of books and bricks and glasses in alternation. Until I saw you again, all the distances between me and everything else seemed uncrossable that morning, a permanent exile; perhaps it was the relief of having a safe haven at last, for I seemed to crash, exhausted and emotionally overwrought into liking you. "Morning, vampire," you said, placing your textbooks on the desk in front of us. "You look awfully sleepy again today. Do you ever sleep?"

"Yeah, but not well, I suppose," I said. "What about you?"

There was a stiff pause. "I'm fine, but I wanted to talk to you about something."

Here we go again, I thought to myself sombrely. "Sure," I said. "What is it?"

You looked down and then back to me again, eyes shining terribly. "I didn't mean what I told you yesterday, when I told you to fuck off. I feel so terrible, I'm sorry."

I was unsure of what to say and kept silent.

"I promise you I didn't mean it. You ought to know I have a habit of saying things I don't mean sometimes," you sighed. "I thought about *us* properly last night. I want this. Only if you want it too."

I paused again, thinking erratically: *You are not damned. You are not damned,* a voice called out to me. Suddenly, I couldn't hear the other. "Actually, I don't know why you're sitting next to me," I smiled sarcastically. "I thought we hated each other?"

You let out a tense, but soft laugh. "If being with you means that I hate you, then I really fucking hate you," you smiled, extending out your arm again. "*Treuga?*"

I reached to shake it. "*Treuga,*" I smiled. "Then I guess I'll have to tolerate you sitting here for the rest of the course..."

"You'll have to," you said definitively. "I'm not going anywhere."

From then onwards, there was nothing but a mutual tenderness between us; to simply talk and get lost for hours. Your ability to concentrate for long periods of time infected me, and I learned by your example, working side by side. Sometimes, we would play the records we liked over and over in shared headphones, the music informing the trajectory of our mornings. I felt disconnected from all that was outside of the world that you and I had created between us.

In those moments, I felt myself turning into another person, a person filled with love. A person that was better. Better because of you. I held onto every single memory, because I knew we wouldn't be making anymore soon. And although we spent most of our time together, we still remained focused in class, nor were we isolated. When the classes merged, we were joined by two other students, Vasileios and Veronika, on our table.

Vasileios and I had been introduced already on induction day when he told me that he was Spanish. I used to jokingly nickname him *Señorita*, but surprisingly, Adeline informed me that he was from Honduras. Turns out, Vasileios was neither. He was Greek. His hair was fully shaved in a neat buzzcut, always dressed head-to-toe in black hoodies and shorts, and had a pair of Poseidon-like eyes. Veronika, on the other hand, was all academics, all smart and root-grown knowledge. She knew this about herself and didn't have a hard time voicing it aloud. "It's hard being so smart all of the time," she would say. I definitely had to get used to her company. Altogether, it felt like a less significant reboot of the TV show *Friends*, but nevertheless, I enjoyed their company.

On Thursday, the weather turned suddenly, unseasonably, insistently lovely. The sky was blue, the air warm and windless, and the sun beamed on the muddy ground with all the sweet impatience of July. But more significantly, it was the day of the gala.

As the day progressed, everyone waited anxiously to see if the weather would hold and it did, with serene assurance. Hyacinth and daffodil bloomed in the flower beds; violet and periwinkle in the meadows; damp, bedraggled white butterflies fluttered drunkenly in the hedgerows. I put away my leather coat and over boots and walked around, nearly light-headed with joy, in my short-sleeves.

I went to Westgate with Adeline, Asli and Serena for lunch to try out a joint called The Street Food and I ordered bean noodles with tofu on the side. "How excited are you for the gala tonight?" Adeline asked, opening up her coke.

"So excited," said Serena. "I can't wait."

"Where's it going to be?" Asli asked.

Adeline took a sip from the glass bottle. "Ashmolean, it's there every year."

I shrugged. "I've never heard of it," I said. "Psychology getting any better?"

All three of them sighed. "No," said Serena. "If anything, it's getting worse...anyways, did you get a new professor?"

"Yeah, I did," I said. "Her name's Louise, she's amazing."

Adeline joined in excitedly. "What have you been studying? I have no idea what Philosophy classes would be like."

I thought to myself for a moment. "There's lots of different things," I said. "Oh–like today, we were learning about how beauty is looked at by different philosophers."

Adeline grinned widely. "Let's hear it then."

"If you insist," I smiled back and reached for my notebook. "Okay, here it is:

> ...*Plato's account in the Symposium and Plotinus's connect beauty to a response of love and desire, but can only locate beauty itself in the realm of the Forms, and the beauty of particular objects in their participation in the Form. Plato speaks of aesthetics, that beauty is metaphysical, that the physical world is only an imitation of forms. To Plato, beauty imitates Form, and thus when things become tangible, they are no longer beautiful, morally incorrect...*

I flipped the page and continued reading.

> *"For Kant, aesthetic judgement branches off into experiences — either that of beauty or sublimity: Kant makes the claim that objects in nature can be beautiful, but not sublime. This claim is manifested in the idea that the sublime can not be found in any sensible form, for it is the beautiful that is concerned with form.*

Kant's critique of judgement outlines how there are universal rules to our depiction of beauty. Pleasure comes from sensations applicable to the perception of beauty. To be imperfect is to exist, he states...

...Hegel differs from both, saying that beauty is where ideas meet matter, how the spirit comes to understand itself. How spiritual freedom makes one truly free, that art is not imitative, but intends us to teach."

I closed my notebook and slipped it into my bag.

"Wow," said Serena, "I should've taken Philosophy. I thought we would have been learning that kind of stuff in Psych."

I smiled modestly. "Psychology is pretty great too," I offered.

Adeline giggled. "Not as interesting as the professor being fired on the second day," she said. But I remember, in that class, not being bound by either Kant, Plato, or Hegel's theories. Instead, it was Aristotles that particularly caught my attention. He said:

To love something in itself, as opposed to loving it because it pleases you or is useful to you, is to love it on the basis of one's rational recognition that it is kalon.

How do we know something is beautiful, Aristotle asks, because we experience it.

Each philosopher tried so hard to find their definition of beauty and yet, I found it so easily. I hope they were envious of me for finding beauty, of knowing beauty was. I hope they were jealous that I knew of beauty and they did not.

Aristotle's theory made me think of you.

CHAPTER FIVE
DUSK AND DESIRES

YOU ASKED ME ONCE WHEN I KNEW THAT YOU WERE FOR ME, and I told you that I had always known. But that wasn't true, and I knew it even as I said it — I said it because it sounded pretty, like something someone might say in a book or a movie, and because we were both feeling so wretched, and helpless, and because I thought if I said it, we both might feel better about the situation before us, the situation that we perhaps had been capable of preventing — perhaps not — but at any rate hadn't.

But I want to be accurate now. I want to be accurate, both because there is no reason not to be, and because I should be — I have always tried to be, I always try to be.

I'm not sure where to begin.

Maybe with some nice words, although they are also true words: I liked you right away. You were always talking about, oh, I don't know — Nietzsche? Mockingbirds? You always found something to discuss and I loved this about you, even though I often couldn't understand it. And every time you looked at me, the look on your face — I still cannot describe it, I felt something crumble inside me, like a tower of damp sand built too high: for you, and for me. And in your face, I knew my own would be echoed. The impossibility of finding someone to offer kindness to another person, so unthinkingly, so gracefully! When I looked at you, I understood what people meant when they said someone was heartbreaking; that something could break your heart. I had always thought it mawkish, but in those moments I realised that it might have been mawkish, but it was also true.

And that, I suppose, was when I knew.

Everything was faded and silent in my room — dirty teacups, an unmade bed, pollen floating past my window with an airy, dangerous clam. My ears rang. When I turned back to my work, ink-stained hands, the scratch of my pen on the paper rasped loud in the stillness. I thought of that evening in your room, now miles away; of all those layers of silence on silence. I didn't want to be alone, quite the contrary. The afternoon light was sober and pale and made my room seem horribly quiet. I stood up and knocked on the twenty-third room. "Hey, Adeline," I said. "Do you want to go on a walk?"

A thin ray of light struck the prisms of a candelabrum on the coffee shop's mantelpiece, throwing brilliant, trembling sharps of light that were distorted by the slant of our cappuccino cups. I looked fixedly at a bright, warm pool of sunlight soaking into Adeline's cheeks right across from me. Most of the time, we talked through the language of experiences, a few too many of them painful, and we found our way to those hurts and tugged them out of each other like following the trail of a map we didn't know was already inside of us. Everything roamed, spiralled, turned down unexpected corners.

Those are the memories that don't hurt my heart to look back on.

"Let's get ready for the gala together?" Adeline asked. "I can't wait."

I hadn't thought about it much but agreed. "Definitely," I smiled. "I looked up photos of Ashmolean, it looks huge. Either way, it sounds really fun. *A gala night*. I wonder what they have planned."

The minutes crept by with a tortuous slowness. The gala was actually a scam, disguised as an academic enrichment night. All students were under the impression that it would be a night of dancing, blasting music and socialising. We spent hours getting ready, switching through piles of dresses and suits, did our makeup and hair for an expected evening full of partying. I looked at myself in the mirror: there was such anonymity, such protection. Even if someone were to accidentally graze my thighs, I was wearing enough layers so that they'd never be able to feel the ridges of scars beneath. Everything was covered, everything was hidden. If I were standing still, I could be anyone, someone blank and invisible.

Upon our arrival at Ashmolean, we were handed a booklet to fill out on each of the museum's artefacts. Safe to say, we were all disappointed and bored out of our minds. Whether from isolation, malice, or simply boredom, people there were far more credulous, and this hermetic, overheated atmosphere made it a thriving black petri dish of melodrama and distortion. Diffusing aurora beamed through the pillared alley, brass sculptures and ancient paintings resided on the walls, unkempt and unloved. Inside the museum were several sets of stairs, each twisted in a perfect spiral and likely a deep walnut, but with the thick layer of undisturbed dust it was hard to tell.

The inner edge was painted antique cream; no dirt and no flaking dents.

You were dressed, immaculate in a deep navy suit, like the heir apparent of some small European monarchy. Viewed from a distance, your character projected an impression of solidity and wholeness which was in fact as insubstantial as a hologram; up close, you were all motes and light, I could pass a hand right through you. If I stepped back far enough, however, the illusion would click in again and there you would be, bigger than life. I saw a group of girls approach you, the select few, pretty ones. Immediately, I felt a fleeting stab of jealousy, a sense of impotence. A character like yours disintegrated under analysis. It could only be defined by the anecdote, the chance encounter or sentence overheard, which was the secret of your appeal and what made you so approachable, colouring your environment wherever you went. We made eye contact and you came straight up to me. That being the case, I was surprised, precisely because you could easily have used your beauty as a weapon. However, your reticence did nothing to feed a secret home in me. It only made you even more appealing, I admired those who did not use what they had at their disposal. *Alis volat propriis.* He flies by his own wings. "How would you like a chaperone for this incredibly, boring night?" you asked.

"I would in fact like that very much," I smiled. "I cannot believe they told us it was a gala'"

"They practically marketed this evening all day," you said before smiling mischievously. "How would you like to make this evening a little more exciting?"

"I would in fact like that very much," I said.

We decided to slip away from the crowd into a nearby room that was left isolated and unkempt. We sat smiling and laughing about something practically meaningless for minutes until your hands glided up the sides of my dress, the warmth crept through with each touch. I think I liked you for your loneliness, your manner of not quite being there in the world, that's what pushed me towards you, the aloofness, disengagement. Such singularity moved me. My hands trailed across your back and your skin was soft like summer rays; your warm skin made me like you even more. I was undoing the top button of your collar, slightly struggling. "Need help?" you asked, chuckling.

I laughed softly. "Come on, Theo," I said. "Give me a break."

"It's fun," you said. "I promise you."

Time ebbed and I kissed every inch of you and was still left longing for more, yearning to be closer. My soul did not understand the notion of time, or calendars or clocks. It only knew that it felt right to be with you and you with me. I grabbed the collar of your blouse and pulled you towards me. After a moment's hesitation, you pushed up the lower hem of my dress. Under your hands, the fabric didn't so much yield as it did bend and crease, like cardboard, and although you were only able to fold it to the inside of my thigh, it was enough to see three columns of neat white scars, each about an inch wide and slightly raised, laddering up my legs. You tucked your finger under the fabric and felt the tracks tinning onto the upper thigh, but stopped further, unwilling to explore more and withdrew your hand.

It seemed, you were not letting yourself ask the questions you knew you ought to because you were afraid of the answers. There had been a silence then, you suddenly stopped and pulled away from me. "What are these?" you asked, grazing a hand across my thighs.

I went very still. I felt my face burning. For a while, we both said nothing.

I pulled down my dress. "It's nothing," I said firmly. In that moment I felt not angry but exposed: not because I didn't trust you but because I didn't want you to see me as less of a person, as someone who had to be looked after and helped. I wanted you, wanted everyone, to think of me as someone reliable and hardy, someone they could come to with their problems, instead of me always having to turn to them.

"It's not nothing," you said darkly. "I know what it is, Alaska."

I shrugged. For a long time, I was quiet, and you were quiet as well.

"Why did...are you still?" you asked, brows furrowed and confused.

"No, no," I said. "I'm not, don't worry."

You looked down at my dress again. I felt intensely insecure. "I'm not worrying, it just...it makes me upset," you said. "You understand why I'm upset, right?"

"It's not important," I snapped.

"It is important," you affirmed. "Why?"

Finally, I said, "a few reasons."

You looked at me with a sombre expression. "Like what?"

I looked down at the tiled floors. They were unusually green and made me nauseous. "They're not relevant," I said. "It doesn't matter anymore." Truthfully, people had always decided how my body would be used, and finally, I knew that I had found a way to take back control over it. Even though I was better now and I didn't necessarily need it, a childish and obdurate part of me always resisted and kept it in the back of my mind. I still felt as though, after everything that had happened after moving to New York, that I had such little control of my body — I couldn't let anyone begrudge me this, just in case I ever had to turn back to it. Just in case something would go wrong, that I would slip again.

You held my face in your hands; the warmth of them pressed against my cheeks. "Can you trust me? I promise I'm not going anywhere," you said.

I nodded and thought to myself for a moment: *Not because I don't trust you,* I said to the version of you in my imagination and to whom I would never have that conversation. *But because I can't bear to have you see me as I really am.*

When you let go of my face, I sharply exhaled and looked to the floor again. "Why, Alaska?" you repeated. I felt sick and struggled to get the words out. I didn't know what it was — maybe it was just the calmness of your voice, the steadiness with which you made your promise that made me realise that you were serious this time in a way you hadn't been before; or maybe it was just the realisation that yes, I was tired, so tired that I was willing, finally, to accept someone else's care.

"Because, sometimes I feel so many things and I need to feel nothing at all—it helps clear them away," I said shamefully. "It's because I sometimes feel so awful, or ashamed, and I need...*needed* to make physical what I felt. The pain and adrenaline was such a sudden rush for me."

You considered this for a moment. "Can I ask you a question?"

I nodded slowly, but hesitantly.

"Did something happen to you that I should know about?" you asked.

I could instantly feel something inside myself become alert. You had the uncanny ability to ask questions or make observations that both devastated and discomforted. I didn't think there was any malice behind it, but it made me wonder what went on in your subconscious.

I stiffened under your hands and diverted my eyes to the tiled floor, rolling to my left side and then away from you. "Jesus, Theo," I said, finally. I withdrew my hand forcibly and moved out of your embrace, creating some distance between us. I was mortified; how obvious was I? Could you just tell by talking to me, looking at me, what had happened all those years ago? And if so, how could I have better concealed it? I was so sharply nauseated that I had to stop myself from physically vomiting and waited for the moment to pass. I could feel you trying to treat me the same as you had, but something had shifted. "Is it okay that I don't want to talk about this right now?" I sighed.

You walked over to me and wrapped your hands around my waist again. "Of course," you said. "But you're okay, right?"

I laughed nervously. "I'm okay, I promise," I said. "Especially when I'm with you. Nothing else really matters to me."

You smiled and looked down. "I want you to know that I understand," you said. "Do you remember what I showed you that night under the bridge?"

I nodded. "I will never forget it," I said. "It was one of the most beautiful things I've ever heard."

You smiled at this and pulled me closer. "I left out a few things..."

"What kind of things?" I asked.

"After my dad...I was so miserable for such a long time. I thought it would last forever, that I couldn't escape it," you said. "So one day, like you said, I felt so many things that I didn't want to feel anything at all..."

My heart began to hurt. I wrapped my arms around you, tightly, almost afraid to let go.

"One night, I ended up on the roof of this old building... and then my mother called. She's my best friend, you know? I trust her more than anyone. When he was ill—my dad—I hated him for a while. When I told her about that, I remember her telling me: you don't hate him, you hate the—"

"You hate the illness," I said. "You hate the person they become, when all you know was the person they were before everything changed."

You sighed. "Correct again, Alaska."

I clasped your hand tightly in mine and brushed my thumb

against it. For a while we both didn't say anything. Our silence was powerful enough. "You know that those feelings were valid," I said at last. "That you had every right to feel how you felt." You leaned your head against my shoulder and I grazed it gently with my hands. "If it means anything," I said, "you have no idea how happy I am that you're still here. I am so grateful to have met you, to know you. And I know, *I know*, that everyone around you feels the same way, Theo."

You looked up at me and smiled. "Thank you," you said and leaned in for a kiss. I let it consume me; everything inside me suddenly slipped away into the warmth of your arms. When you pulled away, you looked at me with such a gentle and adoring smile. "You know, Alaska," you said, softly. "Sometimes it feels like you're the only one who really understands me."

I pressed your forehead against mine until our noses were touching. "You know, Theo. You're the only one who has made me feel like a person again."

The gala finally ended at ten. The sky ran white. It was like a film in fast motion, the moon waxed and waned, clouds rushed across the sky. Vines grew from the ground so fast they twined up the trees like snakes; passing in the wink of an eye, years for all I know...I mean we think of phenomenal change as being the very essence of time, when it's not at all. Time is something that defies spring and winter, birth and decay, the good and the bad, indifferently. Something changeless and joyous and absolutely indestructible. Duality ceases to exist, there is no ego, no "I", and yet it's not like the self-being a drop of water swallowed by the ocean of the universe. You have no idea how pallid the workday boundaries of ordinary existence seem, after the ecstasy of love.

We were getting back to campus, smoking and talking until

suddenly, there was a long pause. "Did you know Melissa wrote our names on the campus ledge?" you asked.

I laughed in disbelief. "I don't know what to say."

We stood looking at each other for a moment, silent, smiling, content. "You're awfully quiet," I teased. "Tell me what's going on in your mind so it can be in both of ours instead."

You took a moment to think, almost calculating how to bring your next words out. "Well, I was talking with her earlier today, Melissa," you said.

"What were you talking about?" I asked, sceptically. A pit grew in my stomach like a fig tree.

"Well, she asked me if we were together, officially," you said. "I said no...but it just made me think about a few things."

"What kind of things?" I asked nervously.

You laughed at my expression and wrapped an arm around my shoulder. "Nothing bad, don't worry," you chuckled. "I meant that the conversation made me think about making things more official between us." We were almost standing by the marquee. "I know we've only known each other for a few days, but I feel like I've known you my whole life," you said. You stopped and looked me straight in the eyes with a smile; the inner hanging lights beamed across your face, illuminating each contour in a warm glow. "How would you feel if your first boyfriend was someone that you wouldn't end up hating?"

At that moment, I realised I didn't want a relationship for property's sake; I wanted it because I was utterly infatuated with you at the time; sometimes I even felt it physically, a sodden clump of dirty laundry pressing against my chest. I cannot unlearn the feeling even now. People made it sound so easy as if the decision to want it was the most difficult part of the process. But I knew better: being in a relationship would mean exposing myself to someone, which I still had never done to anyone up until I had met you; it would mean the confrontation of my own body; much of what it has become has been beyond my control, but my thighs have been all my doing and I can only blame myself. But the wanting, for me, was easy.

I had never wanted anything more.

I paused for a moment, then began to smile. "Are you asking me to be your girlfriend?" I teased.

You took a step closer to me, wrapping your hands around my waist. "Will you, Alaska Greenwood, be my adoring, nine day girlfriend?" I was silent. I couldn't speak, I couldn't react; I couldn't even feel my face, couldn't sense what my expression might be. I hope you wouldn't say one more word, because if you did, I would cry, or vomit, or pass out, or scream, or combust. I was aware, suddenly, of how exhausted, how utterly depleted I was, as much by the past few days of anxiety as well as the past five years of craving, of wanting, of wishing so intensely even as I told myself I didn't care.

But those words, *your* words, made me feel like I was worth something for the first time.

"Of course," I said.

I have never wanted anything more.

After the shout-out, I walked straight through the night. Noises got louder; objects shimmered; my peripheral vision darkened when unexpectedly you flew up and threw your arms around me. Your hoarse breath was loud in my ear and cheek was like ice when you put it against mine. "Dickhead," I exhaled breathlessly. "I thought I was going to be kidnapped."

"To be a modern-day woman," you said, warm arms wrapping tightly around my chest. You were breathing hard, and deep circles of red burned high on your bright cheeks; in all my life I had never seen anyone so maddeningly beautiful as you were at that moment. "'I thought you'd be more happy to see your boyfriend," you teased, and I gently nudged you to the side with a smile. We stood in the deserted streets under the glow of a single lamppost, we were at the gold centre of everything. The darkness around was still, fragile, non-existent under the light. No sound could be made out, except for the occasional batter of crickets in the far-away field, everything dark and quiet as the grave. You drew me in for a kiss, and it was so cold then, and so silent, and I liked you so much.

Outside it was abruptly, insultingly cold, and both of us began sniffling. "Theo," I said, when we were halfway down the street, "I wanted to talk to you about something, but—I don't know where to begin." *Stupid,* I told myself. *This is such a stupid idea.* I opened my mouth to continue and then shut it, and then opened it again: I was a fish, dumbly blowing bubbles, and I wished I had never begun speaking.

"Alaska," you said, "are you having second thoughts?"

"No," I said. "No, nothing like that." We were silent. "Are you?"

"No, of course not."

"I don't want to tell you this," I said, and looked down at the forsythia, its bare twiggy ugliness. "But I have to because I don't want to be deceitful with you. But Theo—I think you think I'm one kind of a person and I'm not."

You were quiet. "What kind of a person do I think you are?"

"A good person," I said. "Someone decent."

"Well," you said, "you're right. I do."

"But—I'm not," I said, and could feel my eyes grow hot, despite the cold.

You had been silent for such a long time that I knew the answer even before I heard it. "Look, Alaska," you had said, slowly. "You don't owe me your secrets." You paused. "But yes, I do wish you'd share more with me. Not so I could have the information but so, maybe, I could be of some help." I stopped and looked at you. "That's all."

When I took your cold hands, I felt the quick pulse of your wrist between my thumbs.

"Okay?" you asked with a smile. "I would just like to be where you are; I would like to trust you and be with you. Only with you. Inside of you, around you, in all conceivable and inconceivable places. I would like to be where you are, only if you want me there too."

"Okay," I smiled back and laughed softly, relieved.

"Goodnight, *girlfriend*," you teased.

"Goodnight, Theo my *boyfriend*," I laughed, and suddenly you grabbed my arm and pulled it towards you, planting a soft kiss on the back of my hand.

Then, in almost a husky and low whisper, you mumbled into my hand, "Good girl," before turning around and fading into the darkness.

Since then, I tried to tell you more things. But there were so many topics I had never discussed with anyone, now five years ago, that I found I literally did not have the language to do so. My past, my fears, what was done to me, what I had done to myself — they were subjects that could only be discussed in tongues I did not speak. I was unclear about explaining myself to myself. I never used to let people come this close. And then there was you, that came and settled in the depths of my soul. No human had ever stood so close to my soul as you stood.

I didn't know this then, but in the months to come I would, again and again, test your claims of devotion, would throw myself against your promises to see how steadfast they were. I wouldn't even be conscious that I was doing this. But I would do it anyway, because a part of me would never believe you; as much as I wanted to, and much as I thought I did, I didn't, and I would always be convinced that you would eventually tire of me, that you would one day regret your involvement with me. And so I would challenge you, because when our relationship eventually would end, I would be able to look back and know that I caused it, and not only that, but the specific incident that caused it, and I would never have to wonder, or worry, about what I did wrong, or what I could have done better.

In spite of this, I was terribly wrong.

But that is in the future. For now, my happiness was flawless.

When I reached my room, I had to lie on the bed for half an hour before I could even think of retrieving my phone. I needed to feel the solidity of the bed beneath me, the silk of the cotton blanket against my cheek, the familiar yield of the mattress as I moved against it. I needed to assure myself that this was my world, and I was still in it, and that what had happened had really happened.

My life, I thought, but this time, I smiled.

CHAPTER SIX
LET THE LIGHT IN

ONCE AGAIN, I WOKE BEFORE DAWN, PERHAPS SENSING THE waning moon. But there was no warmth, only endless rain, and though it was technically night, there was no darkness; the sky was murky, and it seemed as if the moon had dropped, pressing its milky surface against the four dusty glass panels of skylight. I felt an oppressive lightness, got up, threw on a jacket, and walked to Radcliffe Square. The mockingbirds scattered, an alarm moaned in the distance, and a single car passed. July temperatures rose and fell with a harsh temperament.

The improbability of the situation seemed to grow larger and more vivid in my mind; every time I glimpsed into the reflection of my hollow and pale face on a puddle, I would feel sickened: Who, really, would even want this? The idea that I could become someone else's seemed increasingly ludicrous, and if you saw me just once more how could you too not come to the same conclusion? I knew it shouldn't matter so much to me, but I wanted it with a steady fervour that defied logic, and I couldn't bear it being taken away from me now, not when I was so happy, not when I was so close. Something had changed, and for a brief period, I had the strange sensation that the Alaska I knew had been replaced by another Alaska, and that this other Alaska, this changeling, was someone of whom I could ask anything, who might have funny stories about pets and friends and scrapes of childhood, who wore long sleeves only because she was cold and not because she was trying to hide something.

There were no cafes open at this hour, so I returned to the dormitories and lit a candle, somewhat clouded myself. The rain beat against the skylight. April showers in July. The sun was full but not visible, fused in a dense system of clouds.

I reached for *Phaedrus* sitting on my tabletop as rain splintered against the streaked-stained panes. Charioteer and his horses looked back at me, estranged. I flipped slowly through the pages and stopped when reaching Lysias's monologue. *Love is the regrowth of the wings of the soul,* Plato said back to me; years in the past, almost past seeing. Except of course, they were as alive as words were. On the breath of ink wings, spread on a sail made of paper page, this, in translation:

> '... he receives through his eyes the emanation of beauty, by
> which the soul's plumage is fostered, and grows hot, and this heat
> is accompanied by a softening of the passages from which the
> feathers grow, passages which have been closed up, so as to prevent
> feathers from shooting.
> Eros the god that flies it's his name in the language of mortals:
> But from the wings he must grow, he is called by the celestials
> Pteros.'

Mingle not with those you do not love, Plato warns, or you will be condemned to wander the earth nine thousand years without wisdom.

I met Adeline and Asli at breakfast. "Where's Serena?" I asked.

Adeline took a long sip of water. "She's printing something in the office," she said.

I let myself break into a smile. "I have something to tell you guys," I said. "Theo asked me to be his girlfriend last night."

Asli slammed her coffee on the table with excitement. "What?" she exclaimed. "That's amazing."

I couldn't seem to stop smiling. "Right," I said, "I wasn't expecting it but I'm really happy—is everything okay Adeline?" She was sat still and sombre, somewhat obscure.

She bitterly exhaled. "I don't know," she said. "What about what he said to you a few days ago?"

Asli looked confused. "What did he say?"

"Don't worry, it's not important," I shrugged. "What I mean is, it's fine now. He apologised for it, he didn't mean it."

"I'm still lost on what he apologised for–"

"Next time," Adeline said firmly. "Don't come crying to me about him then." She abruptly stood from her seat and left the cafeteria. My expression blanked. Asli and I exchanged uncomfortable glances at each other.

"What was that about?" Asli asked, taking a sip of her spilt coffee.

"I'm not sure either," I said, taking a seat. "I didn't cry to Adeline."

Asli sighed. "I believe you. She's been in a bad mood recently, last night she was mad at me for going out with the Spanish girls."

"That's not really fair though," I said, offended.

"It's not," Asli said. "I don't think she likes that we're branching out with others. If it means anything, I'm really happy for you."

"Thank you," I said, slightly saddened. "I'm happy too."

"Bloodshed is a terrible thing," said Louise hastily. "But the bloodiest parts of Homer and Aeschylus are often the most magnificent—for example, that glorious speech of Klytemnestra's in the Agamemnon—Vasileios, our resident Greek, I'm sure you've heard of the Oresteia; do you remember any of it?"

The light from the window was streaming directly into his face; glinting in the drowsy July sun, ageless, watchful, sly as a child. His brows slightly furrowed as the light poured through the class and collected onto a soaked yellow pool on the ground. "I remember a little," he said, before he began to recite the lines.

His voice in Greek was harsh and low and lovely.

> *Thus he died, and all the life struggled out of him;*
> *And as he died he spattered me with the dark red*
> *and violent-driven rain of bitter-savoured blood*
> *to make me glad, as gardens stand among the showers*
> *of God in glory at the birthtime of the buds.*

There was a brief silence after he had finished; rather to my surprise, Vasileios winked solemnly at me from across the table.

Louise smiled. "What a beautiful passage," she said. "I never tire of it. But how is that such a ghastly thing, a queen stabbing her husband in his bath, is so lovely for us?"

Veronika raised her hand. "It's the metre. Iambic trimeter. Those really hideous parts of the Inferno, for instance, Pier de Medicina with his nose hacked off and talking through a bloody slit in his windpipe—"

"I can think of worse than that," said another student at the end of the classroom.

"So can I. But the passage works because of the terza rima.

The music of it. The trimeter tolls through that speech of Klytemnestra's like a bell."

"But iambic trimeter is fairly common in Greek lyric, isn't it?" said Louise. "Why is it that particular section so breathtaking? Why do we not find ourselves attracted to some calmer or more pleasing one?"

I thought of The Bacchae, a play whose violence and savagery triumphed over reason: dark, inexplicable. "Because beauty is terror, isn't it?" I said. "Whatever we call beautiful, we quiver before it."

"*Akrivos sósto.*" Lousie smiled. "Exactly right. If we are strong enough in our souls we can rip away the veil and look that naked, terrible beauty right in the face; let beauty consume us, devour us, string our bones. Then spit us out reborn."

We were all leaning forward, motionless as Louise continued. "Tell me," she said, "what is a novel that terribly seduced you? Made you feel reborn into another being? Theodore, throw one at me."

You paused for a moment, thinking heavily. "*Il barone rampante* by Italo Calvino," you said finally. "It is the story of a boy called Cosimo who spent his life hidden in the trees, creating his own kingdom."

I turned to my notebook and flipped to the back page, *Il baron rampante by Italo Calvino.*

You looked at it and smiled at me "The *baron* has an *e*, like this," you said, taking the notebook from my hands.

"The baron in the trees," I smiled. "How come it's your favourite?"

"You'd have to read it to find out."

The trees looked schizophrenic and began to lose control, enraged with the shock of their fiery new colours. It was warm again as we walked to the University park on our usual routine. A sudden wind rustled through the birches; a gust of yellow leaves came storming down overhead. We took a sip of our coffees and lit a cigarette each.

The velvety swell of land faded to a soft auburn on the horizon, and the strip of highway was visible — just barely — in the hills, beyond the trees. The very colours of the surroundings had seeped into my blood: just as Oxford, in subsequent years, would always present itself immediately to my imagination in an affectionate whirl of green and red and brown, like a glorious blur of watercolour; chestnut and burnt orange and gold, separating only gradually into the boundaries of memory. But specifically on that day, there in that park, with you beside me and the smell of tobacco smoke in the air, it had the quality of a memory; there we were, before my eyes, and yet too beautiful to believe. "I love this, Alaska," you said, with a dream-like smile.

"Love what?" I asked.

"Everything."

You made me happy just by being near. No matter how hard I tried to avoid the thought, you just seemed like the perfect match for me. There hadn't been a moment where I spent time with anyone else and felt the same way I did around you; the way you label something completely changes your approach to it. I remember you saying this to me. And now, there was this newly formed sense of comfort, of security, even of safety around each other. I remember thinking that this is what it was to be struck by lightning, knowing I would never be untouched by you again.

I thought back to the story of Apollo's gardens. Cleis was a girl who fell in love with Phoebus Apollo, the sun. To take pity on her, the gods turned her into this flower, so that she might watch him with all her life. I distrusted the myth, though certainly it seemed a plausible story at the time, all except for the part where the gods did this out of mercy. They did it for fun, it seemed to me. In Greek mythology, loving Apollo seemed to be among the most dangerous of the heart's choices: the fields and gardens are full of his lovers, multiplied by time into millions.

I thought of you, looking back at their tale. How much more I could have loved you, if there was another one of me. If there were millions. If I had been scattered.

If I had a flower for every time I thought of you, I could walk in my garden forever.

CHAPTER SEVEN
LONDON

I SUPPOSE THERE IS A CERTAIN CRUCIAL INTERVAL IN everyone's life when character is fixed forever, for me, it was that first week I spent at St. Catherine's College. So many things remain with me from that time, even now; those preferences in clothes and books and even food — acquired then, and largely, I must admit, in adolescent emulation of the rest of our time together — have stayed with me through the years. It is easy, even now, for me to remember my friends and your daily routine, which subsequently became my own, were like. Regardless of circumstance they lived like clockwork, with surprisingly little of that chaos which to me had always seemed so inherent a part of my life prior. There were certain times of the day or night, even when the world was falling in, when you could always find Adeline in her room eating packaged greens, or when Serena was on daily walks around High Street looking for clothes. Up until the very end, there were always, always, after-class dinners with Asli, except on the evening our final essays were due, when no one felt much like eating and it was postponed until the next evening. I was surprised by how easily I managed to relax into the cyclical, byzantine routine of things.

Saturday came by, and it was wonderful how many things could happen in only a week. The cold in the sixteenth staircase that morning was nothing I'd known before or since. If I had any sense I'd gone and turned on my electric heater at night. I had only the dimmest awareness that half the population of St. Catherine was also experiencing pretty much what I put myself through every night–bone-cracking cold that made my joints ache, cold so relentless I felt it in my dreams: ice floes, lost expeditions, the lights of search planes swinging over whitecaps as I floundered along in black Arctic seas.

This particular day remains specifically vivid, a brilliant Saturday in July, one of the last sunny days we had in those two weeks. Memories of the London trip that fall from this vantage merge into a sweet and indistinct blur. In spite of this, when I woke, I was as stiff and sore as if I had been beaten, only later did I realise that the true cause of this malady was hard, merciless shivering, my muscles contracting as mechanically as if by electric impulse, all night long, every night.

Outside, students crowded around the tour buses for several hours as the counsellors split us into staircases; meaning that I was happily seated with Adeline (despite her outburst on Friday morning, Adeline and I were doing particularly well; we simply acted as though nothing out of the ordinary had occurred. This isn't to say there wasn't a certain animosity growing in the air between the three of us, we just chose to ignore it.) and Asli, but separated from Serena. When we finally boarded the coach, sun filtered through my eyelids; a bright, painful red, and my damp legs prickled with heat. As the hours passed, the dark gaps between street lights began to grow smaller and smaller, and farther apart, the first sign that our bus was approaching familiar territory, and we would soon be passing through the well-known, well-lit streets of Victoria station.

We got off the coach and crossed the footbridge over the river Thames, the rain so shallow and clear in places that sometimes I heard the droplets click as the water dashed white against the pavement, boiling heavily on our polished clothes. We ran from Victoria Station to a Starbucks in Charing Cross, ordered cold brews, and waited patiently for the rain to subside into a light drizzle. For the entirety of the trip, I fulfilled the unspoken duty of a tour guide, making sure we all knew where we were going at all times, not bound to get lost in the street's loud and marshy crowds. I enjoyed the responsibility and culpability of managing the group, I had already witnessed enough of London during those formative years of my life and instead wished the same experience for Adeline and Asli in spite of the rain.

On our way to Soho, we stopped past Trafalgar Square to take a few photos together, running from store to store, trying on clothes that made our home tickets too expensive to afford by the end. We stopped by Zizi Factory and took a photo of Adeline under their 'sexy French waffles' sign. We sat in a cafe as the sun came suddenly from behind a rain cloud, flooding the streets with glorious light that wavered on the pavement like water. Asli's face burst into a glowing bloom. A terrible sweetness boiled up in me. Everything for a moment was unstable and radiant as a dream. "Are you sure you want to stay here alone?" Asli and I asked, looking at Adeline suspiciously.

"It's fine," she said, "I think I need some downtime."

"But you're absolutely sure?" I asked, unconvinced.

"Yes, really, it's fine," she said. "I might meet up with Serena anyways."

And so, Asli put the book I was reading, my sweater, her newly bought clothes and a bottle of cream soda in a beige sack. I didn't mind carrying it, because it lent her a sailor's air. We boarded the 33 bus and rode to the end of the line to Chinatown. I always loved bus rides across London. Just the idea that you could be so deeply absorbed in a city landscape was magical. I was reading the biography of Alexander Chee when I snapped to the present and looked at Asli. She was like a character in *Brighton Rock* in her minimal-style outfit, silver jewellery and chained purse. My phone buzzed and I opened it to see a message from you. We were planning to meet up in London, but the distance between us caused an issue. I was in Soho, and you had absolutely no idea where you were. We decided to meet back on campus instead.

When we pulled into Chinatown, we lept to our feet filled with the anticipation of a child. I slipped the book back into the sack and took Asli's hand. It felt good to be back in London, it was one of my favourite places, often daydreaming of getting a job there and living in one of the old tenement buildings across from Mayfair. And nothing was more wonderful to me than the breach between Soho and Chinatown with its gritty ambivalence. It was my kind of place: the fading corner shops, the peeling signs of bygone days, matcha chais and fish cakes on a stick, performers dressed in feathers and glittering top hats. We wandered through the gasp of town, strolled the boardwalk and got our picture taken by an old man with a box camera. We had to wait an hour for it to be developed, so we went to the centre of town to a restaurant that served cocktails and seafood.

There was a big-black and white awning flanked by a bigger sign, casual and sparse, adorned with large abstract pieces of art. Everything, save the white walls, was navy: booths, tablecloths, napkins. The big draw was surf and turf: burgers and lobster. It was as darkly glamorous as one could wish for.

We sat on the second floor and immediately were greeted by a waiter and complimentary drinks, signalling to us that this restaurant was real fancy shit.

Me and Asli were just ourselves that day, without a care. It was our good fortune that this moment in time was frozen in a box camera somewhere. We sat in a booth in the restaurant's theatre district sharing burgers and green-sauce appetisers, talking about everything and nothing at the same time. Our heritages provided us with a starting point to easily bounce off each other's company and experiences with mutual repertoire. We shared the same views on almost everything.

After refilling our cocktails, which were suspiciously good despite the extensive amounts of alcohol diluting their contents, we were abrupt in laughter and good conversation like we had been friends for years, even sisters. These kinds of conversations really reinforced the sense of a sisterhood between us, a sense of: *we're in this together, we have each other's backs.*

We paid the check and went further down Soho. The skyscrapers were beautiful, not like mere corporate shells but monuments to the arrogant yet philanthropic spirit of London. The character of each quadrant was invigorating and one felt the flux of its history. The old world and the emerging one served up in the brick-and-mortar of the artisan and the architects. I swiftly clocked Asli, inside and out, it seemed so natural talking with her. "So, Asli," I said, "you know how you've always wanted to see Buckingham Palace?"

"Of course," she smiled, "it's been a childhood dream of mine."

"Well, it's on the way to our bus stop so—"

"Alaska, you're kidding!" she exclaimed, throwing her arms around me.

'No, I'm not!" I giggled with her excitement as if it were my own. "There's a route that passes it! Let me take you!'

"Thank you. This is insane!"

"Don't thank me," I chuckled, "thank the GPS. God, I haven't seen Her Majesty in ages."

Asli's eyes widened ecstatically. "I can't believe I'm going to see—wait," she paused, "isn't the queen dead?" Despite the morbid nature of Her Majesty's passing, we did laugh then, we laughed a lot. We were both laughing so hard, as much from the nervous, self-soothing helplessness of not knowing as from the absurdity of our guesses, that we were bent over in our chairs, pressing our coat collars to our mouths to muffle the noise, our tears freezing pinching on our cheeks. We walked through Mayfair and then Green Park, drinking appleito lemonades from Pret. "Wait," Asli said, suddenly stopping on the cross-path. "What is *that*?"

I scanned around the fields of green grass. "What is what?" I asked, unable to notice anything outside of the usual London candour.

"That," Asli said, pointing somewhere on the patch of grass in front of us. "That thing there."

"I don't get it," I laughed. "What is what?"

"Under the tree!" she exclaimed. "There, look!"

She couldn't have been talking about…"The squirrel?" I asked.

"That's a squirrel? I've never seen one before."

This time, I laughed really hard. A real stomach and gut wrenching laugh. "You've never seen a squirrel? Do they not have squirrels in Turkey?"

"No! But oh my god, it's so cute," she said. "I need to get a picture of it."

We slowly inched our way closer to the defenceless rodent until we were only a mere centimetre away, I was surprised with how close we were able to get without disturbing the creature, hence, our laughter was tumultuous.

Entering the perimeters of Buckingham Palace, we were

greeted by the sounds of bongos and acoustic guitars, protest singers, political arguments, activists leafleting, older chess players challenged by the young. This open atmosphere was something Asli had not experienced, and I marvelled at her reaction to the simple freedom permeating the air around us. "Elizabeth!" she yelled. "We love you! Rest in peace!

I couldn't stop laughing. "Asli," I said, "she's buried in Windsor!"

"Win-what?" she asked.

"It's in Berkshire."

"Oh, in that case," she said. "William! You're so hot!"

We left London feeling extremely satisfied, content in each other's company and the passing festivities of the day. The bus was too full for Asli and I to sit with each other, so I spent the ride in and out of sleep, drifting along with the coach's unsteady rhythm, snapping awake at every speed bump. When I realised getting any sleep would be fictitious, I reached for the book I had with me from the tote bag, it was about Russian psychologists spontaneously combusting into flame. The author thought it mysterious, the sudden acceleration of the body's heat to a temperature that would sear bone. This did not mystify me then, as it did before.

The person writing had never met you.

CHAPTER EIGHT
SO MY DARLING

THIS PART, FOR SOME REASON, IS DIFFICULT FOR ME TO write, largely because the topic is inextricably associated with too many nights in my far memories (sour stomach, wretched nerves, clock inching tediously from four to five). It is also discouraging, because I recognise attempts at analysis are largely useless since the years have passed.

I am sorry, as well, to present such a sketchy and disappointing exegesis of what is in fact the central part of my story and character. I have noticed that even the most garrulous and shameless of victims are shy about recounting their assaults. And still, now even an air of unreality suffused even the most workaday details when repeating them back to you in the park one afternoon. It's not an ideal story, obviously, but I trusted you enough to tell it, I didn't have any alternative to speak of.

But that comes later...

The windshield wipers ticked back and forth for hours. A cop in a rain slicker was directing traffic at the intersection. When I got back to campus I found you sitting at the entrance, reading a book. There was something moon soaked and dawn flavoured about you. Something kissed by the wild and loved by lightning. You looked like the sun as it rose after kissing the dawn. "Hey," you said, glancing up. "Your bus took awfully long."

Seeing you was like an electric shock. Unexpectedly I felt a surge of elation. Rain was blowing through the streets and I walked down the entrance of St. Catherine's College to join you in the shade. "I didn't expect there to be so much traffic on the way back," I said.

A soft breeze passed in between us. "I missed you," you said.

We both smiled at each other. "I missed you too," I said. "But I'm soaked. Let me go change clothes and I'll meet you back here in five?"

You put your book down and smiled–*ah, lovely,* I thought helplessly, I loved the very sight of you; you were wearing a cashmere sweater, soft grey-green, and your brown eyes had a luminous celadon tint. "I'll be waiting inside," you said.

The night was unusually cold; this one colder than most and the heat was on in the dormitory — steam heat, full blast, which made it unbearably stuffy even with the windows open. My clothes were damp with a mixture of rain and sweat. I stuck my head out the window and took a few breaths. The chill air was so refreshing that I quickly got dressed and left the dormitories in hopes of breathing it again.

Then, once again, I was on the iron stairs at yours — rustled thin, no railing — except now they stretched down into a dark infinity and the steps were all different sizes: some tall, some short, some as narrow as the width of my shoe. You were standing on the top of the staircase, smiling down at me, the drop was bottomless on either side. At first, it had been completely dark inside but now my eyes had adjusted I was aware of the faint, greying light, moonlight, just enough to see by, glowing through the translucent walls. Wordlessly, you came down and pulled me in for a kiss, deep and with meaning. "You really missed me," I teased.

"Shut up, Alaska," you said with a smile, pushing through the doors of the exit. The moon was full and very bright. Everything was silent except for the chirp of the crickets and the foamy toss of the wind in the trees. At the sight of your calm, kindly face — so sweet, so agreeable, so glad to see me — something wrenched deep in my chest. "Alaska," you said again as if there were no one on earth you could possibly be so delighted to see. "How are you?"

"Better now," I smiled. "I'm a little tired. How was London?"

You heavily sighed. "London was pretty shit," you said. "It was too cold and I barely knew where I was half of the time."

"Harrods can be pretty intense," I said.

"I thought I was going to die in there," you said, completely serious and so, I laughed extremely hard. You smiled at this. "I'm just happy to be back here with you."

"Me too," I said, wrapping an arm around you.

The benevolence, the spiritual calm, that radiated from you seemed so clear and true that, for a dizzying moment, I felt the darkness lift almost palpably from my heart. The relief was such that I almost grabbed you in my arms; but then, looking at you again, I felt the whole weight come crashing back down, full force. I reached for a cigarette, and the last, untouched was passed to you. Being lonely with you was better than being surrounded by anyone else.

"The way you smoke," you chuckled. "You're going to end up with something one of these days."

"Not with you watching over me like this," I said. "Besides, I'm not addicted or anything—"

"Can stop at any time?" you joked.

I leaned forward and kissed you. "Precisely," I smiled. "How's your essay coming along?"

Suddenly, your expression dropped. "Shit," you said. "I forgot about it."

"Theo, they're due on Monday. It's Saturday."

"I know. Fuck."

I thought to myself for a moment. "How about tomorrow morning, before the Great Debate, we go out for breakfast and work on them?" I proposed.

You smiled widely and with great affection. "That would be great."

"Call it a date," I said.

"If you insist...*babe.*"

"Absolutely not." I laughed as you threw an arm over my shoulders.

You smiled down at me. "I know you like it," you said, "just a little."

I rolled my eyes affectionately. "Maybe just a little. A very *very* small little."

"Baby steps," you said. "Tomorrow I'll have you devotedly in love with me."

I raised an eyebrow. "That's what you call baby steps?"

"Close enough," you said, leaning forward for another kiss.

This walk, from St. Catherine to the city centre, was not an inconsiderable one. It was a mile, at least. A good portion of it lay along a stretch of highway. Cars whooshed past in a rush of exhaust. I was dead tired. My head ached and my feet were like lead. But the evening air was cool and fresh and it seemed to bring me around a little. About halfway, we stopped at the dusty roadside of a Tesco and bought a packet of mangoes to share. Our feet crunched on the gravel. We smoked another cigarette and ate from the mango container, occasionally feeding a piece to each other. Further into the night, our conversations took on philosophy, as that's what we knew and connected over best. "I'm not scared of death, but what comes after," I muttered. "I don't like the idea of the unknown."

"Well, I think we live in a sort of fourth dimension," you said, taking a piece of mango out of the container. "You know, the role of time as the fourth dimension of spacetime, the basis for Einstein's theories of special and general relativity."

I took a drag of my cigarette and leaned into you. "I'm not quite sure what you mean," I sighed helplessly.

"We're always moving forward through time, sure, but it's just as much a dimension as any of the spatial ones," you continued, raising your hands to make a sort of philosophical gesture. I mimicked it back and laughed. "You cannot treat space and time separately, Alaska, they are inextricably linked."

I contemplated this for a moment and nodded. "I guess I just don't want to end up like those suburban American mums with five kids."

You looked at me and laughed. "Like the ones that yell at customer services?"

"Yeah exactly," I said, sleepily. "And their husbands are never home, most likely sleeping with someone else."

"So," you said, taking a drag of your cigarette. "Your worst fear is to end up as a Suburban American mum?"

I immediately realised the denseness of my statement, and embarrassed, stubbed my cigarette on the ground. "Ok, that sounds really far-fetched." I rubbed my eyes, trying to collect my thoughts. "What I'm trying to say is that I'm scared to end up average, that everything in my life and everything that has and will happen to me will eventually amount to nothing."

You laughed again, but this time it was in a more sarcastic, dishonest fashion. "Don't bullshit, Alaska," you said. "I could never imagine you being average."

"I hope—"

"Never *hope*," you said suddenly, looking at me closely as your expression darkened in the moonlight. Despite the archness of your tone — which normally would have irritated me — there was a melancholy undertone in your voice. You drained the rest of your cigarette and set it out on the pavement, smothering out the flame with the underside of your shoe. "Hoping gets you nowhere, hope is bullshit," you said after a pause. "Hope gets you heartbroken."

I fell into another tormented half-dreaming state from which I woke, several hours later, to a soft knock. My room was still dark. The door creaked open and a flag of light fell in from the corridor. Adeline slipped in and closed the door behind her. She switched on the weak reading lap on my desk and sat on the end of my bed and took a deep breath. "I'm sorry, I know you're asleep but I've got to talk to you," she said. "It's about what I said the other day, about you and Theo."

Shit, I thought, *Theo.* "Wait, what time is it?" I asked, eyes barely open.

Adeline looked at me, confused. "Eleven?"

"Fuck," I groaned, sitting up and out from my covers.

"What is it?" Adeline asked.

I rubbed a tired hand over my eyes. "I was supposed to meet him an hour ago to work on our essays," I said, reaching over to check my phone, *no messages*. "It's fine, I think we both overslept. What did you want to talk about?"

She sighed. "I'm sorry," she said.

"Oh," I said, surprised, but mostly sleepily. "Really, Adeline. It's okay, don't worry about it—"

"I don't know. I see so little of you these days," she said straitly.

"I promise you, if I was upset about it I would've come straight to you," I said, somewhat ingenuous. But this seemed like a step in the right direction, so I accepted her apology and said nothing further. "How about lunch tomorrow?" I asked.

"I'd love that," Adeline said, relieved. "Let's go downstairs for breakfast?"

It was Sunday, which surprised me a little; I'd lost track of the days. I went to the dining hall and had a late breakfast of tea and soft-boiled eggs, the first meal I'd eaten since London.

In the dark morning, the sun was the gold centre of everything. It was only a little sunny, the light scattered the gaps of night left in the sky. I walked through campus up to your dorm; life-size saints lined the walkway to the main entrance, each holding a symbol of vocation or fate: a key, a book, a mathematical instrument, and even a golden saw. I sat in a pew several feet from the dormitories and light poured through the high-stained glass windows; I glanced at the grand altars. *Place of sacrifice,* they said.

A janitor left the back entrance open and I made my way up the stairs and to your room. By then, it was around noon and you were still asleep. When I woke you, your face was flushed and pink. "Alaska," you whispered, waking with a start. "Am I dreaming or are you in my room right now?"

I placed a gentle hand against your cheeks. "Dreaming," I said. "Definitely dreaming."

"Okay," you murmured, not having opened your eyes yet, fearing the sunlight would ruin your peaceful rest. Suddenly, you raised your head and looked up at me. "No, definitely not dreaming. What are you doing here?"

I laughed softly. "We were going to work on our essays."

"What?" you said, looking wildly round. "Shit, yeah."

"Don't worry," I said. "I slept in too."

Your head crashed back against your pillow and everything

was silent for a peaceful moment. You raised your head and looked at me again. "Wait, how did you even get in here?"

"I let me in." I smiled childishly and welcomed myself under the covers, pressing my cheek against yours. "The door was already open and you didn't lock yours."

"Stalker," you smiled, rolling your eyes. "Well, I'm awake now."

"How does breakfast sound?" I said, sitting up to push the hair out of my face. "We can go to Joe & The Juice."

"I love Joe & The Juice," you said, kissing me on the cheek. "If this is how I wake up every morning, I'll never lock my door again."

"Are you sure you want to wake up with a stalker in your bed every morning?"

"If the stalker is as pretty as you, I sure as hell wouldn't mind it."

The memories of summer dissolved in my mouth and suddenly, I couldn't remember what a life before you tasted like. I wasn't sure I wanted to remember.

In Joe & The Juice, I felt a warm rush of well-being and wrote straight through the morning. My essay was almost finished, only a few refinery details and tweaks were left, but you were ridiculously behind; you seemed always in motion, stopping only for a moment if you noticed something. Most of the time, it seemed as if the piece was fully formed in your mind. You were not one for improvising. It was more of a question of executing something you saw in a flash, of finding the right idea. You lay your head on your laptop and groaned into the keys.

On the other hand, I understood what matters in the work, rather than the idea: the string of words propelled by one becoming a poem, the weave of colour and graphite scrawled upon the sheet that magnifies literature, to achieve within the work a perfect balance of faith and execution.

From this state of mind comes a light, comes a life-changed.

For the rest of the afternoon, open light spread from the overhead lamp, intense, unforgiving, yet seemingly filled with unique energy. You lay back in your chair, so deflated that neither of us could say anything. Two hours had passed when I finally finished my assignment and we wandered down to the lake, which was shared, discreetly, by several adjoining properties.

The sky was a fierce, burning blue, the trees ferocious shades of red and yellow. We stepped precariously over rocks and branches, balancing ourselves over the ragged craters. We sat by the water and kicked off our shoes and socks. The water near the bank was clear, pale green, cool over my ankles, and the pebbles at the bottom were dappled with sunlight. I slid into your arms, and we sat for a while, talking and laughing in contentment. A wind rustled through the birches, blowing up the pale undersides of leaves, and it caught in my skirt and billowed it out like a white balloon. I laughed and smoothed it down quickly.

We inched closer to the shore, the shallows barely covering our feet. The sun shimmered off the lake in bright waves — it didn't look like a real lake but a mirage. I listened as you, one hand shading your light-dazzled eyes, were telling me a long story about something your dog had done — but I wasn't following very closely: you were like a living reverie for me: the mere sight sparking an almost infinite range of emotions, from indecent to divine.

I was looking at the side of your face, listening to the sweet, throaty cadences of your voice, lying blissfully in your arms. Everything was still and quiet, the shine shining down on us projected a comforting warmth. Our hands seemed to fit together like magnets, there was never a fumble. There was something real and immutable about who you were, that despite my life of guises after New York, something elemental, constituted your very witness of me into reality again.

Your hand glazed my thighs, my mouth closed in on yours as they made their way up, carefully, cautiously. The feelings were too great for me to get any words out, I blurred into you, warm, waning, wanting; my hands scrunched against your leather jacket. Afterwards, we lit two cigarettes and watched them dissolve into spilling currents, dissolve into each other's affability. "I don't think anything could beat this date," you said.

"Oh really?" I asked, taking this as somewhat of a challenge. "How about I take you out for dinner tonight?"

"Only If you want to," you said.

"Yeah I would love to," I smiled. "Take it as me revolting against the patriarchy. I'll even pay for the check."

You softly chuckled and brushed a piece of hair out of my face. "Revolting against the patriarchy? Says the one lying in my arms."

I rolled my eyes and laughed. "Don't make me change my mind," I said, "I'll pick you up at seven, princess."

G.W.F Hegel, in a lecture on September 18, 1806 said:

> We stand at the gates of an important epoch, a time of ferment when spirit moves forward in a leap, transcends its previous shape and takes on a new one. All the mass of previous representations, concepts, and bonds linking our world together, are dissolving and collapsing like a dream picture. A new phase of the spirit is preparing itself. Philosophy especially has to welcome its appearance and acknowledge it, while others, who oppose it impotently, cling to the past.

Reading it felt a lot like falling in love with you then, my spirit moving forward in a leap and taking on a new shape. A shape of someone new and more loving, more open. My past liquified in your hands. You made me happy, and for a moment, it felt like all that I needed. Of course, I hadn't realised it then, but wasn't it strange how when the breeze started to warm, and permeated the roots of my hair, that everything started to seem alright?

The air stilled and silenced, until a lone mockingbird fluttered in the trees. I looked at you watching the bird with great intensity. It leapt from one branch to another, then disappeared into the sky. "I need to talk to you about something," I said suddenly. "But I've never told anyone this before, but I trust you. I hope that means something to you."

You paused and looked down at me in your arms. "Is this about..."

I nodded and sat very still, trying to think, to think about how to let the words out. I took out a pack of cigarettes from my pocket, brought one to my mouth and lit it before handing one to you. "I needed those months to be a love story, otherwise what else could they have been?" I said, watching the spilling currents.

A gust of air wafted through then, dreamy and soft, you wrapped your arms around me and it was suddenly warm again. The warm feel of a body in my arms was something I'd almost forgotten. "What happened?" you asked as I buried my face in the soft, slightly acrid-smelling curve of your neck, feeling myself fall down and down into a dark, half-forgotten life.

"It was five years ago," I said. "I was twelve and he was about nineteen. I don't really remember." I tried to think of some way to vocalise the rest of this epiphany. "Things progressed. I liked him, I liked him a lot. We talked for months, and he was quite popular...not that it matters, but one day, something happened to him with his friends. He stopped talking to them, and started talking to me much more. He gave me the right amount of attention at the wrong time."

I let the words continue to flow, oblivious of your silence.

They couldn't stop. "It's a blur from here. But one day, something changed. Something in the way that he looked at me, but I was so young I couldn't really place what it was."

You brushed my arms gently, and I rested my head against your chest. "What happened then?"

"I said no, and he didn't." I shrugged, unwilling to elaborate. "The rest of the months went by the same. I kept my mouth shut and never said anything. But that wasn't even the worst part for me."

"What was?" you asked, hesitantly. The mockingbird had returned to the tree and was now perched, watching over us.

"One day, he got tired of me and left," I sighed. "Mind you, I still saw him every day at school but something had...turned off. With no explanation, he stopped talking to me. Just like that. I never knew why, and I don't even know why now. I spent years punishing myself, I thought I had done something to make him upset. I figured that I must have done something to push him away. How could he have been in love with me one minute, and gone the next?" I sighed. "But anyways, he moved abroad that same year and I haven't seen him since."

You were completely silent and I figured I understood why. Most people misunderstood the crime of sexual assault. They thought of stolen youth, a child tucked under the arm and spirited away. But it wasn't like someone entering your house and stealing something from you. Instead, someone left something with you that grew until it replaced you. Mind you, they themselves were once replaced this way, and what they leave you with they have carried for years within them, like a fire guarded all this time as it burned them alive, right under the skin. The burning is hidden to protect themselves from being revealed as burned.

I came to realise that the worst thing was not that someone would know or find out what happened. But the worst thing was that I may lay waste to my whole life by hiding this part of me. I mistook my ability to stay silent and keep quiet about all of it as strength. Strength was admirable, after all, and I was ashamed of everything else about myself. My endurance, at least — was something someone could admire. I was too young to know what I believed as my complicity as something taken from me, but in my silence, I became complicit with the continued pain, the risk that risked replacing me the longer I let it stay. But among the things I could not imagine was that anyone would understand, or be kind. This was all I understood. When I asked myself why it was so hard for me to let this secret go, the answer was that holding on to it was the only source of my self-esteem for years. It was all I thought I had.

I remember reading a line in Roland Barthes's *Mourning Diary*, which he started writing the day after his mother's death:

> *'I live in my suffering and that makes me happy. Anything that keeps me from living in my suffering is unbearable to me...I ask for nothing but to live in my suffering.'*

I too didn't want to escape the suffering. It was always more painful when I tried. If I gave into my hurt, let it envelop me, everything would be less of a struggle. Living in that suffering brought me a comfort, an ease, it pulled me in without my awareness, making it harder to escape it when I finally realised how far gone I was.

But now, to have felt the warmth of your love, your admiration and affection, I never wanted to forget the feeling. You closed your eyes and held me tighter in your arms, your eyes were soft and submissive in the afternoon light. "And these," you said, rubbing gently across my thighs. "Came after, I suppose."

"Yes," I said, the world feeling somewhat lighter around

me. "They did, but not anymore. That's not how I want to live anymore."

From the look in your eyes, I could tell that you were the only person I've ever met who seemed to have the faintest conception of what I meant when I said something. To you, I wasn't disfigured, vulnerable, naive — a role I had inhabited for so long that it had become, indelibly, who I was — instead, I was your friend, your lover, and that identity supplanted everything else.

I remembered who I had been after the assault; I had made a life pretending to be normal, someone to whom everything and everyone seemed so impressive and beguiling. But I wanted to be recognised by someone for who I truly was; I wanted to be around someone for whom my past would never be the most interesting thing about me. And I had finally found them in you. I closed my eyes. I lay there for a long time, half-dozing until I became aware that you were saying my name. "Alaska," you said, quietly, softer than I had ever heard your voice before. "Are you happy?"

I paused for a moment to think.

"I don't think happiness is for me," I said finally. "I think I wait for people to hurt me," I said quietly. "And when they do I feel a certain smugness at being right. And, after that, I just feel pain."

You nodded, and for a long time — an unusually long time — looked into my eyes, and I'll never forget how in doing so we were able to glimpse into each other's inner worlds. For one brief moment, I saw the pain that hid behind my words and gestures, and in exchange, I sensed what you held deep inside. But we went no further. We both stopped on the threshold of the other, and we asked each other no further questions. It was then, that I finally felt safe, for the first time in my life, like everything could be alright if I could stay by your side. I had always been afraid that my emotions would be too much for people, that I would always give love to others more than I loved myself, that I wouldn't ever find someone who met me where I am, but then, I met you, and you found me. You were the first person who made me feel good about being me, and only me, not the things that happened to me, only me. You took my hand in yours and looked down at me. "Nobody sees as we do," you said. I nodded.

I suppose the thrill of the battle between good and evil attracted you, perhaps because it mirrored your interior conflict, and revealed a line that you might yet need to cross. It was all the same. We told ourselves, in our storms, that we were strong, you and I. But in reality, it was only endurance. I was not strong, nor were you. Or if we were, it was the adrenaline of the wounded. We were really only broken, moving through the landscape as if we were not, and not taking all our pride in believing we were passing as a whole. But at that moment, sitting in each other's arms, we no longer needed to be strong, we no longer needed to endure anything. We could sit and let time pass over ourselves like a tide. We could sit and hide ourselves from the world.

We did not need to be strong anymore because we had each other.

In spite of this, with time's passing, I've come to realise that you had an uncanny ability to ferret out topics of conversation that made yourself uneasy and to dwell upon them with ferocity once you had. Maybe if I had realised sooner that you had such apathy and disinterest in my scope of history, perhaps I would have kept these details to myself.

Now, I'd rather choke on my words in silence, than allow you to ever see me in any state of vulnerability again.

Late afternoon, the sun spread its warmth. The dry leaves skittered and danced on the path before me, and I ran into Asli on her way to the Sheldonian theatre. The Great Debate, another mandatory activity, was showing in the auditorium. Despite the name suggesting something profound or sagacious, it was not very great at all.

The entire summer program seemed like an education conducted through gestalt experiences: take kids to a place where they don't understand anything, and then take them on tours with other people who understand only a little more than they do. I was growing bored of these trips.

We were late and there were no seats left so we sat on the other side of the hall, Asli leaned back on her elbows with her legs stretched out in front of her, cracking pensively as the high wind rattled the primordial walls. A door banged open and shut until somebody propped open with a brick. Not even fifteen minutes into the introductory speech, some counsellors left, including Ian. The microphones spilled out monotonous, barely comprehensible shrills into the auditorium, lulling myself and others into a drowsy slumber. Every now and then, I'd catch a glimpse of another student with their head hung like a rag-doll or fast asleep in the stands. I sent periodic texts and photos to Serena and Adeline, who were sitting on the other side of the auditorium: we played *Smash or Pass* with unsuspecting victims from the college and guest speakers.

Asli and I took periodic bathroom breaks that lasted a minimum of twenty minutes in attempts to ease the boredom, other students apparently had the exact same idea; we talked to other girls and they were almost as bored as we were, if not more. I took some of their socials and proposed hanging out later but we never did.

The only thing of interest to me was catching your gaze every now and then. But as the hours dawned on, I caught myself more staring than a mutual gaze. When the lights came on, and the circle of darkness leapt back into the mundane and familiar boundaries of the auditorium — low, lumpy seats; the dusty draperies that read *Oxford University* — it was as if I'd switched on the lamp after a long bad dream; blinking, I was relieved to discover that the doors and windows were still where they were supposed to be and that the auditorium hadn't rearranged itself, by diabolical magic, in the dark.

Asli and I went out for lunch afterwards and the cafe we had chosen was like a tomb, illuminated from within by a chill fluorescent light that, by contrast, made the afternoon seem colder and greyer than it was. The windows of the dining room were bright and blank; bookshelves, empty carrels, not a soul.

The cashier — a despicable woman with blonde hair — was behind the desk reading a copy of *Woman's Day* and didn't look up. The coffee machine hummed quietly in the corner and we both ordered warm lattes in spite of the weather changes outside. We climbed the stairs to the second floor, and it was just as empty as we'd thought. "Have you spoken to Adeline recently?" Asli asked.

I place my coffee back on the table. "She came to see me this morning," I said.

Asli's eyes widened with curiosity. "What did she say?"

"She apologised about the Theo situation," I said, fiddling with a packet of sugar.

Asli's eyes gave a blank stare, riddled with adversity. "That's good," she said. "But she's still mad at me."

I managed to tear open the packet and poured it into my coffee, watching the crystals dissolve in the heat. "What makes you think so?" I asked.

"She hasn't talked to me all day, I think she's avoiding me," she sighed. "Speaking of Theo, how have things been?"

I lit up and smiled immediately. "Good, really good, I think," I said, taking a sip of my sweetened coffee with delight. "I'm taking him on a date this evening."

Asli smiled. "That's adorable, where are you taking him?"

"I have no idea," I chuckled. "I wanted to go to Franco Manca, but I knew he would judge the Italian food."

"Has he taken you out on a date yet?"

I blinked. "I mean...we went on a study date at Joe's this morning."

Asli looked at me sceptically. "Who's idea was it?"

"It was his," I lied, feeling strangely protective over you. I reached for my coffee again, almost obsessively. "Oh! There's this rooftop restaurant, near Westgate," I said, changing the topic. "I think that sounds awfully romantic."

"That sounds perfect," she smiled.

"It's great to have someone to talk about this with," I said. "Thank you, really. I'm really sorry if it's a burden. Just tell me—"

"It's never a bother, Alaska!" she laughed softly. "It's fun! You should be having fun, and besides, you always help me with my stuff, so I help with yours."

We smiled at each other, finished our coffees and made our way back to campus. I really loved Asli; our friendship was witnessing another's slow drip of miseries, and long bouts of boredom, and occasional triumphs. It was feeling honoured by the privilege of getting to be present for another person's most dismal moments, and knowing that you could be dismal around them in return.

At seven o'clock, the chill sky, misty with fine rain near the rooftop, made even the familiar landscape of Oxford seem indifferent and remote. The buildings were golden in the sun and the top of Christ Church was entirely obscured, intertwined in the auspicious rays. It was all so beautiful.

I found you so fascinating then, I think it was because there was something a tiny bit inexplicable about you, something I was often on the verge of grasping but never quite did. You were a real mystery, the safe I could never crack and never would.

The waiter presented our menus with affected, sarcastic delicacy, and stalked off. Two teenagers playing dress up was amusing I suppose. We sat down and opened the wine list, my heart burned. You, settling in your chair, took a sip of water and looked around peacefully. "This is a beautiful place," you said.

"It really is—"

"It's almost as beautiful as the girl sitting in front of me," you said, smiling.

My cheeks burned and my heart fluttered. "Shut up and order your food," I remarked.

You smiled. "Yes, *darling.*" I rolled my eyes with affection.

We ordered a glass of white wine and a colourful bowl of rice, avocado, tofu and mangoes, all doused in adequate amounts of soy sauce. We spoke through the evening of curfews, and rebellions, and punishments, and pets and siblings, and what I had worn that had driven my parents crazy, and what groups we had hung out with in high school, and cars you had crashed and bones I had broken, and sports I had played and bands you had started. We spoke of disastrous family vacations and strange, colourful relatives and odd next-door neighbour experiences and teachers, both beloved and loathed. "No way," I gasped. "You used to play the drums?"

"All of the time," you said, reaching over for the bottle of wine and refilling both of our glasses.

"Thank you," I said. "How come you don't play them anymore?"

You shrugged nonchalantly. "I never have the time."

"Why's that?"

You smiled and sighed dramatically. "I'd rather be doing other things..."

"Doing what?"

"Like doing you," you chuckled, "to name a few."

"Charming, Theo," I smiled sarcastically and as our eyes interlocked, I forgot every time you had wronged me. We laughed at the stories you had to tell, about the person you used to be. I didn't even have to say a word the entire night about myself to feel satisfied, to feel loved. Every time I was with you, I just felt like I was getting closer and closer to your soul and that was more than enough. I wanted you to tell me everything about you — even if it took years, took centuries, a lifetime — I would've sat there and listened to it all.

You were a good talker. In happy role reversal, it was you who was the storyteller. It was possible that your tales were even taller than mine. As the day passed, this feeling dampened, but it never disappeared; it lived on me like a thin scum of mould. But as that knowledge became more acceptable, another piece became less so: I began to realise that you were the first and last person to whom I would never have to explain anything. You knew that I wore my life on my skin, that my biography was written in my flesh and on my bones. You never asked me why I wouldn't wear short sleeves, even in the steamiest of weather, or why I liked to be touched: you knew already. Around you I had felt none of the constant anxiety, nor watchfulness, that I seemed condemned to feel around everyone else; the vigilance was exhausting, but it eventually became simply a part of life, a habit like good posture.

You had an infectious laugh and were rugged, smart and intuitive. After hearing your stories, I always felt like I knew who you were. Later, when you were gone, I was forced to realise that I knew nothing about you, absolutely nothing. Either way, in the end, we were more alike than not and gravitated towards each other, however wide the breach. We weathered all things large and small with the same vigour. To me, we were irrevocably intertwined, like Patroclus and Achilles in *The Iliad*. We played similar instruments, declared the most obscure philosophical theories, and often puzzled friends and acquaintances with our indefinable devotion. It pleased me to imagine a presence above us, of continual motion, like liquid stars.

The wine wilted down our throats, like white lilies in a sink. It wasn't necessarily the alcohol that interested me; it was the funny feeling in my stomach that excited me, the thrill of doing something forbidden. Despite the vast amount we ate, we drank even more, the surroundings blurred at a dizzying velocity. You did most of the talking, I just smiled and listened. I was surprised at how comfortable and open I felt with you. This boy I had met was bold and articulate, and I liked to be led, to be taken by the hand and enter wholeheartedly another world. You were masculine and protective, even as you were feminine and submissive. Meticulous in your dress and demeanour, you were also capable of a frightening disorder with your words. They were solitary and dangerous, anticipating freedom, ecstasy and release. But whenever you would look at me and smile, it would break through anything else I was feeling or experiencing.

It was dark by nine and around us, the countryside lay veiled and mysterious, silent in the night fog. The walk back to campus was remote, unravelled land, rocky and thinly wooded, with none of the quaint appeal of Oxford and its rolling hills, its old chalets and antique shops, but perilous and primitive, everything black and desolate.

The quire was ringed by a cobblestone porch — jaded vines, wrapped in timber-woods. From the inside, we could see the light from the lobby, orange and mahogany, bicentennial commemorative trivets mounted and hung upon the walls. Faintly, Chopin, one of his preludes, maybe, ran from the evergreens to where we were standing. We both were a little inebriated; the Chopin was slurred and fluid, the notes melted sleepily into one another. A breeze stirred the heavy, humid arm, ruffling your hair. I looked at you as if you had the entire world in your eyes, the sun, even the moon.

And then, as you started to wage your way between my legs, bringing our lips together, I felt a little less war-torn. I was not sure what peace was supposed to feel like, but I thought it may have felt a lot like you. In the background, the musician ran up another octave, trilling nonsensically on the keys. I smiled at you in between kisses, a little dazed. The quire had set off a ghostly echo, giving all that desperate hilarity the quality of a memory even as we sat listening to it fade around us. You leaned in to kiss me and I bit your bottom lip hard, and then your shoulder. "Vampire," you chuckled, wrapping your hand around my hair and pulling me closer.

I slowly unbuttoned your blouse and your hands trailed across my waist. I kissed your cheek, your hands, your forehead, your lips. Underneath your shirt, my hands meandered up and down; like the locomotion of a crashing tide, a waning moon, a comet; I was so weak in your arms, but for once, I was not afraid. Every now and then, the other would let out a gasp, a short collective breath, before drawing the other in again. We were a mirror image, though not so much in physical resemblance; your dark curls against my straight hazel, brown eyes against my grey; but more as in body language, in sync. "Is this what happiness feels like?" you whispered. "It feels so fragile." Unsure of what to say, I pulled you in closer for another kiss. When we pulled apart, you looked at me for a while and then smiled wide. "You know, I love the way you look at me," you said finally.

"Like what?" I laughed.

"Like you have little love hearts in your eyes all of the time," you said.

What I should have told you then, was that sometimes I

wished you wouldn't look at me like that either: *like you could have loved me...*

Dark wood, potted pals, rose silk lampshades with their swaying fringe. I really had a bit too much to drink. I was sitting sideways on the steps, holding tightly to your arms, and even the vines were listing, like the decks of a foundering ship, piano and all.

Both of us had given ourselves to the other. We vacillated and lost each other, but always found one another again. We wanted, it seemed, what we already had, a lover and a friend to be with, side by side.

To be loyal, yet to be free.

The undying affection between us had been prodded, a bond that could not be severed. The affirmation that came from each strengthened us. Both had stoic natures, but together we could reveal our vulnerabilities without shame, and trust each other with that knowledge. With you, I could be myself, and you did not judge me and vice versa. Shedding all else, what existed between us was a mutual tenderness.

I wanted to spend every single second with you if it was always going to be like this. Strangely I found that I could not stop my hands, my mouth, my mind, they wanted everything to do with you and only you. You made me lose something I spent my whole life seeking out for. My control was my peace, replaced now, by the shape of you. When we kissed to say goodbye, both breathless and inebriated, you drew back and looked at me intently. We didn't say anything, we just smiled.

For a moment, in a swish of black cashmere and cigarette smoke, your arm brushed mine; you were a creature of flesh and blood, but the next you were a hallucination again, a figment of the imagination stalking down the evergreens as heedless of me as ghosts, in their shadowy rounds, are said to be heedless of the living...

But I am getting sentimental.

Sometimes, when I think about these moments, I do.

In my room, I'd been at my desk nearly all night reading Camus' *The Stranger* again. The words were rough going but I was slightly drunk, too, and I'd been at it so long that the letters didn't even look like letters but something else, indecipherable, bird footprints on sand. Suddenly a knock came through my door, and as I went to open it, Adeline was standing in the doorway. "Hey, Alaska," she said.

I steadied myself against the doorframe and smiled at her, as if she was some great angel in disguise. "Hey," I said, "how are you?"

"I'm good," she said. "We still have an hour before the marquee, do you want to go out to town? Maybe grab drinks?"

I made myself an agreement, prior to the course, to savour every moment, live it to the fullest. So although I was slightly inebriated and dizzy, I happily agreed to Adeline's offer. I felt a rush of gratitude towards her, I didn't really feel like being alone again. "I'd love to—wait, can we go down to the office quickly?" I asked. "I need to print out my essay for tomorrow."

She nodded. "Of course."

We went down the backstairs and over to the main office — its grey brick facade flat as a stage backdrop against the empty sky. "Hey, I need to print out my essay for tomorrow morning," I said to one of the counsellors, a man in his early twenties.

His red lanyard flashed through the dark. "No can do," he said. "The printing lady won't be back until the morning."

Shit, I thought. I had skipped the deadline to submit online copies in hopes I could get mine physically printed. To be truthful, it was part of my ego, but nevertheless. "How early will she be in tomorrow?" I asked.

"Seven," he said, looking up at me. "How urgently do you need this?"

"It's due first class tomorrow so—"

"That gives you time. Be here in the morning to get it done," he said, closing the office door in my face.

I looked back at Adeline, annoyed. "I swear, these counsellors..."

We signed out our names and headed into town. We turned to Oxford City Center and, at the top of the rise, I saw the gables of the Sheldonian Theatre, bleak in the distance. The sky was warm and empty. A sliver of moon, like the white crescent of a thumbnail, floated in the dim.

That night, the dream picked up from where it left off: I stood; never feeling more naked, more exposed in my life. When I was a child, and things were happening to me, I used to be able to leave my body, to go somewhere else. I would pretend I was something inanimate — a curtain rod, a ceiling fan — a dispassionate, unfeeling witness to the scene occurring beneath me. I could watch myself and feel nothing: not pity, not anger, nothing. But then, I tried, I found I could not remove myself. I was in that apartment, my apartment, standing before a man who detested me, and I knew then, that that was the beginning, not the end, of a long night; one I had no choice but to wait through and endure. I would not be able to control that night, I would not be able to stop it.

My beautiful apartment, I thought, where I had always been safe. This was happening to me in my beautiful apartment, surrounded by my beautiful things, things that had been given to me in friendships, things that I had bought with money I had earned. My apartment, with its doors that locked, where I was meant to be protected, where I was meant to always feel human and whole...

CHAPTER NINE

MYSTERIES OF MIDNIGHT SUN

FROM THE MOMENT I SET FOOT IN ST. CATHERINE, I HAD begun to dread the end of the course; when I would have to go back to New York, the flat land, and filling distractions, and dust. As the days wore on, and the cold got deeper and the mornings blacker and every day brought me closer to the date on the smeared mimeograph inside my calendar, my melancholy began to turn into something like an alarm.

I woke the next day with a start, to chill sunlight and the thump of Adeline entering my room. It was early, sunrise, late Monday morning maybe; I reached for my phone on the night table and stared back at the digits reading seven-thirty, then made my way down to the office to print out my essay. It was a short walk, but the wind was up and it was terribly cold, making it a harrowing one.

The walk to Pitt Rivers was also especially cold that morning. A November stillness was settling like a deadly oxymoron on the July landscape. Rain was falling in earnest now — big silent petals drifted through the summertime woods, white bouquets segueing into raining dark. My path took me beneath a row of cherry trees, full-blown and luminous, giving way to the twilight like an avenue of pale umbrellas. The big white flakes wafted through them, dreamy and soft. I did not stop to look, however, only hurried beneath them even faster. I loved this place, its shabby elegance, and the history it held so possessively. So many had written, conversed and convulsed in these lecture rooms. So many skirts had swished these worn marble stairs. So many transient souls had espoused, made a mark, and succumbed here. "Good morning," Louise said.

Startled, I turned to see her standing at the other end of the hall. She was without a jacket but otherwise immaculate for such an ungodly hour: trousers knife-pressed, her white shirt crisp with starch. On the desk in front of her were books and papers, a steaming espresso pot and a tiny cup. I walked over to her desk and placed my essay on a paper file. "I'm interested to see what you came up with, Alaska," she said, and I smiled before returning to my seat. Louise kept a gentle but firm distance between herself and her students; and though she was much more fond of us than teachers generally are with their pupils, it was a relationship of equals, and our classes with her ran more along the lines of benevolent dictatorship than democracy. "I am your teacher," she once said, "because I know more than you do." She refused to see anything about any of us except our most engaging qualities, which she cultivated and magnified to the exclusion of all our tedious and less desirable ones. While I felt a delicious please in adjusting myself to fit this attractive if inaccurate image — and eventually, in finding that I had so skilfully played — there was never any doubt that she did not which to see us in our entirety or see us, in fact, in anything other than the studious roles she had invented for us. It was through this perspective that allowed for her to transmute any substantive troubles into spiritual ones.

I knew then, and I know now, virtually nothing about

Louise's life outside of the classroom, which is perhaps what lent such a tantalising breath of mystery to everything she said or did. No doubt her personal life was as flawed as anyone's. But the only side of herself she ever allowed us to see was polished to such a high gloss of perfection that it seemed when she was away from us she must lead an existence too rarefied for me to even imagine.

I sipped on my water, watching the flurry of students pile in and place their essays on the desk. You still hadn't arrived yet, and the clock was nearing two minutes to eight. "Hey," a tired voice said behind me and I already knew who it was.

"Is everything alright?" I asked. No response. "Did you get the essay done?"

You leaned back in your chair and trained your watery, red-rimmed eyes on me. Your hands, folded on the desk before us, gnarled with veins and had a bluish, pearly sheen around the knuckles. I stared at them. "No," you sighed. "I couldn't think of what to write."

I was somewhat annoyed, but didn't let it show. "It's okay, don't worry," I said. "I'm sure that if you talk to Louise she will understand."

You still hadn't said anything and were instead, looking down at the desk, burying your face in your palms.

"The essay isn't even a big deal," I lied (it was seventy percent of our final grade). "I'm sure you'll still graduate."

You exhaled deeply and ruffled through your backpack. "Seriously," I said. "Don't worry–" You arched your eyebrows and looked at your folded hands for a moment. "You absolute dickhead," I sighed, mostly in relief.

"You were really stressed out for me, weren't you!" you laughed, relishing in my discomfiture. The pages of your essay were sitting valiantly on the table.

"Shut up, at least I care." I said, rather startled. I reached over for the stack of papers and flipped through them briefly. "*The acceptance of meaningless*...I love–you referenced Camus?"

"I told you I would!" you exclaimed.

"I didn't think you actually would!"

"I even added a section on Nietzsche," you said.

"Mr Existentialist," I chuckled.

"I'm a man of surprises," you winked, standing up and walking over to Louise's desk. I smiled. We became more ourselves, day by day, hour by hour, even every minute. Our transformation was the rose of Genet, and pierced deeply, blooming. I desired to feel more of your world, yet sometimes that desire was nothing more than a wish to go backwards where our mute light spread from hanging lanterns with mirrored panels. You responded as my beloved half. Your dark curls merged with the tangle of my hair. We learned we wanted too much, we could only give from the perspectives of who we were and what we had.

That morning, we were taught a class on the history of Romanticism, how the sensitive artist was often doomed by a cruel world. "To be Romantic," Louise said, "is to be senseless to madness." What I essentially took away from that class is that I was definitely a romantic. I can't really argue with emotions being the expressive freedom for form; I mean, look at all of this writing. "An example of a romantic poem that I invite you all to ponder on is *Stopping by Woods on a Snowy Evening.* Robert Frost, anyone?" Louise asked.

Veronika's hand shot up like a stark bullet. "The speaker is drawn to the woods and would like to stay there longer to simply watch the falling snow."

Louise nodded, but continued to look around the classroom. Veronika slouched in her seat, seemingly rejected by Louise's gesture. "Alaska, our tenant poet," she smiled, "and how would you interpret such a text?"

I looked at the whiteboard.

The woods are lovely, dark and deep,
But I have promises to keep,
And miles to go before I sleep,
And miles to go before I sleep.

And then to you. *Promises I have to keep...*

"I would say that this poem conveys Frost's attraction to danger, the unknown, the dark mystery of the woods," I said, "and the third, perhaps related but distinct, is his death wish... of suicide. As lovely, dark, and inviting as the woods are, the speaker has to honour themselves first."

Louise smiled thinly, but with an unidentifiable warmth and continued. "You may be wondering what's going to happen to your final presentations now that the classes have merged."

The whole class awaited nervously. "As much as I would love to sit and listen to each one of you present individually, we do not have the time for that anymore. You will be put into pairs, and I will be assigning topics."

I groaned into my sleeves. You laughed hysterically. "You already started yours, didn't you?"

I mumbled something incoherent and buried my face into my palms. "It was the one I showed you on Saturday," I said.

"That was really good," you said, still smiling, almost cocky.

"I know," I sighed. "I'm going to have to start all over."

"Well, if it helps," you said, "you're very cute when you're all worked up and aggravated like this."

"How much could I pay you to move seats?" I groaned.

You slid your hand into mine under the table. "Not enough."

Louise projected a list onto the whiteboard. "...Theodore, you and Veronika will have the pleasure of studying *The Master and Margarita*...and Alaska, you'll be paired with Melisssa on Absurdism."

It was my turn to laugh, and I did so, rather obnoxiously and manically.

"Absurdism? Alaska is doing Absurdism?" you yelled in despair at our table. "She knows everything about Camus!"

Louise overheard and winked at me. I had a strange feeling it wasn't a peculiar given fate or coincidence.

"You love Camus more than you love me," you wailed.

I giggled. "Well, he's *French*," I said.

You dropped your jaw in disbelief. "And what's so good about the French?"

"Well, Adeline is French," I smiled. "Oh! And cigarettes and coffee."

You threw your hands in the air. "I get you those all of the time!"

I smiled and laughed a little harder. "You're very cute when you're all worked up and aggravated like this," I teased.

You rolled your eyes. "About moving seats—"

"Not enough," I giggled. "Don't be too upset, *The Master and Margarita* is actually divine. I did my program last season to the orchestral soundtrack."

"Program?" you asked.

"Skating."

"Ah," you said. "In that case, feel free to do the presentation for me."

I snickered. "Only if I'm getting paid–"

"I'm not going to prostitute you into doing my presentation," you said, bewildered.

"What a shame," I pretended to sigh.

It was getting warmer again. The dirt grass was postmarked from the warm rain, melting in patches to expose the slimy, yellowed grass beneath it; raindrops crackled and plunged like daggers from the sharp peaks of the coffee house's roof. Towards the fringe of the park, the young trees were yellow with the tinge of new leaves; woodpeckers laughed and drummed in the copses and, lying in your arms on a bench, I could hear the rush and gurgle of the melting raindrops running in the gutters all morning long.

I took the pages of your essay and studied them. The airy, oblique style in which it was written did little to dispel my feeling that there was more in it than met the eye. Reading each other's work, though deceptively simple, had a sort of Augustan wholesomeness and luxuriance which never failed to soothe. The prospect of sitting with you then was immensely cheering; you were a charming companion. I spent so much time explaining myself, my work, to others — what it meant, what I was trying to accomplish, why I was trying to accomplish it, why I had chosen the words and subject matter and font and application and technique that I had — that it was a relief to simply be with another person to whom I didn't have to explain anything: I could just look and look, and when you asked questions, they were usually blunt and technical and literal.

I read onwards as you sat across from me, smoking cigarette after cigarette, dark brown eyes fixated on my work. You interrupted me with questions only once or twice and by the time I finished, the sun was fully up and the birds were singing. Spots of smoke were swimming in front of my eyes. A damp, cool breeze shifted in between us. While you were still reading, I looked at you curiously. Your eyes were tired and preoccupied, but there was nothing in your expression that gave me any indication of what you might be thinking. "So?" I asked nervously.

You handed over the pages and smiled. "This is really good," you said. "You're a talented writer."

I smiled widely with childish validation. "Yours too. I love the way you say things," I said, leaning my head on your shoulder. "I don't know why you put yourself down all of the time."

"So you won't?"

I took your hand in mine, the wind curled around us. "Nobody sees as we do."

It was still early when I got back to campus. With one assignment out of the way, I slept for an hour, face down in my pillow, a comfortable dead man's float only remotely disturbed by a chill undertow of reality — talk, footsteps, slamming doors — which threaded fitfully through the dark, blood-warm waters of dream. Day ran into night, and I still slept, until finally the rush and rumble of footsteps and a call rolled me on my back and up from sleep. "Hello?" I asked, picking up my phone.

"Alaska," you said, "there's nobody out."

I rubbed my eyes, slightly dazed. "What are you talking about?"

"There aren't any counsellors out...come over."

I smiled and began to dress. "And why would I do that?"

I heard you scoff on the other end of the line. "I know you're coming. Meet me at the back door and I'll let you in."

Everything was still. Outside, the crickets shrieked with rhythmic, piercing monotony. I looked to the sky and as the angels winked, you opened the back door and motioned for me to follow you. You led me upstairs to your room, which opened upon the small winding staircase. Rays of filthy sunlight filtered through the slanted skylight. It seemed as if the whole world was being stripped of innocence, or maybe I was seeing too clearly. We turned down the blinds and pulled forcefully into a kiss. We were finally alone, properly isolated, and rushed to remove clothing; the nordic sweater, my t-shirt and jeans; they piled messily onto the carpeted floor until it was finally skin next to skin.

And now is as good a time as any to say that you were beautiful. In the dark beside me, you smelled faintly of sweat and smoke, and on that thin-mooned night, I could see little more than your silhouette. Even in the dark, I could see your eyes — dark amber, the kind of eyes that predisposed a certain melancholy and ambiguity. I had noticed all of these features before, of course, but I had never quite apprehended their significance — *sic oculus, sic ille manus, sic ora ferebat*. I envied them, and found those features beautifully devastating; moreover, this strange quality, far from being natural, gave every indication of having been intensely cultivated.

Everyone expects a boy to be beautiful. It's allowed. A man has so much else to do. I know now not to trust a beautiful man. It's like they're still boy, somehow, in an important way.

That's not to say that women hate beautiful men. They may envy them, but that isn't hate. Hate is love on fire, set out to burn like a flare on the side of the road. It says, stop here. Something terrible has happened. Envy is like, the skin you're in burns. And the salve is someone else's skin. *Yours.*

You caressed me with hands that knew exactly what to do. I slid off your trousers, and my mouth glided down to your thighs and then upwards. Your hands wrapped around my hair with a slight pull and my self-hood had been completely uncentered. The control was intoxicating, inebriating alongside the echoes of your voice, your hands ruffling in my hair. Feeling the warmth of your skin made me feel so right; your love kept me gentle, and that's how I knew you were good for me.

As you began to open me up, slowly, from the inside, everything inside me began to warm. The air was now humid, a vast vibration; it had started with the moon, the inaccessible poem that it was. Now we had walked upon it, rubber treads on a pearl of the gods. Perhaps it was an awareness of time passing, the last weeks of the summer. Sometimes I just wanted to raise my hands and stop. But stop what? Maybe just to preserve moments like those for a little while longer. We lie silently after, still, safe in each other's arms. My head rested on your chest, hearing the sound of your heartbeat, feeling the warmth of your skin, and for a while, we fell into a sort of transient sleep. When I woke, I made out the silhouette of you in the dark, tracing over your jaw and brows. "Hey, sleepy," I murmured, burying myself into your chest.

"Morning," you said, stroking the back of my head. "What time is it?"

"Eight," I chuckled. "In the evening by the way."

You smiled dreamily and closed your eyes again. "We still have time. I feel so tired," you said.

"Turn around then."

Your head shot up and you raised an eyebrow. "What? I didn't take for for—"

I groaned and smacked a palm against your chest. "No," I said, "that's not what I meant. When I was younger, my aunt used to give me and my sister massages. But she would tell stories while giving them, drawing them out on our backs with her nails."

"If you say so." You shuffled over onto your stomach as I began to slowly trace the outlines of muscle in your back. "That feels amazing," you sighed, breathlessly.

I smiled. "I told you so." We talked through the night, giggling, wholeheartedly like children. I never felt like I was wasting time with you. We could have sat in silence for hours and it would have still felt so full, and good, and necessary. When I talked to you I was irrevocably happy because you listened without speaking and yet, my words found a home. Yet, quite suddenly, for it seemed, in that moment with you my decision to place so much of my being into your hands had been a rash and foolish one, and made for all the wrong reasons. What had I been thinking of? Years before, I had made a similar heedless decision which had plummeted me into a nightmarish, year-long round of assault, from which I had barely escaped it all.

I suppose I had asked you this in order to revive my flagging need for assurance, in hopes you would make me feel as certain as I had that first day. "Hey," I said, trying to sound somewhat nonchalant. "Will you remember me when all of this is over?" I was expecting a definitive yes, something more kind and so, more reassuring, but as you went silent I felt my heart sink into my chest.

Your eyes were still closed and mouth was kept in a faint smile. "No, I don't think I will actually," you said, and my hands began to slow against your back. You said this all quite calmly, without malice, without empathy, without even much in the way of interest, but I, listening to you, felt a lump growing in the pit of my stomach. "You know, the first few weeks I probably won't forget you, but there will be a time when I wake up and go about my routine and the thought of you won't even occur to me."

I said nothing for a long time, only looking at the shadow of the lamp cast on the ceiling. I was not even sure of what you meant, but for the first time, I had a glimmer of something I had not previously understood; the words were still wholly obscure, but what I saw of it I didn't like at all. "I mean," you continued, "it's not like we're in love, or anything of the sort. At least, I don't think this is what love feels like. I think I would've realised it if I did...you know, *love you*."

I tried to figure out what you were trying to say. The pounding agony in my head was such that I couldn't concentrate on anything. Nausea swelled in a great green wave, trembled at the crest, sank and rolled again. I felt saturated with despair.

Everything, I thought tremulously, everything would be okay if only I could have a few moments of quiet and if I sat very, very still. "Yeah." My voice was flat and strange even to my own ears. "Me too, I suppose."

"Honestly, Alaska," you said, suddenly and very seriously. "I don't think I have the capability to ever fall in love." The walls had fallen away and the room was now black. Your face, lit starkly by the lamp, was pale against the darkness and starry points of light winked from the rim of your irises, glowed in the amber depths of moonlight. *I have made a great mistake,* I thought to myself hopelessly.

"What makes you say that?" I asked, very quietly.

"I'm not sure," you said, "but I would know love if I felt it." Your senile manner was said to be a facade; to me, it seemed quite genuine, but sometimes, when I was off on my guard, you would display an unexpected flash of lucidity like this, which — though it frequently did not relate to the topic at hand — was evidence that rational processes rumbled somewhere in the muddied depths of your consciousness.

I suppose if I had a moment of doubt at all it was then, as I stood in that cold, eerie dorm room, looking back at you. Who really were you? How well did I know you? Could I trust you, really, when it came down to it? Why, of all people, had you chosen me to do this with?

It's funny, but thinking back now, I realise that this was the particular point in time, as I lay there blinking in the deserted room, was the one point in time at which I might have chosen to do something different from what I actually did. But of course, I didn't see this crucial moment from what it was; I suppose I never did.

Instead, I only yawned and shook myself from the momentary daze that had come upon me and slipped back into your arms. Your eyes were visited on mine; they were bright with a horrible relish. The darkness hung about our tiny circle of lamplight as heavy and palpable as a curtain. With a rush of what was almost motion sickness, I experienced for a moment both the familiar claustrophobic feeling that the walls had rushed in towards us and the vertiginous one that they had receded infinitely, leaving both of us suspended in some boundless expanse of dark. My heart was thumping so wildly that I thought it would burst in my chest like a red balloon.

I sat on the bed, breathing hard and stared at you. I became progressively more agitated, everything seemed so out of hand, silhouetted by orange and pink and acid-green auras. The night seemed hot and steamy, no moons or stars, real or imagined. I had the uneasy feeling that if I did not flee I would turn into stone, a statue armed with hyacinths. "I think I need to go now," I said, sounding surprisingly good-natured even to myself.

"Sure," you said. "I'll see you later?"

"Yeah," I smiled sombrely. "Of course."

Down the hill, the lights stayed on. Without warning, I was overcome by a rush of emotion. Afraid I would say or do something childish, something I'd regret, I gave you a kiss before slipping out of the staircase when the lights went off. I pulled on a jumper and shrugged out the door. I had in my mind the idea that I needed to make this end, that there should never be another moment like this.

That time, I wouldn't tell anybody what you said. *It's good*, I thought, somewhat ruefully, for no one would hear what I had, no one would understand. I had learned early to assume something dark and lethal hidden at the heart of anything I loved. When I couldn't find it, I responded, bewildered, and wary, in the only way I knew how: by planting it in myself. I was accustomed to this feeling. I'd had it all my life, but in the past, I tried to make up for it as if it was my fault. I compensated for this with a sweet nature, seeking approval from my parents, from my teachers, from my peers. I wasn't certain whether I was a good or bad person, whether I was altruistic, demonic. Hysteria seemed to follow me everywhere I went and I could never seem to escape it; I supposed that some people were just born with tragedy in their blood.

I walked out of your room alone, in a state of

bewilderment and turmoil. By now my thoughts were so contradictory and disturbing that I could no longer even speculate, only wonder dumbly at what was taking place around me; I had no classes for the rest of the day and the thought of going back to my room was intolerable. I signed out my name and walked blankly around the streets of Oxford; the wintry sun, coming in at a slant through the clouds, gave everything a frozen, precisely detailed look; nothing seemed real, as I felt as though this were some complicated film I'd started watching in the middle and couldn't quite get the drift of.

I leaned against a wall and smoked a cigarette, swathed in clarity, a little shaken, but I knew it was merely physical. There was another sensation brewing I had no name for. I discovered that absence had a consistency, like the dark water of a river, like oil, some kind of sticky dirty liquid that you could struggle and perhaps drown in. It had a thickness like night, an indefinite space with no landmarks, nothing to bang against, where you search for a light, some small glimmer, something to hang on and guide you. But absence was, first and foremost, silence. A vast, enveloping silence that weighed me down in an unforeseeable, unidentifiable state.

Despite this, I strangely had no sense of direction either, like how at a set time, the mysteriousness of twilight and the bottomless darkness of night merely exchanged places—a remote on the border of the edges of consciousness. The past and present, memory and emotions, ran together as equals, side by side.

It was quite dark and I walked the wide and empty streets. I felt a little afraid, and then, in the distance, I saw the familiar outline of Vasileios waving right at me. I felt that he might silently step from the mist and tap me on the shoulder, removing all the hurt. I stopped and took a breath, unable to believe my good fortune. "Alaska! Alaska!" he yelled. "Come over here!"

I advanced slowly, afraid he might disappear like a mirage in the desert. "Hey," I said. "What are you up to?"

He shrugged casually. "Absolutely nothing. Where are you going?"

I looked at him blankly, trying to create some sort of a facade, but my mind was too narrow and vulnerable so I gave up. "Honestly, nowhere," I said. "I'm just walking around."

"Alone at night? You can't do that."

"Trust me," I said sadly. "I don't need any kind of charity right now."

Vasileios took a step back and laughed. "I'm also doing nothing. Come along with me."

"And what gives you the impression that I would want to?" I smiled.

"Well, you have nowhere to go, and neither do I."

I would like to say I was driven to what I did by some overwhelming, tragic motive. But I think I would be lying if I told you that; if I had led you to believe on that Monday evening in July, I was actually being driven by anything of the sort. "Alright," I smiled. "Lead the way."

We walked into a white stucco bar with a singular window. There was no one around. I entered tentatively. It was dimly lit and mainly inhabited by boys, angry-faced fellows, leaning against the jukebox. A few faded pictures of King Charles were tacked on the walls. I ordered a Pernod and water, as it seemed the closest to absinthe. The jukebox played a crazy mix of Charles Aznavour, country tunes, and Car Stevens. In their company, I felt a comforting warmth return to me like provincial flowers. *Tiny flowers spattering the walls, just as the sky had been spattered with budding stars,* I wrote in my notes, the first, solitary entry in weeks.

As Vasileios walked to the counter to order Vodka shots, I

opened a new document on my phone. I hadn't written in weeks and had previously imagined that I would write the words that would shatter nerves here in Oxford, but I hadn't. For you see, some things are hard to write about. After something happens to me, I go to write it down, and either over-dramatise it, or underplay it, exaggerate the wrong parts and ignore the important ones. At any rate, I never write it quite the way I want to. For example, I try to be poetic in the way that I loved you, but it was so passionate that I still cannot string the words together in any way that makes sense. Nevertheless, hurt can be a great motif for writing, and I finally had something to start with. The student I was then was puzzled by the distorting classes, but in truth, the program was so effective it almost recommended itself as a method. The stories I was writing, which I did to entertain myself when I ran out of things to read, were their own kind of milestone, visible to me only much later: there was something I wanted to feel, and I felt it only when I was writing. I think of this as one of the most important parts of my writer's education — that when left alone with nothing else to read, I began to tell myself the stories I wanted to read.

And then there was the story I was living. Whatever I thought I was doing through my experiments in observation. I can see I was a girl losing herself as a way to find herself in the shape of others.

I slipped my phone back into my purse and smiled at Vasileios walking over with our drinks. I felt an uncommon lightheartedness, not sad at all. Vasileios was just the right kind of company at the right time. The rain began in earnest, beating against the bar windows. The light cast a shadow against his face. "One for me," he said, "and one for you," handing over the shot glasses.

"Thanks for calling me over," I said. "I needed it."

"It's not a problem, but why were you walking around in the first place?" he asked, curiously.

"The weather seemed nice," I shrugged, taking a sip of water.

Vasileios looked at me sceptically. "But it's raining?"

"Well, I like the rain," I lied. I picked erratically at the tablecloth and had a hard time keeping my eyes off him as we ate. I felt as though I were in the dining car of a train and had been seated by someone who didn't even speak my language, perhaps, but who was still content to get drinks with me, exuding an air of calm acceptance as if he'd known me all his life.

We took another shot and perhaps saw the oddest thing of all: a hound-pack of shirtless men arguing on the streets, shouting obscenities while throwing signs at each other. Vasileios and I senselessly cocked our heads when the more frail and tattooed man pulled out a watermelon and threw it at the buff one. "Let's place bets," Vasileios said. "I think the tattooed guy is too drunk to throw the first move."

I laughed. "I disagree. I think that the others are not drunk enough to start a fight, so the watermelon guy will."

And I was right. Startled, we leaned forward as the frail man threw a misjudged punch at the other, more buff guy. On our way back to campus through the dark woods, it was so dim I could barely see him. When we emerged from the woods into the deserted, blue-lit streets of St. Catherine, everything was silent and strange in the moonlight. A faint breeze tinkled in the wind chimes of someone's staircase.

I headed straight to my room. My belongings seemed to swell and recede with each thump of my heart; or perhaps the Vodka. In a horrible daze, I sat on my bed, elbows on the window sill and tried to pull myself together. I was gazing at the sparks flying from the lamppost when suddenly I was struck by a harrowing thought. I looked out the window and the answer was so obvious it gave me a chill: *of course, you would forget me*. We'd only known each other for eight days, why should I have assumed that you had fallen in love with me? I felt slightly nauseous at my misguided judgments and lay pathetically against my bed covers.

I suppose it would be true to say that at this point I felt torn in some way, grappled with the moral implications of each of the options available to me. I figured we'd keep seeing each other, but the reality of our aftermath loomed in my path like a beacon. When you confessed then, that you did not, in fact, love me, the notion had not even come to my mind. But in the moment, when you had verbalised these feelings of yours I felt something inside me rotting away, a wound reopened.

It hurt.

I knew I had to let it go; we only had a few days left, thus any problems arriving seemed inconvenient to pursue.

I felt my heart limping in my chest and was revolted by it, a pitiful muscle, sick and bloody, pulsing my ribs. Rain streamed down the window panes. The lawn outside was sodden, swampy. I felt my heart limping in my chest and was revolted by it, a pitiful muscle, sick and bloody, pulsing my ribs; I thought I'd be sick.

I closed my eyes and then, in the recesses of dream, I was being lifted again, and moved, but it was difficult to see where I was being taken: one eye was already swollen shut, and the other was blurry. My vision kept blinking in and out.

"Theo," I gasped, "please, please." I was never one to beg for mercy, not even as a child, but I had become that person, somehow. When I was a child, my life meant little to me; I wished, then, that that was still true. "Please," I said. "Theo, please forgive me—I'm sorry. I'm sorry."

But you, I knew, were no longer human. You were muscle and rage. And I was nothing to you, I was prey, I was disposable. I was being dragged to the edge of the sofa, and I knew what would happen next. But I continued to ask anyway. "Please, Theo," I said. "Please don't. Theo, please."

I was on the floor near the back of the sofa, and the apartment was silent. All along I had been waiting for some sort of punishment for my arrogance, for thinking I could have what everyone else had, and there — at last — it was. *This is what you get,* said the voice inside my head. *This is what you get for pretending to be someone you know you're not. For thinking you have a chance....*

CHAPTER TEN

THE BODLEIAN LIBRARY

WHEN THE SUN CAME UP, I SAW IN THE SMALL, COLD LIGHT of dawn, that the flagstones outside were covered with moss: delicate, nasty, blind and helpless on the rain-dark sheets of slate. I sat up. I pulled on my trousers and flexed my hands, brought my knees to my chest and back down again, moved my shoulders back and forward, and turned my neck from left to right. Everything hurt, but nothing was broken. *My life,* I thought, *my life.* By then, it was eight-thirty. I locked the door and walked to Pitt Rivers, nervously jangling my key in my pocket. The green lawn, filled with gaudy tulips, was hushed and expectant beneath the overcast sky. Somewhere a shutter creaked. Above my head, in the wicked back claws of an elm, a mockingbird rattled convulsively, then it was still. The light outside was very strange. Something about it intensified the green of the lawn so all that vast expanse seemed unnatural, luminous, somehow, and not quite of this world. A British flag, stark and lonely, against the violet sky, whipped back and forth on the brass flagpole.

In class, the grounds were soaked in sunlight, the lake rippling gently at the touch of a breeze. Louise poured tea at the sideboard, so the room smelled, as it always did, of chalk and lemon and Ceylon. "Tragedy in Literature," she said, grandly, placing her mug down on the desk. "I will refrain from telling you to take the tragedies any more seriously than comical literature. In fact, one might argue that comedy must be deadly serious to the characters, or it is not funny for the readers. But that is a conversation for another time."

She took the teacup off the tray, sipped delicately, and set it down again. Louise had never been a lectern and instead paced slowly back and forth in front of the blackboard as she taught. "This period, we will devote our attention to Shakespeare's tragic plays. I know, another dead white man these subjects can't get enough of, but I digress. What might that course of study encompass, do you think?"

There was a brief pause before we began suggesting topics.

"Source material," said Vasileios.

"Structure," said another.

"Imagery," said Melissa.

"Conflict, internal and external," said Veronika.

"Fate versus agency,"

"The tragic hero," I said.

"The tragic villain," you said.

Louise held up a hand to stop us.

"Good, yes," she said, "all of those things. We will, of course, touch upon each of these plays—*Macbeth*, and other problem plays included—but naturally we will begin with *Julius Caesar*. A question, why is *Caesar* not a history play?"

Veronika was first to answer, with characteristic academic eagerness. "The history plays are confined to English history."

"Indeed," Louise said and resumed her pacing. I stirred my coffee and sat back in my chair to listen. "Most of the tragedies include some element of history, but what we choose to call history plays, as Veronika said, are truly English history plays and are all named after English monarchs. Why else? What makes *Caesar* first and foremost a tragedy?"

My classmates exchanged curious glances, unwilling to offer the first hypothesis and risk being wrong.

"Well," I ventured when nobody else spoke. "I think it's more about the people and less about the politics. It's definitely political but if you look at it next to the *Henry VI cycle*, for example, where everyone is fighting over the throne, *Caesar* is more personal. It's about the characters and who they are, not just who's in power."

"Yes, Alaska is onto something," Louise said. "Permit me to pose another question: what is more important, that *Caesar* is assassinated or that he is assassinated by his intimate friends?"

It wasn't the sort of question that needed an answer, so no one replied. Louise was watching me, I realised, with a proud motherly affection.

"That," Louise said, keeping her eyes on my gaze. "Is where the tragedy is."

She looked around at all of us, hands folded behind her back, the midday sun glinting on her glasses. "So, shall we begin?" She turned to the blackboard, took a piece of chalk from the tray, and began to write. We rummaged around in our bags to find notebooks and pens, and as Louise carried on, we scribbled down almost every word. The sun warmed my back and the bittersweet scent of black tea drifted up into my face. I stole furtive glances at you as you sat and listened.

When the clock turned to ten, we were dismissed for morning break. We grabbed our coffees at the University park and walked until reaching a field of jaded evergreens next to the museum. The woods were deathly still, more forbidding than I had ever seen them — green and black and stagnant, dark with the smells of mud and rot. There was no wind; not a bird sang, not a leaf stirred. The dog blossoms were poised, white and surreal and still against the darkening sky. Twigs were cracking beneath our feet, and my own hoarse breath loud in my ears, and before long, the path emerged into the clearing.

The reservoir lay to the left — raw, wet, treacherous, a deep plunge to the water below. Careful not to get too near to the edge, we walked to the side for a closer look. Everything was absolutely still. We turned again, towards the woods from which we had just come.

It was getting darker by the minute and cold, too.

"Hey," you said, "take this," handing over your coat. I buttoned it up and sat on a damp rock that overlooked the reservoir, staring at the muddy, leaf-clogged rill that trickled below and half-listening to the sounds of crickets in the distance. You leaned against a tree, smoking. After a while, you put out the cigarette on the rock and came over to sit beside me.

Minutes passed. The sky was so overcast it was almost purple. A wind swayed through a luminous clump of birches on the opposite bank, and I shivered. We were quiet, looking at each other — *nobody's son, nobody's daughter*. A chilly breeze rustled through the woods and a gust of dogwood petals blew into the clearing. "I love every moment like this," you said. "Especially with you."

"Me too," I said doubtfully, taking your hand as you stood from the banks. We ran through the evergreens, until we approached the base of the woods, and the land took a downward slope. A thick fog lay in the valley below, a smouldering cauldron of white from which the treetops protruded, stark and Dantesque. By degrees, we descended and watched the world sink from view.

You, beside me, stood out sharp and also hyper-realistic with your blushed cheeks and laboured breaths. We began to wrestle until we were lying in a crevice in the field, side by side.

I lit a cigarette and watched as the smoke curled in the wind above us.

"We have ten minutes left," you smiled and quickly, a brazen, fearless look flashed across your face. In one impulsive motion, you rolled onto your side and kissed me, caught me, both hands curled tight around the back of my neck. I was startled but still, oblivious to everything but the unexpected heat of your mouth on mine.

We separated an inch and looked at each other with wide, unguarded eyes. Nothing about you had ever seemed simple, but you were, then. Simple and close and beautiful. A little tousled, a little damaged. You forced my lips apart and stole my breath right out of my mouth, and pushed me backwards until we were lying on top of each other. We broke apart and smiled at each other...and that was all it took for me to forgive you then

In a sense, I had a childlike faith in you. I suppose I let it go because, with you, everything just felt right. I couldn't bear to be the one that ruined it. Even now, I remember the way we were before it all changed. I'm still trying to accept how beautiful things, like our connection, could end. That sometimes people leave, that two human beings don't beat the odds.

I'm still trying to find closure in that.

Back in class, the clock struck eleven. Your mouth quirked up at one corner and slid into the chair opposite mine. I pushed your coffee towards you and watched as you lifted the cup to your lips, still smiling. The others rattled in from the hall, and the spell of lazy tranquillity faded into the air like steam.

We had left off our lesson on *Caesar* and moved on to *Macbeth*, but *Caesar's* familiar words leapt readily to our lips, and with them came a kind of bristling tension, making neutrality impossible. That day, what began as a simple discussion of tragic structure quickly developed into an argument.

"No, that's not what I'm saying," Melissa said, halfway through our lesson, impatiently pushing her hair out of her face. "What I'm saying is that the tragic structure is staring you in the face in *Macbeth*; it makes *Caesar* look like a telenovela."

"What the hell does that mean?" Veronika yelled.

"Language, please, Veronika," said Louise.

A blonde girl from across the classroom sat straighter in her chair. "No," she said. "I understand."

"Then explain it to the rest of us," Louise said.

"*Macbeth*'s a textbook tragic hero, her flaw being ambition."

"And Lady M is a textbook tragic villain," I added, glancing from Louise to the blonde girl, soliciting their argument. "Unlike Macbeth, she doesn't have a single moral qualm about murdering Duncan, which paves the way for every other treacherous thing to come."

"So what's the difference?" Veronika said. "It's the same in *Caesar*. Brutus and Cassius assassinate Caesar and set themselves up for disaster."

"But they're not villains, are they?" Melissa asked. "Cassius maybe, but Brutus does what he does for the greater good of Rome."

"*Not that I loved Caesar less, but that I loved Rome more,*" I recited.

"What I'm trying to say," Melissa said, "is that *Caesar* is not in the same category of tragedy as *Macbeth*."

"So what category is it in?" Louise asked.

"Fuck if I know," Veronika said.

"Veronika, language, please!"

"Sorry, but I think you're all making it too complicated," Veronika continued. "*Caesar* and *Macbeth* have the same set-up. Tragic hero: Caesar. Tragic villain: Cassius—"

I interrupted. "You think Caesar is the tragic hero?"

Veronika shrugged, "who else?"

"It has to be Brutus: *This was the noblest roman of them all: All the conspirators, save only he did that they did in envy of great Caesar; be only, in a general honest thought and common good to all, made one of them.*"

"No," Veronika insisted. "Brutus can't be the tragic hero."

I was affronted. "Why on earth not?"

Veronika then laughed at me. I felt something boil in my lungs. "Because he's got like fourteen tragic flaws!" she said. "A hero's only supposed to have one."

"Caesars is ambition, just like Macbeth," you said, entering the conversation. "Simply, Brutus's only tragic flaw is that he's dumb enough to listen to Cassius."

"Yes, but the play's named after him, isn't it?" Veronika said, the words and her breath coming out in a deep rasp. "That's how it goes in all the other tragedies."

"Really," I said, voice flat. "You're going to base your argument on the *title* of the play?"

"I'm still curious to hear what the fourteen flaws are," you said, backing me up.

"I didn't mean there are *exactly fourteen,*" Veronika said, thickly. "I meant it would be impossible to isolate one that leads him to skewering himself."

"Couldn't you argue that Brutus's tragic flaw is his insurmountable love for Rome?" I asked, looking across the table at you who was watching Veronika with narrowed eyes. Louise stood in front of the blackboard, lips pursed, listening.

"No," said Veronika. "Because besides that you've got his pride, his self-righteousness, his vanity—"

"Those are all essentially the same, as you of all people ought to know." My voice cut across Veronika's and the rest of the class were startled into silence.

"Excuse me?" Veronika asked. I clenched my jaw and I

knew I hadn't meant to say so much out loud. I knew I had gone too far but still stood my ground.

"You heard me."

"Yes, I fucking did," Veronika said, and the cold snap of her voice made you exchange a mischievous glance at me. "I'm giving you a chance to change what you said."

"Try harder" I scoffed firmly. "Are you sure you heard me right?"

You looked over to me and smiled mischievously. I felt your hand slip into mine under the desk. "*All great truths begin as blasphemies*," you whispered.

"*Ladies.*" I'd nearly forgotten Louise was there. She spoke softly, faintly, and for a moment I wondered what was going through her mind. "*Enough.*"

Veronika, who had been leaning forward like she might leap off her chair and throw herself at me, eased back against her seat again. I, on the other hand, wanted to smash her skull into the desk in front of me. After a slightly awkward pause, we exchanged a quick look together.

"For god's sake, it's just a play," said Vasileios.

"Well," Louise sighed, removing her glasses and began to polish them on the hem of her shirt. "Duels have been fought over less."

Veronika raised an auspicious eyebrow at you. I felt an unease pass through my stomach. "Swords behind the refectory at dawn?" she whispered.

"Only if Alaska will be my second," you replied.

"*I've hope to live, and am prepared to die,*" I quoted.

Veronika glanced up at us. "Very well. Vasileios can be mine."

"Hey, don't get me involved in this!"

We returned to Macbeth civilly.

After class was over, I headed straight to Broadbent Lab for an Introduction to Social Science Research/Interview and

Anthropology seminar, hosted by a petite woman in her late thirties named Freya Hope. The seminar had been notably long and boring for the most part, minutes crept by with a torturous slowness. All I wondered was how, in the name of Heaven and a merciful God, was I going to make it through the hours ahead.

We had been there only twenty minutes and I already felt like shooting myself.

An hour had passed and we still had three more to go. My mind had become a cloud of fog as Freya droned onwards with absolutely no sense of candour. Time slowly transformed itself into an endless blur, fast and ongoing. It passed by in flashes and I caught myself falling in and out of consciousness, drifting through each hour immobilised. The only sense of feeling I had was limited between moments of blistering pulses to a dawning numbness that was my bones inebriating beneath my skin.

There was something diabolical about the passing of time, every time I looked up from my screen, I found you grinning at me in an attitude of grateful malice in my peripheral vision. The clock ticked loudly, a jangling, arrhythmic tick. We sat in the fading light, Freya's prompt cards forgotten. A fiery outline of twilight shone around her silhouette, burning red-gold in her hair until the seminar was finally over.

I went straight back to my dorm and took a sleeping pill and went to bed. The sleeping pill was an extraneous gesture; I didn't need it, but the mere possibility of restlessness, or recounting the afternoon full of academic disputes, was too unpleasant to even contemplate.

So I slept soundly, more soundly than I should have, and the afternoon slipped easily away. It was almost late-afternoon when somewhere, through great depths, I became aware that someone was running their hands across my cheek. The weather had turned again, and it took me a moment to realise that I had been shivering, and that the sounds in my dream had been of wind, and that I was being shaken awake, and that my name was being repeated, not by birds, but by a human voice: "Alaska, Alaska." You raised an eyebrow and laughed at me. "All you ever do is sleep," you said. "Why is it you're always sleeping when I try to come to see you?"

I blinked at you. My shades were down and the hall was dark to me, half drugged and reeling, you seemed not at all your bright unattainable self but rather a hazy and ineffably tender source of affection, all slender wrists and shadows and disordered hair; the Theo who resided, dim and lovely, in the gloomy boudoir of my dreams.

I turned over and propped myself on my elbows, but was able to register you only in segments: your face first, and then your hair, and then your body. "How did you get in?" I asked.

"Same way you did on Sunday," you smiled. "How come your doors are unlocked?"

I parted my hair out of my face. "Adeline's been waking me up every morning."

"Is she now?" you teased.

"I'm a little," I said, raising my hand in a strange gesture. "Tiny bit of an insomniac."

"Makes sense with your work ethic," you said, "*vampire*."

I scorned. "Works well with my work ethic," I corrected. "I write better at night."

A narcotic heaviness still clung deliciously to my limbs and I felt sort of marvellous. You wandered around my room but stopped at my desk. You looked down for a moment and grinned widely back up at me again. "Is that what this is?" you asked, holding up my blue notebook.

Shit, I thought to myself, *your letter*. I stood up from my bed and grabbed the notebook out of your hands. "Nope," I said as you were nosing around trying to get a look at it.

"Hand it over," you laughed. "I've read your writing before–unless..." I made a strange face and you laughed. "Unless you're writing about me," you joked with a curious tone.

"Here," I said, throwing my keys at you. "Lock the door before I decide to kick you out."

"That's not a no," you said giddily, locking the door. I sat on the other side of the unmade bed, feet bare and half-dressed. You shouldered off your wet coat and threw it over the back of a chair. Your hair was damp, face flushed and radiant. A drop of water trembled at the end of your long, fine nose. You sniffed and wiped it away. "Don't go outside, whatever you do," you said, "it's terrible out."

A few stubborn drops of water clung to your cheeks. You didn't quite look like yourself, somehow. You seemed so beautifully fragile I was almost afraid to touch you. "When did it start raining?" I asked.

"You probably didn't hear the rain since you were asleep."

I tucked myself back into my covers. "Well, I was trying to forget whatever the shit show in class was," I sighed.

"To me," you laughed. "It was pretty great. Veronika had it coming and–oh, I almost forgot." You reached into the pockets of your overcoat and pulled out a bundle of napkins. "I brought you a sandwich since you weren't at lunch. I'm such a great boyfriend, aren't I?"

I laughed softly. "Don't push it...but thank you."

"You just won't admit it," you said, folding your arms across your chest.

"Oh really?" I said, standing up to grab the container of cold brew on my desk, swinging a sip as it burned down my throat. "How about I show you how great of a girlfriend I am?"

"You can't beat this supermarket sandwich, but feel free to try," you snickered.

On my way back to the bed, I walked over to where you sat and put my hands on either side of your face, kissed you, on the eyelids, on the mouth, on the place at your temple where the honey-coloured hair turned into silky gold.

You started to say something — maybe my name — but only the ghost of a sound slipped out before you stopped, and then pulled me in for another kiss. Your eyes were keen dark brown, but lying so close I could see a little ring of gold around each pupil. Something was moving, working in your mind—accompanied by a tightening at the corners of your jaw, a curl of your upper lips. My hands trailed to your belt and pulled it undone. Soon, my lips trailed down your chest and further. You let out a small shuddering sigh, then breathed more easily. "Good girlfriend?" I asked after.

"The very best," you smiled.

My room was blue with smoke, through which a broad expanse of white linoleum was arctic, surreal. For a long time we lay side by side without speaking, our noses touched and we were wrapped in each other's arms. The silence was short lasting, and soon there were rapid footsteps on the stairs, followed by a loud banging at my door and a delirious burst of French. We lay there for a moment, motionless, staring at each other. "This can't be happening again," I whispered, defeated.

Another flurry of knocks banged against the door. "L'Alaska! Tu nous manques!"

"Oui, Oui!" Someone shouted, and then laughter. It was Adeline and Asli. I exhaled a tight breath and relaxed into your arms again.

"I would have preferred the counsellors," I said, burrowing my flushed cheeks into your chest.

"It's just your friends, don't worry," you laughed.

"Would now be the right time to meet them, I suppose?" I joked. "When we're both half-naked in my room?"

Before you could respond, they yelled again. "Alaska! We know you're in there!"

I stood up and threw on a shirt. My chest ached, but the ache went deeper than muscle and bone like some sharp thing had ripped a little hole right through me.

You looked around my room with curiosity. "Where's your closet?"

"I don't have one," I said, motioning to the shelves filled with stacks of clothing. "Just...stand behind the door?"

"The door?" you said, raising an eyebrow.

"Any better ideas?" I said, walking over to the door and unlocking it. You rushed quickly behind.

I was immediately greeted by Adeline and Asli with their usual exuberance. "Where have you been all day?" Adeline asked. "We're about to head to town with Serena. Do you want to join us?"

"Of course," I said, enthusiastically, forgetting your presence in the room with us. Suddenly, you pushed the door into the side of my hip and it made a sharp, loud banging noise. "Fuck," I yelled. Both of them looked at me, estranged. "I'm sorry, this door...it's broken I think. Maybe in ten minutes?"

"Yeah, ten minutes works—" Adeline's face suddenly dropped and her hand clasped against her mouth. She pointed into my room and I turned to see your shoes lying neatly by the bed covers. *Great, we're so careful,* I thought. "How about we come in for a minute?" she teased playfully.

"It's a mess," I insisted.

"But—"

"Don't worry, I'll be out in a minute—" The door hit the side of my head. "*Ten* minutes," I said firmly. "I'll be out in *ten* minutes."

"You okay?" Asli asked, blissfully unaware.

"Yes—fuck!" I yelled as the door slammed against my hip

bone again. "I'm just re-thinking a lot of my..." I said, pushing the door back into you. "...life choices."

Adeline smiled warmly. 'Suit yourself. We'll see you in ten!"

I finally locked the door and turned back to you, faking a whimper as you pulled me into your arms laughing. "You're an asshole," I said.

"That was hilarious," you chuckled. "I wish I could've seen the look on your face!"

"Ha ha, yes, you're hilarious," I teased, rolling my eyes. "Now get out, stalker."

"Actually," you said, wrapping your hands around my waist and pulling me back into bed. "I think I'll stay a little longer...*ten* minutes?"

I pretended to sigh. "Do I have a choice?" I said, leaning closer under the covers.

You chuckled. "Nope, you can't get rid of me."

I smiled. "Well, there are worse life sentences."

After a little while longer, you left me to join my friends for dinner. The rain soon faded as quickly as it had come, all gone except for some lovely shady patches on campus — white-laced branches dripped rain holes in the crust — and the slushy grey piles collected at the roadside. The Oxford street stretched out wide and desolate like some Napoleonic battlefield: churned, sordid, roiled with footprints. The place where we wound up — a bar called the OXO — was not remarkable for its food, or its decor — folding chairs and Formica tables — or for its sparse clientele, which was mostly rural, drunken and over sixty-five. They were crazy about something called Kamikazes and liked to dye their Margaritas a horrifying electric blue.

We sat at the end of the bar by the television set. A basketball game was on. The barmaid — in her fifties, with turquoise eyeshadow and lots of turquoise rings to match — looked us over. Adeline glanced up and fixed her with a smile of great warmth and sweetness. She had a way with people. They always hovered over her in restaurants and went to all kinds of special trouble on her behalf.

The Bodleian Library was on a narrow road that veered off sharply from the highway and twisted along for many miles, over-bridged, past antique shops and pastures and fields. The place was like a maze. I felt small walking through the rows of timber bookshelves, I always did. It was a carnivorous room, with a high vaulted ceiling and long windows that gazed out onto Oxford. Maroon velvet curtains hung on each side, hems gathered in dusty piles on the hardwood floor.

I finished my Absurdism presentation in about an hour and a half. By then, the library was paved with black cinder, and there were no students all except a few scattered around the exit. A shaft of light splintered painfully in my vision. I clutched the back of the chair, closed my eyes and saw luminous red as the rhythmic noise of shuffling feet fell over me like a bludgeon. The floorboards creaked in the shadows and I turned. "Someone there?" I asked.

"Alaska?" It was your voice.

"Theo?" I asked. "Where are you?"

You emerged from between the two bookcases, your face a warm oval in the dusky orange light filtering through the shelves. A murmur of thunder smothered the sound of the doors closing and the crackling flames. "Shhh," you said, grabbing my hand. "Come here."

"Where are we–"

"Shhh," you repeated, looking back at me with a smile.

You led me behind an over-scaled bookshelf, into a deserted corner, big and loft-like, with gaps of moonlight shining on the floorboards. You motioned for me to sit as the lights went off in the library. We heard a distant voice calling out: *library is closing, library is closing now.*

Suddenly, there was a click. We looked at each other. Then another jangling of keys, two melodious chimes before silence. "What are you doing here?" I laughed.

"I brought tea for us," you said, reaching into your bag to pull out a long, silver thermos.

"How did you even know I was in here?" I asked.

You shrugged and twisted open the silver cap. "I asked your friends."

I chuckled. "Stalker."

"No," you rolled your eyes. "I'm trying to be romantic."

"We just got locked in the Bodleian Library?"

"Exactly," you smiled. "Romantic."

We drank the tea from your thermos. The lamplight was warm and the library still and snug. In my private abyss of longing, the scenes I dreamed of always began like this: drowsy drunken hour, the two of us alone, scenarios in which invariably you would brush against me as if by chance, or lean conveniently close, cheek touching mine, to point out a passage in a book; opportunities which I would seize, gently, as exordium to other pleasures. I set down the thermos and looked at you; I could lose myself forever in that singular face, in the pessimism of your beautiful mouth. "This is beautiful, Theo," I smiled warmly. My voice echoed amidst the sharp surfaces and polished floor.

"Why, thank you, darling," you said.

Another hour went by, or maybe two or three. The sky was so dark that it was impossible to tell how time was passing, unless you measured the minutes by the number of breaths. It was a cosy night, a happy night; lamps lit, sparkle of glasses, rain falling heavily on the roof. Outside, the treetops tumbled and tossed, with a foamy whoosh like club soda bubbling up in the glass. The windows were open and a damp cool breeze swirled through the curtains, bewitchingly wild and sweet. You were scanning up and down the bookshelf until fixating on a brown paperback, slightly above your head. "How about a bedtime story?" you smiled, pulling out a copy of *Heptameron* by Marguerite de Navarre from the shelf. I shifted in your arms until we were both lying comfortably, and you began to read.

I breathed in and held the sweet woody air in my lungs for as long as I could. You laid back, reading peacefully in the moonlight rays. The spell of lazy tranquillity faded into the air like steam as you ran a gentle hand through my hair. I buried my face in your neck, pressing my hands flat against your back so I could feel your heartbeat. You were looking up at me, but in a way you'd never looked at me before, something reckless gleaming in your sea-glass eyes.

When phrases were cast out in your voice, they were intolerably sweet; now, sitting right beside you, it was unthinkable that I should voice them myself. I felt your hands on my chest, your palms warm through the thin fabric of my shirt. My heart stuttered at your touch as you leaned into me, the press of your body threw all my logical objections. My hands moved automatically, without permission, rising to find the crevice of your spine, smoothing the silk against your skin. I could smell your cologne, sweet and lush and tantalising, the fragrance of some exotic flower. Your fingers, softly insistent on the back of my neck, pulled my face towards yours. My pulse crescendoed in my ears, my imagination rushing treacherously forward.

Out of the window, we could see stars, tiny pinpricks of white scattered around the moon and glinted like sequins. The world was perfectly still for one precious instant. Then, there was a crash, a shout. At first, neither of us moved. We lay staring at each other, hoping — silently, desperately, pointlessly — that the wind had simply knocked a bottle off the counter, or slipped on the stairs, or some other clumsy, innocent thing. But before either of us could speak again, a voice inside started yelling.

There was the fumble of a key in the lock, and a few moments later the security plunged through the door. He soldered his coat off and let it fall in a heap on the rug.

"Hello, hello," he bellowed, lurching inside and shedding his jacket in the same fashion. He had not come into the stairwell, but made an abrupt turn into the hallway which led to where we were seated. He was big and red in the face, with a heavy jaw and a full head of white hair; for a moment he stared at us, his smallish mouth fallen open into a tight, round *o*. Then, surprisingly boyish and quick, you sprang forward and grabbed my hand.

"Run!" you yelled and without thinking, I followed.

"Hey!" the guard shouted. "What are you doing in here?"

We continued running, occasionally looking back, until we had finally reached the doors of the library and exited onto the streets passing tourists, students, cars in a streaky blur. When we made it back on campus, we finally stopped running, and burst out laughing under the lamplight. We reached the marquee and the doors faced out on the barren, floodlit terrace — black cinder, privet in concrete urns, a statue artificially broken in white pieces on the ground. Rain slanted in the lights, which were angled to cast long dramatic shadows. We couldn't contain ourselves during shout-out, frequently exchanging glances and giggling silently with each other.

Those days, I took an enormous relish in my new-found lover. Now it appeared that I was safe, a huge darkness had lifted from my mind. The world was a fresh and wonderful place to be, green and bracing and entirely new, and I looked at it now with fresh new eyes.

I went on a lot of long walks with you, through Oxford, down to the riverside. We liked especially going to the little country grocery to buy a bottle of wine, and wandering down to the riverbank to drink it, then roaming around drunk all the rest of those glorious, golden, blazing afternoons after class; I was still young: the grass was green and the air heavy with the sound of bees and I had just come back from the brink of Death itself, back to the sun and air. Nor was I free; and my life, which I had previously thought was lost, stretched out indescribably precious and sweet before me.

It hurts to remember how close we were back then. Maybe I deserved someone else, but I always wanted you.

It rained hard all night. My nose tickled from the dust in the dorm, and the staircase floor — which was poured concrete beneath a thin, comfortless layer of indoor-outdoor carpeting — made my bones ache whichever way I turned. The rain drummed on the high windows, and the floodlights, shining through the glass, cast a pattern on the walls as if dark rivulets of water were streaming down them from ceiling to floor.

Occasionally a car swooshed by in the rain and its headlights would swing around momentarily and illuminate the room. For a moment my face, pale and watchful as a ghost's, would be caught in the headlights and then, very gradually, would slide back into the dark.

In the morning I woke up sore and disorientated to the sound of Adeline entering my room.

"Alaska, it's seven thirty," she yelled, and I simply raised my head and gave her a thumbs up. The rain was falling harder than ever. It lashed in rhythmic waves against the windows of the white, brightly lit cafeteria as we ate another cold, cheerless breakfast of coffee and toast.

"I hope we're all ready to leave the phenomenal world and enter into the sublime." Louise said, walking into the room and placing her coffee cup on the desk. "Tomorrow, you will be giving your final presentations. I hope you are all ready, we will start at nine on the dot, do *not* be late."

There was a heart-stopping ruby-red pinprick of a freckle just beneath your eye. On an irresistible impulse, I leaned over and gave you a kiss.

You laughed. "What was that for?" you asked.

My heart — which, thrilled at my daring, had held its breath for a moment or two — began suddenly to beat quite wildly. I turned and busied myself with my notebook. "Nothing," I said, "you just looked pretty."

"Today, we will be talking about the Romans," Louise said, "we touched on them briefly in the first week, does anyone remember what the main flaw of the Romans was?"

She looked around the classroom until Veronika raised her hand.

"An obsession with order," she said.

"Very good, Veronika," Louise said. "One sees it in their architecture, their literature, their wars. This Fierce denial of darkness, unreason, chaos. Easy to see why the Romans— usually so tolerant of foreign religions, persecuted the Christians mercilessly. How absurd to think a common criminal is rising from the dead. Pragmatics are often strangely superstitious."

She picked up her coffee and took a long sip. "What about the Greeks?"

"The Greeks were different," I said, "they had a passion for order and symmetry, much like the Romans, they knew how foolish it was to deny the Unseen World, gods. Emotion, darkness, barbarism." I paused for a moment. *"Beauty."*

"Elaborate on the beauty part," Louise said with excitement.

"Sometimes the bloody, terrible things are sometimes the most beautiful," I said. "It's a very great idea, a very profound one. What could be more terrifying and beautiful, to the souls like the Greeks or our own, than to lose control completely?"

"Very good, Alaska," Louise said and smiled.

You leaned into our table and whispered. "I would never lose control."

"Is that so?" I asked, raising an eyebrow.

You smiled mischievously. "Yes? What makes you think that?"

Before I could continue, Veronika interjected into the conversation. "It must be so hard to be *perfect* all the time like you, Theodore." At first, I assumed it was a joke until she continued for the rest of the lecture. *You are just so perfect, Theodore.* It was not the tone of her voice, exactly, as much as the look on her face which was so annoying. Vasileios stared, his mouth falling slightly open as we exchanged glances. For about ten long seconds there was no sound but the rhythmic tick tick tick of the clock. I didn't know what to say and so, kept quiet.

But I almost shot myself.

I liked Vasileios a lot in a platonic sense, but with you and Veronika, it was a different story. You were happy enough to be together in company and it soon occurred to me that you were genuinely fond of each other, a keen very pointed streak of malice from me thus sparked toward Veronika in particular. But there was absolutely nothing I could say or do. Perhaps, in my mind, there was a justification for jealousy that couldn't be voiced.

We walked back to the University park and sat down on the dock instead, watching the lake heave in the early morning. The waves here seemed like a mockery of the ocean. The sun looked fake. I sat there, cigarette in hand, until you sat down beside me and leaned against my shoulder, I could feel the rain off your cheek. I made room and you slipped against me, lighting another cigarette. "Do you have any plans after class?" you asked.

I took a drag of the cigarette and exhaled. "No, not necessarily. I'm meeting with Asli in the afternoon, but I'm free afterwards. Why?"

The wind was now warm and danced around the leaves. "Come to my room," you said.

We both smiled at each other.

"Just to hang out?" I teased.

'Like *besties for life*,' you mocked.

I laughed and wrapped my arms around you. "Can I braid your hair and paint your nails then?" I joked.

You gasped with fake excitement. "Oh my god! I would love that!"

"What about face masks? I could even do your makeup. Please let me do your makeup!"

"Okay, okay, Alaska," you laughed. "Don't get ahead of yourself."

When the wicks were over, we flicked them into the lake, where they sizzled upon landing. We watched them float into the dark together. The threads burned out and off. The fire went out.

During lunch, I sat in Waterstones with my books spread across the table in front of me. It was a strange, bright, dreamlike day. The grassy lawn — peppered with the toylike figures of distant people — was as smooth as sugar frosting; a tiny dog ran, barking, after a ball; real smoke threaded from the afternoon mist.

This time, I thought, a year ago. What had I been doing? Driving a friend's car up to Manhattan, standing around in the poetry section of bookstores worrying about my application to Oxford, *reconciling after the assault*. And now, here I was, sitting in a book-filled room, had the greatest friends I had met in my short lifetime and was in a relationship that I believed only possible in the realm of my letters.

Nihil sub sole novum. A pencil sharpener complained loudly somewhere. I put my head down on my books — whispers, quiet footsteps, the smell of old paper in my nostrils. Coffee urns and potted ferns on the inside window ledge peeked through the lettering. Strains of jazz music drifted from the speakers; Van Morrison sang to me about stars and young lovers. When I got tired of reading, I opened my notebook and continued writing your letter.

Dear Theo... sat on the page staring back at me.

I wrote tirelessly through the afternoon. That's when I knew I was in a good writing fix; time started to slow and all the minutes faded into a watercolour blur. Suddenly, there were five minutes to class and I rushed out of the door, probably looking as if I had stolen something.

The Waterstones sign glittered in the sun, and I heard a familiar voice behind me. "I don't think she's noticed us," a faint Italian accent called. Instinctively, I spun around and met your eyes. I smiled, excited to see you. I was about to say hello back, before I noticed Veronika standing beside you.

"Hey," I said after a pause. "How are you...*both?*"

"Not bad," said Veronika, with her deep, husky voice. "You?"

"Fine," I said, eyeing you with a crooked smile. My possessiveness was also a bad habit that needed to be corrected. I couldn't remember when I first began coveting something that I could own, something that would be mine and no one else's.

You immediately picked up on this and replied, "we were just grabbing lunch."

I raised my eyebrow and shook a Marlboro from its pack, lighting the cigarette from the corner of my mouth. My jealousy scraped off as you kept breathing, kept sending more air through yourself. Slow fire. I slipped the pack into my bag instead of passing it to you.

Love melts all our murder. As much as it makes it. We all didn't say anything for a moment.

"Okay," said Veronika uncomfortably. "I'll see you guys in class."

We said goodbye and walked over to Pitt Rivers together. I stayed silent.

"Alaska," you laughed. "You scared her off! How am I supposed to hook up with her now?"

I watched the blue sky mingle with the clouds, turning them transparent, into mist. "Very funny, Theo," I sighed. "You said you were having lunch with your friends–"

"Veronika is my friend," you said, somewhat defensively.

The blue seemed to deepen in the sky; it hurt my eyes so I looked down at the sandy pavement instead. "Because she calls you *perfect* all of the time?"

For a moment, you were quiet and then laughed. "We're presentation partners. You don't need to be jealous if that's what this is–"

"I'm not jealous," I interrupted. "Were you having lunch to talk about your presentation?"

You blinked. "Well, no–not exactly–"

"Okay–"

"She's my friend too–"

"*Theo*." I said. "I know. It's fine"

We walked silently for a while until you wrapped your arms around my shoulders with a smile. "You can't stay mad at me forever," you said.

"I'm not mad," I said as you drew me into a kiss.

"And besides, I kind of like you being jealous. It shows that you care."

Green leaves crunched under our feet, the sounds clung to

the sky and didn't let go. "I'm just the peak of Romanticism," I said.

"Only when you don't hang out with Vasileios," you joked.

I paused for a moment, unsure of how you knew, and then smiled again. "How am I supposed to hook up with him then?"

You laughed and leaned towards me again. "I have a hard time believing you'd want him more than me. You know, since I am *so perfect.*"

I nudged you gently from the side. "You'd have to prove it then."

Christ Church had been built in fifteen-something, according to the National Register of Historic Places. It was age-bladed, with its own rickety little garden in the roll of country lane. When we arrived, the sun had finally come out, but a grey drizzle was still falling. Asli and I headed inside to the sanctuary, and stepping inside, were blinded by a dazzle of candles. When my eyes cleared I saw iron lanterns, clammy marble floors, flowers everywhere, and laid down some groceries we had brought along with us. We ate, and talked, and laughed. Then walked back to campus and spent the afternoon in her room. Sunlight was fading, from the street came dull and dusty bellows of cars hitting the driveway. We finished up some of the food as yellow light streamed through the windows from the street lamp outside.

I decided to take a warm shower.

There must be quite a few things a hot shower wouldn't cure, but I knew little of them; I never felt so much myself as when I was in a hot shower. Everything around me dissolved; my past dissolved, my future dissolved, my present dissolved.

The longer I lay under the clear hot water, the better I felt.

CHAPTER ELEVEN
MY LOVE, MINE ALL MINE

I SEE NOW, HOW QUICK IT WAS. AND IT IS IMPOSSIBLE TO slow down this film, to examine individual frames. I see now what I saw then, flashing by with swift movements.

If lying in bed at night, I find myself an unwilling audience to this objectionable little documentary (it goes away when I open my eyes but always, when I close them, it resumes tirelessly at the very beginning), I marvel at how detached it is in viewpoint, eccentric in detail, largely devoid of emotional power. In that way, it mirrors the remembered experience more closely than one might imagine. Time, and repeated screenings, have endowed the memory with menace the original did not possess. In the moment, I let it all happen quite calmly — without fear, without regret, without anything but a kind of stunned curiosity — so that the impression of the event is burned indelibly upon my optic nerves, but oddly absent from my heart.

It was many hours before I was cognisant of what we'd done; days, weeks, before I began to comprehend the magnitude of it. I suppose we'd simply thought about it too much, talked of it too often, until the scheme ceased to be a thing of the imagination and instead seemed to be the natural, forward-moving step in our relationship.

Never, never once in any immediate sense, did it occur to me that any of this was anything absent of love.

What is unthinkable is undoable. That is something Louise used to say in our Philosophy class, and while I believe she said it in order to encourage us to be more rigorous in our mental habits, it has a certain perverse bearing on the matter at hand. The idea of sex used to be unthinkable to me. Nevertheless, we dwelt on it incessantly, convinced ourselves there was no alternative, devised plans which seemed slightly improbable to get into each other's rooms. A month or two before, I would have been appalled at the idea of losing my virginity to a guy I had met only ten days prior. But that Wednesday evening, it seemed like the easiest, most natural thing in the world.

———

We climbed the stairs hastily, clumsily, impeded by our foolish refusal to keep our hands off each other. We ran down the hall on the second floor, crashing against the wall and locking lips before stumbling into your bedroom. You threw the door shut and pulled down the blinds. You hugged me so hard we fell to the floor laughing and crying. It was a great relief to be held, to feel arms around my whole body, arms that clasped my waist, your face pressed into my neck, absorbing my heat, my love. We collided more than embraced, the whole feverish scene shot through with flashes of euphoria as you clenched your fingers in my hair. I caught your bottom lip between my teeth. We kissed and gasped and grasped at each other like we were afraid to let go. Everything was going beautifully, on the brink of taking wind, and I had a feeling that I'd never had, that reality itself was transforming around us in some profound dangerous fashion, that we were being driven by a force we didn't understand.

Your dark eyes took me in and I wondered what they would look like if you fell in love.

As our clothes came off, my head swam, the floor shifted and tiled under me whenever I closed my eyes. I ran one hand from the nape of your neck to the small of your back, your skin, electric under my fingertips. The warm silk touch of your lips against my neck made me clutch closer — delirious, addicted, furious that I'd ever pretended not to want you, furious that the assault had sheltered me from such an experience for so long, furious at the world for denying me this until now.

My head was so light that without the weight of you on top of me I might have floated away. Inch by inch, my brain and body reconnected. You let me have my way for a little longer, then rolled me over on my back, unwilling to be entirely submissive. My muscles were quivering under my skin. We were too hot to touch and we lay with only our legs tangled together. Our shallow breaths lengthened, deepened, and sleep pulled me swiftly down like gravity.

We didn't sleep long. My eyes opened before I even knew I was awake, and I stared up at the unfamiliar ceiling. You lay beside me, one hand pressed under my cheek, the other arm tucked tight against my chest.

The lamp on the nightstand leaked watery orange light across the bed. I reached carefully over to turn it off but paused, my arm outstretched. Your breath fluttered against the back of my hand. I couldn't help but stare. The delicate line of your wrist was marred by tiny blooms of purple, like budding violets on your skin. I brushed a strand of hair off your forehead, then turned the light off. The room shrank in around me, the eager darkness encroaching at last. I lay and watched you sleep, looking at you just as I had the first time we had met. You were still that same boy with your tousled shepherd's hair. *Nobody sees as we do.*

I was scared then, of the love that I had for you, I knew it would soon ruin me. And I also knew that I would let it.

I sat on the bed and waited until you woke. You leaned on one elbow and smiled. "Want to get under the covers, vampire?", and began tickling me. We wrestled around and couldn't stop laughing. Then you jumped up. "Let's go to the marquee," you said. "It's five minutes until the shout-out."

We had to slip around to the back door, sneaking down the stairs like cat-burglars — it was very tiresome, all that creeping around barefoot in the dark. The night smothered the land with a vice-like grip, its ornamental beauty returned. Like phantom fingers, frost hung serenely off all windows. Upon entering the marquee, the lights were so bright, and I felt so faint with shock that I couldn't do much more than stare at you.

After taking a seat next to Asli, I glanced around to make sure that no one was within earshot; she leaned over to hear what I was going to say but just at that moment, as we were sitting in a huddle and our breath was coming out in clouds, I heard someone call my name and there, at a great distance, you sat smiling at me. I turned back to Asli and whispered what exactly had occurred only minutes prior. She shrieked and laughed, and I smiled so widely my cheeks were sore.

In the sixteenth staircase, nothing moved but the shifting tides of salt in my body and the peculiar shapes of certain clouds and silences were left as skeletal darkness. Furnished vines, oak trees that swayed among the breeze, unforgiving. Asli and I, alone of us all, were encumbered; I sat stiffly on the carpet, straightening my hair, and she lay on my bed, drinking from a flask of cheap rosé. I told her everything, unfiltered and uncaring. We laughed, discussing all the minuscule details that appeared like flashing stars in my memories.

That night, we were girls together and I loved that so much.

CHAPTER TWELVE
FAVOURITISM

IN SOME RESPECTS, IT WAS AS IF NOTHING HAD HAPPENED AT all. We went to our classes, did our philosophy, and generally managed to pretend among one another and everybody else that things were alright. It might seem that this episode would have imposed a certain coolness upon our relationship. While I don't suppose that anyone who has devoted much energy to the study of philosophy or literature can be very much disturbed by sex, neither am I particularly comfortable with it as it concerns me directly.

But, if I dare say it, it wasn't until I had actually slept with anyone, that I realised how elusive and in-complex that sex could actually be, and not necessarily attributable to one dramatic motive. To ascribe it to such a motive would be easy enough. There was one, certainly. But the instinct for self-preservation is not as compelling an instinct as one might think. In one minute, it started, and the next, it was over. I began to reflect heavily on the social influences and stigma surrounding virginity and chastity, the fear and shame that I thought would come with it; but sitting in class again, the billow of oak trees in the breeze, the sunlight streaming through the window, I felt more myself than ever. Nothing had changed and if anything, I just felt happier.

I do understand that this is not the case for most women, though. I remember studying *The Bell Jar* for a personal writing project months prior to my enrolment at St. Catherine. The piece was about Plath's exploration of virtue of her protagonist, Esther Greenwood (what a coincidence), in a time when women were expected to epitomise ideals of purity, chastity and domesticity to adhere to conventional feminine archetypes:

> "The article was written by a married woman lawyer with children and called, 'In the defence of Chastity'. It gave all the reasons a girl shouldn't sleep with anybody but her husband and only after they were married. The main point of the article was that a man's world is different from a woman's world a man's emotions are different from a woman's emotions and only marriage can bring the two worlds and two different sets of emotions together properly...Now the one thing this article didn't seem to me to consider was how a girl felt."

Virtue was frequently equated with a woman's ability to conform to these prescribed gender roles, in favour of fulfilling societal expectations, relating to the preservation of virginity. My main motive for writing the article was mainly because, after the assault, I found myself between a state of celibacy and hyper-sexuality. I began to question my own virtuosity and whether I could fit myself into any ideal of newer intimacy, without shame or guilt afterwards. I had the preconceived notion that sex would make me unclean or impure, just like Esther, but strangely enough, I felt more liberated and in control of myself than ever before.

I woke up very late the next morning. My eyes hurt when I rolled on my cheek. I lay there for a while, blinking in the bright sun, as confused details of the previous night floated back to me like a dream; then I reached for my phone on the night table and saw that it was late, almost nine. Why had no one been up to get me?

I got up, and as I did my reflection rose to meet me, head-on in the bathroom mirror; its grey eyes stopped and stared back. I brushed my teeth, didn't dress, and hurried outside to Pitt Rivers.

I was fifteen minutes late when I pushed through the lecture doors. Presentations had already started and I made my way over to our desk, making as little noise as possible. Louise smiled kindly at me as I took my seat.

Watching the presentations, albeit uninterested and half-asleep, I felt very close to the others in class. I began to realise how, they too, knew this beautiful and harrowing landscape, centuries dead they had the same experience of looking up from their books with fifth-century eyes and finding the world disconcertingly sluggish and alien, as if it were not their home. It was why I admired Louise, and you in particular. Your reasons, your very eyes and ears were fixed irrevocably in the confines of those stern and ancient rhythms — the world, in fact, was not their home, at least not the world as I knew it — and far from being occasional visitors to this land which I myself knew only as an admiring tourist, they were pretty much its permanent residents, as permanent as I suppose it was possible for them to be.

Philosophy is a difficult language, a very difficult language indeed, and it is eminently possible to study it all one's life and never be able to understand it completely; but it makes me smile, even today, to think of Louise's calculated, formal English, the English of a well-educated foreigner, as compared with the marvellous fluency and self-assurance in Philosophy — quick, eloquent, remarkable witty.

When it was your turn to present on *The Master & Margarita,* observing people take in the work I had watched you create was an emotional experience. It had left our private world. Of course, it was what I always wanted for you, but I felt a slight pang of possessiveness sharing it with others. Overriding that feeling was the joy of seeing your face, suffused with confirmation, as you glimpsed the future you had so resolutely sought and worked so hard to achieve.

At the same time, I was hit with a diffuse of sadness. Once the presentations were over, we only had two more days left. All of this, all of it, was now almost over. I brushed away the thought as we were dismissed for break. Since there were so many students, my presentation had been moved to the third and last period of the day. *I should've slept in,* I thought to myself.

You followed me out of the door, a few paces behind, through the hall and down to the park. We ordered a coffee and took a seat, lighting a cigarette in the early morning glow. Neither of us said anything for a moment. You seemed calm enough, tired but calm, and your intelligent eyes met mine with a sad, quiet candour. I was so fond of you, that it was unthinkable that anything unkind should ever happen to you. I thought, with a pang, of how kind you had always been; of how sweet you were in those first awkward days, or turning to me in a crowd with a tranquil assumption — heartwarming to me. "How come you were late this morning?" you asked with a smile. "Fun night?"

"Absolutely," I replied, taking a swing of my latte.

You grinned, wrapping a warm arm around my shoulders. A wave of silence passed through the air as we sipped our coffees in the park. "Hey," I said. "What will happen to us?"

"There will always be us."

The blistering sun rippled through the sky in the afternoon. Tulips sprouted on the sidewalks, illuminating and billowing through the grassy fields. In the town centre, I met with Adeline, Asli and Serena at *Joe & The Juice* for lunch. They ordered tunacados and I, being vegetarian, got another assortment of avocado-toasted sandwiches alongside a sports juice. I hadn't seen Serena in a couple of days, both of us were so busy with assignments and final projects that we hadn't had much time to catch up, especially since she wasn't in the same staircase as Adeline, Asli and I. On the way back to Pitt Rivers, I stopped by Waterstones with an idea in mind.

Walking through the rows of bookshelves, I waited at the counter for the clerk to arrive. "Hi," I said to the clerk. "Do you sell a translated copy of *Il Barone Rampante?*"

Walking into class, I slid down my seat and placed the novel in front of your desk. For a moment, your eyes glistened and shone with excitement before grabbing the book. "No way," you exclaimed, flicking through the pages.

"I told you I'd remember," I said, and you smiled back, childish and warm. "Sign it for me."

I handed over my pen as you took a few moments to contemplate what to write. Then suddenly you began to scribble in all capital letters:

DAL TUO PRIMO FIDANZATO, THEODORE.

I would translate it after the course, I thought to myself.

You immediately opened the novel and scanned through the pages, intent and focused, barely averting your eyes until I was called up to the podium ready to finally give my presentation. Melissa plugged the laptop into the board and we began improperly.

"Religion is important whether you believe it or not. Just like history is important whether you've lived through it or not," I said, glancing at the blur of faces until I made my way to yours. "We are engaged in the most important pursuit of all; the search for meaning. What is the nature of being human? What is the best way to live? How did we come to be? And what will become of us when we are no longer?"

I paused and took a deep breath. "Many of us spend a large part of our lives feeling stuck. We become worried of mistakes we can make, things that can go wrong, the risks in moving forward that we believe the safest option is to keep ourselves stationary instead. The world makes no sense. We set systems to determine our meaning through religion and even philosophy itself, but they never seem to completely work out, simply because of the way the world works, the way reality functions is not under any sort of truth. Absurdism arises out of the tension between our desire for order, meaning and happiness and, on the other hand, the indifferent natural universe's refusal to provide that. The universe is irrational and meaningless."

I looked at you and smiled. "Consider Nietzsche's approach. Like Camus, he thought that life was devoid of intrinsic meaning. But he thought we could give it a kind of meaning by embracing illusion. That's what we have to learn from artists, according to Nietzsche. They are always devising new inventions and artifices that give things the appearance of being beautiful, when they're not. By applying this to our own lives, we can become *the poets of our lives.*"

"The solution Camus arrives at is different from Nietzsche's and is perhaps a more honest approach. The absurd hero takes no refuge in the illusions of art or religion. Yet neither does he despair in the face of absurdity—he doesn't just pack it all in. Instead, he openly embraces the absurdity of his condition. Sisyphus, condemned for all eternity to push a boulder up a mountain only to have it roll to the bottom again and again, fully recognises the futility and pointlessness of his task. But he willingly pushes the boulder up the mountain every time it rolls down..."

In an instant, it was finally over. I returned to my seat and sank into a deep melancholy. The presentations were the last, graded assignment for the course, and now, they had elapsed with nothing else coming forward, nothing else to embark on. I knew we were thinking the same thing, how much we had been through, good and bad, but also a sense of relief. You squeezed my hand. "Do you feel sad?" you asked.

"Time was bound to catch up."

The city air was fresh that day, almost sweet and floral as the pace of living relaxed to a steadier rhythm; small, green trees on the roadside swayed as the strong breeze hit them. I met with Asli in Westgate, browsing through retail stores, interior supplies, and other random things to fill the gaps of time. We sat down in *Pret A-Manger* and ordered a serving of mangoes and lemonades to share. "I can't believe we're graduating tomorrow," I said, reaching for my drink.

"I know," she sighed. "It feels like we only started at St. Catherine yesterday."

"I feel like I just started to get comfortable, in tune with a sort of routine, and now it's practically over."

"You know," she said, placing down her lemonade and fiddling with the mangoes. "I wish my experience was more...it was great, don't get me wrong—but more thrilling. Like, Adeline had that councillor guy, and although it didn't go anywhere, it was for fun. And you and Theo. I didn't find anything like that here."

I thought to myself for a moment. "I think I just got lucky," I said genuinely. "The past few years haven't been the best. I feel like the universe is trying to make up for it in a way. Not everything has to be tied to romance to be a great experience."

"I know," she said. "I sometimes wonder if I could have done anything better."

I looked out of the window; a homeless man sang on the streets, people passed in blurs of colour, the breeze picked up fallen leaves. "Don't blame yourself," I said. "I know it's a cliche thing to say but the best things come when you least expect it. You can't sit around and wait for things to change, or you'll miss it when they actually do. Good things come to those who wait for them."

Asli and I walked back to St. Catherine and spent the rest of the afternoon in her room. Compared to mine, it was more organised; assortments of perfumes lined the shelves, clothes neatly stacked, a small pantry for food. I sat on the floor and touched up on my makeup as Asli applied various, soft-scented creams to her brown waves; the fragrance of different aromatics diffused and billowed through the air as it began to rain again. Fat dewdrops clung to leaves, the fresh evening air wrapped itself around my skin. I had the wonderful sense that the rest of the day belonged to me.

It was six-thirty when I trailed to the back of the twenty-third staircase to find you waiting with the door open, ushering me inside. We climbed the stairs up to your room, where the blinds were already closed. As per routine, you shut the door and I lay on your bed, tired and half-asleep. "For a vampire, you sure do sleep a lot," you laughed.

I rolled over to face you. "Ha ha, very funny," I said sarcastically. "Are you always calling me a vampire because I'm pale?"

You snickered and joined me in the covers. "Half and half,"

you smiled. "Because you are very pale, but you also love to bite."

"I do not."

"Yes, you do."

I sat up from the covers and wrapped my hands around your neck. "You want to see what a real bite looks like?" I said and kissed it slowly before my teeth began to gnaw against your skin.

"Hey, easy," you laughed, turning your head in the other direction.

"I'm not done."

"Like fucking hell you are."

I wedged my lips into the nuzzle of your neck "*This* is a bite," I giggled. You brought your arms to cover your neck, and as I tried to pull them down again, we both laughed and fumbled against the once-made bed covers.

"Alaska, it's going to leave a mark," you laughed.

"I have no idea what you're talking about."

We toppled out from your bedsheets, crashing onto the carpet floor. We wrestled and laughed. "You really are a fucking vampire, huh?" you teased, leaning closer until our lips were a hair's breadth apart.

"Oh my—you're going to kill me when you see this." I sighed into your mouth when you kissed me with another sweet pull.

Revisiting this moment, I realise how I was already so deeply in love with you and I wasn't even aware of it. I had loved you secretly and hopelessly. You were so warm and familiar, solid and safe. Looking at your smile, your laughter, your voice, it all made me so happy. I wanted to cling to your shirt and bury my face into the warm curve of your neck, never to let go. I don't necessarily remember falling in love with you. I just remember holding you in my arms and realising how much it was going to hurt when I would have to let you go.

You helped me meet a version of myself I didn't know existed, and the most beautiful part is, I wasn't even looking when I found you.

I think what hurts is the fact that I thought you felt the same.

You put the radio on and in time, fingers and voices came together, the music happened; the song inside the music awakened. I listened with my eyes closed, toes pushing into the warm carpet. Words came and then the melody. It was a wistful tone that conjured the colour of your eyes. I sang the words of *Patience and Prudence* over and over with you so I wouldn't forget them. Outside, the sky was a splotch of violet and the rain was glittering serenely on the windowsill. "Let's have a little dance," you said, rounding up to my side.

"You know I can't dance," I said feebly, blinking up at you holding your hand out.

"Neither do I, but we always look dumb doing things together anyways," you said, grabbing my hand and putting it on your shoulders as you slid your arms around my waist. You smiled and I leaned forward to kiss you on the forehead. As the song continued playing, we began swaying back and forth; it wasn't right, it wasn't how you usually slow danced, but it was good enough for us.

"I feel stupid." I blushed, looking up at you who was still smiling down at me.

"Then twirl me around and we can feel stupid together," you said. I lifted your hands and spun you around, laughing. You chuckled softly as you almost tripped over your feet, clumsily. When we came together again, we danced slowly on the spot, pressing our forehead together with closed eyes.

> *...My honey I know (I know)*
> *With the dawn that you will be gone*
> *But tonight you belong to me...*

Head on your shoulder, we danced in the sunset glow of your room and suddenly all I wanted to do was tell you that I loved you. In spite of the ventilation being turned on, the room seemed close and intimate. I could hear our breathing, quiet, measured breaths that came and went with calm regularity, two sets of lungs, eating at the tin oxygen. Your lips brushed mine with a soft, possessive bite.

> *...How very, very sweet it will seem*
> *Once more just to dream*
> *In the silvery moonlight...*

We went upstairs to look at stars. There were world above ours, a night sky full of separate infernos so far away they looked to us like they were only tiny lights, easily extinguished. You and I tried to make out the rings of Saturn and Jupiter, but the sky, clear as it looked, wouldn't allow it.

We loved through the night again. You were as cold as the wind every time it started, warm like a tear when we were done. But as soon as we finished, you reached for your phone this time, strolling mindlessly as I stared back, quiet, wordless. I tried slipping into your arms, but you still hadn't said anything or even looked at me. In the silence, I heard every thought, and suddenly I was wide awake. I started going over all the different stages of my past; faces once forgotten swam towards me, I saw the girl in the boarding school bleachers, and the red light of my dark room in New York. At first, the memories were blurred, but over the next few minutes, they started to come into focus again. My thoughts roamed further and further back in time until at last, they settled on the calamity of a warm shower. I walked over to your bathroom and switched the faucet on, stepped through the glass doors and let the water's warmth pour over my skin; the steam coated an overcast against the glass.

The door, already open, made a slight noise; when I turned around, you were standing in the doorway, smiling. "Stop being a fucking creep," I laughed.

You smiled back at me. "You're so beautiful," you said, and everything suddenly seemed alright again, perfect even. It sounds dramatic, but that is how I felt; I felt finally loved; I had found the thing I had been searching my entire life for in you. It was so nice to be anywhere with you. I wanted to stay there, forever and always.

It didn't matter where, as long as I had you.

I joined you back in bed after my shower, nestling into the curse of your arms, we held each other like a prayer unspoken. "I wanted to ask you something," you said.

I sighed, resting my head against your chest. "You need to stop saying that or you're going to make me go insane one day," I said.

You chuckled softly. "You need to stop expecting bad news from me," you said. "I wanted to ask, since tomorrow is our last night, whether you wanted to spend the night here?"

I grinned widely. "I knew you wanted to have a sleepover!"

You rolled your eyes affectionately. "Seriously, do you want to?"

"Of course I do. But what about the counsellors?" I asked.

You smiled at me. "We would already have our diplomas so we couldn't get kicked out or anything. They can't just take them back, you know?" you said.

"And shout-out?"

"I already asked and they said we wouldn't have one. So many people are leaving straight after graduation, so it would be pointless to check attendance."

"Well then, how could I decline that offer?"

"Okay, great," you laughed, tracing a finger gently across the bridge of my nose. "What time is it?"

I reached over for my phone on the nightstand. "It's ten

minutes until the marquee," I said. "I better leave before everyone starts coming out."

"Good idea," you said, getting up from the bed and walking into the bathroom. I got dressed into my clothes again, pulling one of your oversized t-shirts over my chest. Suddenly, a yell came through the bathroom walls. "What did you do?" you yelled.

"What do you mean?" I said, getting up and walking into the vanity space. I stopped straight in the doorway. "Oh my god!" I laughed.

"Alaska, this is criminal," you half-laughed, staring at the salient battleground of marks across your neck.

"Who would even do that to you? Are you cheating on me?"

"'I am actually," you said, "with my roommate," inspecting the marred stretch of purple.

"I think you should wear a—"

"Nope."

I looked at you, eyes wide and confused. "Wait what?" I said. "Or makeup at least? I can give you some later?"

"Nope, you made this mess, you suffer with me," you smiled, wrapping your arms around my waist.

"You're unbearable," I said.

"And you're a fucking vampire!"

The night rippled with aerosols of grey drizzle; a gusty wind was whipping over the hilly, rough landscape as moonlight illuminated the cobblestone path before us. We left your dorm together for the first time; I zipped up my anorak, holding my hand in front of my face and trudged along the sidewalk passing other students on their way to shout-out. You caught up with a group of your friends and walked over to them, leaving me walking steadily in front. The cold penetrated against my damp hair and skin harsher than the moment before. From a distance, I heard their voices taunting me. They yelled and pulled at your neck, shouting obscenities at me.

A tinge of embarrassment coursed brutally through my body; I hugged my arms for warmth, cradling the collecting drops of water across my shirt. The cold was a shock to my lungs. I don't know if this is a 'fair' judgement for me to make, but I felt a little left behind then, unprotected and exposed, a little isolated even. Moments prior, we had been messing around in your room, and now I was walking through the blistering cold alone, jokes being pushed in from behind my naked back; I felt a sense of inferiority as I slowed my pace to catch up with yours. *You made a mistake,* a voice said back to me, *why did you think it would be different this time?*

"I'd thought you'd maybe at least walk with me after we had sex?" I said, my voice light-hearted but protective. I managed a playful smile.

You shrugged nonchalantly. "I am walking with you now?" you said.

"Yeah, you're right," I said, embarrassed. "I'm sorry."

"You say sorry a lot," you laughed.

"I feel it a lot."

Entering upon the white-coated marquee walls, I took my seat next to Asli and leaned my head against her shoulder. "Where were you?" she asked.

I threw up my hands and sighed. "You'd never guess."

"Theo?"

From two rows behind me, I heard another voice call out my name. I turned around to be met with your friends again, they laughed and taunted their words through me like I was transparent, made of glass. They gestured towards you again and teased me: "Did you do this to Theo?" they repeated — part chant, part curse.

More embarrassment, *wonderful.*

"Why? Are you jealous?" I asked, turning back to face the

front. I wanted to die, sink into my seat and the earth below. *Why is your girlfriend a bitch?* I heard one of them say in the background. I didn't hear you respond.

I turned back to Asli, whose face was exasperated and cartoonish. "What happened to his neck?" she laughed.

I groaned. "I'll tell you later."

What follows here is hazy bewilderment and a thick fog that is illuminated only here and there by a few brief memories. Standing in my room, looking out of the window at the inner courtyard, the lamplights caught in the branches of trees, the stars.

Soon, night had completely fallen and I began to pack the things scattered around my room — my figure skates, piles of clothes, my pen and bottle of ink — into a large, dark suitcase under my bed. Unable to sleep, I got up and went outside to breathe the air. The mockingbirds were still there, motionless, covering a portion of the ledge of the garden wall, but I couldn't really tell if they were dead or just sleeping. The field flattened in the rain, but I knew by tomorrow the grass might have been three inches taller.

I wrapped your name tight around my ribs to keep me warm. The sun was hours from rising and I was love-burned, tired, covered in your scent.

In early morning July, the darkness faded. My room, now bare, was lit only by the green and red glow of evergreens, and a shaft of sunlight fell through my half-closed door. It felt as if I had woken from a dream that had been going on for several years; a dull, warm pain in my right leg, my stomach, my chest. In my head, a faint buzzing was getting louder. Gradually, I pulled myself out of the covers and began to dress.

I made it for breakfast and decided to wait for a warm

English breakfast; accompanied by vegetarian sausages, baked beans, eggs and toast. With contentment, I sat with Adeline, Asli and Serena, laughing through the early morning. We finished our breakfasts and made our way to our final lectures. Watching the shining vapour trail of planes on the reddening horizon as I walked to Pitt Rivers; as often happens when one of nature's spectacles combined with my longing and memories, I sensed a slight tugging on my insides.

"Good morning, everyone," said Louise, looking around the classroom for the last time. "I hope we're all ready to leave the phenomenal world and enter into the sublime."

I gazed out of the window. Thyme shrubs, garrigue and kermes oak stretched off into the distance; the air in Oxford was more fragrant and the colours more intense than back home. I slid my hand into my pockets and fussed around with leftover paper receipts. "Today, we will be starting with... drumroll...Nietzsche! By now, you should all be familiar with Mr. God is Dead. If not, please raise your hand–"

Vasileios raised his hand ever-so slightly.

"--let me know so I can change your grade right now," she smiled and he shot it right down.

You had come to class in a raincoat and began slowly taking it off, looking amused at my displeasure. "What's wrong?" you asked, teasingly. "Is someone having a little bit of regret?"

"I have no idea what you're talking about," I murmured.

"Are you absolutely sure?" you said, turning your neck over.

"Never been more sure in my life," I sighed.

Louise turned to the whiteboard and began writing down in an inky-black marker. "What some of you might not know, is that this is one of my favourite quotes by Neitzsche," she said.

"What if some day or night, a demon were to steal after you into your loneliest loneliness and say to you "This life as you now

*live it and have lived it, you will have to live once more and
innumerable times more." Would you not throw yourself down and
gnash your teeth and curse the demon who spoke this? Or have you
once experienced a tremendous moment when you would have
answered him: "You are a God and never have I heard anything
more divine."*

"Neitzche's idea of eternal recurrence has existed in various
forms since antiquity," Louise said. "Put simply, it's the theory
that existence recurs in an infinite cycle as energy and matter
transform over time. Has anybody heard of this before?"

You raised your hand. "Nietzsche's philosophy is concerned
with questions about freedom, action, and will. His idea of
eternal recurrence assumes that our first reaction would be
utter despair: the human condition is tragic; life contains
much suffering; the thought that one must relive it all an
infinite number of times seems terrible."

"Thank you, Theodore," Louise said.

I raised my hand. "Yes, Alaska?"

"Suppose we could welcome the news, embrace it as
something that we desire? That, says Nietzsche, would be the
ultimate expression of a life-affirming attitude: to want this
life, with all its pain and boredom and frustration, again and
again...to love one's fate."

"*Amare il proprio destino*" you said, smiling.

Looking back at you, I had the irrevocable knowledge of
what I would've told the demon, I knew what I would've told
the God...

Never have I heard anything more divine.

Suddenly, Louise approached our desk, eyes wide with
childish, theatrical surprise; she leaned down and spoke to us
in a whisper. "You know, I was walking around the park the
other day, and there were so many squirrels around," she said.
The mischievous, open-ended note in her voice made me

nervous. I stared at the aqueous, rippling circles of light that the crystal vase cast over the tabletop. "So I researched it. Why were there so many squirrels in Oxford?" she asked, looking directly at you. "Apparently, there is currently an epidemic of rabid squirrels that are biting teenage boys on the neck."

We all paused. Oh. *Oh. Right.*

Vasileios snickered loudly as Veronika laughed alongside him. "Somebody get Theodore some makeup!" Louise laughed.

We both exchanged sheepish glances and buried our heads in our hands for the rest of class. "Is someone having a little bit of regret?" I asked.

"I have no idea what you're talking about," you murmured.

"Are you absolutely sure?" I asked, mockingly.

"Never been more sure in my life."

It was far too cold for us to grab coffee that morning, and although neither of us had ever missed a coffee run before, I had the turning suspicion that neither of us wanted it to be the last time either. As you headed to the bathroom, I exited the lecture hall with Vasileios to a nearby *Horseroy Coffee Co.* van set up outside. As I waited for my order, one coffee for me and one for you, I lit a cigarette and let Vasileios take a few long drags.

I pushed through the doors of Pitt Rivers for the last time that early Friday morning. Sitting back in my seat, I slid over your coffee across the desk and into your hands. "Wow, thank you," you said, giving me a soft kiss.

Louise entered through the doors, and began her final lecture; ten minutes passed, and then fifteen, until the hour had passed and we were ready to pack our things and leave. "I want you all to remember," Louise said, "I am so grateful for the time we spent together, and I hope you feel the same way. I won't be at your graduation, so from here on, it's farewell. Continue striving for excellence." We all gave her a tender round of applause and took a Polaroid photo of the whole class together. Still, none of us could make ourselves actually leave the classroom, staying a whole extra hour behind to talk with Louise.

We knew the end was approaching, we saw it somewhere far in the distance, but now, it was there and every single one of us began to feel it. Talking to Louise, I remember the sadness in your dark eyes. I wished I could give it all to me and hold onto it so you didn't have to.

When I had finally left, I headed back to St. Catherine in the scathing rain. In the afternoon, when the lawns were green as Heaven and the apple blossoms had recklessly blown, I was reading in my room with the windows open and a cool damp wind stirred the papers on my desk. *Everything would change,* I thought, packing my things, the madness of my mess.

I was nodding, half-asleep over my book, when someone bellowed my name outside my window. I shook myself and sat up, just in time to see Adeline. I jumped up and leaned over the sill. Far below, I saw her clutching at the trunk of the elm tree. "Alaska!" she yelled. "Want to go grab a coffee?"

I looked out to the rain and sighed. "I don't know, it's raining pretty heavily. I don't want to get wet before graduation later."

"We can get Starbucks?..."

Fuck. Adeline knew I could never say no to getting Starbucks. "You know me too well," I groaned. "I'm coming down."

I used to love the rain, its romantic temperament, its saccharine aesthetic; warm candle lights, late-nights writing, rising autumn; this was all until I got to Oxford that I truly remembered how much I hated being *in* the rain. Walking through the city centre, I grew increasingly more aggravated and, obviously, wet. "My mascara is running down my face, my jeans are soaked, my hair is soaked," I sighed. By the time we made it to Starbucks, we were head to toe soaked, the bottom of our jeans drowned in a watery grave. "It breaks me to have to let go of so many people, including you," I said. "it's almost impossible to realise how lucky I got in these two weeks. If I had chosen another block, another course, or another campus, my story would have been completely different. Maybe, I wouldn't even have had a story to tell at all."

Adeline nodded. We collected our drinks and headed out into town again.

"In a sense, actually in more of a Hegel way," I joked. "It's actually quite beautiful."

Back in the dormitories, I was blow drying my hair and taking periodic sips of coffee as your message lit up against my phone: *hey, I'm outside, let me in.*

The rain was still hollowing at the glass windows of the entrance, relentlessly, when you pushed past the doors and immediately pulled me in for a long, deep kiss. Water droplets hung serenely from the tips of your dark hair and across your face as my hands trailed around your neck. I sighed as you pulled apart. A sly smile warmed over your face and your hands slowly slid under my shirt and below my denim shorts. "Hello to you too," I smiled. "What was that for?"

"Because." Your lips brushed mine again. "You love it and so do it."

We stood in the entrance for a while, my hands against the cold of your rain-stricken jacket, your warm skin brushed against mine. As the rain continued to crash against the windows, we kissed a little more passionately before pulling away. "I'll see you at graduation, vampire," you smiled, disappearing back into the rain like a fragment of a dream.

I headed upstairs to join Adeline and Asli in our shared bathroom. We spent the following hours singing and getting ready for the evening's events. When I had finished my makeup, I got dressed into a rose-coloured, formal dress I had purchased from Urban Outfitters days prior–I loved the rustic watercolour materialisation of the piece, but also the length and ruffles for some elegance. We took photos and bittersweet videos together in our attires before heading to the graduation ceremony.

CHAPTER THIRTEEN
NOVOCAINE

IN THE MAIN HALL, THE OXFORD CREST STILL HUNG PROUDLY behind the podium — *Nova Et Vetera,* I thought to myself as Ian walked up and behind the stand.

"Good evening, everyone. *Nova Et Vetera,*" he said, peering at the crowd from behind his round and glossy spectacles. "We have approached the end–"

A random student yelled amidst the crowd, causing an eruption of laughter.

"Quiet down, everyone," Ian groaned. "I hope, in coming to Oxford University, you have made unforgettable memories, friends, and garnered the knowledge that will take you far in your bright, future careers..."

Everyone seemed unusually calm and at ease and I thought I knew why; we were all avoiding the topic with deliberate unconcern. I leaned back and looked at the silvery, staggering oaths the raindrops made as they blew across the large windows. Minutes passed slowly, and soon, classes were announced one by one to be handed their diplomas. By our usual strain of unfortunate luck, Philosophy, Literature and Modern History was the last of subjects to be called out.

When your name was announced on the last page, I felt a surge of melancholy, seeing you on that stage. Time had flown, as if on its own tiny plane. We smiled at each other as the stage lights beamed down across your face, devastatingly beautifully, like a fallen angel. You saw me looking at you, finally. You smiled and waved, silent. I waved back. I told myself, not even the light should dare to love you.

My name was called out shortly after and I collected my diploma. For the kind of heels I was wearing, gold laced and five inches, sitting at the top of the hall was an abhorrent idea. I collected the certificate and made it back to my seat. "Now," Ian said, "we will be handing out special achievement awards to students in each course who received an exceptionally high grade..."

"It's definitely not me," you said.

"Me neither. It's probably Veronika," I snickered.

"Who?"

I looked at you, confused and bewildered. "Veronika?"

"Who's Veronika?" you asked, completely serious.

I scoffed. "She's—"

"Alaska Greenwood!" Ian yelled out into the microphone. "For the highest attainment grade in Philosophy, Literature and Modern History..."

Wait, what?...

"Oh, shit," you said.

"Oh, shit," I replied, standing up unexpectedly and making my way down the stage.

For the rest of the ceremony, we listened to Beethoven's renditions on the grand piano and heard an array of speeches from select students, one of which was an Asian girl with box-dyed black hair and a wispy fringe. Her speech was...*interesting*. If anything, I'm not even sure if it was approved by Ian, and she rambled onwards for twenty minutes of the ceremony. When her strange, but I suppose memorable speech ended, the hall erupted in applause. I remember that you cheered harder for her speech than when my name was called out.

That night, we were given a formal dinner by the college; the cafeteria was decorated with colourful baubles, wooden figures and candles; the smell of wax and fir twigs lingered around. On the table were large turkeys with potato gratin, lamb ragouts, roasted portions of beef, cranberry sauces and pavlova cakes and pies. There was a party in the marquee; laughter and music floated through the night air.

It was close to midnight now and after dinner, I changed into a short, black dress and walked through the dark to the party. By the time I had arrived, almost everyone was already there. Everything seemed so soft and kind and infinitely forgiving. I noticed a strange beauty in the faces of people previously unbeknown to me. I smiled at everyone and everyone smiled back, bathed in a celestial light.

Veronika offered me a drink. The gesture was, to me, tremendously touching and all of a sudden I realised I had been wrong about these people. These were good people, common people; the salt of the earth; people whom I should count myself fortunate to have known. I was thinking of some way to vocalise this when Veronika came back with the drinks. I drank mine, wandered off to get another, found myself roaming in a fluid, pleasant haze. The music was insanely loud and people were dancing and there was beer puddled on the floor and a rowdy mob at the centre. I couldn't see much but a Dantesque mass of bodies on the dance floor and a cloud of smoke hovering near the ceiling, but I could see, where light from the outside spilt into the darkness, and upturned glass here, a wide lipsticked laughing mouth there. As parties go, this was a nasty one and getting worse, but it was a Friday and I'd spent all week writing and I didn't care. Then I remember feeling awfully sentimental; you found me amidst the crowd, grabbed my arm and motioned for me to follow you out of the marquee. I could see the door propped invitingly with a cinder block and could feel a cold draft on my face.

Gradually I brought you back into focus. Very pretty, in a snub-nosed, good-natured way; dark hair, freckles, dark brown eyes. I couldn't make out what you were saying, though the timbre of your voice was clear even over the noise: cheerful, loving, pleasant.

You stopped to look at me, eyes regarding me with a kind of intimate amusement in the jaded light, then brought my face close to yours. "It's too noisy," I said in your ear.

The party across the way was still going strong and a faint but boisterous rap song throbbed obtrusively in the distance. You gazed at me with a vacant, inebriated composure, standing on the outer edge of the woods. Your hand was in mine, I squeezed it hard. Clouds were racing across the moon. You raised up and gave me a cool, soft kiss. I felt my heart beating fast and shallow. Suddenly, you broke away. "I've got to go, I'm going into town with my friends," you said.

"Sure," I said, sadly. "Am I still coming over?"

"If you want to," you shrugged.

I hated that answer.

"Do you want me to?" I said, lighting a cigarette and passing the pack over to you.

"Of course I do," you smiled.

I loved that answer.

You gave me a quick kiss, then turned and walked down through the woods and back into the marquee. I took a long drag of the cigarette, flicked it on the ground, and watched until you reached the corner, then dug my hands in my pockets.

I went to my room, locked the door and lay down on the floor. On my back, the cool tiles counted themselves. I pulled down my clothes, kicked them across the floor to the door. The only light was a faint steam coming in under the door, a silver gleam. I looked into it and waited for time to pass. The familiar thought of you returned to me, just as a tide returns to its shore.

What do you want of him, I asked myself.

I told myself, *to walk inside him and never leave. For him to be the house of me.*

At around one o'clock in the morning, you returned to St. Catherine and invited me to your dorm. The back door was already open, so I slipped inside and knocked against your door.

I could hear the keys jangling through the frame as you opened the door and locked it behind me. Outside, we could hear the exhilarated screams of other students; rummaging through other staircases, sneaking out of campus, partying in nearby rooms. "I'll go get some alcohol from my neighbour," you said.

"Sure," I said, kicking off my shoes and jacket.

I sat on the bed until you returned with a large bottle of Vodka and two shot glasses. "For my darling," you said with a smile, handing over the bottle. I got some ice and poured two shot glasses full; they clicked across the ghastly wilderness of white linoleum. You sighed and reached into your breast pocket for a cigarette, blowing a ring into the yellowy circle of light beneath the lamp, half into the surrounding dark. I took the pack and lit one for myself. "This tastes terrible," you said, taking another sip of the vodka.

"No yeah," I said, disgusted. "I can't drink this."

"Thank god," you sighed. "Because I can't either."

You placed the cups back on the desk and my hand instinctively wrapped around your waist from behind. The coloured lights spun out in all directions. Flecks of light swam in my eyes. I thought of atoms, molecules, things so small you couldn't even see them.

Something felt different that night compared to all the rest; the hot air brought us closer, the night loomed over us. I suppose that everything was so much more beautiful because we knew that we were doomed by the morning light. When we had sex, something in the air had shifted; like I was sending something of myself through you, until it came out in a soft breath, where I caught it back into myself in a kiss and sent it through you again. I wanted to melt inside those fragments of time.

That night, our very last, will always be a cherished memory to me.

Hours passed and we continued to move through every inch of each other until our hot breaths collected against the walls; sweat bead down my neck as you traced my curves with soft kisses. The sun glowed inside your chest, the moon echoed from your eyes. Through the windows, the moonlight lit only the lower half of you. Your shadow head said all of this. The desk lamp was pale orange, like a firefly on its last burn.

When we finished, I got up and looked through the window to see that the field had sprouted sunflowers on the cabin side; already they dwarfed me. Their golden heads towered on slender green stalks rising as high as ten feet. I'd been wondering why I had you in my life, why we had found each other here, and then suddenly I knew. I looked back at the image of you burning in the warm lamp's light. You smelt of carnations and, very faintly, cigarette smoke. Like a corsage someone left in a bar.

I am in love with you, I realised then. *That's what this is.*

I showered in the blue light of the night around me, before joining you under the covers again. Your arms wrapped around me tight, the moonlight moving silently around us. "Hey," I said, stroking a hand across your cheek gently. "Do you remember the letters I told you about?"

You gleamed up at me. *Heart eyes.* "Of course I do."

I smiled back. "Well, you know I've never shared them before but...I wanted to know if maybe you wanted to hear the beginning of your letter."

"You wrote me a letter?"

"I mean, I care about you...so yeah. I did, but it's not finished yet."

"I'd love to hear it," you smiled. I pulled out my notebook from my bag.

Under the covers, our legs intertwined, and one of my hands roamed around in your hair while the other flicked meticulously through the pages. "Here it is," I said. "If it's not good, don't tell me or I'll cry."

You laughed softly and I began to read:

"Dear Theo...

I can find words for everything, in melodies, in the rise and break of summer sunsets. I will find the words for what you say, and the words you do not, and I will make poetry for them. You are the first thing in a long time that has made me want to write poetry again. Endless pages of writing, all for you, all about you. But I cannot find enough words to fully, ever describe you. We'll dream of a longer summer, but this is the one we have. This is the time we have.

I am overflowing with words I do not have. I fear that this longing will last forever. I pretend it doesn't bother me, but it does. It does. Where am I to store all of this heartache? I look for you at the edge of every garden. I look for you every time I come home. I'm looking for you at the end of my story. I'm looking for you and I think you know.

Soon, I won't be able to look into your eyes anymore, but I know they will be all I think about. I memorised your face as

*though it were my mirror or every night prayer. I will leave
behind my name before I forget you; for you are the only one who
has ever been able to find me.*

*I wonder whether you will hear the words I shall speak each
deep, early morning. When I long for your presence. Still, I ache
for you when I have it all. Nothing ever feels enough until I'm
with you. You're enough, enough for me at least. I forgot what
living without loving you feels like. I don't want to remember. You
were worth knowing, worth finding, worth loving. worth every
single second of it. But now I have to remember you for longer
than I have known you. I don't want to be the one that mourns
everything when everyone has clearly forgotten. It's mortifying to
be the only one who remembers.*

*On our last night, I want to hold you in a way you'd
remember me for. You have no idea what a charming memory you
will be for me. It never took much to love you, but it's going to take
everything I have to leave you. You have a place in my heart that
no one else could ever have. If I could have done it all again, I
would have loved you better. But I could not have loved you more.
If I could ask only one thing of you, it is this: please don't let me
remember you. Please, do not become a memory to me. If I could
ask only that of you...*
I swear, it would be enough..."

A long-lasting silence lived through the air. I put down the
notebook and looked down into my lap. "I'm sorry if it was
underwhelming for you," I chuckled.

You looked up at me, and I noticed a faint glimmer in your
eyes, a furrow in your brows. "You wrote that? For me?" you
asked.

I nodded.

You gave me a disheartened smile and I could tell then that
you wanted to say more, but simply didn't want it clinging to

the air. But in your eyes, a pearly wash shone in the light. I had looked at you, then, and had felt that same sensation I sometimes did when I thought, really thought of you and what your life had been: a sadness, one that seemed to encompass all the poor striving people, the billions I didn't know, all living their lives, a sadness that mingled with wonder and awe at how hard humans everywhere tried to live, even when their days were so very difficult, even when their circumstances were so wretched. *Life is so sad*, I would think in those moments. It's so sad, and yet we all do it. We all cling to it; we all search for something to give us solace.

But I didn't say this, of course, just sat up and held your face and kissed you and then fell back against the pillows. Wordlessly, we absorbed the warmth of one another and just as dawn broke, fell asleep in each other's arms; as if it was the most natural thing in the world, we stayed together, not leaving each other's side. Nothing was spoken, it was just mutually understood.

In the early morning hours, I awoke from a heavy, dreamless sleep to find myself lying in your arms, in your bed, and the sun faintly streaming through the back window at the rear. You were still asleep in a gold chimney of light and for a while, I lay listening to the sounds of your breathing, watching the soft crease of a smile across your face. Behind the curtains, I could see the silhouettes of the trees. A soft light started to illuminate the fragile webs in the corners of the room and the edge of your bed. The portrait of the morning I saw through the window beckoned. I cradled it in my arms and prayed it would wash away.

At that exact moment, I knew it was too late for us.

That we had run out of time.

CHAPTER FOURTEEN
THE FOURTEENTH OF JULY

THE HEART HAS ITS OWN MEMORY AND I HAVE FORGOTTEN nothing. I think about our goodbyes all of the time. The warmness of air, the trees and grass around us. Wreathed in a necklace of polar-white glow, the sun crept up quietly behind, glowing in her full majesty, throwing down water shards of sunlight in vain. With the reprise of autumn on St. Catherine's doorstep, sweet songs lulled into a sombre reprise, looping my aching body like a curse.

I opened one eye, unsure if I should move but reluctant to risk waking you. You'd rolled toward me sometime in the night, and your head was tucked against my shoulder, and your breath raced down my arm every time you exhaled. The strange sudden thought that I didn't want to move struck me, with the surprising lucidity of a sunbeam slanting right into my eyes. Your warm drowsy weight in the bed beside me felt natural, comfortable, *comme il faut*. I lay impossibly still, wondered what I was waiting for, and slowly fell asleep again.

I didn't sleep long or deeply enough to dream. What seemed like seconds later I was awake, dimly conscious of your hushed breaths nearby. My fingers gently traced the contours of your face, purring like a cat in the warm sun. When you finally woke, you looked up at me with a smile. "Good morning, sleepy," I smiled.

You mumbled something, pressing your face into the soft cotton sheets and wrapped your arms around my waist again. "I'll see you at breakfast?" I asked. "I still need to pack."

You threw a pillow at me and smiled. "Shut up and come back into the covers."

We fell asleep again for another few, sacred minutes, until your alarm sang through the room, waking us both. We entered a sort of domestic morning; brushing our teeth together, showering, getting dressed, it was so simple but made me feel so whole. *What if we could spend our entire lives like this?* I wondered. I wouldn't have minded. I would have given up everything for that dream.

"You're all packed up?" I asked, sitting on the bed and watching you affectionately.

"I think so," you said, propping the suitcase upright. You smiled at me and walked over to where I was sitting, wrapping your arms around the crown of my neck.

"I'll see you at breakfast?" I asked.

You nodded silently before unlocking your door. We smiled at each other, somewhat sadly, and without a word, leaned in for a kiss. On the way back to my room, I watched as the dusk dissolved the memories of the night. I could see a soft, declarative wind that was warm, like a lark singing sweet hymns of autumn approaching in the distance. I packed my bags and met with Adeline, Asli and Serena at breakfast. I scanned around the dining hall until I saw you, we locked eyes and frowned at each other. The morning had started to feel overcast and grey with emotions.

We left the cafeteria together and by eight-thirty, had handed in our keys at the office, and stored away our belongings in an empty classroom. Around us, everyone around me blurred into colours, into the light drizzle of rain breaking through the sky. "One more smoke break?" I asked, and you smiled.

The river led out of the woods. It grew wider, the current faster; the water had risen after the last few days of rain. The bank was muddy and soft; the water had the milky freshwater taste of having come through granite, which is why it was so clear there. The sun above turned flat and silver like a dropped dime.

There was a quiet in which we pretended not to know what all of this meant.

I took you in my arms and let our cigarette smoke curl around us in the wind. "You know," you said suddenly. "I was on the phone with my mother last night. Before you came."

"What'd you talk about?" I asked curiously.

"I told her that I loved you," you said, watching the river current.

I just looked at you, not understanding at all. There was nothing in our relationship that had prepared me for such a revelation. All of the signs that you had obliquely imparted I had interpreted as unrequited love. But after all, you had *loved* me?

I looked at the field glistened in the glossy rain, and in fact, did appear three inches taller. Things grow so fast, it is amazing we don't lie awake at night, listening to it all happen.

"I..." I started to speak, but a boil burned against my chest. "I've loved you this whole time. Why didn't you tell me sooner?"

"I only realised it a few days ago. I didn't want things to change between us," you sighed.

I paused for a moment, awfully perplexed, and took a drag from my cigarette. I didn't know quite what to say. "What now?" I asked.

"I mean, we could try long distance? But were both terrible callers–"

"We both know what's for the better," I said, ingenuously. I obviously didn't want any of this to end; if I could've held onto it forever, for eternity, I would have. Though, I wasn't sure if you felt the same.

"We should try, Alaska," you said.

"Okay," I said finally and against my better judgement. "We can try, but…"

"But what?" you asked, disheartened.

I sighed and watched the smoke of my cigarette mesh with the wind. "I really do love you, Theo. I'm going to be really hurt if you just disappear on me one day," I said. "Unless you tell me now, if it's going to be too much, just tell me, don't lie to me."

"I promise you," you said firmly. "I'm not going anywhere."

Though we didn't speak more about it, I slowly prepared myself for the changes that would surely come after morning. I think it was hard for us to bring everything out into the open. Paradoxically, you seemed to want to draw me closer. Perhaps it was the closeness before the end, like a gentleman buying his mistress jewels before telling her it's over.

We walked to the entrance, you pulled me close to you. I could see a sadness in your eyes and I knew without a doubt you could see in my expression how much I didn't want to say goodbye. You trailed the back of your fingers down my cheek and I shivered.

When your transfer pulled into the college, long slants of rain illuminated the headlights and the tires threw up low fans of water. We carried your bags down to the sidewalk and stood next to the car, not knowing what to say. Your hand cradled around the back of my head. I tried to remember how it felt there. I tried to memorise how you smelt just like the carnations of smoke from the park. I tried to memorise how my mouth rested right at the height of your neck, as though your shoulders were made for me to rest my head on them.

I leaned into you and kissed your neck. A soft kiss and nothing more. You lifted my head off your shoulder, tilting my face up to yours, scrolling over my features.

"I thought I was tougher than a word," you whispered.

I wanted to say: *Then never say it.* But your mouth crashed into mine. You were saying goodbye with the way your lips moved over mine, the way your hands caressed my cheeks, the way your mouth moved to my forehead and pressed one single, gentle kiss right in the centre of it. You kissed me like you wanted the kiss to be remembered. For which one of us, I did not know, but I allowed you to take as much as you could from that kiss and I gave you as much as I had.

And it all was perfect, until you released me. You practically pushed away from me, as if putting distance between us would make it any easier. You walked backwards until you were at the edge of the curb, and all my words were lodged in my throat. I pressed my lips together and tried not to let them loose. We stared at each other for several seconds, the pain in our goodbye was evident in the air between us.

You gave me a sad, lonely smile before getting into the backseat and closed the door. I couldn't make out your face through the tinted windows. I stood watching you, and the ghost of my own distorted reflection receded in the curve of dark glass until the cab turned a corner.

Just like that, you were gone.

I stood in that deserted street until I could no longer hear the sound of the motor, only the hiss of the powdery rain that the wind kicked up in little eddies on the ground. I wanted to shout something after the taxi, but it had already vanished. I knew that this moment was very important for me, but at the same time, it felt as if it wasn't yet ripe, like a photo still lying in a developing bath. I stood on the sidewalk, a magnetism planting my feet into the cobblestone, feeling the memories of our world cave in on me. Eventually, the image of the taxi faded away and I pulled myself off the curb.

I don't know what to say to you except that it tore the heart out of my body to say goodbye to you that morning in late July. From then on, my heart began to grieve, to ache, like an open wound.

Months later, I became obsessed in spells with trying to identify the exact moment in which things had started to go wrong, as if I could freeze it, preserve it again, hold it up and teach it before a class: this is when it happened. This is where it started. I'd think: Was it when I flew to Marseille? Was it when I called you with that ultimatum? And, more impossibly, was it when you did whatever you did to me that made me send you that letter?

But really, I would know: it was when you walked into the blue cab that afternoon. It was when you allowed yourself to be escorted in, when you gave up everything and flew back to Italy.

That had been the moment.

And after that, it had never been right again.

AFTER

"...for you love me and you suffer."

Italo Calvino, *Il Barone Rampante*

CHAPTER FIFTEEN

TIL' FOREVER FALLS APART

EARLY DAWN CAST YOUR SMILE UPON THE LAND, BUT MY curtains were closed. Oxford was still warm, disrupting my plans; I could only ever leave my sister's home when it was cold.

She got up first and bounced up to open the blinds. In her early twenties, she had thick blonde hair and was friendly and polite to everyone she met. I would often see neighbours and colleagues standing around her when she spoke, listening spellbound. The secret was in her voice; soft, not too deep, not too high, with the merest hint of an accent, it encircled her listeners like an invisible lasso and drew them in. She was very highly thought of in her job as a chartered student veterinary nurse, the only thing that mattered to her was always her animals. When she got home from work in the evenings, she would cook for us both; teriyaki udon, calabrese chilli sauce with tagliatelle pasta; she always made time for me but was utterly devoted to her cooking, trying new and explorative recipes each night, which after Oxford, felt as though I was eating at a five-star restaurant for a week; her girlish smile always gave her an air of optimism.

After St. Catherine's College, I resumed the life of a citizen. It took me far from the world I had known, yet you were ever in my consciousness; the blue star in the constellation of my personal cosmology. It seemed, for the most part, that I submitted my grief towards you into my dealing with the rest of the world. I was insulting, rude, quick to start a quarrel with my sister every time she came home from work. As troubling as this was, these eruptions of hysteria were infrequent. But they made it plain how upset I was, and how disagreeable I might make myself if provoked. We hadn't spoken since Saturday morning and I began to miss you a lot more than I thought I would. Things kept happening and I always found myself wishing I could tell you about them.

My sister and I spent two days in Oxford before taking the bus to St Albans for the weekend. The place always reminded me of a grouchy, but essentially loveable old man who dozed all day. As in many parts of St Albans, the houses were made of brick; they had plain shutters and reddish, weathered roof tiles bathed in the soft light of the setting sun.

Bare cheek on the cold window. The roar and rush of the bus was so loud I thought it would swallow me up. It was like all the times I'd ever been sick, all drunken throw-ups I'd ever had in the bathrooms of stations and bars. Same old bird's eye view: those odd knobs at the base of the bus, sweating porcelain, the hum of pipes, that long burble of noise spiralling down.

Immediately, I thought of you and I started to cry. The tears mingled easily with the cold air, in the luminous, dripping crimson of my cupped fingers, and at first I wasn't aware that I was crying at all. The sobs were regular and emotionless, as mechanical as the dry heaves which had stopped only a moment before; there was no reason for them, they had nothing to do with me. I brought my head up and looked at my reflection in the window with a kind of detached interest. *What does this mean?* I thought. I looked sick. I felt sick. Nobody else was falling apart; yet here I was, shaking all over and seeing bats like Ray Milland in *The Lost Weekend*. I saw the shape of an asylum seeker; obsessively searching for greener grass on sunny days. I dreamt of refuge to that rainy place, my heart yearned for your familiar fallen in; but the only place I found solace was already gone, consumed by itself.

The present quickly began to feel like the past, time eating away. It was a summer day, and I wanted to be wanted again; more than anything else in the world. It made me think back to how, in the *Second Sex*, Simone de Beauvoir described the way women lost their identities when they fell in love with men:

> 'The centre of the world is no longer where she is but where her beloved is; all roads leave from and lead to his house. She uses his words and repeats his gestures, adopts his manias and tics. "I am Heathcliff," says Catherine in *Wuthering Heights*; this is the cry of all women in love; she is another incarnation of the beloved, his reflection, his double: she is he. She lets her own world flounder in contingence. She lives in his universe.'

I suppose I had to get used to living a life without you; I had to forget what it felt like when all I wanted to do was remember.

We reached St Albans towards evening. The gravel crunched beneath the wheels as our bus came to a halt in front of the station. There was something eerie about the building; its facade was overgrown with moss, its roof dilapidated. It smelt of the past. The streets were dark; bombed-out, abandoned. I had not been out of the house since the week before in Oxford, except to meet with Adeline a couple of times. I spent the days writing; finding comfort in my words when no one else seemed to offer me any, including you. The whole sky was mine to write on, blown open to a blank page. I wrote so I could breathe a little easier; for a moment, the noise of space blotted around me, and I could only look and look at my writing: even in my distress, I had the presence of mind to understand that I was responding less to the words themselves than to the memories and sensations they provoked, and this my sense of violation was a personal reflection, specific only to myself.

We took a taxi down the main street; the trees in the drive were in full leaf and the yard was overgrown and dark. Bees droned in the lilacs. My aunt, mowing the lawn, nodded and raised a hand at us. I had a lot of thinking to do about directions I should be taking. I wondered if I was doing the right thing. Was it all frivolity? It was the nagging sense of guilt I experienced that made it truly hard to collect my thoughts and manifestations.

Sat around the table, my uncle read us the newspaper, my aunt served us baked sockeye salmon. As always there was a sense of camaraderie at the table. Their mainecoon cat slunk over and began to twine round my ankles. Their house was shadow and cool. There were sheets on some of the furniture and dust balls on the hardwood floor. After dinner, the cat followed me into the kitchen, clawing at my legs while I made myself something else to eat. I carried a sandwich into my room, and shut the door.

The following morning, I felt for the first time physical pain without being hurt again. Those two weeks together quickly began to feel like an illusionary dream, the only thing bringing me back to them was the sound of your voice. Despite this, we hadn't talked since Saturday morning, and my longing for you began to feel somewhat all-consuming; every time I saw the date change I felt a sense of shame.

We took the bus to Milton Keynes Rink in the afternoon. I hadn't been skating regularly since the summer had started, yet my defining sense of self was still entwined within the laces of my skates. When we arrived, we paid for a public session and headed into the arena; couples clung desperately to the boards, coaches taught their students, laughter reflected off the ice like some cruel juxtaposition. As I touched down upon the ice, I felt a wholeness that had been so-long absent. Everything came back to me swiftly, with a harmony only silence could match. I skated into the heart of the rink, every thought transformed into feeling. The friction of my skates accelerated and already premature weakening of the ice's surface, precarious veined beneath the transparent layer. Free of all expectation or desire, I spun, and was at once the loom, the thread, the strand of gold. I bowed my head and lifted an arm toward the sky, surrendering, drawn by the gloved hand of my own conscience.

The two hours passed quickly, and soon, my feet were sore and swollen; covered in red blemishes and blood stained on my boot's tongue. We ate dinner at Zizzi's. It was a miserable dinner for me. I remember hardly anything about it except that it was a very bright day, and we sat at a table too close to the windows and the sunlight glare in my eyes only increased my confusion and discomfort. And the whole time I only thought about finishing the letter, the letter, the letter...

At that point in time, my writing appeared disjointed, incoherent, and to my astonished eyes — unquestionably genuine. I always skimmed it briefly and remembered so little about what I had written only nights prior. It was filled with profanities of various sorts which made it difficult, even in the most desperate of circumstances, to imagine myself sending the rest of it to you.

Nevertheless, I continued working on it, every minute and hour of the day, including the bus ride home. The rain beat tirelessly against the windows. I invited longing back into my life. I hadn't seen or spoken with you for some time. I sat to ready myself, contemplating the call I was about to make, when the phone rang. "Hey," you said when I picked up the line. You sounded weak, but your voice strengthened as you heard mine.

"Hey," I said, and held myself still. "How are you?"

"Things are going well," you said. "But it's so hot here in Italy'"

"It's better than rainy Oxford at least," I chuckled.

"That's for sure..." you paused for a moment and then sighed. "I miss you."

"I miss you too," I smiled. "Too much actually."

You laughed and the mere sound made my heart flutter. I wished to reach through the phone and hold you again; to feel the warmth of your skin, not only your voice. As more time had passed, we were as we had always been, breathlessly finishing one another's sentences. "So, what's going on in your life?' you asked.

I looked at the rain coating the bus windows. This time there were no tears, only flawless comfort. "Well, I'm heading back to Oxford for a few more days. I might even see Adeline, I'm not sure yet," I said. "Then I'm flying to Marseille for the rest of summer."

"Marseille? I should come down and visit you," you chuckled.

"That would be the dream, wouldn't it?" I smiled.

"You know...I talked to my mother about you last night again."

I raised a curious eyebrow. "What did you say?"

"That I found my future wife."

I rolled out of bed and noticed it was late, and I had planned to meet Adeline in the evening. I raced through my morning ritual, going around the corner to the *Pret A-Manger*, grabbing an iced coffee, lemon roll and packaged mangoes. I took the bus to the city centre and spent all afternoon in the Bodleian library, reading the Jacobean dramatists. Wester and Middleton, Tourneur and Ford. It was an obscure specialisation, but the candlelit and treacherous universe in which they moved — of sin unpunished, of innocence destroyed — was one I found appealing. Even the titles of their plays were strangely seductive, trapdoors to something beautiful and wicked that trickled beneath the surface of mortality: *The Malcontent. The White Devil. The Broken Heart.* I poured over them, made notes in the margins. The Jacobeans had a sure grasp of catastrophe. They understood not only evil, it seemed, but the extravagance of tricks which evil presents itself as good. I felt they cut right to the heart of the matter, to the essential rottenness of the world.

I had always loved Christopher Marlowe, and I found myself thinking about him, too. He was a scholar, the friend of Raleigh and of Nashe, the most brilliant and educated of the Cambridge wits. He moved in the most exalted literary and political circles; of all his fellow poets, the only one to whom Shakespeare ever directly alluded was he; and yet he was also a forger, a murderer, a man of the most dissolute companions and habits, who 'died swearing' in a tavern at the age of twenty-nine. His companions on that day were a spy, a pickpocket, and a 'bawdy serving-man.' One of them stabbed Marlow, fatally, just above the eye: *'of which wound the aforesaid Christ. Marlowe died instantly.'*

I often thought of these lines from his, from *Doctor Faustus*:

I think my master shortly means to die
For he hath given me all his goods...

And of this one, spoke as an aide on the day that Faustus in his black robes went to the emperor's court:

I'l faith, he looks much like a conjurer.

For a long time after, I walked around Oxford aimlessly — past ruined parks, blasted statutory, vacant lots overgrown with weeds and collapsed apartment houses with rusted girders poking out of their sides like ribs. But here and there, intercepted among the desolate shells of the heavy old public buildings, I began to see new buildings, too, which were connected by futuristic walkways lit from beneath. Long, cool perspectives of modern architecture, rising phosphorescent and eerie from the rubble.

I went inside one of these new buildings. It was like a laboratory, maybe, or a museum. My footsteps echoed on the tile floors. There was a cluster of men, all smoking pipes, gathered around an exhibit in a glass case that gleamed in the dim light and lit their faces ghoulishly from below. I drew nearer. In the case was a machine revolving slowly on a turntable, a machine with metal parts that slid in and out and collapsed in upon themselves to form new images. An Inca temple...click click click...the pyramids...the parthenon.

When night fell over the city, the rain had stopped but the sky was overcast and the wind was blowing hard. Someone was ringing the church bell and not doing a very good job of it; it clanged unevenly to and fro like a bell at a seance. I sat outside, on a wooden bench beneath a yellow light bulb, waiting for Adeline to finish her second Great Debate at Balliol and come out of the theatre.

People strolled to their cars, dresses billowing, holding hats to head. And when I finally saw Adeline standing in the dreary Oxford light, I thought that I was dreaming. Without realising it, I had come to think of her, too, as a ghost: but to see her, wan but still beautiful, in the flesh, my heart burst, I thought I would die, right there. I was terribly glad to see her and she, I think, to see me. I stood up and held out my arms. "Adeline," I said, pulling her into a deep embrace. "I missed you so much."

We loitered all evening in a dark little bar on High street, smoking cigarettes and drinking Irish whiskey. "How have things with Theo been? Are you guys still talking?"

I shrugged and drank off the rest of my glass. It was clear the subject made me uncomfortable. "It's complicated," I said.

"It shouldn't be."

"That's all right."

Adeline was consumed with curiosity, she was staring down into her drink. "Oh," she said, "you were very kind to him."

In the rainy twilight, we walked back to Balliol through the city centre. The lamps were lit. "Do you miss him?"

"Of course I do."

What was more, ever since arriving in Oxford, I'd kept catching glimpses of people I thought were you: dark figures dashing by in taxicabs, disappearing into office buildings. I wanted to tell Adeline; I needed to tell somebody and it was always fun to tell her a story. She leaned forward and hung on every word, reacting at appropriate intervals with astonishment, sympathy, dismay. And so, I told her everything; when I was finished she bombarded me with questions I pleasantly answered. We were crossing a bridge. Yellow streamers of lamplight shimmered bright in the inky water. Adeline closed her eyes, dark-lidded, dark shadows beneath them. Her gaze was steady and impassive in the dim light. Above her ear, beneath the wire stem of overhead lights. We spent the rest of the evening talking about Balliol, the people, her friends, and her business classes. We had a tearful goodbye, and promised to keep in touch.

She turned from me and walked inside Balliol. I watched her back receding down the long, gleaming hall. A lone traffic light rocked on a wire over the empty intersection. It wasn't until I'd dropped Adeline off and was being driven, at a rapid clip on the bus, towards the dark centre of town, that I realised how poorly I had been apprised of the situation I was heading into.

It has always been hard for me to talk about you without romanticising the memories we shared. In many ways, I loved the memories more, most of all; and it is with you that I am most tempted to embroider, to flatter, to basically reinvent. I think that is because you yourself were constantly in the process of reinventing the people and events around you, conferring kindness, or wisdom, or bravery, or charm, on actions which contained nothing of the sort. It was one of the reasons I loved you: for the flattering light in which you saw me, for the person I was when I was with you, for what it was you allowed me to be.

Now, of course, it would be easy for me to veer the opposite extreme. I could say that the secret of your charm was that you latched onto young people who wanted to feel better than everybody else; that you had a strange gift for twisting feelings of inferiority into superiority and arrogance. I could also say that you did this not through altruistic motives but selfish ones, in order to fulfil some egotistic impulse of your own. And I could elaborate on this at some length and with, I believe, a fair degree of accuracy. But still that would not explain the fundamental magic of your personality or why — even in the light of subsequent events — I still have an overwhelming wish to see you the way that I first saw him: as the wide of young boy who appeared to me out of nowhere on a desolate strip of road, with a bewitching offer to make all my dreams come true.

But even in fairy tales, these kindly gentlemen with their fascinating offers are not always what they seem to be. That should not be a particularly difficult truth for me to accept at this point but for some reason it is.

It's funny. In retelling these events, I have fought against the tendency to sentimentalise you, to make you seem very saintly — basically to falsify you — in order to make my veneration of you seem more explicable; to make something more, in short, that my own fatal tendency to try make interesting people good. And I know I told you earlier that you were perfect but you weren't perfect, far from it; you could be silly and vain and remote and often cruel and I still loved you, in spite of, because.

The following morning, Oxford, suddenly, was green and bright as Heaven again. Most flowers had been killed by the rain except the late bloomers, honeysuckle and lilac and so forth, but the trees had come back bushier than ever, it seemed, deep and dark, foliage so dense that the way that ran through the woods was suddenly very narrow, green pushing in on both sides and exacerbating the sunlight on the dank, cobblestone path. I arrived at Waterstones a little early to spend the day writing and reading. The mirror over the fireplace was the centre of attention, a cloudy old mirror in a rosewood frame; nothing remarkable, but it was the first thing one saw when one stepped inside and now even more conspicuous because it was cracked — a dramatic splatter that radiated from the centre like a spider's web.

I browsed through the bookshelves, and settled on reading *Before The Coffee Gets Cold*, by Toshikazu Kawaguchi;

immersing myself into the world of time travel, mystical chairs and regret. With a coffee in front of me, I closed my eyes, and inhaled deeply. It was my moment of happiness. I always wanted to do things without having to worry about what others thought.

I simply lived for my freedom.

> *'No matter what difficulties people face, they will always have the strength to overcome them. It just takes heart. And if the chair can change someone's heart, it clearly has its purpose.'*

I put the book back on the shelf and began to write.

Why couldn't I write something that would awake the dead? That pursuit is what burned most deeply.

Poeta nasciter, non fit. The poet is born, not made.

I suppose I was getting over the physical loss of you, but never the desire to produce a string of words more precious than the emeralds of Cortes. Yet, I lived with the memories of your dark hair, a book of Calvino. And in the folds of faded violet tissue a necklace, two violet plaques etched in Italian, strung with black and silver threads, given to me by the boy who loved Nietzsche. I remember reading this: the artist seeks contact with their intuitive sense of the gods, but in order to create their work, they cannot stay in this seductive and incorporeal realm. They must return to the material world in order to do their work. It's the writer's responsibility to balance mystical communication and the labour of creation.

I left Mephistopheles, the angels, and the remnants of their handmade world, saying, *I choose Earth.*

You called later that day and we talked about everything and nothing at the same time. I remember you laughed and said something I didn't quite catch, some Horatian-sounding tag about being too good for sorrow. I was glad to hear that you seemed quite your bright, serene old self. I was still inexplicably fond of you, but strong emotion was distasteful to me, and a display of feeling normal by modern standards would to me have seemed exhibitionist and slightly shocking. But, your cheery, socratic indifference to matters of life and our relationship probably kept you from feeling too sad about anything for a long time, including our forgone distance.

I spent the rest of the days in Oxford wondering how my love for you was intensified by your absence. I wanted to speak of something not dead or divine — unlike Christopher Marlowe — I wanted to speak to you, *all of the time*. I couldn't figure out how to express the inexpressible nature of my longing for you in a way that would hopefully have made your heart ache as mine did.

Suddenly, I had lost the words that were so dear to me.

CHAPTER SIXTEEN

SHADOWS IN THE SUN

WHEN I HAD FLOWN TO MEET MY FAMILY IN MARSEILLE FOR the rest of summer vacation, you were nearly, completely unresponsive. I began to question how I could stay loyal to someone who was almost never home. The truth was, I really cared for you, and believed our communication was strong enough to overcome your long absences. These extended periods on my own afforded me the time and freedom to pursue literary growth, but as time passed, it was revealed that the trust I believed we shared was repeatedly violated, endangering us both and compromising our connection. This gentle, intelligent, and seemingly modest boy I had met weeks prior, seemingly had a lifestyle in Italy that was inconsistent with what I believed was our quiet bond.

Ultimately this would destroy our relationship, alongside the respect I had for you, and the gratitude I felt for the good you had done as I stepped into uncharted territory.

Though I wasn't aware of this yet.

FROM YOUR FIRST BOYFRIEND, THEODORE.

That's what sat on the messy pages of *Il Barone Rampante* in front of me. I traced over the scrawl of ink with my forefinger and smiled to myself, before putting the book down and going outside. It was a beautiful night, full moon, the sand was silver and the beach houses threw square black shadows sharp as cutouts on the sand. Most of the windows were dark: everyone was asleep, late to bed.

The ocean waves flowed from high places to low places; by the nature of gravity. My emotions also seemed to act according to gravity. When in the presence of someone with whom I had a bond, and to whom I had entrusted my feelings, it was hard to lie and get away with it. The truth just wanted to come flowing out. This was especially the case when I was trying to hide my sadness or vulnerability. It is much easier to conceal sadness from a stranger, or from someone you don't trust. But I saw you as a confidante with whom I could share anything. The emotional gravity was strong. I mistakenly thought that you were able to accept anything — forgive anything — that I let anything flow out. A single kind word from you could cut the cords of tension that ran through me, yet since arriving in Marseille, I hadn't heard from you in a week. I had sent several text messages, none of which you replied to.

You could have called. It wouldn't have hurt any less, but maybe I wouldn't have had to spend those days waiting, wondering when I was going to hear from you again.

I was stuck between wanting to wait for you and wanting to forget you. I didn't know which one was better so somehow I was doing both at the same time. I felt myself to be inside an airtight and airless bubble, invisible to everyone. The colourful buildings that lined the streets were seemingly colourless, and faced the wrong way for light of any kind at any time. The weeks a long shadow I walked through.

I needed light to be seen.

I went to the town centre. It was eleven o'clock in the morning. I ordered two iced lemonades and drank them in quick succession. Then I ordered a third, having a hard time keeping my cigarette balanced between my fist and middle fingers. I passed a gaunt, stylish woman — a print dress, harlequin glasses, sharp nasty face like a poodle — carrying a stack of folded towels to the beach. I immersed myself for hours reading *Il Barone Rampante*; the waves bead against the shore, my cigarette hung from the corners of my mouth. The dualistic nature of Calvino's story engendered a new archetypal figure, that of the active nonconformist. The revolutionary dissenter who rejected the establishment struggle for the improvement of his fellowmen in apparent seclusion.

A boy straddling two worlds.

A boy just like you.

The branches were waving high bridges over the earth. A light wind was blowing; the sun shone among the leaves, and to read, I had to shield my eyes with my hands:

> *Cosimo looked at the world from the tree: everything was different seen up there.*

That evening, I went to the hotel entertainment club with my sister. The band had a ragged edge, the music erratic, angular and emotional. I liked everything about them, their spasmodic movements, the drummer's jazz flourishes, their disjointed, orgasmic musical structures. I felt a kinship with the alien guitarist on the right. He was tall, with straw coloured hair, and his long graceful fingers were wrapped around the neck of his guitar as if to strangle it.

I continuously wrote to fill my nights with something more meaningful than you.

Unsurprisingly, it didn't work.

When my pleas finished and my handwriting became a passionate scrawl, I fell down on my bed and went to sleep. Eventually, I learned how to manage the memories. I couldn't stop them — after they had begun, they had never ended — but I had grown more adept at anticipating their arrival. I became able to diagnose it, that moment or day in which I could tell that something was going to visit me, and I would have to figure out how it wanted to be addressed: did it want confrontation, or soothing, or simply attention? I would determine what sort of hospitality it wanted, and then I would determine how to make it leave, to retreat back to that other place.

A small memory I could contain, but as the days went by and I waited for you, I recognised that the long eel of a memory, slippery and uncatchable, and it whipsawed its way through me — its tail slapped against my organs so that I felt the memory as something alive and wounding.

At eleven o'clock I woke, made some changes, and opened my laptop to type it up. I had missed breakfast and decided to head down to the beach instead. I pushed open the room door and stuck my head out for a moment, then went outside. The innkeeper glanced from his paper and gave me a supercilious up-and-down look. He was one of those prissy retirees one sees in New England, the sort who subscribe to antique magazines and carry those canvas tote bags they give as gift premiums on public TV.

I gave him my best smile.

After a few days in Marseille, I got used to my holistic, insouciant routine; waking up late, applying light-to-no makeup, drinking coffees and smoking cigarettes. I spent every afternoon at cafes writing; drinking more coffee and eating croissants, flirting with servers, more smoking and reading. Then, I spent every evening at the beach; attempting to tan, swimming in the cold sea, drinking more coffee and reading even more.

It was on one unidentifiable afternoon in the wake of the blistering sun that I decided to call you. You answered on the second ring. "Hey–" you said before I interrupted.

"If I never reach out to you first, am I ever going to hear from you again?" I asked.

You were silent for a moment. "It's been a week, Alaska?"

I sighed and looked to the sun for answers; she didn't give me any. "I thought maybe you'd write something at least."

"Alaska," you sighed. "Why are you in a mood with me? You trust me right?"

I could tell that was not what you were thinking, or I was thinking, or what you had been about to say, nor did I understand its relevance, but I answered anyway. It was an easy question. "Of course," I said.

There was a slight pause before you continued. "Then what's the problem?"

I was silent for a moment; my head hurt from the sun and I began to feel slightly nauseous. "There's no problem," I said. "I'm sorry. I just missed you, I suppose."

"If I don't call you for a week, it honestly doesn't feel like that big of a deal for me," you said. "I can't always check in on you...it would be better if we only did one call a day maximum, but that's also a lot for me."

"*Maximum?*" I asked, slightly hurt by this objection.

You sighed into the carrier. "It won't work for me

otherwise, and you..." you chuckled. "You're a lot of work. At least you're pretty."

I didn't say anything. Regardless of what you felt for me, there was denying that what I felt for you was love and trust of a very genuine sort. "Thank you," I mumbled. "So, how's everything else been?" To me, you seemed my only protector in the world. I figured it would be better to hear from you sometimes instead of never. When our call finally ended, I went back to reading, flicking mindlessly through the pages.

Well, that's the summer taken care of, I thought.

I opened the window in my hotel room that faced the back; I heard people talking, listening to the radio, moving around. I stepped up onto the balcony. Through the screen door window, I could see a dark, cool lobby and, behind the desk, a man of about sixty, his half-moon glasses pulled low on his nose, reading a copy of the Bennington banner. I lit a cigarette and smoked it in the cool, evening moon. I dressed standing at the window looking out at the dark beach, hands clasped behind my back. I rummaged through the bureau drawers — serene, preoccupied; lost, apparently, in my own abstract concerns. I headed down for dinner and continued writing through the evening afterwards.

In a mixture of coffee, cigarettes and sun — a diabolical trifecta at best — I ended up with stage one heatstroke after my first week in Marseille. For the amount of time I spent in the sun, I really couldn't have expected anything different.

In the morning, I vomited after going to the beach and spent the rest of the day cooped up in my hotel room, blinds shut, AC on and a glass of iced water on the bed stand. I took slow sips, feeling the coolness penetrate the linings of my stomach; and the immediate cold relief rushing from my lips to head. I took a nap and woke a few hours later to rays of sunlight peeking through the blinds; I had no plans for the rest of the day, except for: *ice, sleep, repeat.*

I decided to call you and you answered on the third dial. "Hey," you said.

"Hey," I responded. "I have heat stroke."

"Shit," you laughed kindly. "Have you thought about not having heat stroke?"

"You're a genius! Why didn't I think of that?" I groaned sarcastically. I heard you laugh even harder on the other line of the phone; suddenly my headache seemed to fade and the sunlight was unblinding and kind.

I smiled to myself and rolled around in the covers. "How are you?" I asked.

"Better than heatstroke," you chuckled.

"Charming, Theo," I said.

We talked a little while longer. I was jarred — a little spooked, as well — at our blatant reference to something referred to, by mutual agreement, almost exclusively with codes, catchwords, and a hundred different euphemisms — like nothing had changed at all.

"Seriously though, how have things been?" I asked.

"Good. I've been setting up my drum kit all day."

"You're playing drums again?" I asked, excitedly.

"Yeah–wait," you said, disorientated momentarily. "How did you know I played the drums?"

I paused for a moment, confused. "You told me? When I took you out–"

"I don't remember telling you that?"

A bright knife of terror plunged through my heart. I listened to you, dumbstruck. I acknowledged your world as you willingly entered mine. At times, however, I felt mystified and even upset by these sudden transformations. When we breached moments of intimacy like these, I felt shut out because it seemed more for you than me — it seemed you were starting to forget me already, filling your spoken prophecy, though, I didn't expect it to have occurred so early in our relationship. "I remember everything," I said, disheartened.

There was a brief pause until I heard your voice through the carrier again. "Good for you," you said, monotonously.

"Good for me?" I asked, hurt.

"Yeah," you said, without a care in the world. "Good for you."

There was another pause.

"You know, talking to you, Alaska," you said, "feels like talking to the ghost of somebody that doesn't exist anymore."

From that moment, I started to recognise the silence as signs. We had been through this before — at the beginning of St. Catherine — when you couldn't make up your mind about our relationship. I had a troubling feeling the same conflict was transpiring in you again, but miles away this time. I started to feel somewhat abandoned, the emotion was too familiar for me, and now, it was more-ever present than before.

To compound this — all these unpleasant recollections to the contrary — so much remained of the old Theo, the one I knew and loved. Sometimes when we'd call, I would have such a strong pang of affection mixed with regret. I forgave you, a hundred times over, and never on the basis of anything more than this: a look, a gesture, a certain tilt of your head. It seemed impossible then that I could ever be angry at you, no matter what you did or said.

Unfortunately, those were the moments you chose to attack. You would be amiable, charming, chatting in your old distracted manner, when in the same manner and without missing a beat, would lean back in your chair and come out with something so horrendous, so backhanded, so unanswerable, that I would vow not to forget it and never forgive you again. I broke that promise many times. I was about to say that it was a promise I finally had to keep, but that's not really true. Even today I cannot muster anything resembling anger for you.

In fact, I can't think of much I'd like better than for you to step into the room right now, dark hair and eyes, smiling with curiosity and saying: *'hey, Vampire, what are you up to?'*

After midnight it was still sultry and humid in the air. The men and women were still on the dance floor, and with the sun gone, it was finally okay for me to venture into the night. The night, as the saying goes, was a jewel in my crown. The pulse and pitch of the band, and my mild heat stroke symptoms, spiralled me into another dimension. Yet with all of that swirling around me, I could feel another presence as surely as the rabbit senses the hound. I suddenly understood the nature of the electric air. I missed you a lot more than I thought I would, but I grew tired of waiting. Nevertheless, there was a part of me that was desperate to know if my absence had done any damage to you. That there was a possibility that you too, experienced long restless nights due to the thought of me. That your heart was broken in the same places as mine. I wanted to know that I was not the only one hurting from our physical separation. But your lack of engagement often made me doubt this possibility.

In fact, you seemed just fine.

In spite of my newly found fulfilment in Oxford, in Marseille my texts continued to be left on read, no replies, my calls were unanswered; and in consequence, I grew impatient. This knowledge had a strange effect on me. Of course, I was attached, but I was also seventeen. I don't say this simply to excuse my desperation, but rather an explanation to coincide with the lack of love I had experienced prior to meeting you. I suppose I was scared that, you too, would leave me behind, abandon me all over again.

Looking back I realise that this wasn't such a far fetched judgement after all.

I walked to the dock, cigarette in hand, a cocktail in the other. Your presence was slowly replaced by heaps of sea foam and sand, building up against the coastline. Nothing moved but the shifting tides of salt in my body; the peculiar shapes of certain clouds took the build of your autonomy. Like smoke, their tassels towered in the wind, they spread their lungs beneath the earth as fish. I took a deep breath before exhaling slowly, the warm air permeated through me like a burning flame.

I sent you a photo of the dark moon shining across the waves: *this reminds me of you.*

Flicking out my cigarette, I stood from the sun-lounger and headed back inside to sleep. In the silence of the evening, I wondered thoroughly of the dead, of their storms, their far-off boys. I wondered how their days had ended because I didn't know how to get through mine.

I survived before you, why couldn't I survive after you?

I suppose I was always drawn to the wrong things: I liked to drink, I liked to smoke, I didn't have a god, respectable politics, ideas, ideals. I liked to write love letters and never send them. I was settled into nothingness; a kind of non-being, and I accepted it. I didn't want to be interesting anymore, it was too hard.

What I really wanted was only to be soft, a hazy space to live in alone.

July was ending as my misery grew. I smelt of vanilla and cigarettes, no one made me happy anymore. The taste of alcohol was just a bit too familiar. I didn't want to think of you or the wrong I'd done; but nostalgia haunted me from every corner and the regret bit at me from the moment I woke.

Selfishly, I missed you.

Saturday morning and all I could do was wonder if I ever crossed your mind. I wished I could write to you; someday finish my long and beautiful letter. But things aren't often beautiful when the only purpose for them is beauty. I draped the sheets on the lumpy mattress that seemed to contain the impression of a long, rugged body — I arranged my things around the bed stand; but I found that I could not write. Instead I pulled out my copy of *Il Barone Rampante*, and flipped to the eleventh chapter:

> 'He (Cosimo) understood many things in life. I would say that he always carried with him the troubled image of the cavalier avvocato, as a warning of what a man who separates his fate from that of others can become, and he was successful in that he never came to remember him.'

I read to page two-hundred and fifty and had another fifty to go. I hoped that I could call you when I finished it.

I went downstairs and the desk clerk greeted me with gentle humour. I passed a man sleeping in the lobby, an oversized coat and crushed felt hat, shaking off the residue of a hashish dream. I sat on the beige couch in the lobby, unable to bear the heat again; bees buzzed loudly in the honeysuckle. I had sent you a sultry and romantic message the night before and looking back at it in the daylight, no reply, I felt slightly sick in the stomach and quickly deleted it. I went back to my loft and washed in the shower to be freshly clean. I combed my hair away from my face and wrapped an old French robe made of tea-coloured linen around me.

For a while, I lay in bed waiting for the afternoon sun to

die-out. I could not stop wasting time. It was crazy; I wanted to do something with my life but instead I went to sleep, or sang in the shower or sat on the beach and stared at the ocean. I couldn't even tell you about what I saw, and even if I did, I wasn't sure if you were going to respond. The cicadas kept dying outside, and as I dreamed, my mouth grew thick and venomous with silence.

In the evening, I walked down to the beach again; I always knew that there would be something new and wonderful for me to look at, to touch, to catalogue; glass negatives, salt prints of forgotten poets, gravures of beach houses in the moon. I had brought my notebook to the beach and sprawled on the sand writing nothing but fragments, poems and the beginning of stories, imagined dialogues and unattainable love.

Aphrodite, I pleaded to the moon drenched night sky. *Tell me; if love is meant to heal, then why does it destroy those who choose it?*

From somewhere beyond the clouds, I heard the goddess laugh.

And I knew.

Even as our relationship waxed and waned, something about you implored me to return. I wanted things to transpire as normal, as if nothing had happened, yet you were not repentant. You weren't willing to go backwards, and still seemed to be harbouring an inner turmoil you refused to voice. Although, when we called, you were mostly good to me, I could tell still you were always somewhere else. I was accustomed to you being quiet, but not silently brooding. Something was bothering you, something that was not about being so far apart from one another. You never ceased to be affectionate to me, but you just seemed troubled. I felt powerless to penetrate the stoic darkness surrounding you then.

This was the time when your aesthetic became so

consuming that it was no longer our world, but yours. I believed in you, but you had transformed our relationship into a theatre of your own design. The velvet backdrop of our fable had been replaced with metallic shapes and black satin. The white mulberry trees draped in heavy nets. I paced while you slept, ricocheting like a dove skidding the lonely confines of a Joseph Cornell box. Our wordless night made me restless. Something in the change of weather marked a change in myself as well. For I felt a longing, a curiosity, and a vibrancy that seemed to stifle as I walked the streets of Marseille.

For someone that claimed to love me, you sure did ignore me a lot.

I went for a late night swim; the water was cold and desolate, the only light shimmering from a distant lighthouse; every now and then, it would cast pearly rays over the waves in ripples. The silence, for me, was the most comforting seal of satisfaction in a seemingly desolate world; falling on my ears with the pitiless clamour of a pneumatic drill. Cramped into the stretch of a soft monotony, the cold night disguised itself like a soft melody as I made my way under the waves. The thought was this: that all my life had been murk and depths, but I was not a part of that dark water. I was a creature within it.

It was the most peaceful I had felt in days.

Returning to my hotel room, I took a warm shower, did my makeup and changed into a white dress. My hair wasn't dry yet, but I let it fall over my shoulders and soak the hems of my cotton straps. Suddenly, my phone buzzed on the counter and I reached forward to pick it up.

That's not fair, Alaska. I've been trying to figure out the perfect reply.

I stared at your message, blankly, for a full five minutes before sending a response. I realised that I was meeting the person you actually were, underneath your performance of competence. I knew how this interaction was meant to go: you yelled at me. I yelled back at you. A détente, one that ultimately changed nothing, one that was a piece of pantomime, was reached: I would submit to something that wasn't the solution but that made you feel better. And then something worse would happen, and the pantomime would be revealed to be just that, and I would be coerced into accepting something I didn't want. I would be lectured and lectured and lectured and I would lie and lie and lie. The same cycle, the same circle, again and again, and again, a churn as predictable as the changing seasons. My life, a series of nothing but dreary patterns: love, pain, this, that.

Not this time, I thought.

You know what's not fair? That I have to wait days just to hear from you.

You saw the message and didn't respond. I called you immediately.

"Honestly, Theo," I said. "Tell me that I am as forgettable as you are making me feel. You tell me you care, but have done nothing yet to show me." I heard you laugh across the line. "This is just so funny to you, isn't it?" I exhaled in frustration.

You chuckled. "Alaska, I'm high right now."

"What?" I asked, aggravated at your unusual incompetency.

"I'm high right now, I can't talk."

"You always can't talk, being high won't make a difference," I scoffed. "I've been playing by your rules for a month already. I leave you alone, I stopped texting, I stopped calling. What more do I have to do to make you at least act like you care about me?"

I heard you sigh and ruffle a hand in your hand. "I'm trying to think of a good response, I don't even know what to say most of the time."

"Whatever you feel. I don't care if it's perfect," I sighed. "Whatever you say, it's enough for me."

"You don't have to delete the messages," you said after a pause.

"I don't have to wait for a response either."

A moment of silence passed. Your snide remarks upon the subject were so exhaustible and tireless, I think because in spite of my good-natured laughter, you must have been dimly aware that you were touching a nerve, that I was incredibly self-conscious about these virtually imperceptible differences of privacy, and rather less imperceptible differences of manner and your care. "Do you still love me?" I asked suddenly. I didn't even realise the severity of the words as they left my mouth, but once I had said them, there was no going back. Still, I felt acutely the hopelessness of ever trying to get to the bottom of anything with you but never failed to try.

You were like a propagandist, routinely withholding information, leaking it only when it served your purposes. "What?" you asked, caught off-guard.

"It's a yes or no question," I said. "Is it that hard to answer?"

Your words, usually so deliberate, were fought with contradiction; it went from neat and precise to a childlike scrawl. When you spoke next, your voice was crackly and distant. "I didn't think you'd corner me like this."

"This question shouldn't make you feel cornered, Theo."

"I don't think there's a way for me to answer this that'll satisfy us both," you said. "I don't not have feelings."

I breathed out wearily. "I'm not asking much of you," I mumbled.

"I don't know," you sighed. "I don't see why that even matters now."

"I'm afraid that it does matter. More than you might think," I said. "Just say whether you want me or you don't want me. That's all it takes and I'll leave you alone."

"Alaska," you said, in a tone which simultaneously

welcomed me and let me know that I had called at a bad time. You sounded really stoned, bug-eyes and sweating. This was probably more than you had bargained for: bright lights, too high, having to deal with a hostile Alaska. "It's not that easy. I don't think you get it."

"What's there not to get?" I asked. "You told me you loved me."

A hush fell over the line. "I never said that," you said finally.

I shook my head, not understanding at all. Every time I reached out, it felt like all I was doing was trying to haunt, to drag you back in time, to tell me again what happened. "Yes, *you did.*"

Another silence ensued. My peace amounted to nothing but the darkness of night blanketing my limbs through the holes of colourless sky. "We can discuss this later," you sighed. "When I'm not high, okay?"

"Just go," I whispered. *You always do.*

"I promise you I'll call later."

"Sure," I said.

But even then, I couldn't believe you.

My back was aching from the stiffness of rushing courses. When we called, the sound of your voice brought me a moment of peace; I could feel the emotions running over me like a strong tide and suddenly I missed you so much it felt gross, it felt wet, it felt nauseating. But once over, I woke up in a cold sweat to your voice in my head, on and on for hours.

My thoughts were holding you when my arms couldn't.

At the evening club, the moon sat proudly in the dark sky; sweaty groups of people danced in groups, bar men on roller skates rushed from drink to drink, the music was blasting so loudly I couldn't hear myself think. I sat in the corner, watching from a distance and sipping on some-sort of a tropical cocktail I had tried to order over the noise. Shadows shifted under the bright lights and the humid air was making me slightly nauseous. I felt awfully pathetic. *Why am I even waiting?* I thought to myself depressingly. As the music grew louder, and the air more sticky, I grabbed my belongings, stood up, and made my way back inside and to my hotel room, the darkness caving in around me.

I gave up all hope of hearing from you after five hours.

Lying in bed, I wished I could stop myself from thinking. But all sorts of things had begun to occur to me. For instance: why had you let me into your life, only two weeks (it seemed years, a lifetime.) Because it was obvious, now, that this decision to do so was a calculated move. You had appealed to my vanity, allowing me to think I had been loved. *Good for you,* you said. I could picture you leaning back in your chair; I could still remember the tone of your voice as you said it: *good for you, you're just as naive as I thought you were*; and I had congratulated myself on the glow of your praise; when in fact — I saw this now, I'd been too vain to see it in Oxford — you'd led me straight to it, coaxing and flattering all the way. Maybe you'd divined in me — correctly — this cowardice, this hideous pack instinct which would enable me to fall into step without question. And it wasn't just a question of having kept my mouth shut, I thought, staring with a sick feeling at my blurred reflection in the window pane.

Six hours had passed when you finally decided to call me again. My eyes were on the brink of closing, sand stuck to the roots of my hair. Sunburnt and tired, all I wanted to do was fall asleep and let the day fall into darkness.

I picked up the phone anyway. The name *Theo* glared back to me, bright, white, like a shining constellation connected by each letter; on the other hand, the little red heart looked distorted in the moonlight glow of my room. "Hey," you said. "I was quite high when you called."

"I could tell," I said, flatly. "Let's cut to the chase. Yes or no?"

I heard you sigh. "Alaska, it's complicated."

My head began to hurt as I rubbed my temples. "It's a yes or no."

"I hadn't really thought about it, to be honest."

"It's been six hours?"

"You counted?"

"No," I said. "*I waited.*"

Your tone was suddenly affronted and defensive. I heard you groan and exhale sharply. "Can you please stop victimising yourself?"

I stammered, feeling utterly confused. "Victimising myself?"

"Yeah," you said, hints of aggression flooring in your tone. "It's starting to piss me off, Alaska."

"Theo, don't switch topics–"

"I'm not, you always do this," you said.

I furrowed my brows and looked down at my phone. "Do what?" I asked in disbelief.

"Act like you're the only one who matters!" you affronted.

I stared blankly at the wall in front of me. The walls looked thinner, the room looked magically smaller. "You think I'm being selfish?" I asked, very upset now. "I've been sticking to *your* rules, what *you* want, *your* schedule...If anything, it seems as though you don't care to consider me unless it's convenient for *you.*"

"That's not true..." you whispered.

"Then why are you always acting like it?"

"I do not–"

"It doesn't matter now," I sighed. "Just answer the question."

Breathing in deeply, I could hear the strain of your exhale

through the carrier. "I can feel you settling in and I'm having doubts."

"Okay," I said, wearily. "I-I mean, you're allowed to have doubts."

"I feel like there's something missing here," you mumbled. "I can't place it, we just don't have this-"

"Love?" I asked.

Minutes passed and nothing was solved. "I don't know," you repeated.

"So, that's a no."

"It's an *I don't know*," you said. "Alaska, I just need to be a hundred percent certain with you, and I'm not right now-"

"Theo, stop doing this to me. Please don't do this to me," I pleaded. "We have a good thing, okay? I-I mean, what? What do you need from me? This...this is good. You just have to give it a chance, just try for me-"

"I can't," you whispered. "*I can't.*"

There were moments of spontaneous brightness when my mind appeared emancipated, but that was mere epiphany. "God, Theo," I wailed. "You always talk about how you want love and that you don't think you'll ever find it. You're always looking for love and I'm here! It's standing here right in front of you and you can't..." I inhaled shakily.

I heard you take a deep breath in. "We understand each other better than anyone else," you said finally. "You're the first person I feel like I've ever been level with in a relationship before, that means a lot to me. We're so similar it's crazy, we can talk for hours like we're running out of breath. I care about you, Alaska. I care about you a lot."

I paused for a moment, unsure of what to say. The shadowy room closed in and crawled towards me now. "But you don't love me?" I asked.

Silence.

"No...I don't love you, Alaska."

I hung up the phone.

Even in the agony of loss was passion, was love, and measured against death that sort of pain was a feast, also, and required a knife to carve it.

Or so it seemed.

CHAPTER SEVENTEEN

UNTRUST US

OMNI LUCI EST UMBEA. THERE IS A SHADOW TO EACH LIGHT.

Everything else returned: years and years of memories I had thought I had controlled and defanged, all crowded me once again, yelping and leaping before my face, unignorable in their sounds, indefatigable in their clamour for my attention.

I woke gasping for air: I woke with the names of people I had sworn I would never think of again on my tongue. I replayed the night with you again and again, obsessively, the memory slowing down so that the seconds could be analysed. I had visions of taking an ice pick and jamming it through my ear, into my brain, to stop the memories. I dreamed of slamming my head against the wall until it split and cracked and the memories tumbled out with a wet, bloody thunk. I had fantasies of emptying a container of gasoline over myself and striking a match, of my mind being consumed by flames.

That morning, the sun was too hot, the sea too cold, alcohol tasted like liquid soap and nothing felt right. The pain I felt was, if anything, was more intense, and weighed down on me even more greatly because of the physical distance.

Alienation and loneliness became a cable that stretched hundreds of miles long, pulled to the breaking point by a gigantic winch. And through that taunt line, day and night I waited for your call; a message, an apology, *anything* really.

After eating breakfast, I headed down to the beach again to read more chapters of *Il Barone Rampante* — I was hoping to finish the book by the end of the first week, but found myself only being able to handle a few chapters of Calvino's prose at a time — I decided to take my time with it, picking up on every small and large intricacy of the novel, annotating the sidelines. This was something I was terribly fond of; making my books my own. Back in New York City, my room was filled with books, scattered across the floor, resting on selves — I found room for them everywhere, really. Every single one of them was annotated, their pages lined with inky smudges and jarred handwriting; these books were mine, and I treasured them dearly regardless of enjoyment. I read a few chapters before lying down on the sun loungers for a few hours, letting the sun prickle and glaze over my skin.

I could not smile at it.

I tried to rest, but my mind felt needle-pricked. Now that you had named my loneliness, it hung from everything, up and down the sand paths, trying to shake it from me. I sifted and resifted my memories of you, all those hours we had leaned against each other. That old sickening feeling returned: that every moment of my life I had been a fool.

Providing this context, I would like to mention that I am not proud of the decision I made next, if anything I'm slightly embarrassed by it; but I was seventeen (an excuse I realise I must stop myself using in excess to explain some of the empty-headed decisions I made) and in love (this one, strangely, seemed more reasonable).

There are times when I do not choose healing. I'm

stubborn. I choose self-destruction instead hoping that I will learn what it's like to have wounds again. And learn and learn and learn again. It's so cruel to want to love so much but the feeling of chaos was often too intoxicating to ignore. If I were a different kind of person, I might say that this whole incident was a metaphor for life in general: things get broken, and sometimes they get repaired, and in most cases, you realise that no matter what gets damaged, life rearranges itself to compensate for your loss, sometimes wonderfully.

But I was not that kind of person at the time. These were days of self-fulfilment, where settling for something that was not quite what my first choice of a life seemed weak-willed and ignoble. Somewhere, surrendering to what seemed to be my fate had changed from being dignified to being a sign of my own cowardice. There were times when the pressure to achieve happiness felt almost oppressive, as if happiness were something that everyone should and could attain, and that any sort of compromise in its pursuits was somehow my fault.

Because of this, I gave you a second chance. I ran back into a burning house to save the things I loved.

"Hey," you said, answering the phone. "I didn't think I was going to hear from you again."

I chuckled quietly, mostly to myself. "I hope you're not disappointed."

"No, no," you said. "I was worried. I didn't want it to end like that."

"Then why didn't you call me?" I asked.

"I wanted to give you space, I figured you were probably hurt."

"I was," I said. Looking back, I wish I would've stopped there; I would have saved myself a lot of hurt in the long run. "But, I still really care about you," I sighed. "I don't really want to lose you."

"I don't want to lose you either.'"

We both paused to think for a moment.

"So, what now?" I asked. "Where does this take us?"

"We can take it slow, keep talking and see where it takes us again?"

"Yeah," I smiled. "I think that would be good."

"Nuovi Inizi?" you asked.

"Nuovi Inizi," I chuckled.

We talked for another hour and it was almost as if the call from last night never happened. It became easy for me to wipe away your words, just like the tide pulling in hard clumps of sand, swallowing it hole and disappearing into a deep blue.

I gave you more space, only checking in every few days, and for a while, it seemed to work. You were more responsive and kind, we quarrelled less and laughed more. I kept my love quiet but still felt it blossoming with every time I heard your voice. I remember falling asleep on the phone one night, and when I woke up several hours later, you were still there. We talked through the morning before hanging up. It was painful, but I was used to keeping things to myself; like an old habit, I retreated back into it silently and with unfortunate ease. Nevertheless, I continued to waste hours of my day away just waiting just to hear from you; obsessively checking my phone, silencing notifications only to turn them on again a few minutes later.

In retrospect, it seems our resolve was awfully simple and complex, but often, that's how things often are in life; not everything that happens can be profoundly comprehensive, it's only until later that the consequences build their way back through the sand.

As summer ended, I only thought of you; the air was warm but never as warm as your touch. I had two more days left in Marseille; I sat at coffee shops, gently sipping on steaming cups of coffee amid flurries of joyful tourist goers, as the smell of salt and warm sand wafted through the air. The sun billowed against the bright sky, I watched smoke twirl skyward like wisps of ancient myths; the ocean was a vivid blue, clear and cold. After finishing my drink, I removed my sandals and let the tides wash over me, consuming me in blue. Every now and then, I'd hold my breath under the water as the waves came in, letting salty crystals prickle against my skin; and when breaking the surface, the warm sun's glow would crystallise them. It was terribly peaceful, *what if life could always be this way?* Birds hummed in the distance, the sand was gold and scorching — everything was psychedelically tranquil again.

After swimming I headed to the sun-beds and finished reading the last pages of *Il Barone Rampante.* As soon as I closed the book, I called you. Strangely enough, it was you I was still angriest at, and you who had betrayed me, and you who was always at the subject of any of my outbursts–but, it was also you I was best able to tolerate on a daily basis, and you who I wanted to speak to in the same quantity. I was more or less irritated with everyone else. "I just finished reading *The Baron In The Trees,*" I said excitedly.

"How was it?" you asked. "I really love that you read it."

"I really enjoyed it," I said happily. "Calvino writes beautifully, like prose almost."

'That's why I love him,' you smiled.

"I get that now. You know, you remind me a lot of Cosimo–his love for philosophy, literature, adventure..."

"Have you read *The Nonexistent Knight?*" you asked.

"I haven't."

"Then you have your next read," I heard you say with a smile. We spent the next few minutes updating each other on our days, plans and other meaningless topics; somehow you always made them enjoyable to hear, no matter the topic, I was utterly devoted to every word. This does not mean that my admiration was felt mutually, if anything, it was the exact opposite. "If I'm being honest,' you interrupted, suddenly. "I'm not listening to anything you're saying."

I suddenly was so sharply nauseated that I had to stop what I was doing and wait for the moment to pass. "Oh...I'm sorry," I said, disheartened. "It's alright." A strange feeling had risen in me; a sort of humming in my chest, like bees at winter's thaw.

I walked through the illuminated trees, through the quiet orchards, the groves and brakes, across the sands and up the cliffs. The birds were still, and the beasts. All the sounds were the air among the leaves and my own breath. The sky bent its arc over me, clear and bright. I stared into the blinding waves, the white-flaring sun. No one seemed to disturb me. On my last day in Marseille, the sun was high in the sky; blistering and golden.

Like the saying goes:

Aut viam inveniam aut faciam.

I will either find a way, or make one.

I could feel us trying to treat our relationship the same as it was, but something had still, obviously shifted. Because of this, I was acutely aware that our end was near, but was still willing to be whatever you wanted me to be, whether it was friends, lovers, or both; I wanted desperately to be in your life still, to exist alongside you, as long as you would have had me. I would have done anything to have felt loved again and didn't really care how needy, or how desperate, or how miserable it sounded, because at the time, I craved the idea of that life with every inch of my being.

"Hey," you said, picking up the phone that sunny afternoon.

"Hey, how are you?" I asked, a pit silently brewing in my stomach. I thought I was going to be sick.

"Everything's good over here," you said casually. "What about you?"

"Everything's been good too," I said and paused to take a deep breath. I exhaled ever so slowly. "But I wanted to ask you something."

"Anything," you said, blissfully unaware.

"Things have been going well for a while and..." I struggled to get the words out. My heart beat against my chest. "I wanted to ask, what are we? We haven't really talked about it for a while, and I just want us to both be clear on what's going on." You were silent for a moment. "I don't want to spring this on you, I'm really sorry if it sounds unreasonable–"

"No, no, it's completely understandable," you said. "I'm happy you asked."

"'I didn't want to corner you with the question, so I'd be more than happy to give you some time to think about it, if you need it."

"I think time would be good," you said. "Is two weeks fine?"

You need two weeks? I thought solemnly to myself. "Okay," I sighed. "But I probably won't reach out to you until then, but feel free to contact me whenever you want."

"Alright, should I give you a call then?" you asked.

"That works," I said.

Two weeks...

"Would you be in a relationship with somebody that didn't love you?" you asked suddenly, interrupting my thoughts. The bluntness of your question hit me with a sort-of whiplash sensation. I didn't really know what to say.

To be honest, I don't even remember what I said.

257

When the call had ended, I was left with an anxious, almost nauseating feeling all over my body, penetrating from my head to toes. I already knew I had a long two weeks ahead of me, I hoped they would be kind.

Unsurprisingly, they weren't.

CHAPTER EIGHTEEN
THE WAITING GAME

WHAT IS MORE 'AUGUST' THAN THE STILLNESS OF TREE leaves on a calm morning, when they seem to listen to the song of light of the rising sun? Arriving back in Brooklyn, I felt a bottomless sadness, so completely alone. Like one of my stuffed animals at home that I was too old for now, that sat on the shelf in my closet, mashed against the back wall. The smell of coffee in the morning, sunbeams on the tiled floor of the parlour. Subdued clattering from the kitchen, pages of the newspaper crackling at dawn; it was as if nothing changed, nothing at all. Our summer felt more of a fairytale than the reality.

DAY ONE.

It was raining as I passed the churchyard closed with an iron gate. I noticed I was praying to the beat of my feet. I hurried on. It was a beautiful evening. The rain, which had been falling lightly, now fell with great force. I wrapped my coat around me.

It was warm and glowing in my apartment, yet still,

everything distracted me, but most of all myself. Without your arranging hand, I lived in a state of heightened chaos. I set my laptop on an orange crate. The floor was littered with pages of onionskin filled half with unwritten poems, meditations on the death of Mayakovskt, and ruminations about Rob Dylan. The room was strewn with records to view. The wall was tacked with my heroes but my efforts seemed less than heroic. I sat on the floor and tried to write. Slowly, things I thought would happen didn't. Things I never anticipated unfolded. I wanted to be a writer but I wanted my work to matter; in these moments, it felt like whole worlds were trapped inside of me waiting to spill out.

Because all I wanted to do was write, not fuss around with words.

But getting frustrated with my writing — and it was impossible not to think of my work as my colleague and co-participant, as if it was something that sometimes decided to be agreeable and collaborative with me, and sometimes decided to be truculent and unyielding — I just had to keep doing it, and doing it, and one day I'd get it right.

I begun the evening with Boccaccio's *Decameron:*

> *And it pleased Him that this love of mine, whose warmth exceeded all others, and which had stood firm and unyielding against all the pressures of good intention, helpful advice and the risk of danger and open scandal, should in the course of time diminish in its own accord. So that now, all that is left of it in my mind is the delectable feeling which Love habitually reserves for those who refrain from venturing too far upon its deepest waters. And thus what was once a source of pain had now become, having shed all discomfort, an abiding sensation of pleasure.*

The *Decameron* was a collection of love stories told by ten people running from Florence during the time of the Black

Plague. They told stories to pass the time rather playing games, at the direction of the Queen, travelling with them. Seven women, three men. Everywhere they looked, people dying. What a pleasure it must have been, I thought, as the story flew up the pages in front of me in sections.

To survive.

DAY TWO.

When the sun was up, it was hard to see much through the grime-streaked windows. Defunct timetables papered the walls, cigarette butts and chewing gum were stomped deep into the linoleum. I went through all the upstairs rooms, then to the attic. Lampshades and picture frames, Ormandy party dresses yellowed with age. Grey wide-plank floors, so worn they were almost fuzzy. A shaft of dusty cathedral light filtered through the stained-glass porthole that faced the front of the house. I went down the back staircase — low and claustrophobic, scarcely three feet wide — through the kitchen and pantry, taking a swing of white wine, and out onto the back porch. I slipped outside into the night. The rain ceased falling and it seemed like the whole of the city had been covered in an undisturbed layer of mist—white and fleeting as snow.

I was very tired. All around me the messages written in chalk were dissolving in the wetness. Streams formed beneath the charms, cigarettes, pages. Pearls of flowers left on the plot of earth above Jim Morrison floated like bits of Ophelia's bouquet.

I was still waiting for you to tell me on your own terms, I was waiting for the evening calm, I was waiting for our time to come again; the oblique light, that pause between day and night. Peace would come, surely. But I could imagine no other peace than that of our two bodies bound together, of our love given over to each other infinitely—I had no other homeland but you at the time. I didn't care that I was potentially settling for a fraction of a relationship with you, when I knew I was deserving of much more.

I was willing to settle for whatever you gave me because a fraction of you was better than nothing at all.

The story I read that night, though, was a good one: Tosca, the lover of a handsome painter, Cavaradossi, betrayed him in order to protect him from his torturer. Tosca could save her lover by giving herself to the torturer, and she said she would in exchange for a mock execution. He came to her and she instead, impulsively, stabbed him to death with his dinner knife, in his chambers. She then visited her lover in prison, assured him of his safety, rushed to his side after the firing squad, only to find he really was dead. The torturer's murder was discovered, and his police came for Tosca, who then flung herself from a parapet to her death.

DAY FIVE.

I haven't been angry in years. And yet I've been angry since before I remember happiness.

I can't say it was this or that was the reason. There was no reason and every reason.

I spent the majority of the day at the ice rink, letting the familiar cold rush through me with a revitalising freshness. It felt good; spending hours focused on something other than you, dedicating myself to physical exertion as a response to the abundance of loneliness I was feeling on the inside. Every morning, I would head to the rink as soon as the sun dawned upon the city scape. And then, in the evenings, would return to the rink and continue to train. There was nothing I loved more, except for maybe literature, that I could find such a transportary escape in; but alongside that, came the recurring longing for a life separate from needing to escape at all. Couldn't I simply exist and find comfort within that itself?

I closed my eyes and could see the tale of Tammamo, her hand closing her husband's eyes, breathing in the air to make the fire breathe, his family, watching her. Enough, she'd be thinking. Fire on her lips.

It ends with me now.

And although I had fretted over whether my life was worth-while, I had always wondered why myself and so many others went on living at all; it had been difficult to convince myself at times and yet so many people, so many millions, billions of people, lived in misery I couldn't fathom; with deprivations and illnesses that were obscene in their extremity. And yet on and on and on they went. So was the determination to keep living not a choice at all, but an evolutionary implementation? Was there something in the mind itself, a constellation of neurones as toughened and scarred as tendons, that prevented humans from doing what logic so often argued they should? And yet that instinct wasn't infallible — I had overcome it once. But what had happened to it after? Had it weakened, or become more resilient? Was my life even my choice to live any longer?

Nevertheless, I walked the days with your name lying on my tongue, like a swallow of water that I couldn't take down my throat.

DAY SEVEN.

School arrived. I did well. At home one Friday, I wheeled myself into the bedroom, into bed. I spent the entire weekend in a sleep that was unfamiliar and eerie, less a sleep than a glide, weightlessly moving between the realms of memory and fantasy, unconsciousness and wakefulness, anxiety and hopefulness. This was not the world of dreams, I thought, but someplace else, and although I was aware at moments of waking — I saw the lights above me, the sheets around me, the sofa with its wood-fern print across from me — I was unable to distinguish when things had happened in my visions to when they had actually happened. I saw myself lifting a blade to my arm and slicing it down through my flesh, but what sprung from the slits were coils of metal and stuffing, and I realise that I had gone under a mutation, that I was no longer human, and I felt relief: my culpability had vanished with my humanity.

Is this real? The voice asked me, tiny and hopeful, *are we inanimate now?*

But I could not answer myself.

Again and again, I saw those years in New York. As I had gotten weaker, as I had drifted from myself, I saw them more and more frequently. I felt my past was a cancer, one I should have and thought I had treated long ago but instead ignored. Now the memories had metastasised, now they were too large and too overwhelming for me to eliminate. Now when they appeared, they were wordless: they stood before me, they sat, side by side, staring at me, and this was worse than if they spoke because I knew that they were trying to decide what to do with me, and I knew whatever they decided would be worse than I could imagine, worse than what had ever happened before. At one point I saw them whispering at each other, and I knew they were talking about me. "Stop," I yelled at them, "stop, stop," but they ignored me, and when I tried to get up to make them leave, I was unable to do so. "Theo," I heard myself call, "help me; make them leave, make them go away." But Theo didn't come, and I realised I was alone and became afraid, concealed myself under the blanket and remained as still as I could, certain that time had doubled back upon itself and I would be made to relive my life in sequence.

It'll get better eventually, Louise promised me. *Remember, good years followed the bad.*

But I couldn't do it again; I couldn't live once more through those years, those years whose half-life had been so long and so resonant that had determined everything I had become and done.

By the time I finally, fully woke up on Monday morning, I knew I had crossed some sort of threshold. I knew I was close, that I was moving from one world to another.

The longer I waited, my brain knew your answer, but my heart wasn't ready to accept it yet. I knew from the moment you had to think about it, there wouldn't have been a chance for us to be together again. Nevertheless, I clung onto the idea of a maybe, of a possibility again; I clung onto the chance of *hope*. Everybody would sacrifice something for a little bit of beauty.

Right?

When a week had passed and I still hadn't received any sort of answer, I was worn down to the edge of insanity, leaving me with the fate of a tormented child. Missing you was the agony I had never felt so terribly before. As if all my breaths of calm were stolen and swept under panic. It pried at my eyes, filling them with a yearning that flowed past reasonable vision. I lay awake thinking of you, so obsessed I became ill. The sensation stayed with me for some days. I was certain it couldn't be detected; but perhaps my grief was more apparent than I knew. The light poured through the windows upon our photographs and the poem of us sitting together for the last time, creating silence. Myself, destined to live, listening closely to a silence that would take a lifetime to express.

During that week, I had read a lot; a pathetic attempt to distract myself from the waning thoughts; I grasped desperately for anything, hoping it would speak to my soul as you did. I picked up *Notes On Heartbreak,* by Annie Lord and spent the midnight hours getting lost in her feminine reprise and tales of romance. "*We met in Philosophy class...*"

I almost threw the book (and myself) out of the window.

It seems that we were destined to be intertwined; only separated by memories, wishes, distance and your empty hand. It left me feeling wholly incomplete. You were missing from me and I didn't want to miss anymore, I was irrevocably tired of it. Reading the novel sent shivers through my body, a pang in my heart, dishevelled fingertips and a bruised tongue; something I loved shouldn't have caused that much pain — whenever I thought about you, all I thought of was how much I had lost in my life — you felt like my home, but it was starting to feel like you weren't anymore. I knew that there was something to be said for all of this missing, but I did not know what it was.

I closed the novel, giving up all hopes of solace in literature, and instead, decided to call Adeline. We'd been calling every day now. Our friendship felt like a grace miracle, a shining star amidst the night; she reminded me that when I was looking for love and it seemed like I might not ever find it, that I probably had access to an abundance of it already, just not the romantic kind. That kind of love might not kiss me in the rain or propose commitments. But it would listen to me, inspire and restore me. I had so much to gain and learn from this kind of love. I could carry it with me forever.

I vowed to keep it as close to me as I could.

DAY EIGHT.

August evenings were especially stricken with melancholy — as if the ghosts of all past summers came rushing to haunt my heart. I felt awfully pathetic, waiting, desperate. A lot of the feelings of abandonment that persisted during the time of the assault fired through me with a new intensity, and I was stuck, reliving them for the first time in years; leaving me incomplete and slightly torn.

I arrived at the ice rink, my sanctuary amidst the chaos of life. The cool air brushed against my face as I stepped onto the smooth, glistening surface. The familiar sound of blades slicing through the ice filled the air, a soothing melody that whispered promises of clarity. With each glide and twirl, I lost myself in the rhythm of movement; the world outside faded away, leaving only the crisp air, the sound of my skates, and the feeling of the ice beneath me. It was there, on that frozen stage, that I found solace and release, where the weight of my thoughts and worries melted into the ice. I felt the tension in my mind unravel, replaced by a sense of freedom and clarity. In those moments, on the ice, I was truly alive, and the world made sense again.

DAY TEN.

I wrote through the day in a local coffee shop, my notebook and laptop by my side, my eager co-conspirators as I worked through the letter and started the process of editing it. Reading over my writing from during the course was painfully nostalgic; maybe we were not as good as I convinced myself we were. I began nitpicking certain scenarios and realising moments I had chosen to act oblivious to at the time: every insult I let pass by, every cruelness, I drank like water so it would no longer be seen, be heard, be felt. I realised how I had taken it and put it inside of me.

I didn't say a word. I never let out a peep.

But the past cannot be changed, forgotten, edited, or erased. It can only be accepted.

The irrationality of my ultimatum came and hit me in the face with a blunt force, why would I ever propose such an idea? Was I dreaming of some war-torn ending, cars blown and worlds destroyed? Was pain all that I knew that now I chased it, relentlessly, wherever I went; seeking any sort of comfort I could find in destruction? To be honest, I wasn't really sure and neither am I now.

But our restrictions left me feeling free inside the silence, which, inside the cafe, was as thick as the drapes that protected the dark room from the light that would bleach the colour from the chairs and yellow all the books. Even in their pristine cases. The relief of nothing to say. I'd always prized silence for the absence of other noises. In that cafe I came to see how one could prize silence for being articulate, as well.

DAY TWELVE.

Sometimes the scattered thought of you ran like a jagged red seam of the fire inside me and I burned from the inside out, like a lightning-struck tree: the outside whole, the inside, that carried the lightnings charge, a coal. At other times, I felt empty, transparent, a child of the wind. Touching nothing, nothing touching me. And alternating between these states with no warning as to one would turn into the other.

He's gone, I told the moon.

Nothing came back to me.

I saw the end from afar, but my eyes had always fooled me. Waiting for your decision, my heart had slowly started to come to terms with the fact that your answer would not be what I desired for. The mere fact that you had to think about it was enough proof for me to begin the process of mourning our relationship and everything I believed it was.

When I turned to face grief, I saw that it was just love in a heavy coat. Whatever else one may say about grief, it certainly lends one diabolical powers of invention; and I spent two or three of the worst nights I had, then or ever during the wait, lying awake drunk with a horrible taste of liquor in my mouth and worrying about what you were deciding to do. I knew that I could never be friends with you; maybe because your eyes reminded me of the nights we spent together. I couldn't look into the eyes I once saw a future in and pretend to see nothing. On the other hand, I knew that I could not be in a relationship with somebody that didn't love me. It wouldn't have been the first time, but were you really worth diminishing my worth to inexplicable value? Was I really going to settle for a half-love, a fake-love, a love that wasn't mutually felt? *No,* I thought to myself, *I can't let myself do that again.* I have learned better, if much at all.

From that moment I knew, I knew that whatever your decision would come to — which wasn't looking in my favour anyway — it would be the end. This choice of mine was, of course, painfully and half-heartedly decided upon, but I knew that nothing was deemably possible.

And even if I could go back, I wouldn't belong there anymore.

DAY FOURTEEN.

Even a slow angel moved faster than you knew how to.

As per usual, I spent my morning and evening at the rink, and the interlude between them writing. The letter was still the centre of my focus at the time; having that mode to express myself freely was desperately liberating. It had already been two weeks without hearing from you; I caught myself frequently planning out messages, hovering over the call button — I used writing to suppress those desires and write them somewhere safe and consequence free. What I had already written was dreadfully blunt, candid, and frank, but sometimes it's tiring to poetise pain. Not everything can be made beautiful, especially the truth.

The right words always seemed to come too late for me.

As the wait got longer, and the sun droned shorter, there was a deep brooding pit of sadness in my heart. Writing the letter left me somewhat haunted by the ghost of who you could have been, what we could have had, or how things used to be. And even if I could live without you, I felt as if I would never smile or laugh in the same way that I used to; that my eyes would never hold that same kind of unknown happiness before they had cried untold amounts of tears. Writing exposed me to the sad reality of that you were not the person you promised, or even pretended to me that you'd be; and progressively, reading back my own words, I had come to terms with the desperation and embarrassment that came with sharing our past. I was constantly living in a state where it felt like I was begging, begging to mean something to you. I was ultimately losing my mind trying to understand yours. I tried to remind myself that I had lived without you before, and must, by logicality, be able to live without you again. But sometimes, as the night darkened and cornered in my room, it really didn't seem to feel that way at all. The only thing that brought me back to my senses was writing. Every time I opened up those ink-scrawled pages, I was met with the senseless ways I had devoted so much to you for little in return, often causing me to question every inch of who I thought I was at the time.

What mattered now, though, is what I chose to do with that revelation as the clock struck midnight.

CHAPTER NINETEEN

C'EST LA FIN, MON MERVEILLEUX AMI

YOU WOULD BE A MOTHERING CLOAK, A VELVET PETAL. IT was not the thought but the shape of the thought that tormented me. It suspended above, then mutely dropped, causing my heart to pound so hard, so irregularly, that my skin vibrated as if beneath a lurid mask, sensual yet suffocating. We had weathered painful shifts in our relationship, also the critical tongues and envy of others, but we could not stem the tide of the terrible fortune that befell us. Every fear I had once harboured seemed to materialise with the sadness of a bright sail bursting into flames. My youthful promotion of you crumbled into dust returned with pitiless clarity. I saw your impatience to achieve denouement in another light, as if you had the predisposed life line of a young pharaoh.

I could not bear to stay home alone. I washed and changed clothes, slipped on my raincoat, and ventured into Brooklyn alone. It was quite dark, and I walked the wide and empty steps of Brooklyn Museum. I took a seat and manically busied myself with small tasks, thinking of what to say, when, instead of calling you in hope to speak of working together again, I knew I had to wait it out. I called Adeline again, and though I hadn't talked to her in a few days, it was as if no time passed, and she was happy to hear from me. It was a quick call, and when we hung up it was completely silent, save the rustling of autumn leaves and the rain, which were becoming more pronounced. On the unmasked walls were plastic flowers, cigarette bums, half-empty wine bottles, broken rosaries and strange charms. The rain began in earnest and suddenly, as if by some dark miracle, you called.

The graffiti surrounding me were words in French:

C'est la fin, mon merveilleux ami.

This is the end, beautiful friend.

I picked up the phone and for a moment — a painfully long moment — we were both silent. "Hey," you said eventually.

"Hey," I replied, anxiously fiddling with the strings of my hoodie. "So..."

I heard you take a deep breath before exhaling patiently. The whole night stood still for a moment; the moon, the stars, the sky. "I don't want to continue this relationship anymore. The only reason I would stay with you would be for sex. That's it."

My heart sank. I didn't say anything. I couldn't say anything.

"To be honest," you continued, taking another long breath. "I never thought this was going anywhere after the two weeks."

I had screwed up.

"I didn't even want to give you my number, really. I was worried you were going to reach out. I had no idea how to react when you actually did."

I had been careless.

I paused for a moment, trying to come up with something to say. But I couldn't. My reaction to your admission was more emotional than I had anticipated. Nothing in my experience had prepared me for this. My thoughts were meshed with affection and flamboyance. I had prided myself on being non-judgemental, but my comprehension was narrow and provincial. I started to cry. I had your attention; I had it now, but I didn't want it. Your words lay exposed in the air. Finally, I answered. "You would only stay with me to have *sex?*"

"Yes," you said, somewhat shamefully, but I disregarded it.

The horrible shock had started. I begun to breathe heavier and my thoughts came out in a hysterical mess. "Oh my god," I mumbled through tears. "You fucking played me!"

"No, *no. Alaska,*" you exhaled somewhat desperately. "Let's not get ahead of ourselves–"

"Why did you let me love you so hard if it was nothing to you?"

"I...I don't know," you stuttered.

"You said you...I thought that...you're just a liar!" My head started to hurt. When I started to talk, it was painful to hear myself stumble over my words that I'm afraid I blocked out much of what I said. "I fucking trusted you with everything."

"You weren't wrong for that–"

"No, I was. *I was,*" I said, flatly and slowly, after my initial shock had lessened somewhat.

"That's not my fault," you said. The air clung to my limbs with a narcotic heaviness. We were both silent for a moment before you spoke again. "I never asked you to trust me."

I paused again, feeling something shift violently inside of myself. "What the fuck, Theo?" I spat. "Why would you even ask me to be in a relationship with you if you didn't see it going anywhere?"

"I don't know!" you started to yell. "I thought that I was doing you a favour!"

"A favour?" I scoffed.

"Yes, I just...I just felt bad after what you had told me and—"

"You slept with me because you...*pitied* me?"

"I'm sorry, Alaska," you mumbled.

In such an ingenuous way I couldn't possibly do anything but laugh. As is true of most incipient band things in life, I had not really prepared myself for this possibility. And what I felt was not fear nor remorse but only terrible, crushing humiliation, a dreadful, red-faced shame I hadn't felt since the assault. And what was even worse was to hear you, knowing more acutely than myself, that you knew about it. I hated you — I was so angry I wanted to kill you — but somehow I was not prepared to hear you say something like that. "Don't... don't fucking say that you're sorry. You are not sorry, Theo," I whispered. "I can't believe it. Did you ever even feel anything towards me?" I asked, heavy with despair.

"Sometimes," you said, almost in a whisper too.

"Sometimes," I laughed through my tears. "When was sometimes then? When we were having sex?"

When you didn't say anything, I knew that I already had my answer. I felt stunned, yet I had to wonder if you'd put into words what I had myself divined. I wasn't sure why you said that; and what you had said, I never asked for an explanation. It wasn't as if you were doing me a favour (except having sex with me, apparently). I wondered if you realised that you were presenting yourself as mean spirited, or merely speaking the truth. "God, I shouldn't have done it with you! I trusted you, you knew about everything and you still had sex with me," I exhaled.

You breathed heavily and drew out a painful sigh. Nothing could have prepared me for what you said next. "You can't say you didn't enjoy it," you said, suddenly crude. "You sounded like you enjoyed it."

A sharp silence paused between us.

"How fucking dare you?" I yelled back. I had a hard time keeping my voice down. There were windows open in the upstairs apartment that faced the back; I heard people talking, listening to the radio, moving around.

"I never asked you to develop feelings–"

"What else would I have done?" I said, sinking into myself every second. "You told me you loved me."

"No I didn't," you spat. "I would clearly remember if I did."

I laughed again in disbelief. "You clearly don't. I told you that I love you too."

"It'll pass."

I was gasping with exertion, with misery. "You have to be actually kidding me."

"I just...I never saw us as a thing," you said.

"So?" I asked. "Neither did I, but it...it changed. You changed that for me. Why can't I change that for you?"

"Look, Alaska," you said suddenly. "I have to go to dinner but–"

"Dinner is more important to you? That's what you're prioritising now?" I spat. "Your fucking dinner?"

"I–"

"You know what, just fucking go. It won't make a difference," I said, hanging up the phone. I put my head on my knees and wept; wept for the wrong turns and the summer wasted: wept for myself, for being so blind, for having over and over and over again refused to see. A cold draft was blowing in the air. I felt shaky but oddly refreshed.

Nihil sub sole novum, I thought as I walked back down Brooklyn to my apartment.

Any action, in the fullness of time, sinks to nothingness...

"Had fun at dinner?" I asked, sarcastically, picking up the phone again.

You groaned into the line and exhaled sharply. "Alaska, you're being rude."

"I'm being rude?" I asked, appalled. "Don't you get it?"

"What am I supposed to get?" you said, and I was recognising again, as if you were a stranger, and how little I really knew about you. "Don't be dramatic."

"Can you take this seriously?" I asked. "At all?"

"We keep going round in circles. And you, you just won't fucking give up. What more do you want from me?"

I took a shaky breath before speaking again. "Does this not matter to you at all?"

You sighed heavily. "I don't know what you want me to do in this situation."

Silence. I couldn't quite figure out what to say.

"Did you ever think we were going to work out?" I asked finally.

"In all honesty?" you asked. "No. But it wasn't because of you." I rolled my eyes, I had heard that one too many times before. "I just don't love you."

I rubbed my temples erratically and picked at my skin. "I understand that. I'm not upset about that, I knew you didn't when I gave you the ultimatum and you had to think about it," I confessed. "I would never force you into a relationship you didn't want, even now I'm not asking to get back with you." I took a deep breath and exhaled. "I'm upset at your reasoning behind it, and everything you keep saying. Like that you would only stay with me to have sex. I never asked you to say that!"

You huffed and soughed. "I didn't mean the sex thing, okay?" you sighed. "It came out wrong."

"You still said it," I shrugged. "I never asked you to."

"Alaska," you said, I could hear the annoyance in your tone. "Do you want me to be honest?"

"That's all I've ever wanted," I said painfully, hesitantly.

"You were just...just too needy for me," you said. My heart sank deeper. My thoughts now passed in fractures, a sharp pain pulsed at my forehead.

To my horror, I realised that, in a way, of course messed up and all, you were right. As ghastly as it had been, there was no denying that. You had thrown all subsequent events into a kind of glaring technicolour. And, though his new lucidity of vision was frequently nerve-wracking, there was no denying that it was not an altogether unpleasant situation.

"Needy?" I scoffed. "I was finally vulnerable with someone and you took it for my weakness. All I only ever wanted was for you to see me above all of those things."

"I never asked for that," you mumbled with anger.

"You didn't have to!" I yelled. "It meant that I trusted you, that's what a relationship is supposed to be. *Trust*."

You didn't answer that. Things still weren't clear, but for the life of me, I couldn't think of the right questions to ask. "Why did you keep talking to me for two months? Why didn't you end it earlier when you had the chance?" I asked. "You asked me to do long distance, only to have led me on!"

You sneered. "I never asked to do that."

"Yes you did! Why are you lying?" I wailed, huffing in my tears through each desperate inhale. "Answer me. Why?"

"Same reason as before..."

"Say it," I demanded.

"I felt bad," you admitted. "You were clearly in love with me. I didn't know what to do or say!"

"You could have told me the truth!" I pleaded.

"That's what I'm trying to do now and look at how you're acting!" you howled into the phone. "I didn't want to hurt you–"

"You didn't think that this would hurt more?" I asked in

disbelief. "Leading me on for two months, calling me needy, easy, telling me you would only be with me for sex?"

"Alaska!" you yelled. "Can you stop bringing up the sex thing? I already told you I didn't mean it. You keep saying this and that, saying that I played you or just used you for sex, that's not what happened at all. It's ridiculous..." You went on and on.

A black buzzing noise echoed in my head. I can't stand this, I thought, I've got to leave, but still you continued, and I still listened, silent, vast, arctic. I felt sicker and blacker to hear your voice every second. "It's not ridiculous. You said that."

"I didn't mean it, I know I shouldn't have said it, it just came out," you defended hopelessly. "Just trust me—"

"Trust you?" I yelled. Tears had fallen across my cheeks, swelling the soles of my lips. My voice was war-torn and raspy. "You want me to trust you? Where has that ever gotten me?"

"You said nothing could make you change the way you felt about me," you said, voice low and husky.

"Then I guess we're both liars."

I heard you take a sharp breath. The temperature in the room seemed almost to drop.

"Alaska, there you go again, fucking victimising yourself. You're making this into a bigger deal than it needs to be." Your voice chilled me to the bone. I had always thought of you with only a veneer for what was, at bottom, a warm and kind-hearted nature. But as I heard you then, your voice was mechanical and dead. It was as if the charming theatrical curtain had dropped away and I saw you for the first time as you really were: not the benign sage, the indulgent and protective lover of my dreams, but ambiguous, a moral neutral, whose beguiling trappings concealed a being that was watchful, capricious and heartless.

"You keep forgetting I'm an entire person and not some

vague fucking concept that you dreamt." I said this intending to hurt you, and with pleasure I saw that I had. I was so angry, so furious: there was no word for what I was. Hatred sizzled through my veins. You wanted to see me for who I was, and now, you were getting your wish. Now you were seeing me as I truly was.

Do you know how badly I could hurt you? I wanted to ask you. *Do you know I could say things you would never forget, that you would never forgive me for? Do you know I have that power? Do you know what I really am?* My life, the only thing that was mine, was being possessed: by you, who wanted to keep me alive and true. *What is life for?* I asked myself.

What is my life for?

Oh, I thought, would I never forget? Is this who I am after all, after those years?

It was then that I heard your phone hit across a blunt surface and your voice echoed from across the room. Now — I still shudder to remember. "What the fuck is wrong with you?" you spat. "I don't care about calling you, just so that you feel less lonely." Your words — helpless, wild — hit me like a blackjack.

Suddenly, and for the first time, really, I was struck by the bitter, irrevocable truth of it; the evil of your own words. It was like running full speed into a brick wall. Feeling completely helpless, I wanted to die. "Stop trying to fix me, Theo," I spat back at you. "What am I to you? Why were you with my anyway? I'm not your fucking charity project. I was doing just fine without you."

"Oh yeah?" you asked. "Sorry if I'm not living up to being the ideal boyfriend, Alaska. I know you prefer your relationships heavy on the sadism, right? Maybe if I assaulted you a few times I'd be living up to your standards?"

I was quiet then. Very painfully and very achingly quiet.

A shaft of light splintered painfully in my vision. I clutched the back of the chair, closed my eyes and saw luminous red as the rhythmic noise of my sobs fell over and over again like a bludgeon. I felt about you the way I once felt during the assault, you were another person to whom I had, rashly, entrusted myself, someone in whom I had placed such hopes, someone I hoped could save me. But when it became clear that you would not, even when my hopes had turned rancid, I was unable to disengage myself from them, I was unable to leave.

"I'm sorry," you whispered. "I shouldn't have—"

"Fuck you," I hissed.

"Yeah, I get it," you said. "I'm the asshole, I'm the bad guy."

"I never said that," I argued.

"Well, you're acting like it."

"I'm trying to understand where all of this is coming from, do I not at least deserve that?" I asked.

"I don't care about what you think you deserve or don't—"

"You don't really care at all!" I yelled. "Oh, right, unless it's sex—"

"You know what, I'm done with this," you said. "Go fuck yourself."

You hung up the phone.

I found oddly, that I felt nothing — not fear, not hate, not anything. The worst had happened and now I was free. I had a relationship, and it was awful, and now I would never need to have one again, because I had proven to myself incapable of being in one. My time with you had confirmed everything I feared people would think of me, of my past, and my next task was to learn to accept that and to do so without sorrow. I knew I would probably still feel lonely in the future, but now I had something to answer that loneliness; now I knew for certain that my loneliness was the preferable state to whatever that was — terror, shame, disgust, dismay, giddiness, excitement, yearning, loathing — I felt with you.

It was still dark. Birds were chirping in the eaves. Blinking in the glare of my desk lamp, I was struck with a wave of revulsion so strong it was almost nausea. Horrific as it was, the present dark, I was afraid to leave you for something better, another permanent dark. I had seen this shadow before in my life — stupid terror; the whole world opening upside down; my life exploding in a thunder of crows and the sky expanding empty over my stomach like a white ocean. Then nothing. Rotten stumps, sow bugs crawling in the fallen leaves. Dirt and dark.

Without warning I had a vision of you — twenty years later, fifty years, and of myself — older too, sitting around you in some smoky room, the two of us repeating an exchange for the thousandth time. At one time I had liked the idea, that the act, at least, had bound us together; we were not ordinary friends, but friends till-death-do-us-part. This thought had been my only comfort in the aftermath of Oxford. Now it made me sick, knowing there was no way out. I was stuck with you, with all of the memories, for good.

How about your first boyfriend being someone you don't end up hating? My flesh crawled, remembering the ironic, almost humorous twist you'd put on the last words — oh, god, I thought, my god, how could I have listened to you? You were right, too, about the hating part at least. The call was over in a moment, but in a strange way it had persisted, manifesting itself in different lights like one of those pictures on the cover of horror paperbacks in the supermarket: one page, a smiling blonde-haired child; turned the other, a skull in flames. Sometimes the structure was mundane, silly, perfectly harmless; though early in the morning, say, or around twilight, the world would drop away and there loomed a gallows, mediaeval and black, mockingbirds wheeling low in the skies overhead. At night, it cast its long shadow over what fitful sleep I was trying to get to escape your memory, but you followed me into my dreams. Someday, I thought, somehow, I would find a way to tell someone, one person. And then I had, someone I had trusted, and that person had left, and now I didn't have the fortitude to tell my story ever again. But then, didn't everyone only tell their lives — truly tell their lives — to one person? How often could I really be expected to repeat myself, when with each telling I was stripping the clothes from my skin and the flesh from my bones, until I was as vulnerable as a small pink mouse? For now, my privacy, my life, was still mine. For now, no one else needed to know. My thoughts were so occupied with you — trying to recreate you, to hold your face and voice in my head, to keep me present — that my past was as far away as it had ever been: I was in the middle of a lake, trying to stay afloat; I could not think of returning to shore and having to live among my memories again.

And then, that evening, in which I knew my efforts would not satisfy me any longer: I needed to cut myself, extensively and severely. The sharp yelps that seemed to come from some other creature within me, I knew they would be quieted only by my pain. I considered what to do.

But if I didn't do something — then I didn't know. I had to, I had to. I had waited too long, I realised; I had thought I could see myself through; I had been unrealistic.

I got up from bed and walked through the empty apartment, into the quiet bathroom. The counter glowed whitely, ignored but beckoning, pleading to be headed, the salvation it offered as flimsy as paper. For a moment I stood, unable to move, and then slowly, reluctantly, walked towards the drawers and opened them.

I looked down into its black, clutching its frame as I had those nights before, wondering if I could bring myself to do it. I knew that it would appease the voices. But there was something degrading about it, so extreme, so sick, that I knew if I were to do it, I would have crossed some line, that I would, in fact, have become someone unrecognisable to myself again. I shut the door behind; my lungs began to burn, my legs became weak, I could not help but collapse onto the cold, hard floor. My hands shook with such vigour I clenched them together and held them against my mouth, trapping the cries that fled my soul. I sat on the floor, wailing my silent song of pain, sinking my talons into my arms, waiting for it to go away.

Finally, finally, I unstuck myself from the frame, my hands shaking, and slammed the door shut, slammed the bolt back into its slot, and stumped away from it.

The next morning, I awoke an outcast on a cold star, unable to feel anything but awful helpless numbness. I was filled with so much anger, burning me from the inside out; it boiled and bubbled until reaching the edges of my mouth. If only I could yell and scream all the bitterness out. I wanted to claw my brain out every time I thought of you; worst of all, it sickened me how much I still loved you after how much you took from me, how horribly you spoke to me, after all the times you showed me that you didn't care. I hated myself for still loving you despite all that you put me through.

As the day went on, my mood transpired from fits of hopelessness, sadness, perhaps even depression, but quickly transformed into a seething rage; by stages I grew to abhor you. Ruthless as a gun dog, on the phone you picked up with rapid and unflagging instinct the traces of everything in the world I was most insecure about, all the things I was in most agony to hide. These were certain repetitive, sadistic games you would play with me. They were unpleasant enough, these private inquisitions, but I cannot find words to adequately express the torments I suffered when you chose to ply these in our last conversation.

The damage which you presented was, after all, not immediate but slow and simmering, a sort which can, at least in the abstract, be postponed or diverted in any number of ways. I can easily imagine us there, at the appointed time and place, anxious suddenly to reconsider, perhaps even to grant a disastrous last-minute perception. Fear for your own freedom might have led you up the gallows to slip the noose around my neck, but a more urgent impetus was necessary to make you go ahead and kick out the chair, then watch me dangle helplessly until I was lifeless, hanging, swinging in the cold wind.

I went to the ice rink. I needed a distraction. A timeless place, free from both and everything like a dreamless sleep. When I made it to the arena, there was a wet chill in the air. The sky deepened, casting a blue light on the ice. I removed my pair of battered figure skates from my bag, and dutifully wiped their blades before placing guards over them.

Stepping onto the ice, it was very cold, but with my jacket and happy absence of ventilation, I was able to skate for great lengths of time. The rink was my second home, the act of skating my true lover. I gave myself completely, feeling the vibration of water moving beneath the surface, layers of ice melting. In the silence of the arena I was completely self-possessed, conjuring my own melody, a firebird rising from the ashes of a delicate nocturne, both a blessing and a curse to her captors. After a few laps around the rink, I already could feel any misgivings dissipating. I skated until the sun retreated, and afterwards, sat on the flat benches, taking time to unlace my books and clean off the blades.

I had no fear of returning to your memories in the dark; I had trod the same path a thousand times and knew every stone underfoot. But I needed somewhere to put down all of my longing, all of my pain. When I got home, I opened my laptop and typed through the night, only to fall asleep at six in the morning; light billowed through my windows, illuminating every crack and crevice in my room, the cityscape was radiant in the morning glow, promising the grace of a new tomorrow.

I decided from that point onwards to devote myself entirely to my writing.

Vulnerability is clumsy but it's the only thing worth anything. As the letter got longer and longer, you were the blood in my poems. I was trying not to hate you, but how else could I have dealt with it? As the computer light reflected against my face, my head hurt. I wished I had a pair of sunglasses. I wasn't supposed to be at the rink until seven, but my room was a wreck, I hadn't done laundry since the call; it was too hot to do anything more taxing than lie on my tanged bed, write, read and sweat, and try to ignore the bass of my neighbour's stereo thumping through the wall. It was a helpless feeling then, to know that no matter how hard I tried, however much I exerted myself, I was never going to make you love me back. For the first time since St. Catherine, I reread the first letter I wrote to you. It took everything in me not to go back and change everything I had written; add in the knowledge I had then, integrate smart remarks and comments of the future unknown to me at the time. But I needed to leave those memories behind and let the feelings that came during them stay alive. For in those moments, they were true. Unlike writing, I could not change them, I could not change the way I felt. But when reading back over how loved you were, how cared for you were, and then knowing how much you took advantage of it made me sick. I had to push my way through the intimacy of my own words and try not to ruin them. Those memories existed, and I needed to let them exist. I couldn't change the past, I could only accept it and move on.

Perhaps I understand that now; that there are moments or a series of moments in life when you must wear a different pair of shoes, walk in another direction from the one you had planned, and however well you succeed in your pursuits, there will always be an element of regret.

I bolted awake one night, swathed in darkness, my entire body immobilised; as if the connection between my mind and muscles had been severed. I always had trouble sleeping when there was any light proliferating inside of the room, and always made sure to close the curtains when I went to bed. Still, I felt the presence in the room of someone else, concealed in the darkness, watching me; whoever it was held their breath, hid their scent, changed their colour and receded into the shadows. This thought brought me a sort of tranquillity, I lay visualising the individual observing my pain as if it were not my own, a different entity, separate and far from myself.

Since Marseille, I thought your recurring absence was always the problem, the trigger to my reoccurring spirals of hysteria — but perhaps, it had been something deeper, more suppressed all along — the more time we spent away from each other, the more I was faced with the mistakes I made, but simultaneously chose to reject. My inherent lack of love was causing me to excessively project love onto others; I realised that my heart opened up wider to love others, waning and intense, leading me to feel as if the energy was not reciprocated. I began to think whether there was something, some habitual quality that was crooked and warped; like the far side of the moon, forever cloaked in darkness and maybe that dark, hidden side would one day outstrip the outside and completely consume it.

During the first week, I sat in bed every night staring face-to-face with our nostalgic memories; my mind began to think about everything at once but nothing at the same time, trying to figure out how to fill in the empty space that I'd been feeling all day; to remove the uncomfortable feeling that was burning me on the inside, like all of my organs were being swallowed.

The days passing faded through my fingers like loose threads, and each day evaporated as quickly as the rest. I was reminded of the days where it took real effort, real concentration to return myself to my current life, to keep myself from raging with despair and shame. To keep myself from reaching into my closet for the bag of pocket razors. I knew that was not my life anymore, but the intense loneliness of the night felt as though it could break me — as if our memories acted like a long string that needed to be pulled out of my brain, yet no matter how long I'd pull, they'd still continue.

The process of writing the letter felt like I was floating in a small bubble of water, encased on all sides by walls and ceilings and floors of ice, all many feet thick. I knew there was a way out, but was unequipped. I had no tools to begin my work, and so, my hands scrabbled uselessly against the ice's slick. I had thought that by not saying who I was, I was making myself more palatable, less strange. But now, what I didn't say made me a stranger to myself; or how you had said it, an object of pity and even remorse. At the end of the day, I always found myself alone. It was not a physical loneliness; not something that could have been fixed by the touch of a lover's hand or a false love made up of people that adored me. It was the pain of knowing no one saw me.

After all, how could anybody notice me if I wasn't truly there?

On the first morning of the second week, I felt myself tumbling towards despair; I felt myself giving up. Not necessarily because I was depressed, but because I was exhausted. At least nobody was telling me to move on; I didn't exactly want to move on, I didn't want to move into something else; I wanted to remain exactly at this stage, forever. Denial is what sustained me, and I was dreading the day when my delusions would lose the power to convince me; I needed the world to not come too close to me, to let me remain as I was, encased in this bubble of memories. I always had the repulsive need to be something more than human.

I found within myself a sort-of anger, waiting to burst from my mouth in a swarm of stinging black flies. Where has this rage been hiding? I wondered. How could I make it disappear? In this case, my anger was projected onto you; someone I loved and cared about, and this, deeply ashamed me. I had never really been able to truly believe your interpretation of me, as someone who was brave, resourceful, and admirable. Wherever you would say those things I often felt ashamed, as if I'd been swindling you: Who was this person you were describing? Your words reminded me of how trapped I felt, trapped in a body I hated, with a past I hated, and how I would never be able to change either. I was reminded that I was merely one with nothingness, a scooped-out husk in which the fruit has long since mummified and shrunk, and now rattles uselessly; I experienced that familiar prickle, that shiver of disgust that affected me both in my happiest and most wretched moments, the one that asked me who I thought I was to inconvenience so many people, to think I had the right to keep going even when my own body told me that I should stop.

One night as I stood looking out at the cityscape, I felt awfully stuck. Red and scarlet vines all over my eyes shone like foil in the moonlight. There was so much I still had to say, but I couldn't allow myself to reach out to you again; I couldn't disrespect myself that way again. The following weeks felt like being stuck in a cold cemented room, from which several prongs exist, and one by one, I was shutting the doors, closing myself from the room, eliminating my chances to escape. But why was I doing this? Why was I trapping myself in this place I hated and feared where there were other places I could go? This, I thought. Was my punishment for depending on others: one by one, they always would leave me, and I would, by nature, be alone again; but this time it would be much worse, because I would remember it had once been better with you. I had the awful sense, once again, that my life was moving backwards, that it was becoming smaller and smaller, the cement box was shrinking...

Usually I knew how melodramatic, how narcissistic, how unrealistic I was, thinking in such ways and at least once a day would scold myself for it. And then, in the cold night, I heard a voice, one unfamiliar but calm and authoritative speak to me. *Stop,* it said. *You can end this, you don't have to keep living like this.* It was such a relief to hear those words, and I stopped, abruptly, and faced the moving clouds in the sky.

I woke, frightened, because I knew what the words meant, they both terrified and comforted me; I had the feeling, as unhappy as it was, that I was at my most valuable during my time with you, where I was at least something singular and meaningful to someone, although what I had offered was being taken from me, not given willingly. But now, as I moved through my days, I heard that voice in my head and was reminded that I could, in fact, stop. I didn't, in fact, have to keep suffering. I argued with myself: why did you have such control over me? I was so tired; knowing that I didn't have to keep this going anymore was a solace to me, somehow; it reminded me that I had options, that even though my subconscious struggled to obey my conscience, it didn't mean that I wasn't still in control of myself.

This epiphany made me understand that I was no longer rooted, but gold flowing.

On the third week, I slowed through day after day. My motivations other than the letter had been murky to me. When I had finally finished writing, I felt a new-found sense of clarity, like my soul alongside my memories had been purged from myself, taken somewhere far away and made beautiful. I spent a couple days revising and editing the letter until I was happy with what I had written. My days centred around writing and skating again, everything else faded into the background of my life in a watercolour blur; my thoughts and neurones were re-wired, things came back to me in more detail and understanding. I finally had started to feel like things could be alright again.

Our mentality changes due to the environment we put ourselves in. This time, the distance between us made me clear. Oxford was a liberating, experimental time of my life that I knew wouldn't last long enough. It proved how fickle I was. I could choose to stay immobilised, or embrace grief; for grief only exists where love lived first.

That night, when I finished the final draft of the letter, the whole world was seemingly made of gold. The light came from everywhere at once. The earth's wounds had healed and my peace had held. *It had been long enough,* I whispered. I felt strong again.

I thought about what my fire could do if I set it free.

———

Sometimes reality comes crashing down on you. Other times, reality simply waits, patiently, for you to run out of the energy it takes to deny it.

Weeks later, in the garden, the autumn leaves were so new they shone like blades. I ran my fingers through the soil, testing it's ache. Now that you were gone, would I be like Achilles, wailing over his lost lover Patroclus? I tried to picture myself running up and down the beaches, tearing at my hair, cradling some scrap of old tunic you had left behind. Crying for the loss of half my soul.

There was such a time, but now, I could not see it.

That knowledge brought its own sort of pain. But perhaps that is how it was meant to be. In all honesty, it wasn't until you left, with me chasing after you, that I finally looked around and felt the depth of your destruction. And there I sat, soaked to the bone, in a smouldering field of wildflowers, trying to water the earth and bring them back to life with my tears that were locked somewhere deep within me. As the wildflowers started to wilt, I looked around again and I realised that I was utterly alone. So I took the flowers in my arms but as I touched them, they crumpled and turned brown, disappearing the more I tried to hold onto them. Desperation, I finally plucked them, roots and all from the earth.

I could no longer hold them.

I could no longer hold you.

I had to release you — I loved you most of all — but I loved myself more, and that is what you did for the people you loved: you gave them their freedom.

That night, I sent you the letter.

Dear Theo,

There is still a part of me that insists what I'll tell you cannot be told. That insists that if the truth were known I would be destroyed. I try to write you this letter and freeze, lose my path, lose my thoughts, my drafts, my edits, all of my purpose. I look up at the ticking clock in front of me and stop.

You have killed my love. You used to stir my imagination. Now you don't even stir my curiosity. You simply produce no effect. I loved you because you were marvellous, because you had genius and intellect, because you realised the dreams of great poets and gave shape and substance to the shadows of art. You have thrown it all away. The simplicity of your character makes you exquisitely incomprehensible to me. When you left, you left with my soul in your hands and my heart in your teeth and I knew I would never get either of them back. You can keep them, I don't really need them anymore. I remember the words you spoke and the words you cannot erase. I remember everything; I made a vow to never forget you and I wish you had done the same.

I'm tired of making things sound so poetic about our time together when in reality, I suppose they never were as real as you made them feel. I cannot make poetry out of everything, especially the truth. It may not be pretty to read anymore, but these feelings inside me are not beautiful either, they are ruined. Just like how your final decision was to ruin me and everything we'd ever built together. I already knew that you wouldn't want me by the end of the two weeks, the fact you even had to consider taking me back was the answer all along. What you cannot seem to understand is that is not the reason causing my hurt, that is not why I am angry or upset. It is because of the words you said after, after you had already taken everything from me and brushed it to the side like dirty laundry. You left like I was never a reason to stay.

When I begged you for some sort of answer, all you could respond was "I don't know," or sentences equally, if not more painful and confusing to the hurt my heart was already feeling. You then called me stupid, naive. God, I felt so stupid, I still feel stupid, for letting you that close to my heart, for trusting you like no one else in my life before.

I should've never told you anything, never let you touch me, never let you get to know the real me, when all I got to know was the fake you. I wish I had given my firsts to somebody that loved me all the time, not only sometimes, not only when they felt powerful over me, not only when I felt easy to them.

I told you everything about me, what made my identity and the things that shattered it along the way, and you still chose to touch me, still chose to do those things with me when you knew you were going to leave me behind. You never saw anything going past the two weeks. So, tell me why you explained that to me on the phone and not before you kissed me, not before you touched me, not before you slept with me, not before you took and tainted all the firsts I had left to offer the somebody that could've loved me properly. You took them from me with no remorse, only pity. You said you only stayed in contact with me because you felt sorry for me, felt bad. I wasted a month waiting for you because you said you wanted it, only for you to have been the one to have led me on the entire time. And I wasted the time I could have experienced with a better loving else, I wasted the trust that somebody else would have held onto with care, with delicacy, with love to you, and you don't even care. On that call, you sounded tired, the ravage of life seemed more pronounced than just a month ago. Strangely, I still wanted to hold you, take all of your pain away rather pathetically but my tongue was heavy from the hurt, my words scattered off my ghosts, who could only watch, mute at what I was trying to do as everything I tried to say failed.

"I never asked you to trust me," you argued, almost spat. Those words closed in on my chest, stealing any last bit of hope and renewing it only into a pounding hurt. I don't know if I'll ever trust somebody the same way I gave my trust to you unwaveringly, unasked and unknowing. And if ever come close to it, if I ever get close to loving someone again, the memory of you will pervade at my mind and draw me back in again. I never will forgive you for ruining that for me. I will never forgive you for the words that broke my heart. I will never

forgive you for taking away my best friend, the person that I once knew as Theo. The way you spoke to me felt like neither, only a stranger, a stranger that knows all of my deepest scars.

But I never expected you to become my deepest scar yet.

I hope I never dream about you again, I hope I never think of you again. This has turned from a letter of childlike love, to one of hate, one of anger. I considered rewriting the before of our story, rewriting them from the perspective and knowledge I have of your intentions now, but that wouldn't be true. Let the world know how brainwashed I was into loving you, let them make fun of me for not realising sooner or listening to friends, let them know how badly, how gravely this mistake of mine was. Let the world know that I am a girl with "no boundaries", one you describe as "needy", as "easy", and let it take advantage of me the same way. But most importantly, let the world see how I really felt about you at the time, how much I loved you then.

Let them know how badly you hurt me in the end.

In spite of this, I don't hate the good memories, the laughs, the smiles, the time shared together. I only hate how tainted they've become. I don't know how far I have to go to feel like I'm enough for your understanding. All I know is I'm tired of waiting, tired of caring, tired of my heart pounding against my skull.

I thought that I would rather break the world than lose you, but it wasn't the world that had it out for me all along.

I should've been more careful, more delicate with my memory baggage. If I've learned anything in these tiring seventeen years, it's that when it comes down to love and trust, there is no one to fall to but yourself. But when I met you, I truly felt like you were so much more different than all of the others, different from the ones that broke my heart and left scars in my skin. You were my blue star, my constellation, my glimmer of hope. Kharisma. But it turns out that I think you might have been worse than all of them.

Never have I gotten so close to love and touch, but it was only an illusion, only temporary, for you anyways. I told you about my loud *past, my loud thoughts, my loud desires, and I can only remember now how you never asked for them. And when I had given them to you, neither did you care. I held onto everything you gave me, told me, and I nurtured it in my soul and heart and bones.*

I just wish you'd have done the same.

I remember the day I began to fall for you. We were under the bridge in Magdalen Boat House, smoking cigarettes and laughing against the rain. When you read me the passage on the Mockingbirds, I was awfully silent for I had never heard anything so divine. I wanted to imprint those words on my skin, in my bones, in my heart. Despite everything that happened, I hope you know how beautiful those words, your words, were. I will spend every day until my last breath trying to remind you.

Se credessi nei defunti che ci guardano queste sensazioni diventerebbero per me verità, ma ahimè sono costrette a rimanere soltanto un piacevole sogno...

I never knew I could fall in love with words until I heard them come from you. If only I knew how fake, how tainted and cruel they would become. You were the cure to my loneliness for a while, and now the reason it may be everlasting. Truth is, I didn't expect to get this attached to you. It was real for me. I don't know what it was for you, but for me, it was real. It meant more than it should have. It would've taken all my strength to quiet my heart. I was willing to be with you forever. And that's what hurts the most.

But now I begin to grieve for somebody that is still alive, and I hate every second of it. How odd is it to be haunted by someone that is still breathing? I can't tell if this version you has only been brought out through the current adversities, or it had been the reality of you all along. I'm unsure which pain is worse — the shock of what happened or the ache for what never will. Your words now, above the hurt, disgust me more than anything else. I may be currently writing this in a place of anger, but you have truly given me nothing else to change the way I feel. If anything, you criticise and back yourself down so much that you cannot even bring yourself to try. You could not deal with my love, you cannot deal with my pain, but especially the fact that it was caused by you. Sure, I loved you then, but now, I can't even cry at the thought of you. I am too full of anger, both to you, and myself. How do I move on when all I've ever wanted has been ripped from my grasp by the same one that gave it to me?

You never really told me outright and clearly how you felt in those moments over the phone, I could just tell there was more, and you simply didn't want it clinging to the air. Either way, I had always loved everything about you.

Even what I didn't understand.

I loved you even in my ignorance. I loved you when I didn't even know. I loved you when we met, and you smiled, because you knew.

Seventeen is an inconvenient time to be in love, you see, but our memories will remain in my heart and mind forever. I will always see you in the wind, in the corners of coffee shops, in a passing bird like your father or little flowers. And I hate to stand the thought of that, I hate to think of how long it will take me to let the memories of you go, while you are inching yourself to forgetting every waking moment. Sometimes, right after you told me about your father, I would look at you and wonder what it felt like, to have the print of a once loved stranger all the way inside you, right into the way you shaped your thoughts.

But I know now.

You live in the childlike idea that your actions equate to you simply being, "a dick", "an asshole", an excuse at its weakest. This perspective makes me realise that you will never truly take accountability for the things you did and said. It doesn't stop me from hoping you will one day understand. But like you said, hope gets you nowhere. Hope gets you heartbroken.

But I've come to realise that hope is the only thing stronger than *fear. Every day I hope. I will continue to hope, no matter how much pain that might bring me.*

And so, I hope you find love, Theo. Even if it's not from me. I hope you find the kind of love that rings through your bones, the kind that quiets the voice inside of you. I hope you forgive yourself for the mistakes you made, the past you kept alive inside of you. I hope you learn to let those things go — of the things you had to do in order to survive.

I hope you find the kind of love that takes your breath away, as you stole mine. The kind of love that changes you.

There is so much to feel in the world.

I hope you feel it all.

You have the ability to make people feel truly seen, which you did for me. That gave me the courage to start opening up to other people. For the first time in my life, I didn't feel alone; which allowed me to imagine something bigger for myself. And I want you to know that no matter how much you hurt me, I won't ever close myself off again. Meeting you cracked my heart open and now it is forever changed. Because of that, I will carry a part of you with me wherever I go. I guess what I'm trying to say is, thank you, for everything.

Even if it was fake, thank you for making me feel like I mattered.

I was scared of the pain I'd feel if I let you go, until I realised how much pain I was in just trying to hold on. Leaving what we had behind was excruciatingly painful, but it forced me to see what I refused to. I held my hands over my eyes for you. Just and only for you. Know that I did that all for you.

But now, I'm finally okay with you not acknowledging it. Because I know I did all I could for you. I thought that if I loved you hard enough, you would love like I do. If I gave you all that you desired for, even if I didn't want to, even if I know now that it was all you wanted, that maybe you would love like I do. The only reason I can still believe in love after this, is because of the way I love others.

Nobody sees as we do, right? Right...

I think it's time I let you go. And that's so hard to do because some part of me will be in love with you for the rest of my life — but daydreaming, running in place, it's not healthy — so this is me, cutting the cord.

This is me doing what I should have done months ago: saying goodbye.

You know everything that happens after this point in the letter. It's all here. Every day we spent together and even a few days we didn't. Every thought I've ever had in your presence...or close to it. I don't expect you to read it, all I can ask for is that somebody, someday somewhere picks my soul up off of these pages, these sonnets of my summer sorrows, and thinks: I would have loved her.

Before...

THREE GENTLE REMINDERS

1. The truth is — genuine connections is ease. It is peace. When you find it you will know. You will feel seen. You will feel respected. At the end of the day, the human beings that surround you in this life should not exhaust you, or hollow you out, or leave you feeling like you are hard to love. Do not romanticise the things in this life that hurt. You cannot love someone into loving you, or being ready, or meeting their potential; you cannot close their hands around your heart if they are not willing to hold it themselves. You have to let them go. You have to focus on the people in your life who bring you back home to yourself. You have to focus on standing up for that kind of connection here, because it exists. It exists. Trust that it will find you.

2. It is often in your weakest moments that you have the opportunity to be the strongest. However, this does not mean putting on a brave face and pretending that heaviness does not exist. This instead means sitting with your feelings, and

experiencing them as they are — letting them wash over you like rain. This means choosing to confront the voids instead of filling them in or numbing them or distracting yourself from the fact that they exist. In an age of extreme stimulation, in an age where we can sweep our pain under the rug, and focus on everything outside of ourselves that is readily available and seeking out attention, it takes a lot of courage to face what hurts. To look it in the eyes, to give it a name, to understand that you cannot outrun yourself forever. That is what makes it an act of strength. That is where the healing begins.

3. Stay open to this world. Stay open to this world because it is filled with human beings, and experiences, and feelings that will deeply, and beautifully, grow you and inspire you and remind you that there is so much out there just waiting to be discovered. All it takes is one chance encounter, one singular moment in time, to completely change your life — to expand the way you see happiness and hope; to crack your heart open, to introduce it to levels of feeling and caring that you never knew existed. Yes, it is risky to be vulnerable, to be unguarded in this life, but it is far riskier to stay closed to all of the possibility that exists within it, to stay fortified and safe and tucked away from feeling. At the end of the day, you are here to risk your heart. You are here to connect. Please don't ever forget that.

CHAPTER TWENTY
WHAT ONCE WAS

Endless August into endless September. Sunny days hit the snow and made me hate light, cold that snapped at my nose numb and then burned me once I was inside. I spent the days reading.

Everyday the waves of pain ran cold and then hot and then cold again. I shook and the hours passed. My limbs were lighter and softened, my back bubbled over with ease. Inch by slow inch, I drew myself to my feet; the thought of returning to you was now like white coals in my throat.

I could not go back.

There was only one other place in all the world I knew were those woods I had dreamed of so often. The deep shadows would hide me, and the mossy ground would be soft against my ruined skin. I set that image in my eyes and walked towards it.

I felt the shade close over me. It had rained a little and the damp earth was sweet beneath me. So many times I had imagined lying there with you, but whatever tears might have been in me for that lost dream had been parched away. After sending the letter, I strangely felt more liberated than I ever had before; I had said everything that needed to be said, and what came next was a new-found freedom. Slowly, I felt myself returning, proliferating in the same, old place my humanity and self met.

I closed my eyes, drifting through the families of a peaceful slumber, the first in months.

Slowly, my restless divinity began to make headway. My breath eased, my eyes cleared. My arms and legs still ached, but when I brushed them with my fingers I touched skin instead of char. The sun set, glowing behind the trees. Night came with its stars. It was moon-dark. It was that, I think, which gave me heart enough to rise.

The grass was damp, flattened by high-autumn rain. In the starlight, the city looked small, bled grey and faint when you called me. My stomach twisted. I had not thought how my confessions would take your greatest pride from you. *Too late,* I thought. Too late for all the things I should have known. I picked up the phone and before I could even say anything, your voice came through the other line. "I'm so sorry," you said, hollow and fragile.

What?...

I hear you painfully inhale and sigh. "I'm so sorry, Alaska," you said, almost in a whisper. "I'm sorry for everything. I read the letter...thank you for sending it."

"Thank you for reading it," I said calmly. "I didn't think you would."

The night air tingled across my skin. "It was quite long, that's why it took me the entire day to get back to you," you said. "But after I read it, *god,* reading what I said even disgusted myself. I realised that you wrote it exactly how it was, exactly how I said things. It was hard to read, but must've been harder to hear. I'm so sorry."

"Thank you," I said, taking a moment to think, unsure of

what to say. "I can't forgive you, I hope you can understand. But it does mean a lot to me."

"I understand," you sighed. "But, if there's anything I could do to make things right, I would be more than happy to—I was even thinking of writing a letter back to you," you chuckled nervously. "But I didn't know if that would have been something you would have wanted."

I took a moment to think to myself. "I would really appreciate that, actually," I caught myself saying. "If you would be happy to do that, it would mean a lot to me," I said. "I'm not going to force you to write it, if you don't want to, then don't."

"I want to," you said, definitely.

I took a sharp inhale and stuttered over my words. "But... don't send it to me in a month when I'm trying to move on with my life. Send it while it actually means something."

"I'll give myself a time limit," you said, and then came a pause. "You're a great writer, Alaska."

I smiled to myself. The air seemed a little warmer. "Thank you," I said. "Well, you're the only person I've ever really shown my writing to—other than school essays and stuff."

"You should let the world hear you," you said.

"I wouldn't know what to say," I mumbled.

"Whatever feels right."

There was another brief silence. "I guess I'm stuck waiting again," I gave a disheartened laugh.

I heard you lightly chuckle, the same way you did those weeks in July. "How does two weeks sound?" you teased.

I groaned. "This two-week shit is becoming cliche."

"Touché, Ms letter writer," you smiled and the breeze felt cold again. "I will always be here if you need me, remember? I'm not going anywhere."

I didn't believe you.

I was trying to figure out how to phrase things in my mind.

Nothing sounded right. "I don't know if that would be good for us—good for me at least."

"I understand," you softly chuckled.

"That's all I've ever wanted," I sighed to myself. "For you to understand."

The days moved slowly, dropping like petals from a blown rose. I tried to remember the feel of your skin beneath my fingers, but the memories were built of air and blew away. Someone will come, I thought. All the ships in the world, all the people. Someone must. I stared out into the horizon until my eyes blurred, hoping for some message, some text, even a call again.

There was nothing.

I pressed my face into my covers. Surely there was some divine trick to make the hours go faster. To let them slip past unseen, to sleep for years, so that when I woke again the world would be new. I closed my eyes. Through the window I heard the rustling of city life singing in the streets. An eternity later, when I opened my eyes, the shadows had not even moved.

This is what it will be like all my days, I thought, *waiting.*

Despite our reprise, shadows were gathering in the corners of my room again. Outside, mockingbirds had begun to scream. At least I thought they were mockingbirds. I felt the hairs stir on my neck, thinking again of those dark, thick trunks. I went to the shutters and closed them. I locked my door. The apartment walls felt to me leaf-thin. Any claw would tear them open. *Stop it,* I told myself.

I spent the days writing, reading and lighting tapers and carrying them down the hall to my room. The feathers of my bed murmured against each other, and the shutter-wood creaked like the ropes of ships in a storm; all around me I felt the wild hollows of the city swelling in the dark.

Thinking about your letter caused fear to slosh over me, each wave colder than the last. The thought crawled across my skin and shadows reached out in the shape of your hands. I started into the darkness, straining to hear past the beat of my own blood. Each moment felt the length of a night, but at last the sky took on a deepening texture and began to pale at its edge. Their shadows ebbed away and it was morning. I stood up, whole and untouched. When I went outside, there were no prowling memories, no slithering tail-marks, no gouges clawed in my mind. Yet I did not feel foolish.

I felt as if I had passed a great ordeal.

I pressed on through the weeks. If my past had given me anything, it was endurance. Little by little I began to live easier: to the sap moving in the plants, to the blood in my veins. I learned to understand my own intention, to prune and to add, to feel where my strengths gathered and speak the right words to draw it to its height. That was the moment I lived for, when it all came clear and the last memory could sing with its pure note, for me and me alone.

I sat at my heart watching the stars turn through the window. *Peace,* I felt. Peace as a garden in sunlight, blossoming deep from the ground.

So you see, in my way, I was eager for what came when your letter entered my inbox at midnight.

CHAPTER TWENTY-ONE
GREY LINES

Dear Alaska,

I've spent most of my life preparing to write something as important as this letter. But for the first time, I realise that I'm not that great of a writer. So many things come to mind that I want you to read, but I just keep deleting words because I don't like how they sound and I don't want to give you something mediocre.

As usual, I want to give more than I am able to.

The least I can do is try to tell the story we both know, but this time from my perspective, being as honest as I can. I know you'll understand. I know now that's all you ever wanted from me.

I am writing this letter in hopes that you will forgive me. You deserve better. You always have. I'm not asking you to seek me out. I'm just asking that you reward the words on these pages in hopes that it can allow you, and maybe even me, to walk away from this with as little damage as possible...

I remember the first time I talked to you. In a matter of fifteen minutes we were able to discuss numerous philosophical and literary currents; I think we were about to run out of breath. When I got back to my room,

I ran and jumped like a baby because I was overjoyed at the prospect of meeting you. It seemed too good to be true honestly.

The next day we kept talking about absolutely anything, having both extremely deep discussions and extremely dumb ones. We were really hitting it off. I awkwardly asked you to sit with me and you happily agreed. That opened the doors to many more discussions and jokes that just felt right and still, felt a little bit too good.

I'm now trying to remember whether the date under the bridge was before or after this... either way, that was quite the fucking date. It was fun, romantic, relaxing; at that moment I had no real worries about us, I was just enjoying it. I talked to you about my dad, and later you talked to me about the guys that ruined you in the past... I guess I'm one of them now.

I wish I could change that.

When we were finally able to be in the same room alone, we didn't have to say or do much, we both knew what was happening. Still, I was extremely anxious, feeling super hot and sweaty and my heart was pounding. We got gradually closer to each other, to the point where our noses were touching, and then we kissed.

The next day, class was very awkward for me, I'm guessing it was somewhat the same for you... every time you touched me I just felt observed by everyone and didn't know how to react. Once lessons were finished, I felt comfortable being completely honest with you and immediately told you that something was off and tried to describe to you how I felt. I don't think you liked those words, in fact you just left without saying anything.

After dinner, I caught you by the dormitories and although I didn't really have any answers yet, I still wanted to talk to you. Matters progressed and when we were in my room, you were sitting on my bed and I was sitting next to you; I told you that I only wanted you sometimes and not all the time. Simply thinking about it makes me feel like a humongous asshole; still, that was the conclusion that I arrived at after analysing my feelings....but as I was sitting next to you, looking at your black outfit and feeling your silky smooth hair on my shoulder, I was attracted to you and I desperately wanted you. We both couldn't resist each other; I was touching you and you were touching me, the desire just kept growing and this all happened in what...six days?

If I have to be completely honest, this is as far as my chronological accuracy can go. After this I have lots of memories mixed up together with no real sequentialism. Still, I remember our morning routine with the many coffee trips we used to take, the times we sneaked in every bathroom to kiss just for a minute, the times we were able to sneak in our rooms and...well, you know what we did. Especially the last night. It was unique, meaningful and so much fun. I felt good, I felt safe, it felt like a proper goodbye; but now I know that you wish it never happened. If I knew that one day you would feel disgusted or ashamed for what we had done together, I would have never had done it. The guilt that I feel will never be worth it, even though I still remember the beauty of those moments.

In this very moment I'm a bit emotional and lots of fragmented memories keep showing up in my head; us singing and dancing in my room, the lovely dates at the park and the fucking expensive cigarettes you made me buy, the gorgeous and very "cheap" dinner we had on the rooftop... it's a real shame that after all of this I was able to make you hate me. The next day was a hurtful goodbye; the last minutes we spent together felt like hours, we couldn't find anything to say that would make things a bit better. I will always remember your face watching me leave; like the hearts in your eyes had shattered.

But then...then we started texting. At first it was fun, especially the calls when we joked and laughed like old times but then it started to feel more and more like talking to the ghost of a person that I had already said goodbye to; a responsibility that I didn't want. I talked about you to a lot of people, as you were still a big part of my thoughts and you still are, but I was starting to be annoyed by the messages I was receiving and I wasn't sure of what to do. I honestly thought that I could just do whatever I felt like; reply when I wanted to, maybe call sometimes and, who knows, maybe you would even come to Italy and we could spend some more time together.

Now I know that it doesn't work like that.

When we didn't text for a week it honestly didn't remotely feel like a big deal. For me everything was the same except I didn't have to answer anything; Once again, I had underestimated your feelings and how important this all was to you. So then you called me while I was in the woods with my friends, and I was very high so everything was much harder and felt much worse, and you kept repeating how I didn't care and I didn't show any care and how bad you felt all those days, until it all came down to the big question: "do you love me?" Oh god, I really hoped that the answer to that question could have been a yes. I like you, in many ways, and I like talking to you and we understand each other much more than anyone else, but something was missing and I couldn't lie to either of us. So, after many twisted words and awkward silences, I said : "No, Alaska, I don't think I love you," and you hung up.

After that, I don't remember how, probably with some Italian charm, I was able to get things back to "normal" for a couple of days, until you hit me with the ultimatum of rekindling our relationship with each other.

We like to think of them as just labels, but we know that it's not true. The way you label something completely changes your approach to it.

But that's not the point; you asked me that because you rightfully couldn't trust me and so you needed to be sure I was going to give myself to you, and as I analysed everything I felt for you in the past I realised that I wouldn't be able to give you that safety. I asked for a lot of advice from a lot of people, and not a single person had told me to actually go for it. So, once I was sure of my decision, I called you, once again underestimating your feelings and you as a person. I said it as if it wasn't a big deal, and once you made it clear that it was actually a *big deal I just wanted to get out of it. Suddenly, you became just an annoying problem that I had to deal with; and that's when I became a complete dick.*

I said a lot of bad things that I regret saying because for some reason I felt attacked by you; the more you made me feel like a bad guy the more I became one. And so, in the matter of hours, I ruined for you everything that had happened between us. I stabbed you right in the stomach with words I didn't know were that sharp, and you started bleeding out all the love you felt for me. And once you told me that I cut you and you were bleeding, I said "oh come one it's not that bad" and stabbed you again to prove my point, all until you had no blood left.

I hope you'll understand this metaphor, it's the best way I can explain things.

After that the discussions went on for a while, until you said something about me taking advantage of you just to have sex and brag about it or something like that; I couldn't take it. That was not what happened, that was not how I experienced things and those were not my intentions. Suddenly your words felt so bad that I told you to fuck off and hung up. Albeit, not a decision that I am proud of.

After a few weeks, you sent me the letter. I was pretty scared, both for the content and the quantity of it, so I waited a bit to read it. But once I started reading it... fuck, I couldn't stop. You are a very talented writer, Alaska. That letter made me feel things; I didn't think anyone could ever consider me the way you did, and in the same document you made me realise how badly I disappointed you. I remember sitting on the floor crying after reading it, and all I could think of was: "I have to call her". So I called you again, and we talked again, and you accepted my apology again, even though you weren't able to forgive me. At least now I know that you know that I know.

And this is pretty much how we left things. A question that you often ask me is: "so now what?"...Now what...Now what...I have no fucking clue. I never know where I'm going, I'm scared of knowing where I'm going, and when someone wants to come with me I either don't tell them the destination or make one up. This is because I don't have the answer to that question, and I don't know if I ever will. Now I'm here, writing anything that comes to my mind and hoping that this might have a good impact on you, hoping that you might be able to forgive me some day and hoping to find a direction for all of this. I guess that the main thing I want you to know is that you really meant something to me, that you aren't just a trophy, that I didn't have bad intentions and that I'm incredibly sorry for how I acted and how I made this story end.

I'm sorry Alaska, I might not be the person you thought I was, but don't let this ruin your future, I am not worth it. This life of yours was made to be lived. So promise me. Promise me you'll live. That you'll reach from the stars, howl at the moon and dance with the sun. Promise me you'll dive into this world, head first, navigating your way, day by day. That you'll do what it takes to make your soul sing; to make your heart beat with hope and compassion. That you'll take your sweet time devouring all the things grand and small that light you up. That you don't wait for life to happen and you go out and make it happen.

And when the world gets too heavy and your bones are tired and you're so utterly exhausted, I'll always be here. Although you don't know her yet, be in love with your future. I can't wait to meet her too.

As Umberto Eco said:

Never leave a sentence unfinished, otherwise you end up...

Theodore.

I reread the letter several times before shutting off my phone and staring blankly at the walls before me. Time stilled and the air had an unfamiliar taste to it, stale and empty. I didn't really feel anything; nothing that I didn't know already. I thought surely if I'd hear from you again, I would be an emotional wreck.

But I wasn't. My hands weren't shaking. My heart wasn't aching.

I brought my fingers to my throat to see if I even had a pulse. Because surely I hadn't spent so much of those past weeks building up an emotional wall so high, that even words like the ones you wrote couldn't penetrate it.

But I was scared that was exactly what had happened. Not only would you never break those walls back down, but I was afraid you'd forced me to build them so thick and high that I would hide behind them forever.

I suppose having the letter, the physicality of your confession brought me a sense of peace — but I still couldn't find a distinct answer between the lines to provide me with any solace. I still was asking myself, what comes next? If anything at all. You were right about one thing, though.

I owed you nothing.

The only thing the letter made clear to me was this: we were the perfect match, but we were not the perfect love. The central paradox of our love was my longing for closeness, which inherently manifested your fears — the more you received my love and attachment, the less you began to value it. I made myself a home in you which we both couldn't sustain. Esther Perel discussed this issue in her book *Mating in Captivity*:

> "Love rests on two pillars: surrender and autonomy. Our need for
> togetherness exists alongside our need for separateness. One does

not exist without the other. With too much distance, there can be no connection."

She goes on to say that the paradox is that if we merge too much, we eradicate the sense of two separate individuals who remain intrigued with and longing to connect with each other. If there is no distance to transcend, then there is, essentially, no one to connect with anymore. After reading your letter, I understood that, I understood what you meant during our last call: the loss of freedom and gain over control of one's independence again. The saddest part was realising we could have made it work. If you were truly in love with me you would have fought for me. But I know you didn't, and that just meant that I loved you more than you loved me. Even if it's cruel, sometimes things like this happen; for every inexplicable and inexpressible reason, but the world keeps spinning on anyways. You must move with time if you wish not to get left behind.

I suppose now is a good time to say, if ever, that I couldn't find something in me to hate you for what you said. I tried, but I simply couldn't. I didn't think of you with anger or resentment, only a little pain, but a pain that I could push through. Nevertheless, I stared down at the letter in disbelief. I knew I should have been angry that you lied to me for so long, but being in your head was somehow justifying your behaviour to me. Now when I looked back on that call, I could see that you weren't entirely to blame. You were expressing your opinion, and even though I disagreed with you and the way you delivered it, you never were the best at communication.

You went into defence mode, and I was in attack mode, and things just went south from there.

I put down my phone and looked out into the night. The stars shone over the cityscape, bright and luminous, like paint flickers across a black canvas. The air, cold and sharp, fizzled through my lungs and out of my nose spewing trails of mist in front of me. I closed the balcony doors and lied in bed for a while.

Your letter brought with it an aching finality that I had a hard time processing emotions for, there wasn't anything else to do, to think about, to start again or leave behind.

It was over.

I closed my eyes and listened as the sounds of the city scape faded in the distance. It was a rare, quiet night in New York City, where everything for the first time started to feel alright.

I realised that even if these feelings of peace may not last long, may come in waves and transpire into anger, sadness or pain, that in that very moment, I felt okay.

And if I could feel okay then, when everything was still so raw and potent, I knew that one day, I would be able to feel that same peace again.

CHAPTER TWENTY-TWO

WELCOME AND GOODBYE

IN ALL THE WORLD ONE MAY ALWAYS HOPE TO RECAPTURE something lost. But sometimes we are obliged to set the memory of certain things in a dresser of small regrets. Yet occasionally I discover in the folds of an old notebook, a letter, or insignificant tastes of coffees that had once embodied our happiest of afternoons.

I experience a moment of respite when all sense of bad remorse vanishes.

"I read your letter," I said into the phone. This was the first time I had seen your face in months; yet nothing had changed. It was painful to see the boy I once knew and loved mean nothing to me — something disturbing about recalling a warm memory and feeling utterly cold. "Thank you for writing it, it means a lot to me."

You smiled in that same catty and peaceful smile. My heart hurt. I couldn't even look at you anymore, all I saw was this stranger that once meant everything to me. "It's the least I could do," you said.

We were both unsure of what to say next.

I looked down and took a deep breath. "I'm afraid I have to ask you again," I said. "What's next?"

"I guess..." You paused for a moment. "This is *goodbye*."

"I guess so."

There was more silence, but this time it wasn't sharp, nor was it painful, only dull like an ache.

"You don't...you don't hate me, right?" you asked.

"You really hurt me," I sighed. "But no. No, I don't think I could ever truly hate you."

"Thank you," you exhaled sharply in relief. "Do you...do you still love me?"

I sighed heavily. "I don't regret the time we spent together. Sure, the memories are tainted now looking back on them, but in the moment I was happy with you; truly and divinely happy. I can't rewrite that...I can't rewrite how my heart feels right now either."

I looked at you, your look of love and reproach and I understood that my love for you could not save us. My love for life could not save us. It was the first time that I truly knew you were going to disappear. "Don't say anything," I said. "Let's just leave that out there just for a second on its own."

"It'll pass," you said eventually, and looked at me with such a deep apology that it was unbearable and I almost burst into tears.

"I know it will," I whispered.

I know it will.

There was so much I wanted to ask you, so much I wanted to say; but somehow I knew there wasn't time and even if there was, that it was all, somehow, beside the point. "Are you happy?" I said at last.

You considered this for a moment. "Not particularly," you said. "But you're not very happy where you are either."

"I don't think happiness is for me," I shrugged.

"Don't say that, I think you will be one day."

"Thank you. I know you will be one day."

A silence settled between us momentarily.

"Tell me something kind to remember you by," I said.

You chuckled softly. "I was just thinking the same thing," you smiled.

"I think we were doomed by our similarities," I joked back.

"Yeah, perhaps. Too similar for our own good."

"Kind of tragic," I said.

"Louise would've loved that," you laughed.

"Mr tragic villain."

"Ms tragic hero."

We both laughed together for a while longer. The world went quiet for us.

My heart hurt again.

"I wish you all the best, Alaska," you said finally. "And I'm sorry I couldn't give it to you."

"I wish you all the best, Theo," I said without missing a beat. "But I wish I could've been there to see it."

Another deadly silence hung in the night around me.

"I guess this is really it...imagine if this would be the last time we ever spoke," I quietly chuckled.

"I promise you we will see each other again," you said firmly, but somewhat desperate. "I promise you."

"Another coffee and a smoke?" I whispered.

"Always."

We both smiled at each other.

Suddenly, your expression softened. "You're so pretty," you said, and suddenly, it felt like my heart broke again into several pieces. I wish, even now, that you never had said that. After a long silence of being lost in my feelings, I managed to mutter just two words "Thank you". I didn't know whether that one phrase could contain all these feelings or whether it conveyed how I felt. But every part of me at that moment was invested in those two words.

"Goodbye, Alaska," you said.
"Goodbye, Theodore."

———

I felt as if I had just had a dream, a month long and summer long dream, but the coffee in front of me was empty and my mouth still had a sweet taste in it. I stood looking at the sky, the clouds the colour of a Raphael, a wounded rose. I had the sensation you had painted it yourself.

Flocks of gulls gathered above me. The blue hour was fast approaching. In the distance I heard a call. In the stretch of timelessness, I stopped. I suddenly thought of you, your brown eyes, your dark locks. I heard your voice above the gulls, the childish laughter, and the roar of waves. It was then when I saw it, a mockingbird. It looked at me intently, with calm eyes before flying into the night.

I smiled.

Something drew me back into a light sleep, so peaceful, like an ancient child. A sleeping youth cloaked in light; I opened my eyes with a smile of recognition for someone who was now a stranger. I looked through the window to see the moonlight billowing against the cityscape; Light shining from a dead star.

That, by the way, was a phrase of Louise's. I remember it from a lecture of her own on *The Iliad*, when Patroclus appears to Achilles in a dream. There is a very moving passage where Achilles–overjoyed at the sight of the apparition–tries to throw his arms around the ghost of his old lover, and it vanishes. *The dead appear to us in dreams*, said Louise, *because that's the only way they can make us see them; what we see is a projection, beamed from a great distance, light shining at us from a dead star...*

EPILOGUE

On a quiet, peaceful night in Oxford, the city's ancient charm unfurled like a well-worn tapestry beneath a celestial masterpiece. The moon, a pale, silvery crescent, presided over the night sky, casting gentle glows upon the cobbled streets and historic spires. As the city exhaled from the day's commotion, a tranquil hush descended. Whispering leaves rustled softly in the cold breeze; old-fashioned lamp posts bathed pathways in warm, inviting light, symphonies of century-old tales murmured by timeworn stones of passing buildings.

Oxford, for me, was the city where time slowed, where the weight of history was felt, and where the gentle night whispered the promises of new stories to be written. Oxford's beauty was an ode to the ages, a timeless reminder that the past and present could coexist in perfect harmony.

The night outside the coffee shop was tranquil, the streets bathed in the soft glow of street lamps. The world was at rest, and finally, so was I. I cradled a cup of espresso, savouring its bitterness, allowing each sip to sink into the depths of my stomach and burned its warmth through the walls. I sat alone at a corner table, my pen poised over the pages of my notebook, I looked out to the city scape and continued to write:

Dum spiro spero. While I breathe, I hope. For I am alive. I feel the air fill my lungs and the moon kiss my cheek. She taught me there is beauty in the darkness too, that even when I don't feel whole, I am enough. These things are enough and enough is everything.

Six months had slipped by, marked by our silence. I hadn't heard from you since that last call, and our months of no contact now felt like a merciful reprieve. I felt the joy of walking quietly through my days, feeling my life wrap gently around me. Oxford was a world away from the bustling streets of New York; the city which had once been the backdrop to our whirlwind romance now stood as a stark reminder of change; I'd started to see the truth that had eluded me for so long.

For a while, I hated you most for not having the courage to ruin us grandly. To break all the dishes and burn down the house. Instead you sunk quietly into the arms of a beautiful weak little bird. Denied me my spilled blood, my great war, everything except your confession. And then one Sunday in December I had woken and had known: Theodore was gone. You were gone from me forever. You were never coming back. I would never see you again. I would never hear your voice again, I would never kiss you again, I would never feel your arms around me. I would never again be able to unburden myself of one of my memories. I had Theodore for seventeen. There was no comparison. You had been the first person I loved, but another person who had seen me as an object to be used and pitied. In spite of this, I was unable to conceive a life without you, because you had so defined what my life was and could be.

That night, I couldn't sleep because I knew that it was over between us. But I'm not bitter anymore, because I know what we had was real. And if in some distant place in the future we would see each other in our new lives, I'll smile at you with joy and remember how we spent a summer beneath the trees, learning from each other and growing in love. The best kind of love is the kind that awakens the soul and makes us reach for more, that plants a fire in our hearts and brings peace to our minds. And that's what you gave me. That's what I'd hoped to give you forever.

But I had to let go; I may think of you softly from time to time still, but I would cut off my hand before I ever reached for you again. Even if I wanted to, you removed my number and erased every memory of our time together. I could no longer find you for you chose to no longer exist to me. You disappeared from my world without a word, a sound, a touch. For a while, I was hurt and angry. I screamed and cried. You told me you would always be there, and suddenly vanished as quickly as the snow fell.

But now I realise it truly was for the better.

You ought to know, you were my best friend. You were. I know you didn't love me and I loved you. I don't hate you for that. It just made me sorry that there wasn't someone else who could have loved me better. I expected too much from you because I was willing to do that much for you. I also made a home out of you because I assumed you had done the same. That was not your fault, but mine; though I had love inside me, I didn't know how to use it; sometimes it cut you like a barb.

You taught me a lot, even though it hurt at the time. Some people search their whole lives to find what I found in you, and for that, I was deeply grateful.

In the following months, cities and continents moved around me. I decided to move forward alongside them, alone but not lonely — I always had your company in the back of my mind. I even visited Italy but kept my silence. I figured you didn't want to hear from me. I still tell myself that it was better this way. I understood that no matter how deeply hurt I was, I would come out of this alive.

I always did.

The healing was not the destruction. It was not the day I knew it was finally time to uproot my life. It was not the moment I told you that you were no longer welcome, or the minute I walked away. The healing was how I gradually allowed my soul to drip into my days again; it was never about whether or not I had the courage to light fire to what was, it was whether or not I was willing to plant a seed in its place and to grow what was always meant to be. Because of this, I nurtured my love for literature and writing, finding solace in the written word. Devoting myself to literature had become my salvation. In the quiet corners of libraries and bookstores, I rebuilt myself slowly, one word at a time.

I lost myself in books, in art, in the haze of new horizons. I lost myself in curiosity, in knowledge, in passion. I lost myself in feeling it all; in feeling all the world and all the stories and lessons it had to teach me. I started to write a novel about us, about silence. The things people don't say. And from that I learned to never lose myself in love; never lose myself in another person.

I was my own home and vowed to never forget it. Although I don't know her yet, I'm in love with my future, Theodore. I can't wait to meet her.

My past, and the memories alongside of us still linger from time to time, but I learned how to carry them differently; no longer as bounding chains but instead as scars of years of resilience. Since the assault, I had spent years seeking solace in the arms of others, believing that love could become my refuge and promise for all those years I had spent suffering.

But I was wrong.

After the call, I was torn between loving you and beckoning to be free; because I was deprived of it all at the time, even the smallest things; and after we had met and you offered them to me and I didn't have to beg, or cry, or scream like before, I held onto everything else you had to offer me. I came to realise that the love that I thought I felt for you at the time was nothing but a shield, a mask to the vacancy of the past behind me. I was so desperate to be understood that I would grab people and shove them inside my heart, shower them in affection — where they stuck out like splinters, and it would hurt every time I felt something.

This isn't to say I didn't care about you, in fact, I still carry a certain fondness of you in my memories. *I always will.* You'll always occupy a special place in my heart. But, it was not infinitely love. It was passion; it all happened too quickly. I couldn't keep up with the array of emotions I had at the time and categorised them as the only feeling I was somewhat familiar with, which was attachment. But after the last call, and the months slipped through my fingers like jaded vines, I began to unravel the feelings that had ensnared me during our time together.

The realisation was painful, but simultaneously liberating. I understood that in order to let go and move on with my life, the same way I assume you did after St. Catherine, I was required to confront my inability to navigate my own emotional solace instead of projecting it onto you. You were never mine, and in a sense, I was never yours. I was young and caught up in my mind about all the possibilities that came alongside your love. The idea of this does not sadden me anymore, instead I'm met with a wholeness, a closure I've never really felt before. The times we shared together only live in my mind as memories now, and I've gladly let them go and moved on from them. They are still dear to me, I look back at them and smile, but not as a lover, not as a dreamer, just an observer. When we met, my heart was still grieving and yours already belonged to your independence. I suppose I enjoyed the idea of loving you, of thinking of you, romanticising your whole being. It brought a spark to my life that I was desperately missing out on for a while. You were an escape for everything going on in my life, and I have a feeling you knew it at the time too.

I had to understand that I was not afraid to walk this earth alone.

From that point onwards, I was finally able to accept it all: in the deepest recesses of my soul; that one heart was not connected to another through harmony alone. They were, instead, linked deeply through their wounds. Pain linked to pain, fragility to fragility. There was no silence without a cry of grief, no forgiveness without bloodshed, no acceptance without a passage through acute loss.

That is what lay at the root of true harmony.

But of course, I wonder from time to time. What if we had met now, instead of back then? Would we have fallen in love? Would you have stayed? These thoughts do not reside, instead they come and go in waves, like the waning moon, like the changing seasons. Some nights I miss you so much it hurts to breathe, to think. I can't stand to pick up my phone knowing your name isn't going to be on the screen. I was trapped in these thoughts of you and me, buried in the memories that seem like they're from another lifetime. But in the end, I wasn't really sure what I was holding on to. You never really gave me anything to hold on to.

Nevertheless, I could not help but make beauty out of the

little things, my heart is still too big for small feelings. You're still the boy I met when I was seventeen in the summer, the boy I wrote all of this poetry about, but now I see you in a different way; in the way you notice the falling autumn leaves, eyes like planet mars, an elliptical galaxy...but not in the way you stop to take a photo of them. I do not hold onto you anymore, not the thoughts, not the memories. They exist, and I smile, and I let them go.

I'm glad to have known you, Theodore, glad to have loved you, but most importantly, glad to have let you go. I'm happier this way, and I can tell that you are too.

That's the last thing I want. *You happy.* I know when you read all of this writing, you'll get it.

Leaving the dimly lit coffee shop at night, I felt the weight of the day's exhaustion slowly lift with each step into the crisp air. The aroma of freshly brewed coffee lingered on my clothes, a comforting companion in the chilly darkness. I looked around at the cityscape, the desolation and radiance of the Oxford streets. Clutching around the darkening hems of my notebook, I savoured my newfound sense of freedom. The centuries-old buildings stood as silent witnesses to my transformation. With each step, I let go of the past, its weight dissipating like a fleeting shadow. The echoes of my history whispered through the cobblestone alleys; they no longer bound me.

But, just as I was turning the corner, the distant sound of a familiar accent bellowed in the distance, vibrating against the moonlight. I turned around and the night stood still.

Shattered.

Fate had a curious way of bringing lost souls back together.

THE END.

ACKNOWLEDGMENTS

Thank you dearly and most of all to Bibi Tuken Tegi, whose dauntless efforts on behalf of this novel leave me speechless. Thank you for always being enthusiastic about my work, willing to read multiple drafts and to talk story-telling, myths and love; for cheering me on through the writing process and all of my pursuits outside of literature. Without you, who gave yourself over the life of this book with such generosity and dedication, this novel wouldn't have been possible.

Much love to my radiant and potent mother and father, whose magic transformed my life, and was patient with me through the months of sleepless nights writing. My father for his humour and all the loving, inspiring conversations. My mother for her irrepressible support in difficult times and for her belief in me. Thank you both for all your support and guidance of me and my work (and for letting me buy a million coffees in the past few months. I hope this novel is enough to adequately repay your bank accounts).

And — despite the risk of sounding like a Homeric catalogue of ships — the following people must all be thanked for their aid, inspiration and love: Victoire, Sydney and Aslihan, for their unstinting support. Our friendship is the greatest gift of my adolescence. My admiration for you could fill another novel. (I hope to hear your reviews on our group chat soon).

There are not enough words in the world to adequately express my adoration of and gratitude for Adelya and Ayau, whose patience with me makes me want to weep. Thank you always for the insight, crucial wisdom and great warmth that carried me throughout this journey and for always being with me no matter how hard the times were. You are both the stars in my life. Never stop shining so bright. (Thank you for always keeping me humble and making sure the decisions I make, like this novel, aren't delusional. And an additional thank you for continuously listening to my rants about love).

Thanks to Ben Tipton for his time and literary insight on an early draft. I continue to be grateful and inspired by Eva Snape in every English Literature class. Speaking of which, so many of my divine classmates were supportive of this book's journey that I cannot possibly list all of them, and must settle instead for a heartfelt Thank you: Nic Achilles Rey, Daniella Cardoso Fernandes, Katie Azriella Ward, Karolien Labuschagne, Felicity Ariel Chloe Kristianson, Ioana Steliana Scripcariu, Aryana Stiube and Maya Hamdy.

My deepest gratitude to Mia Applegate for her unrelenting support no matter how many miles away. My warm flame, never stop burning. The gravest of thanks to Safin Ikhsan for her unrelenting support in my pursuits. You have inspired for me all kinds of stories.

Love and hugest appreciation to Louise Vincent who introduced me to philosophy and reignited my love for literature. Deepest gratitude to Radu Muresan for my beautiful cover art and Speedy 876 for decisively working with me on the prologue. Thank you to Eric Lang for his help during the publication process. For patient and incisive feedback, for all their faith in my work, and for being generally sublime: Jenna Moreci, Abbie Emmons, Patti Smith, Alexander Chee, Donna Tart, and Haya Yanigahara, for infinitely inspiring my writing and daily pursuits. I am forever grateful for your existence.

In loving memory of Jude St. Francis, I hope you have

found the peace you had long sought out for, and can now rest peacefully in my mind and soul. Your life has taught me more than words could ever describe. I hope now that you are happy. You deserve nothing less.

Finally and essentially: I not only never could have, but never would have, written this novel without experiencing the love of my *primo fidanzato*. Thank you, Leonardo, thank you dearly for being with me for every page. There are not enough words in the world to adequately express my adoration of and gratitude for the time we spent together. I will always cherish you in the deepest recesses of my soul.

(and less poetically, thank you for not suing me for writing this novel)

AUTHOR NOTE

I started writing this novel when I was a student at Oxford Royale in 2023. During the course, I met a wide range of incredible people who showed me the true value of friendship and loyalty in my life.

I also fell in love. If that wasn't obvious already.

Sonnets Of Summer Sorrow is mainly autobiographical and deeply rooted in reality. The character of Alaska came to me fully formed. The internal logic of her character, the inevitability to her life never quite changed because it was my own. One of the things I tried to do in this novel was glide a lot between past and present tense. This idea that if you're living with trauma; trauma isn't something that happened in the past and there's a hard defining line between the present. But trauma is something that's waiting in the next room, behind that curtain next to you. And the idea that you live with trauma every day and some days you can live with it a little less intensely, but other days you can't, is something I really wanted to convey; to mimic the sensation of living in your past when you are trying only to live in the present

Months before I started writing the novel as I imagined it (the characters, the layout etc.), already existed in the form of a letter. I knew the archetype of both Alaska and Theodore, mostly because I had the honour of experiencing their relationship in real life. This is a good enough time to say, if any, that the letters included in this novel were, in fact, real. The structure of this novel was written in the style of the letters I wrote as a child, and the real letter I sent to "Theodore" after Oxford Royale. I included them in hopes that the novel would demand a total surrender to the characters' lives and the worlds that had been created. It purposely violates and trespasses into the character's most intimate and vulnerable moments through the form of this long, tragic letter.

One of the major themes in the novel was memory and never really escaping it; the idea of being obsessed with something vaporous. That memory is something slipper and vast; uncontrollable — and someone, like Alaska, who is trying to control and manage memory, feels herself losing against it. What she needed, the right and the way to be angry, to express anger, to be entitled, to demand that life offered her more, were things that she didn't have. This makes a person who is forced to cope with limited abilities and a limited sense of what they can do in the world turn to a very small often and very sad outlet.

This story of unconditional and unqualified love is one that deeply resonated with me, and throughout the writing process, I was forced to face my own grief in hopes of turning it into something beautiful. I've always written and dreamt of the notion of true love, and it wasn't until I experienced it for myself that I realised how disillusioned an individual could become with the idea of total surrender. What I wanted this novel to be, was an intimate and close look into the reality of these themes, and that even though love can exist, it is never right to sacrifice your own happiness for something intangible.

I wrote this novel for the girl who loved books and soon became the woman writing them. And so, for all of the dreamers out there, never forget to hope.

For hope is the only thing stronger than fear.

ABOUT THE AUTHOR

Alaska Ayaleem Tuken Tegi is an emerging author of contemporary fiction. This is Alaska's debut novel. Alaska wrote Sonnets of Summer Sorrow when she was seventeen.

Work Email: Alaska.literature@gmail.com
Instagram: @alaskategi
*Bookstagram: @_alaskareads_*

Printed in Great Britain
by Amazon

31153285R00199